PRAISE FOR SEELEY JAMES

Jacob and his sidekick god, Mercury are two of the best characters ever created

—Secret World Book Club

It wasn't only the story that kept me riveted. It was characters that I loved or detested with a passion.

—DreamBeast, Vine Voice

Plenty of edge of the seat suspense, a splash of well-timed humor, and adventures that leave you wanting more

—Susan Gainoutdinov

An excellent fast-moving action thriller

—Eric Crown, Founder of F500 company, Insight Enterprises

I fell in love with the characters and can't get enough of them. I felt every ounce of rage and desperation.

—CarolAnn Review

DEATH AND DECEPTION

A JACOB STEARNE THRILLER

SABEL SECURITY #9

SEELEY JAMES

Published by
Machined Media
12402 N 68th St
Scottsdale, AZ 85254

DEATH AND DECEPTION: A Jacob Strearne Thriller, released July 21st, 2020
Print ISBN: 978-1-7333467-5-7
ePub ISBN: 978-1-7333467-4-0
Distribution Print ISBN: 978-1-7333467-6-4
Sabel Security #9 version 2.31

Formatting: Machined Media
Cover Design: Jeroen ten Berge

In loving memory of my great grandchildren:

Aaliyah 2013 – 2020
Jeremiah 2018 – 2020

CHAPTER 1

THE MAN KEPT HIS PISTOL leveled as he took the empty chair.

Captain Luis Vaquero froze, a forkful of *ropa vieja* halfway to his mouth. Had the Mexican cartels come to Cuba? He glanced around the deserted hotel patio for help. His sailors were gone. The staff had disappeared. In their place stood two black-clad gangsters.

Vaquero turned back to the concrete block of a man with a bald head, a black camp shirt, and a vaguely familiar green tattoo on his wrist. A warm breeze ruffled the palapa's palm-thatched roof. Twenty yards to his left, the surf rolled gently in and slid back out. He set his fork on the plate.

As calmly as he could, Vaquero asked in Spanish, "Who are you?"

The man replied in English with a British accent. "That is of no matter, Captain Vaquero. You will answer a few simple questions and then you and your people can go back to the shipwreck, pick up all the doubloons you want, and run off."

Vaquero's heart sank. Pia Sabel had promised the discovery would remain a secret until the Cuban government could bring in specialists. He thought it was under control. His ship kept watch offshore. There had been no overhead flights, no news reports, no influx of suspicious craft near the resorts on Caya Coco off Cuba's northern coast. Not even the few off-season tourists on the island had ventured out to the site. There had been no indication the news had leaked.

"What shipwreck?" Vaquero asked. He got a better look and recognized the man's green tattoo. A white crescent moon with five stars in the center of a green circle ringed with red. The military roundel of Turkmenistan. What were Turkmen doing here?

The man slammed a stiletto into the tabletop in a swift and alarming move that exposed a muscular bicep. The knife vibrated in place. The man said, "I ask the questions, Vaquero."

"Fine." Vaquero tried hard to remain calm and in control, but the stranger's violence shook him. "Ask."

"Who is the archeologist in charge then?"

"Archeologist?" Vaquero squinted, trying to reconcile the British accent with a Turkmen. "Cuba is a poor country. Our expert is an American who teaches at the University of Alabama. My orders are to secure the area until he can mount an expedition."

The bald man leaned back, looking a little confused. "How did you verify the ship was the *San Andrés?*"

"I verified nothing. The capitalist Pia Sabel brought her yacht here for an engagement party. They were the ones who found the wreckage. One of her guests claimed it was the *San Andrés.*"

Vaquero remembered the Americans fondly. They were gracious and helpful. They wanted nothing from him, the site, or the Cuban government. But they were ridiculously wealthy and crushingly unaware of the disparity between them and the average Cuban. Vaquero commanded the largest ship in Cuba's navy, yet Sabel's yacht, the *Numina,* was twice the size of his frigate. She and her friend took him to see the wreck in a plexiglass submarine that cost more than Vaquero would earn in ten lifetimes. They were so rich, they left millions in gold and silver untouched on the sea floor.

The bald man tapped the table with an impatient finger. "But the *San Andrés* sank with the *Espiritu Santo* and the *San Esteban* off Padre Island, Texas in 1554. The Spanish records are clear. The other two wrecks have been found."

Vaquero shrugged. "The woman who found the wreck, one of Ms. Sabel's party, had served in the US Navy and specialized in underwater recovery. She verified the find based on a lead-lined box containing the captain's log, charts, and instruments. And two cannons, I think. Maybe three. They looked authentic to me. But then—"

"You are not an archeologist." The bald man's voice betrayed his annoyance. "Well then, either someone forged the records four centuries ago or your find is a fraud."

"This is not for me to determine," Vaquero said. He stared at the plate of *ropa vieja*. The finest skirt steak he'd seen in months cooled on his plate. His mouth watered. His stomach growled. The scent of tomato sauce wafted to his nose. He picked up his fork.

The intruder casually laid the muzzle of his pistol on his forearm, aiming the barrel at Vaquero. The fork dropped.

"What did they take from the site?" the bald man asked.

"Nothing. We arrived the day after the discovery. They allowed a full search of the yacht. They didn't care about the gold. The lady, Ms. Sabel, said it would cost her more in taxes than it was worth." Vaquero laughed. What a problem to have. And Sabel had looked exasperated when she said it, as if the last thing she wanted was more money. Americans.

"What about this then?" The bald man held up his phone. On it was an Instagram thread with twenty-eight pictures. "On it, he says you made them take it with you."

Pictures of that stupid box. Bigger than a shoebox, smaller than a microwave, and heavier than the stone it was made of. That's what the bald man wanted? All the threat and posturing over that ridiculous thing?

"Are you serious?" Vaquero couldn't believe the man's stupidity. "I'm no archeologist—"

"Yes. Yes." The intruder waved his pistol impatiently.

"—but even I know that is a fake."

The bald man looked at his phone, then at Vaquero. "Why do you say that?"

"Please. It's alabaster. Rare for New World art, especially for something so large. It has Latin writing on one side and Mayan glyphs on the other. I don't know about those chicken scratches on the third side."

"Mesopotamian cuneiform."

Vaquero thought the man was joking. When he saw the bald man's piercing stare, he realized it was no joke.

"If you say so." Vaquero pointed to his meat, asking permission to eat.

The intruder shook his head. He asked, "Have you heard of the Poison Stone?"

"No."

The bald man looked skeptical. "His post says you refused to take it. Why?"

"It's a fake. They were trying to do something. I don't know what. Go viral on Instagram. Play us for fools. Maybe there was a bomb inside. That guy just wanted to be famous. Pathetic."

The bald man's voice rose to incredulous. "You do not know who he is?"

"Of course. He's that American war hero. Big deal. Maybe he misses the spotlight and wants someone to pay attention to him. Maybe he has PTSD or takes drugs. He's crazy. That much you can tell from the look in his eye."

"And you let him walk away with this?"

"Cuba wants no part of whatever game he was playing."

The bald man rose, the pistol dangling at his side. He held his phone to Vaquero's face, showing a picture of the American. "Where can I find this Jacob Stearne now?"

IN HER VANCOUVER STUDIO, GU Peng sensed the curve of the stone with her eyes closed. Sometimes the marble refused to speak to her gaze. When that happened, she allowed it to talk to her palm instead. And it did speak. The imperfection gently scraped her skin. Keeping her eyes closed, she ran the sandpaper over it, pushing the rough edge ahead of each stroke, one granule at a time. Gentle movements would inevitably force it to yield to her desires.

When the sandpaper flowed like water over the stone, she opened her eyes and blew the dust off for one final examination. She rubbed her cheek on the marble. Beauty must glow from the details. The neck of the young woman's bust had to be perfect before she could expect anyone to feel its power.

Peng experienced the bust returning her caresses with clarity and light. She had succeeded. Exhilaration filled her spirit. Her granddaughter memorialized in stone. Perhaps now she would find peace.

Peng's phone rang with an odd trill. She grabbed her walking stick and worked her way to her phone on the worktable. A video call. A quick glance showed it was Danny calling on Chalk, the high-security voice encryption app he insisted the Cubans could neither ban nor hack. She checked herself before answering. White marble dust smeared her face and smock. Her hair fell past her shoulders, gray and bedraggled, the braid unraveling. She searched the buttons, hoping to answer it voice-only.

As her finger hovered over the button, she saw Danny's image. He looked so young and beautiful with his fashionable stubble and his long auburn hair gelled back. On closer examination, his rugged face appeared stressed. His eyes were alert and active, darting to one side then the other.

She answered, "Danny? You at Caya Coco?"

"They're here," he whispered. "When I arrived, they were duct-taping uniformed officers at gunpoint."

"Knight of Mithras?" Peng's blood ran cold. They were ahead of her. And by merely minutes. How had she let that happen? "You sure them not drug lord?"

"They have the Turkmen tattoos on their wrists. Six of them. Many more waiting at the loading dock. Three went to the patio, one of them just sat down with Captain Vaquero."

She hoped Danny hadn't heard her gasp. This was no time for weakness or fear. This was the time to act as she had at Tiananmen Square. That is, the way she acted before the tanks came. She waved the liberty flag through the crowd thirty years ago. She would wave that flag again one day. She took a deep breath and steeled herself. "Danny, you safe place?"

"Yes. Wait." Danny moved out of the camera's range. A moment later he came back. He said, "I can hear them when the breeze carries their voices this way. I'm moving to a better place. I'll have to call you back after they leave."

She clicked off. Her fingers squeezed the phone hard enough to hurt.

Gu Peng felt a stab of guilt. Danny had always been such a helpful young man. But now that her best friend's only child had blossomed into full adulthood, she regretted bringing him into the Brotherhood of Claritas. In just a matter of days, the Brotherhood had transformed from a klatch of harmless mystics into a secret force of zealots on a dangerous path. She had prepared them as best she could, but they were untested. Were they ready to take on the ruthless Knights?

The unimaginable had come to pass. After 466 years, the Freedom Stone had been found. Peng had all but given up on the myth, her constant and singular dream since fleeing her homeland. Could it be real? Could it be harnessed? Could she navigate the rapidly changing dangers they faced? Or was she an old woman fooling herself with fantastic tales of witchcraft? She brushed marble dust from her cheek.

Waiting for Danny's call felt like an eternity.

While the minutes dragged on, she stared at the bust of her granddaughter. Shanshan would be proud. Peng cursed. Shanshan might still be alive had she not pursued freedom in her homeland. She had sacrificed everything. The Freedom Stone had to be real. It had to work. It was her last and only hope.

Her phone rang. Voice only. She answered.

"They shot him!" Danny's panicked and breathless voice echoed from the tiny speaker. "They just shot Captain Vaquero! Ohmygod."

"Danny? You safe?"

"Yes."

"And the other?" Peng blinked back tears. This was no time to break down. Danny and the Brothers needed her strength. But she couldn't help it, she saw the tanks again. Driving. Driving. Relentlessly forward, over every sleeping bag, every tent, every human being. Crushed.

"I'm fine for the moment," he said. "The hotel staff hid us in a storeroom. We think the Knights left. They're checking."

"Good," she breathed. "It good thing you safe. I wish same for Captain Vaquero. Poor man. You hear all they talk about?"

"Some. Vaquero told him a man named Jacob Stearne took it to Professor Hidalgo in Mexico. He's a Mayan expert. Stearne felt it belonged in a Mayan museum."

She felt hope returning to her. For once, there was a chance, a slim chance, they could get ahead of the Knights of Mithras. "Where we find Jacob Stearne?"

CHAPTER 2

JENNY LED THE WAY THROUGH the Mayan jungle deep in the Yucatán.

I found her presence mesmerizing. I'd follow her anywhere. At home, we lie on the sofa reading books together. Those are rare and cherished moments of peace in my life. I love that she tolerates my passion for jazz. I love that she showers my cooking with praise. I love that her recovery has progressed past the difficult stages and she was taking life head-on again. All of which reminded me of why I'd proposed.

Our relationship had been rocky for the first six months. We had made it through the worst rocks intact. Her belief that marriage was an outdated tradition was the least of those rocks. Once I presented her with a ring, she changed her mind. Her hostility toward the ancient ritual melted away.

Her mother and father didn't melt away when I asked for their blessing, separately, due to a nasty divorce many years ago. You'd think people would eventually be exhausted by the bitterness. But—humans. At least I presented them with something they could agree on. I'm just glad Jenny ignored their advice.

Three weeks later and we were out on an adventure hundreds of miles from modern civilization. When I announced the right thing to do with the alabaster artifact was to drag it out to Professor Hidalgo at his remote dig site, Jenny jumped right in. She claimed it was time for an adventure on our own. Our other adventures had involved people like the neo-Nazis who strapped her in a suicide vest and the arms dealer who held us hostage under the threat of sarin gas. We thought a little time camping and hiking would make for a relaxing and stress-free vacation. Even if one of us had to carry what felt like a hundred pounds of stone.

My bride-to-be pushed ahead of me through a tangle of vines.

"We're going to have a wonderful life," Jenny said, picking up the conversation we'd let sink into silence while we picked our way through an overgrown part of the path. "We'll establish Stearne Security together. We can finally step out of other people's shadows. You won't be 'Sabel Security's top operative' and I won't be 'the VP's daughter.'" She paused, then snarled, "And we can prove Dad wrong."

She was right about me. I didn't want to be anyone's operative but my own. I'd been hung out to dry once too often for one lifetime. From now on, I would do my thing, not someone else's thing. But Jenny's last sentence came out with such heat it worried me. I waited for an explanation. A hundred yards later, she hadn't offered one, so I said, "Want to talk about your Daddy issues?"

She huffed. "You know how he is. I've never been enough for him. He cuts me off every time I start talking. He undervalues my opinion."

"Undervalues?"

"You know what I mean. Demeans and dismisses it. Like, 'That's nice, honey.' But he never heard what I said in the first place."

For years, Bobby Jenkins and I had been best buds because I'd been assigned to his security detail and knew a few of his secrets. Then I asked permission to marry his daughter. Immediately, the drug kingpin— I mean, founder of Jenkins Pharmaceuticals—accused me of being a gold digger and told me I'd never see a dime of his money. Ever since then, he'd undervalued my opinion before I opened my mouth. I said, "Yeah, I do know what you mean."

"And I'm not talking about recently. It's been like that my whole life. Before the divorce, back when I was eight, he'd listen to my brother talk nonsense, then ignore me. I don't mean he's a misogynist or anything, He listens to Pia like she was preaching the Gospel. It's just that I remind him of Mom. He can't deal with the marriage he wrecked."

Having a bit of background about her mom and a certain General Thompson—who Jenny resembles in an uncanny way—I had reason to believe her dad might not be entirely responsible for wrecking the marriage. But I decided to keep that to myself.

"Anyway," she went on, "I'm looking forward to Stearne Security being a big deal. Maybe bigger than Sabel Security. Then we can champion the important causes. Fight for freedom, that kind of thing."

Mercury, messenger of the Roman gods, floated up alongside me riding on his ridiculously tiny wings. He said, *Y'know what, homeboy? If you don't find this woman something to champion, she's gonna champion you.*

I said, *We're just dreaming about the future, that's all.*

Mercury said, *A hundred aurei says she has you whipped in a week.*

I said, *We've been over this. No one's used aurei in two thousand years. It's dollars now.*

Mercury said, *Whatever, brutha. She's gonna take your manhood and stuff it in a jar. You'll be painting pink polish on her toenails before you know it.*

Oh. Hold up. I might have left something out. See. Most guys come home from the wars and reintegrate into civilian life with minimal problems. But. Some guys come home and live in mortal fear of open spaces. Other guys come back wound up tight like a grenade with its pin pulled. A few guys self-medicate their way back into society. There's a US Army study known as *Red Book* that says soldiers serving three or more combat tours are a "growing high-risk population." I pulled eight.

But I didn't have any problems. None at all.

Because I had a god on my side.

I'm not talking about some mute and invisible deity that preachers and rabbis and imams talk about in hushed tones. I'm talking about a black, toga-wearing, foul-mouthed god in the flesh who smacks the back of your head when you don't listen. I'm talking about a god revered for thousands of years by millions of people. A god who helped me out when I most needed it. Don't go shaking your head like that. Open your mind. Expand your reality.

Why am I so special? Because he and his buddies—Jupiter, Saturn, Minerva, Juno, Venus, the whole lot—fell on hard times back in 390 AD when Emperor Theodosius decreed everyone had to worship Nicene Christianity. Mercury's temple, the biggest in Rome, was trashed that year. Terrible way to treat the gods. He and his buddies have been trying to sell tickets to their reunion tour ever since.

I know what you're thinking: Jacob's insane. You're not alone. My caseworker back in the Army said the same thing. He and a bunch of fancy psychiatrists labeled me "problematic" and "a catastrophic nightmare waiting to happen." Their diagnosis? PTSD-induced schizophrenia. The fact that Mercury's black and tries to talk street sends them over the edge. I don't know why. It says right there in the Bible, Genesis 1:27, "God created humankind in his image." And we all know homo sapiens originated in southern Africa, so there you have it. God is a black African. Spelled out in the Good Book whether or not it upsets your religious sensibilities.

Apparently, no one else can see or hear him. I'm the only one blessed—or cursed—with his heavenly oratory.

Lost in thought like that, I missed where Jenny had taken the conversation. Something about how we could make our marriage last.

"That's what I love about you," she said. "You're the order to my chaos. The yang to my yin."

"Is that a good thing? Chaos? And who's yang?"

"Of course, it's a good thing," she laughed. "Yin and yang are the Chinese concepts of duality. I'm talking about balance. The forces of order and chaos are not in conflict; they create a balance. You keep me balanced."

I kill bad guys for a living, I don't get all that stuff about duality. When I hear that word, I think of books without pictures written by dead Germans. But I'd sure as hell figure it out for Jenny. I want my marriage to last a lifetime. Like my parents, not hers.

"We were both in the military, that's an orderly world." She stopped hiking to face me. "You thrive on that. I didn't. I made it work, but I thrive on chaos."

She didn't like the way I was squinting at her, confused. She added, "When I say chaos, it's not the kind you're thinking of. Not like a terrorist throwing a bomb in a bazaar. It's chaos as in unstructured creativity. Like when you're solving a problem. You need chaotic thoughts to discover a unique solution. Or as Nietzsche said, 'One must still have chaos in oneself to give birth to a dancing star.' There are other times when you need order. Like. Hmm. Like when you drive down the

street, everyone has to obey the rules of the road or else you have ...”
She tried to come up with an analogy.

"Rome?"

"Exactly." She laughed and resumed the trek. "You are my balance.
Yin and yang, negative and positive, male and female. We fit together."

"Oh, I get it. Like tunnels and trains?"

"Jacob! Is that all you think about?"

"Yes."

"Nine more miles to the professor's site," she said. "Then, if you're a
good boy, and we can find a secluded spot ... did I mention you have to
be a good boy?"

"How about a bad one?"

CHAPTER 3

THREE HOURS OF HIKING LATER, we entered the dig site of Professor Benito Hidalgo. We walked along an ancient shoulder-high wall with piles of recently stripped vegetation at its base. Anywhere else, it was a beautiful spring day in early March, but in this part of Central America, it was hot and humid.

As we approached the center of activity, an older rich lady came out and stood in the middle of the path. You can tell rich people in the jungle because they look like they stepped out of a Hemingway safari, only with modern fabrics and colors. A man with a rifle slung on his shoulder stepped out of the brush behind her. She crossed her arms and said, "Whoever you are, I'm Carlotta. This is my dig. Turn around and get out."

"We're here to see Professor Hidalgo," I said. "We called ahead. I thought it was his dig."

"I'm paying for it. Who did you call?"

"His office at the university. They said they'd reach him on the satellite phone to tell him we're coming."

The guy with the rifle said, "Si, we get your call. Follow me."

"No one told me," Carlotta said.

We marched past her and her scowl. Her frown was so fierce, my grandmother would love to borrow it for special occasions. We came to the main clearing, a quarter-acre plaza of excavated paving stones, broken and tossed around by tree roots. On two sides, large military tents staked out the plaza's edge.

Mercury floated out of the heavens and landed beside me. *You are not doing this, homie.*

I said, *Why not?*

Mercury said, *Dude, do you get paid to help the meek? Look at them. Grad students. They don't have a peso between them. Leave them to Jesus.*

I said, *I'm not doing this to get paid. The thing belonged to the Mayans at some point. These guys should decide which museum gets it.*

Mercury said, *Did somebody forget who quit his cushy job at Sabel Security? Did somebody forget he set up his own company? Did somebody forget he has a commission from Mikhail-Caesar-Yeschenko to find Yuri Belenov?*

I said, *This'll only take a couple days. You've been bitching about this trip from the beginning. Leave me alone.*

Mercury said, *You're telling god to leave you alone? Nice. Did you forget Yeschenko offered you an advance and instead you came here? You're gonna run outta cash and then you'll be calling for divine intervention—again. Happens every time.*

Did I mention it's a difficult relationship? I'd rather be a Christian, Jew, Muslim, Hindu—anything else. But those gods never show up when I need to kill people. Bunch of pacifists.

So. He's all I've got. Most of the time he's right about things. But where money's concerned, the Roman god of commerce has strong feelings. Although, he had a point. The wedding planner had maxed out my credit cards (Jenny wanted what she wanted, and her dad thought I was a gold digger, so no love there). Very soon, I'd have to get that advance out of the notoriously tight—not to mention murderous— Mikhail Yeschenko.

An American woman approached us. Early thirties, wearing a dirty plaid shirt and equally dirty khaki shorts that showed off mud-covered knees. After a shower, her jet-black hair would frame her deeply tanned face nicely. She said, "Are you Jacob Stearne?"

One by one, grad students and volunteers appeared out of the trees. A dozen crammed the clearing and stared at us. One guy helped me out of my pack. I laid my artifact on a table and started to open the blanket I'd used for padding. Then I realized it would be better to wait for Hidalgo. Unwrapping for the expert would be more dramatic.

"How did you know his name?" Jenny slid in front of the woman. One of the rocks we'd overcome in our early relationship was her excessive jealousy. I hoped we weren't regressing.

"He's the Hero of Paris, right?" the woman asked. "Everyone knows him. Didn't the French President give him the key to the city?"

Jenny's mood switched to excited. She chatted with the woman. It turned out her name was Cherry. With a self-conscious laugh, Cherry took the initiative to point out she was working on her PhD in Mayan history and had never been a stripper.

PhD or not, she was wrong. The president of France hadn't given me a key to the city. He tossed a medal at me in a short ceremony set up by Sabel Security's marketing department. Neither he nor I wanted to be there. When you save a couple hundred church goers from a mass shooter, you just want to go home and chill, not make a big deal out of it. And no president gets excited about giving national medals to a foreigner. But they dragged us together for the awkward photo op. It was one of the many reasons I'd decided to leave Sabel Security and open my own firm.

A short, older man with a lean and weathered face, gray hair, and a confident ease appeared from the gathering crowd. Up close, the depth of the lines on his face made him look older than I'd first thought. He offered a hand and said, "It is a pleasure to meet you, Señor Stearne. I am Professor Rafael Tum of the University of Guatemala. Thank you for undertaking the arduous journey to our remote and humble dig."

His accent sounded like an upper-class Englishman with just a hint of Spanish. Yet his short, muscular build, and dark, ruddy skin looked as Mayan as anyone I'd met on the trail.

I said, "You're welcome."

Rafael searched my eyes as if he'd lost something. "Dr. Hidalgo will be along in a moment. We are honored that you chose to shoulder the responsibility of the Freedom Stone. Not everyone would ignore the dangers and make such an arduous trek."

Mercury stepped between us. *Not everyone, my brutha, because most mortals would listen to the voice of god and toss that damn thing back in the ocean.*

I said, *It's historical. It's archeologically important. I think.*

Mercury said, *It don't bother you that this fancy-ass professor of whatever just used the words dangerous and arduous while talking about it?*

I said, *Why did he call it the Freedom Stone when you've been telling me it's the Poison Stone?*

Mercury said, *Some people see it differently. Some see blue and others see yellow. Don't matter. The damn thing is Pandora's box. Toss it back in the ocean.*

I said, *We're here. We're giving it to the descendants of the Mayans who wrote on it. It's the right thing to do.*

Mercury stomped off.

Rafael Tum kept his suspicious gaze on me. I rewound where we'd left the conversation.

"No big deal," I said. "Hardly dangerous at all. A long walk but worth it to return it to the right people. Say, what was that you said about responsibility?"

The gathered students and volunteers parted. A tall middle-aged guy made his way through them. He looked European with pale skin and dark brown hair. He stepped close to peer down at me. He wanted me to know he was in charge. At six-one, I'm bigger than most but not always the tallest. This guy had a couple inches on me.

The tall man pointed at me and spoke with a light accent of perfectly articulated vowels and consonants. "You are Jacob Stearne, Señor? My office says you have something for me."

Professor Tum slipped behind Hidalgo and the others. He came to rest with his shoulder against a tree yet kept his gaze on me. Cherry tracked around until she pulled up next to Rafael. They whispered to each other while watching me.

I pulled back the blanket and let the alabaster shine. Hidalgo glanced at me, then leaned in close and turned the box so the Mayan glyphs faced him. In unison, the others leaned in with him.

"Very interesting find, Señor Stearne." He tapped his chin in thought. "You are familiar with the myths about the Poison Stone, yes?"

All eyes rose to me, waiting for an answer.

I'd expected a larger scale of gratitude. Something like what ol' man Tum said. Instead, I felt like a mouse surrounded by bobcats. Mercury had told me his version of the artifact. It had sounded strange and unreliable. I coughed. "Uh. No. What myth is that?"

Hidalgo straightened up and pointed at the artifact. "There are rare but detailed stories in the oral tradition of certain Mayan tribes about an alabaster box. You have not heard these?"

I raised my hands at my side, palms up.

Hidalgo harrumphed and turned back to the box. His examination grew more intense. "Tell me, Señor, why did you post twenty-eight pictures of this on Instagram if you have not heard the tales?"

Mercury face-palmed and shook his head. He had told me not to brag about Jenny's prowess as an underwater salvage operator. She was the one who found the *San Andrés*. She was the one who figured out it was a thousand miles from where it was supposed to be. She was the one who found the captain's logbooks that identified the shipwreck. I thought she should get props for that. But we promised the Cubans we wouldn't tell anyone about the treasure.

Lots of things had gone wrong for her since she got out of prison, and this was the first thing to go right. She had discovered a major archeological treasure. I was bursting with pride for her. Since the Cuban captain thought the box was a fake, I felt it would be OK to talk up that part of her find to our friends—as long as I left out the location and the stuff about caskets of gold and silver. I'm proud of my fiancé. So bite me. But I didn't tell Hidalgo all that. Instead, I trimmed it down to the essentials. "I figured it tied the two continents together a thousand years before Columbus. That is, if it's real. I thought you'd be the guy who would know."

"Where did you find it?" he asked. There was a chuckle under his question. As if he thought I would lie.

In my peripheral vision, I sensed Jenny shaking her head. I said, "In the Caribbean. I'd rather not say exactly where because the locals weren't interested in treasure hunters storming the area."

"I see," he said with some snark.

Everyone stared at me for a long time. Then a few snickers rippled between them. Like people trying very hard not to laugh. I got the impression they didn't believe me. Maybe Mercury was right—I should've left this thing alone.

"Excuse me, Benito," Carlotta said. She pushed him aside with her hip.

She examined the box, placed her hands on either side, and pressed buttons I hadn't noticed before. There was an audible click. She pulled the top off and set it aside. Inside was a black chunk of glass a little larger than a football, shaped like a couch pillow, and smooth like a river rock. It looked almost like obsidian, but clearer and with gold flecks embedded in it. Carlotta grabbed it and raised it with great difficulty as if it were heavy. She held it to her chest, staring at it as if it were a baby. She rubbed her cheek on the surface.

Everyone stared at her in disbelief.

She carefully laid the rock back in the alabaster box and replaced the lid. It clicked again. She turned to Hidalgo, then glanced at the volunteers and students. She said, "So many people are hungry. Uneducated. Helpless. I … I have to help them. I must leave. At once. There is so much to do. So many in dire need of help. I'm so sorry for the way I've treated you, Benito. Everyone, for that matter." She made eye contact with the group, one at a time. "I'm sorry."

Everyone watched her run to her tent. She grabbed what she could carry and came back out.

No one said a word. I got the feeling they couldn't wait to see her leave town. I'd only known her for ten minutes and I was glad she packed. But her last apology sounded out of character and that had the group speechless.

Carlotta didn't wait for a response. She disappeared down a trail in the jungle.

A moment of stunned silence followed. Someone said, "Alrighty then."

Hidalgo shrugged and turned back to the box. He turned it to the Roman side and examined it in detail. It was a bas-relief carving depicting an important event. Commemorating stuff was something the Romans loved to do.

After a long and awkward silence, he pointed at it and said, "Have you any idea what this is about?"

He was making fun of me. Obviously. It was written in early Medieval Latin, a variation of Classical Latin that evolved when the Christians took over Rome. It's not as well-known as the other forms because so little of it survived. But when you have the Roman god of eloquence following you around like a stray dog, you can perform a miracle now and then. Maybe they would be impressed and take me seriously.

My other option was to wrap up my package and walk away. Which was clearly what Jenny wanted. She thought the mood of the crowd was getting ugly. She shook her head gently and moved her gaze to the trail.

I turned to Mercury. *How about it, can you help me out?*

Mercury leaned over my shoulder. *Hey homie, think he already knows what it says?*

I said, *He's the world's leading authority on the Mayans. How would he know Latin?*

Mercury said, *Open your mouth and I will speak through you. They will be in awe of your brilliance.*

I said, *No tricks?*

My used god's ventriloquist act had produced mixed results in the past. He thinks it's funny to make me evangelize for the Roman Pantheon. Which is even more embarrassing than you might imagine. Other times he comes through with articulate Churchillesque speeches that make me proud.

I started talking and Mercury filled my mouth with words.

"It commemorates the Romans putting this box on a boat and sending it off the edge of the world." Heads tilted my way out of curiosity. "The guy on the left is Stilicho, Regent for the underage Emperor Honorius. The date translates to the winter of 408 AD. The map on the right shows what the Romans considered the edge of the flat Earth. Today we know that's where the Canary Current travels from Gibraltar to Africa's West Coast. From there, conceivably, the raft could've been swept into the North Equatorial Current—same thing happened to Christopher Columbus—and carried into the Caribbean."

I felt pretty good about that bit. It sounded like I knew what I was talking about. Sometimes Mercury pulls through.

The group stayed silent for too long after I'd stopped talking. They were suspicious. Still bent at the waist, Hidalgo turned to find Rafael Tum in the crowd.

When their eyes connected, Rafael shrugged and said, *"Mas o menos."* More or less.

Hidalgo rose to his full regal posture and looked down his nose at me. He pointed a finger at the boat depicted in the center of the carving. "And what does it say here?"

"That says they commit the Poison Stone to Neptune."

The group laughed. Hidalgo approached me with a scowl.

His voice rose and his face turned red. "The mythical Poison Stone was a chant, a god, a curse, a gift depending on which of the oral traditions you believe. They say the man who possessed it walked a tightrope over rivers of blood, chambers of knives, and burning coals in the cenotes of hell chased by Kisim, the skeletal god of death. Those who carried the Poison Stone carelessly toppled kings and destroyed whole cities, scattering their populations. He who carried it wisely destroyed only himself, going mad and throwing himself into Xibalba, the realm of death. They warned the Spanish not to touch the Poison Stone. The Conquistadors took it and shipped it back to Spain, only to lose it at sea. And you expect us to believe you found it? And this is it?"

Hidalgo pointed at the alabaster box.

"Well. Yeah. Kinda. I thought you'd be interested."

"You are a liar! A fraud!" He stuck his finger in my chest while his people jeered. "You carved this yourself. The Mayan glyphs are faked. A child could see through your deception. This is nothing but a forgery. There were no Roman artifacts in the Mayan world. Get out of here and take that abomination with you!"

CHAPTER 4

WE LEFT HIDALGO AND HIKED the path of shame until we couldn't hear their taunts anymore. About three miles.

Along the way, I shouted at Mercury, *I should've known you were making it up the minute I heard 'Neptune.' Rome had gone all-in on Christianity by the 380s. Why did I ever listen to you?*

Mercury said, *Chill homeboy. I got a little carried away is all. Caught up in the moment, y'know? Don't that ever happen to you?*

I said, *If you're a god, how come you didn't know Hidalgo was setting me up? There was no writing on that little boat. Now, I gotta lug a hundred pounds of rock all the way to the Mayan ruins at Tikal. And then I don't know what I'm going to do with the damn thing. Thanks for nothing.*

Mercury said, *Why you blaming me, yo? I told you not to mess with that thing. Leave it at the bottom of the ocean, I said. And what do you do? Haul it up and show it off like you got yourself a new toy. Why would you listen to god? Why—*

When he goes on a rant, I tune him out. Everybody wants to yin, but nobody wants to let me yang back. Or whatever.

I figured Guatemala was our best route home. According to my Sabel Satellite phone, we'd crossed the border into Guatemala half an hour earlier. We made camp on the edge of a small clearing.

Tikal was another forty miles south. There weren't any trails. We would head out cross-country in the morning. With a little luck and some perseverance, we could make it there in a long hiking day. Jenny ran 10Ks; she could probably do that in twelve hours. Whatever the case, we were twenty-four hours from civilization and a flight home. I'd dump the rock at the nearest tourist shop. Maybe I could get twenty bucks.

I set up the tent while Jenny stirred a pot of beans on the campfire.

"You wanted adventure," I said to Jenny. "Did you figure on public humiliation?"

I joined her on a log by the fire. She nuzzled my shoulder and purred. "We're literally in the middle of nowhere and some rando chick recognized the Hero of Paris. I'm happy." She patted my chest. "She was talking about my hero of Paris."

Her positive vibe gave me a warm feeling. I hugged her. Having a woman's admiration was a whole new world for me. Before Jenny, women had always asked things like, *What's wrong with you?*

I said, "You don't mind that she was hitting on me?"

"Cherry? Hitting on you?" She laughed. "Are you one of those guys who thinks any time a girl smiles at you it's because she wants you?"

"Whaaat? You mean, it's not?" I hugged her. She wrapped her arms around me. "Then why are you smiling at me right now?"

She laughed again. "Well, truth be told, I was thinking about, you know, yin and yang, order and chaos, trains and tunnels."

We heard a whistle. Melodic. Like someone whistling a tune.

I rose and moved toward the edge of the clearing. Beyond our circle of light, the jungle was black as a cave.

"Someone there?" I called out.

"It is I, Rafael Tum," the professor's voice answered.

He came through the trees and approached the light. He looked concerned. Jenny stood behind me, using my shoulder as a shield before recognizing him and stepping out.

"So what brings you out here in the dark?" I asked.

"Hidalgo is a self-important fool," he said and dropped to the ground cross-legged with the ease of a child. "You, Jacob, are far worse."

His dis felt harsher than the ridicule Hidalgo unleashed back at the dig.

"You walked all this way to tell me it's a fake?" I asked. Jenny and I went back to the log and sat, never taking our suspicious gaze off Rafael. I still had trouble hearing an Englishman and seeing a Mayan. "I've heard. You can go home now. That's where I'm going come sunrise."

"You are worse than a fool," he said, "because you know the artifact is real and yet you parade it around like a child with a prize toy."

"Hang on. I don't know anything about it. The Cubans told us it was fake, but they weren't specialists. We brought it here to the expert and he confirmed it's fake. So, it's a fake. We're done. Going home."

"Hidalgo." Rafael scoffed. "A walking doctoral thesis on ignorance. Why did you bring this up from the bottom of the ocean when you know it causes death and destruction?"

"Hey, that's not fair." Jenny doesn't like other people attacking her man. "We don't know anything about it."

"Oh?" Rafael cocked his head. "In 525 AD a monk created the *Anno Domini*, AD, system for numbering years from the birth of Christ onward. Before that—for example, in 408 AD—Rome numbered years based on emperors. At that time, they numbered years from the beginning of Emperor Diocletian's reign. The date carved on the box reads January 14th—of the year 124." Rafael pointed at me. "Yet your betrothed, a soldier with no formal education in Roman history, converted that obscure number with ease. How?"

Jenny snapped her gaze to me.

I kept my eyes on Rafael and said, "Maybe I looked it up on the internet."

"You accurately translated a good deal of the Roman inscription. Not just for Hidalgo but in your Instagram comments. The Romans typically used little text and let the artwork speak the rest. How did you interpret Roman symbolism from the internet?"

Well he had me there. I sure as Orcus wasn't going to tell him how my immortal companion gave me the inside scoop on all things Roman. That was always a conversation stopper. Not that I cared about the conversation stopping, but I hadn't worked up the nerve to tell Jenny about the winged messenger of the Roman gods. Only a handful of people—those who'd witnessed heroic deeds that could only have been accomplished with divine intervention—knew about him. Jenny had seen some of my miracles, but I didn't want to spook her. OK, so, I had chickened out. But I was getting there.

I said to the nosy professor, "It's a hobby of mine."

He nodded just like my grandfather did when I lied to him.

How come old folks never challenge you, they just give you that knowing glance that makes you feel three inches tall?

"What was all that mystical gobbledygook Hidalgo was saying?" I asked. Jenny squeezed my hand to let me know she was on my side.

"He was trying to scare you with the myths about that box."

"Didn't work," I said and poked the fire with a stick. "I don't believe in myths."

"Nonetheless, you would be wise to remain vigilant." Rafael smiled at me. "The power—and therefore the danger—of a myth lies with those who believe."

"Danger, huh?" I scoffed. "So, who are you?"

"I am a linguist. My specialty is dead languages. I found my calling when I went to boarding school at Eton. My undergraduate degree is from Oxford, my masters from Barcelona, and my PhD from Harvard. I'm familiar with Latin because sixteenth century priests and conquistadors often wrote home in Latin. But my specialty lies in the many dialects of my people, the Maya."

We were impressed. He gloated in the firelight for a moment.

Eton and Oxford explained why he spoke English with a frozen jaw, like the Brits.

Jenny ladled out our stew, and again offered Rafael a portion. He turned it down. We began eating.

"I must tell you, Ms. Jenkins," Rafael said while we ate, "you cut a regal figure behind the controls of that beautiful submarine. You must be fast friends with Pia Sabel for her to loan it to you."

"They grew up together," I said to cut off any further discussion of our young billionaire friend. "She threw an engagement party for us on her yacht and there was a six-person submarine onboard. We played around with it and lucked into finding the *San Andrés*, that's all."

His eyebrows shot up. My casual description of using half a billion dollars' worth of aquatic toys impressed most people. He was impressed. He didn't need to know she had been pulling out all the stops to keep me from leaving her company. We'd had a falling out over ethics. Hers. I'd left and hung out my shingle as a security specialist. Then she announced my engagement party. I wasn't too proud—or too stupid—to turn down a couple weeks splashing around the Caribbean on her four-hundred-foot dinghy before starting my self-imposed vow of poverty. A man needs to be flexible when opportunities arise.

"How fortunate for you," Rafael said. "And yet how unfortunate."

"Unfortunate?" I didn't like his attitude. Jenny squeezed my hand again, this time to calm me. "Danger. Responsibility. You came here to tell us something, so just spit it out. What do you want? Is it the Poison Stone? Wait, you called it the Freedom Stone. Whatever. It's yours."

"Absolutely not." He held up both hands refusing the gift. "I refuse to touch it. In addition to my profession, I am a member of an ancient order called the Keepers. We monitor myths and watch for corresponding events in our era."

"Are you going to tell us it's a magic stone and we're cursed or something?" Jenny asked with a hint of sneer.

"Thousands of years ago, people found a rock." He gave Jenny a patient smile. "Anyone who touched it ended up sick. The ancients labeled that rock evil and stayed clear. Today we call it uranium. Not so long ago, people fashioned the atomic bomb from it. The ancients were not wrong about the evil. Although that raises the question: is uranium magic?"

"Magic until science figures it out," she said. "So, is this thing good or evil?"

"Marie Curie used radium to cure cancer. She died of exposure to it. Is radium good or evil?"

"OK." Jenny's head bobbed with reluctant agreement. "Depends on how it's used."

We both dove into our camp stew to contemplate his concept and to avoid his critical gaze. He watched us as if expecting us to have an epiphany of some sort. Apparently, we weren't Oxford-smart. We didn't get it. I glanced over at Mercury for divine help. He gave me a finger wave and laughed. I mopped up my stew with bread and finished it.

"You believe in myths," Rafael said to me. "You do not flinch when you encounter the inexplicable. You do not question. You believe."

Mercury stood behind the professor with his arms outstretched. *He's talking about me, brutha. Can ya feel it? He senses my divine presence. He knows you're the chosen one.*

I said, *Oh yeah? If he senses you, talk to him. Ask him to stand up.*

Rafael Tum rose from cross-legged to standing without using his hands. He paced the fire circle.

Mercury swept his hands around in a big arc before pointing at Rafael like an assistant drawing attention to the magician's big trick. *Standing, homie.*

I said, *Not because you asked.*

"How do you figure that about Jacob and myths?" Jenny asked.

"Jacob posted many pictures on Instagram along with a highly educated and detailed analysis of the Roman portion. He did that because he believed in something."

I didn't want to get into any mythological weeds right then, so I changed the subject. "What was that about danger and myth-believers?"

"There are people who believe the ancient myths. People who will do anything to attain and keep power, to protect their position. No doubt they've seen your posts by now. They will stop at nothing to take the Stone from you."

"They can have it," I said. "I'm out."

"And if their purpose is to fashion it into the equivalent of an atomic bomb?" the old professor mused. "Your responsibility is to make sure it doesn't fall into the wrong hands."

Jenny and I shared a curious glance.

Rafael went on. "Would you give it to people if you knew they planned something evil?"

"OK, I'll hide it," I said.

He frowned and glanced between Jenny and me. "And let them torture the location out of you or your loved ones?"

"We'll give it to the good guys," Jenny offered.

"How do you know who they—"

A panicked voice came to us through the jungle.

The professor and I raced to the edge of the clearing, beyond the firelight.

"Rafael! Rafael!" Cherry's rattled and breathless voice came to us before we could see her. "They came. Like you said. There must be forty of them."

Out of breath, she staggered to the fire, a backpack on her shoulders and another in her hand. We guided her to the circle and took her packs.

"Just as you feared." She gulped the water Jenny offered and tried to catch her breath. "Armed men. Swarthy. They had that green tattoo you described. Knights of Mithras." She struggled to catch her breath. "They rounded up Hidalgo's team at gunpoint."

CHAPTER 5

HALF AN HOUR LATER, WE'D broken camp. Rafael insisted it would be best to flee the invaders. It crossed my mind that Rafael could be leading us into an ambush, although it didn't seem likely since neither he nor his assistant were armed. Jenny could handle them easily.

Using advanced techniques to cover his trail, Rafael led the women deeper into the uncharted rain forest. Since Jenny had a Sabel Satellite phone like mine, I could catch up with them later using GPS. I went back to Hidalgo's dig site with my only weapon, a Glock 18C. I had to see about this army of Knights Cherry had described. She didn't seem like the type to make up a story, but civilians often succumb to their vivid imagination when threatened. No one wants to be the coward who ran.

My Sabel Visor gave me an advantage over any potential enemy. Night vision with a thermal overlay allowed me to identify humans better in the dark than daylight. Sabel gear is the best in the world. As I neared the edge of the site, I realized that someday soon I'd have to surrender all my Sabel toys—the Glock, the satellite phone, the visor, even the Sabel Darts. Painful thoughts.

I came across the first of Cherry's Knights standing guard a quarter mile from the dig. He was alert, well-trained, and carried an AK-15, the latest Kalashnikov rifle. On his wrist was the tattoo Cherry mentioned, the roundel of the Turkmenistan military's elite units, a white crescent moon with five stars inside a green circle with a red border. It wasn't his fault he couldn't see me. He lacked any kind of night vision. Which told me these guys were daylight operators. Being an expert in night operations, I had a small advantage. I kept a significant distance and moved past the sentry without incident. I made my way through the trees to the tents circling the plaza.

Floodlights had been set up at one end, creating long, dark shadows behind bright subjects. A squad of men carrying AK-15 rifles and wearing black camp shirts and shorts set off on patrol to my left. If they made a standard sweep of their contained area, I had ten minutes. If they were smart and doubled back to confuse a potential enemy, I had two. I analyzed how they worked. They were professionals displaying a level of discipline rarely seen outside the US Army's special ops units. I doubled down on being careful.

Moving to the back of the largest tent, I peered in through a vent. It was an office of sorts. The tent had been tossed over. Chairs and tables and maps and shards of pottery lay strewn about. I crossed through a slice of light between tents to the next one over and checked it. A bunkhouse of sorts. Also trashed with pillows and tangles of sheets on the floor. People had been hauled out after bedtime.

Rounding the edge of the bunkhouse, I could see the plaza and a group gathered there. The grad students and volunteers were on their knees, their hands bound with tight zip ties, mouths gagged with socks. They were lined up in three rows of five. I had a view between the rows. They faced the harsh lights. Beneath the lamps stood a stocky, bald guy—the head honcho. He slapped a collapsible baton against his open palm while he talked to someone. I couldn't make out the words.

Near me, the guy who'd backed up Carlotta with a rifle on our arrival struggled against his zip ties. A guard in black quickly approached him and smacked a baton hard across the guy's back. He barked in pain through his gag.

Two men patrolling the plaza with AK-15s headed toward me. Their eyes, unaccustomed to the dark, hadn't spotted me yet.

I backed into the darkness and made my way to the wall Jenny and I had passed on our way in. It gave me something to hide behind. While the frontside of the wall had been stripped of vegetation, the other side was higher and packed with trees and the Mayan equivalent of kudzu. I jumped the wall in a bound, hurtling myself into the dark on the other side.

Jungles are not quiet places. Howler monkeys scream over the din of insect orgies and territorial bird fights. On top of that, there are hundreds of mammals singing lonely love songs to attract mates. Before we set out on our adventure, Jenny and I looked up the creatures of the Yucatán. There are iguanas, deer, anteaters, kinkajous, coatis, and jaguars just to name a few. I landed on the only javelina for miles around. It looks like a pig but is actually a peccary with a nasty attitude.

He squealed his way out from under me, squared off two yards away, gave me a wicked glare, and pawed the ground like a New York City subway rider. I crouched below the wall and held my hands out, cooing softly, trying to calm him. We stared at each other until he said *Fuck you* in peccary and trotted off.

The men in black on the other side of the wall didn't trot off. They'd heard the squeal and came to investigate. I flattened against the wall, which was waist-high on my side and shoulder-high on theirs. I could hear them talking fifteen yards away. Not Arabic or Pashto, the languages I knew and recognized, but most likely Turkmen. One of them flicked a flashlight beam ten yards south of me. It swept across the trees until it went past my position.

In that moment, I could only think about Jenny. While I held my breath, I began to realize why heroes never have a significant other. My risky behavior—sneaking into an enemy camp because I didn't trust the reconnaissance of a grad student—endangered her future as well as mine. As a bachelor, I never thought twice about slinking around armed killers. If they found me, I could shoot my way out or die. No big deal either way. But now, someone was counting on me as her life-long partner. I'd been through her therapy sessions and helped her escape a crippling case of Rape Trauma Syndrome, RTS. She was almost back to being the accomplished officer she'd once been. As much as I needed her, she also needed me.

Slowly and carefully, I pulled my pistol and considered my options should the guy lean two inches farther over the wall to inspect the noise that drew him. I did the math on enemy troop strength. I'd seen a four-man squad leave on patrol. One man guarded a point on the perimeter. Twelve men guarded Hidalgo's team. One leader. Two more were looking for me. Most likely, there were eight perimeter guards and possibly another patrol. That gave me at least thirty-two. There could be other patrols as well. Cherry hadn't been too far off. And she could've been right about forty.

Mercury crawled up next to me, nose to nose. *If you pull that trigger once, homie, you gonna need to pull it thirty-nine more times and nail each one without a miss. How many rounds in your magazine?*

I said, *Seventeen in this one and one more magazine in my pocket.*

Ooh, that ain't gonna cut it, bro, Mercury said. *Do you have any more back at your camp?*

I said, *I wasn't planning on taking on an army with automatic rifles. I brought enough to scare off a few narcos. So. Can you help me out here?*

You think I can pull bullets out of thin air or something? Mercury asked.

I said, *Or something.*

Mercury said, *You promise to tell Jenny about me?*

I said, *Yes. Absolutely. Maybe.*

The man with the flashlight flicked it off.

I waited. The pair didn't move or make a sound. They were smart, using their ears. My patience outlasted theirs. They started talking, a light argument in their native tongue. From the tone, one guy insisted he saw something while the other teased him about wildlife. They moved off in the opposite direction.

Mercury said, *You're welcome, brutha.*

Carefully, I rose and peered over the wall. These guys were good, they had moved to an area that gave them wider visibility. If they turned one degree to the left, they would see me.

I crept toward the plaza on my hands and knees, occasionally checking on the two guards. Finally, I came to the end of the wall. Going any farther would put me in plain sight of several people. I kept my head low, just high enough to see over the wall.

At least I was within earshot of the leader, Mr. Baldy. I could make out half of what he was saying. He held a Volquartsen Scorpion pistol with a distinctive Q Erector silencer attached. The hardware choice of assassins, it was light, accurate, and quiet. The top-of-the-line suppressor reduced noise to twenty decibels, roughly the volume of someone whispering *BANG*. Mr. Baldy was serious about his work.

Some of his words floated to me as he turned slightly in my direction. "…this Jacob Stearne?"

I caught a hint of British accent, which didn't fit his Central Asian origins. Maybe he had an English education like Rafael.

I couldn't hear Hidalgo's reply. His tone of voice was mournful and pleading. The opposite of the bellowing professor who'd sent me packing.

I clicked the video on my phone and tried getting some footage for later analysis. It was dark, they were far away, but maybe it would catch something I missed.

There was a chance I could get a shot off. Hitting a man at this distance was possible. Upsetting his interrogation was probable. Saving Hidalgo was unlikely. The most common reaction of a man losing control of his situation was to strike out at the most vulnerable. In this situation, that would be Hidalgo. I felt like I had to do something disruptive to change the balance of power. After that, I could worry about saving the professor.

I checked my adversary. Mr. Baldy moved like a concrete wall, slowly and deliberately. His square, bald head sat on a short, thick neck with an anvil of a jaw. He was muscular, with gym-muscles that moved weights up and down but might or might not be useful in hand-to-hand combat.

Suddenly, something bad transpired between the two men. Mr. Baldy shouted angrily. Hidalgo struggled to back away. Mr. Baldy leaned in, leading with his chin.

Hidalgo shouted, "No, no! Captain, I told you all I know. Please for the sake of—"

Mr. Baldy raised his pistol. I couldn't hear the report, but Hidalgo's head snapped forward. The back of it bursting outward. His body collapsed.

I couldn't believe it. I'd seen plenty of executions. I'd executed people. But they were always hostiles in a theatre of combat. Not an innocent college professor. Not for the crime of being unable to answer a question. The shock was overwhelming. I peered down the iron sights on my 9 mil then remembered I was outnumbered—and Jenny needed me.

The grad students and volunteers screamed so loud I could hear them through their muzzles. The group began writhing and twisting. Three guards pulled someone else from the group. A woman I hadn't seen earlier. A guard yanked the gag from her mouth.

Mr. Baldy raised his pistol and said with a British accent, "You get one chance. Where did Jacob Stearne go?"

He knew my name. Why would he care about me? Who was this guy?

"Calakmul," she cried.

It was a lie. I hadn't told them anything about my destination. She just blurted out something to avoid a death sentence. It turned out to be the wrong thing.

Mr. Baldy said, "I just came from there."

He fired. The woman collapsed next to Hidalgo.

Again, I was shocked. Murdering innocent academics to find me? Was this about the Stone? What did Professor Tum call it, dangerous? I aimed my Glock at Mr. Baldy again. It was a long shot for a pistol. Handguns are short-range weapons, 25 to 50 yards on the range. This was 120 yards at least. With a moving target. Too far for a realistic shot.

Mercury pulled my wrist. *Dude, you can't win here. You'd be committing suicide.*

I said, *I gotta try.*

Mercury said, *You might pick off one or two. Then they descend on you in droves.*

I watched as a nightmare unfolded before me. One by one, he dragged harmless academics to the front, asked questions they couldn't answer, and executed them. I'd seen plenty of wartime horrors, but nothing as cold, calculated, and pointless as this. Mr. Baldy was a raging psychopath.

I said to Mercury, *I can't stand by and watch this. He wants me. Jenny is a terrific woman, she'll be sad for a while, but she'll move on. I'm turning myself in.*

Mercury said, *You'll die for nothing, homie. No matter what he does with you, he's not going to let these witnesses live.*

CHAPTER 6

Captain Batyr Amanow sensed the tension and unrest building like ice on a lake before it cracks. His men didn't approve of the bodies lying at his feet. Leadership is a minefield of difficult decisions. This was necessary. They should know that.

When the Soviet Union fell, many former republics fell into lawless anarchy. Innocent civilians were set upon by brutal criminal gangs. Terror and uncertainty ruled the cities of his youth. Back then, strong leaders emerged. Tough measures were required to reinstate rules. Rules that protected everyone equally. When the Protector offered him the opportunity to flee his family's squalor at the age of eight, he jumped at the chance. The Protector showed him the benefits of orderly discipline and he never thought of his home on the Caspian Sea again.

Now, he was hearing hints of dissent in the voices of his men. Dissent can lead to chaos in the ranks. The Protector hadn't entrusted Amanow with this mission just to lose his command before he achieved his objective. His brutal methods had unsettled some of the Knights. A problem he would deal with immediately. Looking over the bodies of the disrespectful academics, he could understand how the carnage might upset the weak. Using the comm link, he summoned everyone to the plaza.

While waiting for the most distant patrols to come in from the jungle, he had the Knights stack the bodies near a large ceremonial stone. He climbed to the top. When the last patrol arrived, he held up his hand, then slowly gestured to the dead.

"Long ago," he said in a strong and confident voice, "the Knights were chosen by God to lead the nations. God chose this time, under the leadership of our Protector, to reveal the location of the Poison Stone. The Protector chose us—just as he chose the Guardian—to follow in the sacred footsteps of the hallowed Knights of Mithras. It is not an easy path, my friends. There will be many difficult decisions that require strength and resolve.

"Imagine how hard it must have been for the Knights who followed the *San Andrés* through a storm that sank three-quarters of the fleet. They stayed on their mission, their hearts true to the cause, until they could sink the ship a thousand miles from its last known location. Did they leave witnesses who could locate the sunken ship? Not a soul."

He paused to look each man in the eye. None shrank back. That lifted his heart.

"These are perilous times for civilization," Captain Amanow continued. "All over the world, police officers are disrespected, attacked, and spat on. Terrorists roam freely, threatening the lives of peaceful citizens. Watch the news in any country and you see violence, chaos, and crime. You have heard the carefully crafted lies coming from rich countries. You have heard their media outlets making up myths to confuse us. What keeps a society safe is no longer important as long as an individual can worship anything he makes up. And where do they worship? At the altar of anarchy. Crime is up fifty percent around the world. Everywhere you turn, immigrants invade this country and that. Syrians invaded Europe. Mexicans invaded America. Uighurs invaded China. Who will invade your country? Who is willing to sacrifice his child so the next terrorist can have a warm place to sleep?"

Several heads began nodding. It felt good to see his words at work.

"It takes a strong man to stand in the gap left by overeducated elites who pride themselves on their diplomas. What do they know?" He pointed at the bodies. "Did they tell the truth when I asked simple questions? They covered for an American warrior who fled with the most dangerous artifact in the history of civilization. Why? Because they are insulated in their ivory towers, they keep themselves safe from the lawlessness that permeates the streets. They leave us to wallow in lives that have been abandoned, ignored, neglected.

"You know the Protector. He alone has looked out for you. He alone stands against the forces of globalization. He alone stopped the incursion of the West. He alone protected your children."

Captain Amanow checked every pair of eyes in the group. They were with him. They made him feel strong. It was a great feeling.

Once again, he gestured at the corpses. "There are difficult decisions to be made, gentlemen. There are horrific deeds and tremendous trials ahead of us. We are up against one of the single greatest soldiers to ever march across a battlefield. You must dig deep inside yourself and ask, am I man enough for the days ahead? Will I stand idly by and let riots of freethinking engulf my city? Will I let extremists bomb children in their classrooms? Or will I stand with the Protector and take up arms against the forces of evil? Well? What do you say, men? Are you with me?"

Gu Peng felt her heart soar at the sight of so many Brothers of Claritas gathered in unity. At the same time, she felt the weight of responsibility for these enthusiastic young people. Yes, she insisted on rigorous training in case the Brothers had to battle the veteran Knights. Yes, they had acquitted themselves like the finest warriors. But that was all it was, training. The Knights were far more experienced, disciplined, and accomplished. She could not yet count on Jacob Stearne to help them. Now the time had come, the Brothers must rise to the occasion. Nonetheless, doubts crept in her mind. Was challenging the Knights for the Freedom Stone the right battle to fight?

The Brotherhood had been a worldwide circle of friendship, hopeful myths, and strange rituals when she'd joined so long ago. After Tiananmen Square, the Brotherhood took her in, nursed her battered body back to health, mended her crushed leg, and gave her a reason to live. Had they believed the stories of a simple rock that could free people from bondage? For so many years she found comfort in believing the hopeful stories. But now, it was real. They had all seen the evidence. The Brotherhood's experts had agreed unanimously: Jacob Stearne had indeed found the Freedom Stone. And the poor man had no idea what the five factions would do to him to obtain it.

With her walking stick tapping out her pace, she followed the stone path down to the grassy shore of Lago Petén Itzá in El Remate, Guatemala. The brave young men and women of the Brotherhood of Claritas lounged on the grass in the warm evening. Torches lit their open space. But fear and anxiety colored the light of their auras.

Branches of despair must be pruned to allow the seeds of hope to grow in their place. Peng had been on both ends of the spiritual spectrum. She knew how easily the vitality of others could fertilize a large circle. For optimism to spiral outward, it needed space and energy. And a spark.

As she approached, they rose and greeted her with respectful hugs and kisses. Danny and Mark pulled a large round of wood fashioned into a coffee table to the group's center and motioned for her to stand on it.

Danny's inner circle of friends hovered around him. She leaned to him and said, "Danny, you water a tree at its drip line, not at its trunk."

He looked a question at her before understanding. With a quick whisper, he dispersed Fiona, Mark, and the rest of his companions to the outside edges of the gathering.

"Ms. Gu, please tell us why we came to this place," Danny said loud enough for everyone to hear him.

Everyone quieted and looked to her expectantly. She climbed the low table. Giving a speech in English shook her confidence. There was no melody to the language. Still, it was the language of the young volunteers before her. She took a deep breath and begged the spirits to give her strength. She held her hands out from her shoulders, palms up, and slowly raised them to the heavens above.

"Mother of star," she began, "we thank you for blessed life we enjoy. From childhood we thrive bosom of freedom. For that, we eternally grateful. But you never promise life tranquility. You draw our soul to Brotherhood. We swore on light of ancestor, as Brother swore thousand and thousand year before, we protect all people from bondage. Now you choose today, you choose my people, we stand up—face down tyrant. We set world to right path, free path.

"Five hundred year ago, all Brother give life to deliver Freedom Stone to Europe. They hope defeat feudalism. Instead, they defeated. All lost at sea. As result, Europe mired in monarchy, enrich few royal with slavery and plunder. World remain under dark cloud of despot, Dark Age and Renaissance. They trample life ordinary people around world. Then, for brief, shiny moment last century, representative democracy peak. By late 1980, forty-six percent of country in world led by elected official. Today, only thirteen percent of country—just six percent of world population—live in free democracy. Fascist and dictatorship already take over world."

She waited patiently while they discussed these details and debated their concerns. She gave each person time until they reconnected with her gaze. Then she raised her hand to speak again. A few hushed the others. When they fell silent, she continued.

"We at terrifying crossroad for humanity. Throughout world, police brutalize and attack those who seek only express themself. They kill reporter and label anyone who call out transgression—dangerous radical. You hear lie of despot. You see video smuggle from closed territory. The heart of cosmos call us shine *claritas,* brightness on those who hate.

"For century, we prosper and flourish. Those day—no more. Bitter hatred sweep across globe. From Hong Kong to Caracas, people who dare question authority—the dictator imprison and beat them. Syrian flee endless war, they turn back. Mexican children, they cage. Muslim in China, they re-educate. Who stand up for oppressed people? Who sacrifice themself for better world?"

On the outside edges of the group, Danny and his friends responded with positive commitments. She smiled and caught his eye. Now she knew it was not she who brought him to the Brotherhood. He had drawn himself to his destiny.

"It take strength oppose authority. We need summon strength to fight violence with action they not expect. We make chaos for them. Why? Because they respect nothing. When we appeal their humanity, they bury our light. Their idea: safe street is empty street."

Everyone leaned back, considering her words. Danny and his friends voiced agreement with her. Mutterings of "she's right" and "it's time" rippled from the edges to the center and grew in volume.

"You blessing of universe. You endow with energy of ancient light. We not do this because I say so. We do this only unanimous consent. We one council. Together we stand against oppressor. Together we turn table and beat Knight of Mithras. This time, no quarter. This time, no hesitate. This time, Claritas."

Gu Peng pushed her fist to the sky. "What you say? You are with me?"

CHAPTER 7

I DON'T KNOW IF I was burdened by or saved by my love for Jenny. Watching Mr. Baldy execute fifteen academics from my hiding place behind the wall left me sickened. It was the opposite feeling from Paris. I'd never felt so far removed from being a hero. I cursed myself for not being better prepared. If I'd brought one of Ms. Sabel's H&K MP7s, I could've taken them all down.

With no options, I ran to meet Jenny and the others. After getting a couple miles between me and the scene of the crime, I called the police at Calakmul. Between my Spanish and their English, they thought I was a drunk tourist playing a prank. They finally agreed to check it out the next day. And that would take all day because of the remote terrain. Their answers didn't fill me with confidence. I resolved to take down Mr. Baldy myself. I couldn't let a madman like him kill again.

But I'd have to get in a better position to attack before taking on a significant force like his.

Running a zig-zag route through the rain forest to throw off any trackers, I caught up with Jenny, Cherry, and Rafael. Jenny had determined Cherry couldn't go any farther without rest and had stopped about ten miles south of Hidalgo's site.

I told them the horror I'd seen, of Hidalgo and his whole team being killed in cold blood. Rafael and Cherry wept and consoled each other. They had worked for weeks with these people.

When they gathered themselves, I thumped Professor Tum's shoulder. "You knew they were coming?"

He stood up to me. "As I told you, the power of myth lies with those who believe."

"Who are these guys?"

"The Knights of Mithras," Rafael said. "They believe the Poison Stone destroys civilization."

"A stone?" My doubt twisted my tone of voice. "Uranium had to be refined and harnessed to destroy civilization. What the hell could be in that box?"

"What the box contains does not matter—"

"I know. It's what they believe that matters." I ran my fingers through my hair, shocked to imagine what kind of supernatural bullshit these guys believed if they were willing to slaughter people to get it.

"We should give it to them," Jenny said.

"What do they do with us after we turn it over?" I asked. "They just killed everyone who saw it."

"Who can we give it to?" she pleaded with Rafael.

"No one," he shrugged. "It is your responsibility."

"What about that group you belong to?" I asked. "What was it called, the Keepers?"

"Ours is a simple cause, we quietly advocate for good. We have no military capabilities."

"That's convenient." I poked Rafael. "Then we need you to arrange for the Guatemalan government to take this off our hands. It's not ours and we don't want it."

"I have no connections with the government."

"Don't give me that. You went to English boarding school. That takes money. Which means you come from a wealthy family. In a country like Guatemala, that means your family is in tight with the government. What are they, orange exporters? They own a big coffee plantation somewhere?"

Cherry snapped a frightened look at Rafael. He ignored her.

"Telecom." Rafael sighed and held up his hands. "You are right about my family; they are 'tight' with the government. They own a good number of officials. Unfortunately, I am not tight with them. My dissension over the treatment of peasants distanced me from them. When I took the wrong side in the civil war, they disowned me."

If my recollection of history served me, Guatemala went through thirty years of civil war that didn't end until the late '90s. There were horrific mass murders committed by both sides, but the government won in the end. That made Professor Tum a man without a family or a country. That's why an Oxford-Harvard man was second fiddle on Hidalgo's dig instead of leading it himself.

"What do you recommend we do with it?" I asked.

"Find one of the factions that will take good care of it." He paused, waiting for me to ask who that might be. When I didn't, he said, "You might consider the Brotherhood of Claritas."

"Brotherhood? Knights? Keepers? There can't be that many secret societies."

"Masons, Elks, Orange Order, Illuminati—You know they exist, yet you never question their charters."

I had to think about that for a moment. My thinking stretched into a long awkward silence.

He sensed my distrust and turned to his camping tent. "I will rest now. You will do as you please."

"Aren't you going to tell me why the Brotherhood would take good care of it?" I asked.

"You never asked about the Knights of Mithras. I suspect you know more than I."

He bent to his knees and crawled in the tent's open flap. Cherry followed him in. Without making eye contact, he zipped it closed behind them.

I sent Jenny to bed and kept watch. There wasn't much to watch because the Knights had no night vision gear. They wouldn't get moving until first light. Then they would move quickly.

The Knights of Mithras turned over in my head. From what I recalled of Mercury's many boring history lessons, Mithraism was a secret Roman religion known only to the initiates. Mithras evolved from a Zoroastrian god and dovetailed into the Roman pantheon. The cult was popular in the Roman military, but the Christians managed to wipe out any records of its existence by the fourth century. Which happened to be about the same time Stilicho put the rock out to sea. All we know about the cult today stems from iconography depicting Mithras hanging out with Sol, the Roman sun god; Mithras slaying a bull; and Mithras being born from a rock. Have they been underground since then? I wondered if Mercury considered Mithras a real god since he started out in Persia.

Not even close, homie. Mercury stood at the edge of the clearing with a bright-green frog the size of a table next to him. *Persian gods ain't no better'n Greeks.*

The frog shot a ten-foot ribbon of tongue out of his mouth, plucked a fly off my earlobe, and snapped it back before I had time to react.

Dude! Mercury smacked the frog with the back of his hand. *You trying to gross out the mortals? Get back in yo' human skin.*

The frog popped into a dark, muscular figure with bulging eyes and a headdress of feathers and skulls. He wore a breastplate of polished seashells, and an illustrated loincloth. A wide black streak stretched across his eyes, and his lips were painted white. He chanted something angry and loud and shook a stick that rattled.

I stuck out my fist for a bump. I said, *Vucub-Camé. How's it hanging, bro? Haven't seen you since Tokyo.*

The Mayan god, Vucub-Camé, or Seven-Death in English, smiled at being recognized and bumped my fist. The last time I'd seen the local deity, he'd had a cosmic hangover after partying with his roommate from god college.

Then a realization hit me like an ocean liner banging into an iceberg. I slapped my palm to my face and took a deep breath.

I said, *Holy shit, this is bad. This is really bad.*

He's honored you remember our time in Japan, Mercury said. *Whatsa matter with that, homie?*

I said, *My hallucinations are compounding now. I gotta go back on my meds. Gotta go back on my meds.*

Mercury said, *Don't be doing nothing rash, my brutha. We're all cool here. Seven-Death is here to help us out.*

I said, *Do I want to know how? Never mind. Let's pretend this never happened and I'll handle things my way for once. OK?*

Mercury snapped back a step, deeply offended. *Oh, hell no. You could screw up a one-year-old's birthday party. You need to hide the Poison Stone and Seven-Death is here to show you where.*

I said, *What good will that do me? They'll torture Jenny and me, probably kill the other two for shock value.*

Mercury put an arm around me. *Don't you trust me yet, homeboy? You have to hide it where no one will ever find it. Someplace where the only way they'll get their hands on it is if you show them. You have to be alive for that. And once you get them into Seven-Death's crib, you can get the drop on them.*

For once, he was making sense. Which worried me. Were the doctors and psychiatrists right, this Mercury-stuff was all in my head? Would I end up hiding the artifact in plain sight while deluding myself into believing it was really hidden? That kind of thing could go horribly wrong. Get me killed. Jenny too. The whole idea sounded crazy to me, and I'm the one they say is crazy. Was it possible? Would it happen? Could I follow a mythological god into the lair of another mythological god and expect it all to work out in real life?

Sure. Why not?

I shouldered the backpack and followed the gods into the darkness.

We didn't go far before we came to a huge hill that towered over the treetops. After we climbed it, Seven-Death pointed to a sapling growing out of a rock at the very top. I looked at the sapling. I looked at the rock. I looked at Mercury. Seven-Death pointed to the tree, shook his stick, and gestured for me to pull it sideways. I did. The roots were wrapped around the rock. When I pulled the tree, the rock came up as if the tree was a lever. Mercury and Seven-Death trotted down into a hole under the rock.

I looked up to the heavens. Rain clouds were thickening in the dark. Out loud, I said, "Jesus, if you can hear me, would you please drag me back to sanity right now? Your buddy Mercury is getting weirder by the minute."

After waiting a long time for my Road-to-Damascus moment, I gave up and stepped into the unknown under the rock.

A narrow stairway led into absolute blackness. The stone treads were barely six inches wide, half the standard in America. The riser was easily two feet, three times the depth allowed back home. For the first fifty steps, the stairs squeezed between two stone walls. It was as if the

Mayans had built a pyramid on top of another pyramid and left a small gap between.

Mercury called to me from the third turn. *Your professor friends haven't found this pyramid yet, bro. It's completely covered in dirt and plant life. You're the first mortal down here in twelve hundred years.*

I'm honored, I said. *I'm still going back on my meds when we get home.*

Mercury turned to Seven-Death, *Don't listen to him, he's always talking smack.*

When we sank below what I calculated to be the base of the hill. I could no longer feel the walls on either side of me. It felt as if the staircase was suspended in a huge cavern. The echoes of my footfalls on the stone came from farther away with each step. I had the sense the space was gigantic. And dark. So dark, I turned on my phone-light.

The stairs continued down into the depths. Far below me was a shimmering lake of silver. Seven-Death waited at the bottom.

Mercury said, *Don't y'all freak on me here. That's a lake of hydrargyrum, what you call liquid mercury, just like the one they found under the pyramid at Teotihuacan. See, building shit like that is what true believers do for their favorite gods.*

I remembered reading about the discovery on the Smithsonian website. A flood accidentally exposed the entrance at the base of the Temple of the Plumed Serpent. Far below was a long tunnel to a series of secret chambers. One was filled with liquid mercury that reflected torches. The ceiling had been painted with stars and planets. I looked up. Yep, this place had them too.

Mercury put a hand to his mouth to shield his words from Seven-Death. *Not that I want a lake of liquid metal, ya understand. I'd rather have you finish that temple you started in your backyard. You could put a statue of me in it—and take out that damn barbeque grill. Show a little respect, is all I'm saying.*

Seven-Death motioned for me to follow him across the lake on a path of steppingstones. When we reached the other side, we ducked through a series of caves. A tightrope carved in stone formed the path. One cave had knives strewn about on the floor. The next looked like a river of blood. The next was freezing cold. Finally, we came out to a ceremonial chamber with an altar in the middle.

I pulled out my alabaster albatross and laid it on a stone altar covered in carvings of Seven-Death. I looked at him. He pointed to a small altar stone nearby that was roughly the size of my artifact. The carvings on it were of a different god. He smeared clay over the glyphs to conceal them. It looked like a large lump of modeling clay when he finished. He pointed to my backpack. I put the altar in my pack and hoisted it. It was a good deal lighter than the alabaster box. That would make the rest of my trek a heck of a lot easier.

We made our way back through the caves and back across the silver lake. When we reached the staircase, I noticed piles of skeletons at the base.

Mercury said, *The unworthy have a bad habit of slipping on the steps. You good, though. You be in tight with me.*

He and Seven-Death smiled big and slapped me on the back. I winced a smile back at them and made my way back up. Seven-Death grunted from the bottom and waved. I waved back. He was staying. Or my madness was clearing up. I wasn't sure which.

I got back to the top as a light rain began. I pushed the tree upright and the stone fell back into place.

The rain started falling harder.

Half a mile from camp, I found Cherry standing in the rain playing with her satellite phone.

My approach scared the wits out of her. When she caught her breath, she said, "I, uh, I couldn't sleep. What are you doing out here?"

"Looking for El Dorado."

She frowned. "That's a Columbian legend."

"No wonder I couldn't find it." Looking back at her footprints in the mud, I noticed hers paralleled my path. I glanced at her phone. A GPS map glowed on the screen. "Looking for the way back?"

She nodded. "I'll just follow you. If that's OK."

I nodded and jogged back with Cherry keeping pace. I went straight to my tent and climbed in with Jenny.

CHAPTER 8

WITH LITTLE DOUBT THE KNIGHTS would be on our trail at daybreak, I squeaked in a couple hours of sleep. I rousted everyone at first light and started the long march to civilization.

It's good to have goals in life. I had three: 1) get Jenny to a safe place; 2) hunt and kill Mr. Baldy; 3) catch the next flight back home. Maybe grab a shower at a hotel if there was time. The shower beckoned me. I could picture the soap clearing three days of jungle grime off my skin. I could also picture clearing three days of jungle grime off Jenny's skin. Followed by candles and a hot oil … I had to take several deep breaths to keep focused on my satellite map.

Professor Tum pointed us toward the nearest town, Uaxactun. We made it there by mid-afternoon. It was little more than a collection of tin-roofed sheds near a few ruins.

Rafael checked in with the proprietor of a one-room museum nestled in a row of dilapidated tourist shops. The museum curator sent us to the bodega down the road to find the only vehicle in town bigger than a motorcycle. The owner of the rusty pickup agreed to take us to the Hotel Jaguar at Tikal. He thought we could rent a car or find a taxi from there. Maybe. The four of us climbed in back because he didn't have a passenger seat anymore. We bumped and bounced and banged down the twenty-four miles of gravel road in little more than an hour.

Our driver's cousin, owner of the hotel, had no cars and no taxis but offered to give us a ride to the next town south after he served the dinner crowd. He gave me a deal on a couple rooms to use for showers and changing. Despite having harbored dreams of lovemaking all day, neither of us could shake the idea that the killers were tracking our path through the rain forest, getting nearer by the minute.

Stearne's Law came to mind. *Paranoia is the result of acute situational awareness.* It happens the instant you run into danger when it suddenly dawns on you that everyone really is trying to kill you.

We met up with Rafael and Cherry for dinner at the restaurant and talked in somber tones.

The hotel manager had a minivan. Exhausted, I nearly fell asleep on the ten-mile drive to El Remate. But we stopped in heavy traffic half a mile short of our destination.

"Roadblock, Señor," our driver said.

He got out and walked through the stopped cars, heading toward two police pickup trucks. Three officers wearing dark blue uniforms with gold trim checked the occupants of cars.

Mercury appeared next to me. *Say, homie, you ever get the feeling the cops around the world are setting up roadblocks just for you? Is that Stearne's Law?*

I glanced around to make sure he hadn't brought any dinner-table-sized frogs with him. I said, *Why would they be looking for me?*

Mercury said, *Because you don't listen to the holy messenger when he speaks to you. I said, throw that damn thing back in the ocean. What'd you do, brutha?*

I said, *We're not going there.*

Jenny looked at me. "Going where?"

"El Remate," I said. "I think the cops might have the wrong idea about who killed Hidalgo."

All my traveling companions turned to stare at me. Then they followed my gaze out the windshield.

Our driver directed the attention of a cop toward us. The two of them began walking back our way. Behind them, the other two officers spread out and paralleled the road. A simple flanking maneuver.

"We must run," Rafael said. He reached over the back seat to get his pack. "With utmost urgency."

"No," I said and grabbed his arm. "I have video of the Knights. I'll explain things to them. They'll be reasonable."

"This is Guatemala, Jacob." Rafael grabbed my arm. "Not New York

City. Reason does not reign where corruption rules."

It took me a second to translate that into American. Facts didn't matter, only the benevolence of the local ruler.

I said, "You were a left-wing radical. You were hassled by the Man. I get that. But I'm American. I believe in the rule of law. And I have an embassy to back me up."

He gave me that knowing, patient grandfather look again. As if I were hopelessly naïve.

Jenny gave me the same look.

The flanking cops reached the sliding door before our driver got to us. They yanked me out and threw me on the ground and cuffed me and gave me a kick. I think the kick was preemptive.

Minutes later, we were in the back of a pickup truck again. This time cop-trucks. Minutes after that, we were in a one-room cinderblock building with three worn-out desks and two wooden chairs in an open area with a cage made of chain link at the back.

Rafael and the ladies were shoved into the cage. I was handcuffed to the main man's desk. The main man leisurely paged through my passport. His men dug through our packs. I quickly realized the three of them were the entire force. Each man had a desk but, due to shift changes, they only needed two chairs.

One officer went through Jenny's pack while the other went through Rafael's. As long as they didn't go through mine, we were OK. But they would get to it eventually. Having a very real pre-Columbian stone altar might be considered motive by some cops. I started thinking up excuses, because *Given to me by god* wasn't going to fly.

The main guy tried to stare me down. While he may have run into a few tough guys in his corner of the rain forest, I'd been through well over a decade of combat duty. I gave him my soldier stare. The one that comes from facing death so many times you're not entirely sure you survived. This could be the afterlife for all I know. If it is, it's boring. But, should the need arise or my mood swing, I could always rip his trachea out with my bare hands.

He flinched.

The guy working on Jenny's pack found my pistol and laid it on the desk. The main guy's eyebrows rose. Next, he found my M9 bayonet knife and tossed it on the counter. Then, my extra magazine.

The guy rifling through Rafael's things froze. At first, I thought he'd found something. Instead, he looked over his shoulder at me. He peered at me, tilting his head. He rose and went to the main man and started to speak.

Having regrouped from his flinch, the main guy introduced himself to me in Spanish, cutting off his officer's words. I shrugged. He understood the language barrier and looked back to the cage. He called something to the others in Spanish. All three answered him. He chose the professor.

The guy rifling through Jenny's underwear ran to the cage to retrieve the old man. Since that stopped him from moving on to searching my pack, I was relieved.

Rafael said, "Our good lieutenant, Carlos Soto, has concerns about your extensive travels."

I said, "Work."

Rafael elaborated. I could tell because he used a whole lot more words than the one I gave him. The lieutenant asked his next question. Rafael answered without consulting me. They went back and forth.

While they talked, the cop who stared at me hadn't stopped staring. Without taking his eyes off me, he tapped his lieutenant's shoulder with a light, tentative knuckle.

I tapped Rafael.

The professor glanced my way, then gave me an update. "He wants to know your business with Hidalgo. I took the liberty of telling him."

"Did you tell him I was the one who reported the shooting?"

"Indeed. The problem appears to stem from the facts. You see, you and Jenny were the last known travelers in the region."

The cop who kept staring at me moved his focus to his phone while Rafael and Soto continued their discussions. When he found something, he tapped his lieutenant's shoulder again. Lt. Soto batted him away as if he were an annoying fly.

I interrupted to insist they look at the video on my phone. When Rafael translated, they handed it to me. I unlocked it and dialed up the video. I'm not a professional photographer. I didn't know videos taken in the dark, backlit by bright lights, would turn into a sea of indistinguishable silhouettes. They could've been dancers at a jungle rave. Fail.

Rafael and Lt. Soto turned their attention to my pistol. The lieutenant's voice rose in anger as he stabbed a finger at my Glock 18C. That could be a problem. Any weapons enthusiast would know Glock sold the pistol only to the Austrian counter-terrorism unit, EKO Cobra. A handful of people knew the only other company to secure the pistol was Sabel Security. It was fully automatic and capable of emptying its seventeen-round magazine in less than a second. Judging by the look on his face, Lt. Soto recognized the model.

The staring-cop returned his gaze to me and tapped the lieutenant again. He was brushed off again.

Rafael turned to me. "He has grown somewhat stubborn about your choice of firearms. It's not about the one you have with you but rather what you might've left behind in the rain forest." Rafael went on to explain their deliberations and how Soto didn't care that I was the one to alert the authorities of the tragedy.

While he spoke, the staring-cop shoved his phone in front of the lieutenant and started talking. The two of them looked at me, then at the phone. The lieutenant tugged at Rafael. They went on at length in Spanish with one word standing out amongst the rapid-fire words, "*París.*"

An hour wait in the bowels of Élysée Palace, twelve minutes of etiquette instructions from Sabel Security's protocol officer, four and a half minutes with a photographer and the French president—and six months later, half a world away, my life was saved. Guess it was worth it after all.

The cops took selfies with me, the Hero of Paris. I smiled.

The negotiations turned to where we would stay the evening. While the cops were nice, they never completely bought into our story about the Knights of Mithras. They thought it sounded like a telenovela. So, Rafael changed the story to the drug cartels the Mexicans were famous for and the cops nodded with grave concern. Lt. Soto wanted us to stay in town while he cleared things with his chain of command and the Mexican

Federales in the morning. We wanted to get as far from the Knights as possible, but we opted for staying on the good side of law and order. They repacked our bags and dropped us at a nearby hotel.

We checked in, paid for two rooms, walked back out, and took a cab to a different hotel—in case Mr. Baldy showed up and persuaded Lt. Soto to tell him where we were.

Our final hotel was nice, freshly painted, and sprawled along a lake. It was a jumble of two-story buildings with eight rooms each, laid out resort-style for privacy, with a wandering path connecting everything. A pontoon boat and a water taxi waited for guests at the end of a long pier.

Feeling good about having the cops on our side and looking for Mr. Baldy, Jenny and I decided to take another shower. This time, just for fun.

CHAPTER 9

Anxious about our pursuers, I slept like a rabbit at a coyote convention. Visions of turning the tables on a platoon of disciplined, aggressive soldiers were dampened by reality. While I knew I could and would take down Mr. Baldy, I still lacked the right firepower. As Jenny slept, I got up to wander. I holstered my Glock at the small of my back and covered it with my untucked t-shirt.

Rafael wasn't any better off. I found him wandering aimlessly down by the lake in the navy-blue pre-dawn light.

I didn't want to tip my hand about taking out Mr. Baldy, so I said, "I want to get out of here. Get back to the USA. When will Soto let us go?"

"You assume the Knights won't follow you to the States?" he asked. "Or follow me back to my hallowed campus?"

The first one was a good question. The second raised a different question in my mind. When did the professor become my problem?

"You and Cherry should come with us." I visualized Sabel Gardens, a guarded compound sprawling over a hundred wooded acres along the Potomac. "I have friends with lots of resources. We'll be safe."

As soon as the words left my mouth, I realized that would entail crawling back to Ms. Sabel, begging for help after my second final goodbye-no-I-won't-reconsider on her yacht just three days ago.

Mercury walked on the lake next to us. *Don't go getting all proud about it, homie. Just cut your balls off, tuck your tail between your legs, and tell Pia-Caesar-Sabel you can't deal with the real world. Don't forget who told you not to leave her in the first place.*

I said, *That's because you think I can make her worship you. We tried that. It didn't work. She's still an Episcopalian.*

Whoa, dude. You think you're done? Mercury smacked my shoulder. *Did Amelia Earhart give up just like that? You gotta go back and try harder.*

I said, *I don't think Earhart's the best example—*

Mercury said, *C'mon, brutha, get your shit together and do what's right for Jenny.*

Rafael tugged my arm. "You saw what evil deeds the Knights of Mithras are willing to commit, yet you would endanger your friends?"

"Well, uh." Now that he mentioned it, that would be a tough ask: Oh, hey, Ms. Sabel, I've only been self-employed for three days now but I've already failed and am being pursued by vicious killers—can I camp in your guest house?

An older Chinese lady with gray hair in a loose braid and relying on a walking stick strolled toward us alongside a tall, skinny young man. They stood out as an odd couple. She was sixtyish and he was early twenties. As we passed each other, the young guy said, "Buenos días."

We responded and kept going. Behind me, I could feel the Chinese lady stealing a glance my way.

"What do you recommend?" I asked Rafael.

"Keep the artifact with you—and keep moving."

At least he hadn't noticed I'd swapped the Stone for Seven-Death's used altar. Cherry never asked why I was walking the jungle with the backpack. So far, so good.

"What about you?" I asked.

"Young man, I will remain by your side. I would never abandon you. Before you think I'm acting heroically, it is anything but. Indeed, my fate is intertwined with yours until someone prevails. I see you are anxious to contradict me. Hold your tongue a moment longer. To forge my own way would render me an open target. I would suffer the same fate as Hidalgo in their pursuit of you."

He had a point. Hidalgo didn't know anything, and they killed him. Same for his people. Rafael and Cherry were in just as much danger. And like the Stone, they were now my responsibility. Great.

We made our way to the open-air restaurant where the women waited for us. The sun rose over the lake while we discussed options. Jenny advocated for returning home and putting our faith in Pia Sabel. Rafael refused. Cherry stayed quiet. I created a hybrid plan from all the options but didn't tell them what it was. I didn't want any arguments until her flight left.

Lieutenant Soto raced in, out of breath and ghost white. He bubbled up a lot of Spanish while staring at me with bulging eyes.

Everyone at the table responded at the same time then turned to me as if I understood.

Rafael raised a hand and said, "I will escort him."

He rose and gestured for me to follow Soto. As we walked through the maze of buildings to the front desk, Rafael said, "Lt. Soto was instructed early this morning by his headquarters to continue the interrogation."

I found it odd the officer wouldn't look at me. Last night, when he was in charge, he eyeballed me as best he could. I pulled his elbow, forcing him to face me. Rafael pulled up behind us, curious about what I wanted.

Soto still wouldn't look at me. He twisted away, heading for his pickup. His official vehicle was parked diagonally at the back of the parking area, half of it obscured by trees. His uniform was disheveled, as if he'd slept in it. He seemed like the kind of guy who took pride in his rank and therefore the uniform that distinguished it. He had dirt in his ear but was clean shaven. His cop-belt was missing. He was alone.

"We're renting a car," I told Rafael. I grabbed Soto by the collar and pulled him back. "I'll drive. Explain it to him."

I went to the desk to make arrangements. Two minutes later, an attendant pulled a new Toyota Agya to the entrance. We squeezed in. Soto didn't make a peep. When he thought I wasn't looking, he stole glances at me. He looked afraid. Of me to a certain extent, but certainly about his future.

"Tell him I know what's going on," I said to Rafael.

The professor was in back. He didn't question me. He simply spoke to Soto in reassuring tones. He patted Soto's shoulder. The cop didn't look soothed. The old man had no concerns. He wasn't nervous. His stint as a revolutionary had prepared him well.

We took the long way around, up a series of backroads to the main drag between Tikal and El Remate. Soto reluctantly guided my turns. We reached the outskirts of town in the opposite direction from what anyone at the station would expect. Driving down the two-lane paved road, we passed shops opening for the day. Owners swept the dirt floors clean. Closer in, the houses and stores had cement floors. A restaurant owner set plastic chairs and tables on his stone patio. Four small children clung to each other and their mother on the back of a motorcycle.

I shoved Soto into the footwell and slowed as we neared the police station. In the light of day, it was dirtier than I expected. Rain sloshed mud on the walls near the ground. The tin roof was just as rusty as every other roof on the street. I counted ten men within twenty yards of the building. None of them fit the local profile. They were the Knights of Mithras I'd seen at Hidalgo's dig. In daylight, the Turkmen tattoo, the size of a large watch, stood out. One guy bore a striking resemblance to Joseph Stalin, walrus mustache and all.

The other official pickup was parked out front, unmoved since we arrived last night.

"Those are the Knights?" I asked Rafael.

"It would appear so," he said. "How did you know it was an ambush?"

I explained how the dirt in Soto's ear told me the man had been shoved to the ground at some point after he'd shaved. His rumpled uniform came from being roughed up. I said, "I'm guessing the Knights met him when he arrived for work this morning. Our hotel ruse last night pissed them off. They forced him to find me. I'm guessing there are at least two gunmen waiting to ambush me from the bushes back at the hotel. That's why his truck was parked funny. Damn, I should've figured it out quicker. We have to get back. Check all that with him. And tell him to call his deputies. Tell them to stay away from the Station. And get backup."

I tossed my phone to Soto, figuring the Knights had taken his.

Rafael confirmed everything as I raced back to the hotel.

Jenny had served six years in the US Navy and could handle herself in tough situations. But the Navy doesn't do a lot of close-quarters combat. The Knights weren't amateurs. Which meant the women were in trouble.

Soto called the police headquarters for the Department of El Petén in Flores. It was on the far end of Lago Petén Itzá. They sent everyone they had. All twelve officers on duty were piling into vehicles to make the hour-long drive. All we had to do was survive the next hour.

I called Jenny while Rafael called Cherry. Neither answered.

We pulled into the hotel parking lot. Soto's truck was gone.

CHAPTER 10

I RAN ALONG THE PATH between the buildings to the hotel's restaurant and stopped before crossing to the palapa. I could see a waiter and busboy standing at an odd angle behind a serving bar. They looked like their feet had been nailed to the floor. They were too stiff, their gazes locked on a distant horizon.

With a snap of my fingers, I caught the bus boy's eye. I pointed at my eyes, then around the floor. He tilted his head to the wall next to me, indicating a hidden Knight. I twisted back to the right, stuck my left toe out around the edge of the wall until I sensed my attacker's movement. I stepped forward, untwisting my body, and leading with my left elbow. As I snapped blindly around the corner, my upper arm slammed into the bridge of a man's nose. His head hit the wall behind him. He went down with a groan.

The waiter and busboy exhaled. Rafael asked if this was the only man. They told him there were two more who had chased the women.

Jenny's phone lay on the floor. I scooped it up and ran for our room. Rafael followed right on my heels.

Mercury matched me stride for stride. *You ever notice the old man, bro? He's older'n your dad and he's kept your pace. Thirty-mile jungle jog, no sleep, racing around this morning.*

I said, *Could you tell me something useful? Like, where the fuck is Jenny?*

Mercury said, *I could tell you that, sure. But what's more interesting is wondering how long ol' Rafael was a revolutionary before he gave it up for teaching school.*

I said, *If you don't tell me where Jenny is, I'm calling the nearest imam and going Muslim.*

You? Do something disciplined like pray five times a day? Sheeyit, dawg. Who you kidding? You hang with me because you're too lazy for anything else. Would you walk to temple every Saturday morning like an Orthodox Jew? Would you spend two years knocking on doors for the Latter Day Saints? Go ahead, call the imam. But first, quit thinkin' about your own self and go to Rafael's room.

I changed course for Rafael's room and rounded a building in time to see two men in hot pursuit of the women.

One of them grabbed Jenny's wrist and yanked. She pushed off backwards, toppling both herself and her pursuer. A good but risky defense strategy to remove his advantage. Cherry stopped and shrieked. The man pinned beneath Jenny wrapped an arm around her to keep her from rolling off. That was the risky side to her maneuver: countermoves. As I raced toward them, he raised a large hunting knife, ready to strike.

Out of nowhere, a young blonde woman appeared an arm's length from Jenny and her attacker. The blonde hooked the man's wrist with her ankle and spun on her other foot, forcing his wrist to the ground. She pinned his wrist, surprising the man and giving Jenny enough time to struggle to her feet.

I arrived a second later and drove a devastating boot to the top of the man's head, stunning him.

The blonde took off running and disappeared.

Before I could shout thanks, the second man shoved Cherry into the room. Jenny slammed her shoulder into the door, preventing him from locking us out. I took three big steps, pounding my shoulder into mix. The door swung open. The second attacker flew backward, stunned and pinned to the wall. I fell to the floor because, unlike the movies, that's what happens when you commit your full body weight to opening a door.

Jenny pulled the door back and smashed it into the attacker a second time. That stopped his struggling for a fraction of a second. She repeated the process several more times. While she did that, Cherry tossed me a backpack.

Rafael took the time to deliver an extra kick to the head of the man lying on the ground in front of the doorway. Then he motioned for me to toss his pack to him. I did.

Jenny said, "I couldn't carry yours. Go get it and meet us on the dock. I have a plan."

I ran for my room, hoping her plan was a good one because I had nothing. I barged into my room and grabbed my pack with Seven-Death's replacement altar.

I stood still a moment, listening to the sounds around me. In the distance, I could hear tromping feet. The Knights' reinforcements were arriving in numbers.

I shouldered the pack and ran down the path to the boats. Four Knights rounded a corner fifty yards back. I passed the old Chinese woman with her walking stick and her young friend. In the light of day, she looked older and he looked younger. They stepped aside as I ran by. Behind me, I heard one of my pursuers face-plant on the walkway. Did the Chinese lady trip him? No time to look back.

Jenny helmed the water taxi as Rafael cast off. She was backing it up when I jumped aboard. I crashed into Cherry and Rafael. They did their best to keep me upright, but my momentum and weight sprawled all three of us across the bench seats. Jenny cranked the throttle and powered across the lake. I took a second to admire her ingenuity in making our escape.

Although it was not as exciting as you might think. A water taxi is no speedboat. We were going about as fast as a decent runner can sprint. The men chasing us opened fire with pistols. I scrambled to the bulwark and returned fire while Jenny zigged.

Without realizing I'd bumped the selector to full-auto during my crash-landing, my first magazine emptied in half a second. My objective was to scatter the killers. It worked—at the expense of a lot of ammo. The Glock 18C uses a standard 9x19mm Parabellum, but Guatemala has few firearms stores in tourist towns. I wasn't sure when I could find more. I reserved the remaining magazine in case of another encounter.

They hadn't expected that kind of firepower. They headed up the hill as fast as their feet could carry them before figuring out I wasn't keeping up the assault. The Knights regrouped and made their way back to the dock.

We were out of range, but they got busy untying the pontoon boat. I couldn't imagine it was any faster than our water taxi, but it couldn't be much slower either. They jumped aboard and followed us.

We were in a slow-motion boat chase, the kind James Bond never, ever gets into. Why does this stuff happen to me? Why couldn't there be a jet ski or a cigarette boat on the pier?

It took an hour to get to Flores. The Knights started a mile behind and fell back by a few yards every few minutes. Which meant they would see where we landed and be behind us by five minutes. And they had radios to guide their minions. I'd counted thirty-two back at Hidalgo's dig. They had plenty of resources.

During our flight from El Remate, Rafael told me Lt. Soto had chosen to wait for his backup to arrive. He couldn't abandon his town or his officers to help us. Which was understandable and admirable. Soto had warned us that the garrison at Flores had sent all available personnel to aid him in El Remate, leaving their city unguarded. Which meant I was the lone defense against our four pursuers. As long as the other Knights didn't arrive in Flores ahead of us, we could make it to the airport and charter a plane or rent a fast car.

I spent the trip chartering a plane. All I could get was a single engine turboprop. The good news was: that's all anyone could get. It wasn't a big airport. With any luck, we'd be on that plane and gone before the Knights in the pontoon boat tied off at the city dock.

Mercury sat on the bow. *You ain't got no luck, homeboy. Not until you come clean with Jenny.*

I said, *I will. Just has to be the right time and place. You can't just spring stuff on people. I mean, I can't just say, Oh, by the way, I'm in tight with a god who hasn't been worshipped in fifteen hundred years.*

Mercury looked hurt. *Say what? I been worshipped plenty. I got worshippers all over the world.*

I said, *I'm not talking about the kind who push their belongings around in shopping carts.*

Mercury frowned. *Dude. You wanna be that way? Then check out this here.*

He pointed at the only dock sticking out of the city's seawall. Ten Turkmen lined it.

CHAPTER 11

WHEN I POINTED THEM OUT to Jenny, she gave the dock a wide berth, keeping us out of range and slicing across a small bay. She said, "Look for somewhere else to land."

I scanned the coastline ahead of us. Nothing but rocky seawalls as far as I could see. Jenny studied Google Maps on her phone.

The Knights tried to run parallel to us along the shore. Due to the arc of the bay, they would have to run much farther to meet us. They would be a threat, but not until after we landed.

The pontoon boat crew saw our avoidance maneuver and narrowed the gap by cutting across our course correction.

"I'm going to run us aground," Jenny yelled above the straining motor. "There's a dirt lot a mile short of the airport. We can sprint the rest."

We glanced at each other; certain we could handle it.

Jenny looked us over as she realigned her course. "We'll be going twice as fast as a San Francisco trolley. It'll be a violent landing."

We traded glances again, this time with less certainty. I knew I could handle it. That was about the speed of an airborne assault landing under fire. Tuck and roll. Rafael had kept up on our trek, but could his old bones handle that kind of jolt? We lined up on the bow, ready to jump on impact.

Jenny revved it up, then revved it down, putting the boat on top of a little bow wave to cushion the impact. An instant before we hit, we tossed our packs and jumped in different directions, tucking and rolling. The little boat ran up the gravel embankment before groaning to a stop. When I rolled up to standing, Cherry came up next to me. The boat had shifted, blocking our view of the other two.

We grabbed our packs and tracked around the front to find Rafael staggering to his feet with Jenny's help.

Bullets pinged off the water taxi's metal hull. The deeper draft of the pontoon boat stopped them fifty yards offshore. I aimed without firing. They instinctively ducked.

We ran.

Rounding two concrete buildings, we ran up the main drag in Flores. We passed a municipal stadium, a tire dealer, a disco, and several restaurants on narrow sidewalks next to a four-lane road. For two more blocks, we had a wide grassy patch between the curb and a fence topped with razor wire. After that, there was no sidewalk, curb, or shoulder. We ran on a narrow strip of ground alongside a wall. The gopher holes and broken bottles lining the way slowed our progress. We stumbled and charged on, keeping our steps light in case the ground beneath each footfall gave way. Progress slowed, but the terrain would slow the Knights as well.

Cherry was not an athlete. Before long her jog turned into a walk. Her resolve didn't fail her, her lungs did. I took her pack from her without asking. She looked at me with protest in her eyes, but quickly understood. Our lead on the killers wouldn't last long. Admirably, she picked up her pace, breathing hard. I noted that she had never complained throughout our ordeal.

In half a mile, we came alongside the airport runway. A cinder block wall topped with rusty barbed wire kept us from taking a shortcut. Half a mile ahead of us, I could see the only plane on the apron. Our plane. The terminal loomed six football fields down the road. Three minutes at our pace.

I looked back. No sign of the Knights. I doubted we were safe, but that gave me hope. Rafael and Cherry were running out of breath.

The professor tripped on a tree branch hidden by the knee-high weeds. I took his pack from him before helping him to his feet. Jenny and Cherry kept going, knowing there was nothing they could do. We regained speed and determination as we neared the terminal's short driveway. Safety was in sight.

Three trucks roared up the road behind us. Several Knights rode in the bed of pickup trucks. They opened fire with semi-automatic assault rifles, laying down a spread of bullets in the dirt behind us.

I dropped the packs and aimed at them, hoping to bluff them again. This time, it didn't work. They laid down another wall of bullets at our feet.

I picked up the packs and ran to catch up with my friends. They had spread out, the bullets scattering them in different directions. Cherry tripped on a pothole and went down. The Knights fired a line of bullets into the dirt between us and Cherry.

I squeezed off a shot at the driver. He kept coming but braked.

At first, I thought I'd scared them. Then I realized they'd slowed for a different reason. In the back, a man rose with a grenade launcher. He fired at my plane. My eyes followed the rocket in disbelief. It hit the engine compartment square on. White hot shrapnel flew out in every direction, some hitting the wings where the fuel tanks exploded in a fireball.

While my eyes told my brain what I didn't want to believe, a second truck flew into the drive behind me, cutting between Cherry and me. Two men jumped out while another held a rifle leveled at me. He didn't shoot. Not wanting to tip my hand about being low on ammo when I was outnumbered, I held my fire.

The two men tossed Cherry into the bed of the truck. She screamed for help.

The driver floored it, burning rubber on his exit. The first truck cranked around in a tight circle and left. The third had already turned around.

My mind instantly snapped into tactical analysis. They could've shot me between the eyes and taken my pack. They didn't. Which means they know I don't have the Stone.

So what were they doing? They hadn't been shooting to kill. They wanted one of us. No doubt to bargain for the Poison Stone. Rafael was right. The myth was only as strong as the people who believed it. And the Knights of Mithras were believers. They believed in it so hard, they were willing to murder archeologists and blow up airplanes in broad daylight. Taking them down wasn't going to be easy.

Could I even do it? Without my friends from Sabel Security? I faced thirty-two men armed with rifles and at least one grenade launcher. Those guys weren't from around here and you don't shove a grenade launcher into your checked bags. At least, I've never gotten away with it.

There was no way they could've pre-positioned hardware ahead of my arrival in Flores. Or even Guatemala, for that matter. I could've easily gone home the way I came, through Mexico. That meant they had bribed someone in the military. And they'd found someone they could bribe while on the run. Or they had help from high up. None of which was a good sign.

Rafael Tum screamed in agony. At first, I thought he'd been shot. I ran to him. Jenny reached him at the same time I did. He turned to me, tears streaming down his face.

He clawed fistfuls of my shirt and cried, "You have to get her back. You have to save my niece!"

CHAPTER 12

IT WAS A TWO-HOUR TRUCK ride from hell. No one said a word. Cherry Crocker had never been so scared in her life. She told herself to stand up and take it. Her uncle had suffered incredible hardships. He had been tortured by paramilitary agents and survived. Many of his comrades had not. In 1980 alone over 3,000 Guatemalan citizens had been labeled subversives or criminals and summarily executed. Her mother's brother had managed to emerge as a powerful leader of the insurgents, a fact she had only learned while in college. Her mother had always refused to acknowledge Rafael Tum existed. Even when Cherry asked about the pictures of him in her mother's childhood photo albums.

If Uncle Rafael could survive torture to lead the insurgency, so could she.

A stocky bald man strode into the tent and glanced at her before gasping. He turned to the guard outside and shouted in Turkmen. He crossed the small space to her and untied her hands from the post high over her head. In a British accent, he said, "My apologies, Ms. Crocker. They were not to treat you as a criminal. You are a guest under my protection."

"Lovely invitation—at gunpoint." Cherry rubbed her wrists. "Are your guests allowed to leave?"

"Soon." He stepped back to give her room. "Before you go, there is an especially important person who would like to meet you. He is known as the Guardian. He has asked to meet you in person. He will explain certain facts about your uncle and your heritage. After you listen with an open mind, you will be free to go."

Cherry looked him over. He was built like a running back with thick muscles and no neck.

He gestured to a camp table with two folding chairs. "We are having *shurpa*, a mutton dish. Are you vegan like so many other Californians then?"

"What do you know about me? You know Uncle Rafael. You mentioned my heritage."

"Patience." He waved away her concern. "You've been on the run for two days. You hardly ate breakfast this morning. You must be famished."

A man brought in bowls of soup filled with chunks of mutton, onion, and potatoes and left them on the table. Strong spices wafted from the bowls. Her stomach growled. She took her seat, confused about the method of this man's torture. Should she trust the soup?

He took the first spoonful and noticed her watching him. "Would you like to trade bowls?"

"This is fine," she said and immediately regretted it. She should've insisted on trading just to read the expression on his face.

"Allow me to introduce myself, I am Captain Batyr Amanow. I am the leader of an expedition for an ancient organization known as the—"

"Knights of Mithras." She spooned some soup. A chunk of mutton melted on her tongue. She tasted hints of bay leaves. It was delicious.

"We are not who your uncle believes. This is one of the things we'd like to explain. Ours is a simple cause, we quietly advocate for good."

"You murdered Benito Hidalgo."

Amanow leaned back as if she'd slapped him. "Is that what your companion, Jacob Stearne, alleges? Did he offer any evidence other than his word? Did he mention the US Army asked him to resign after his many struggles with sanity? You know, reality becomes an elusive thing for men who have snuffed out hundreds of human souls."

Cherry felt confusion clouding her thoughts. "He was a hero in Paris. The president of France—"

"Have you read the alternative facts about those events?" Amanow leaned across the table. "Eyewitnesses saw him murder two innocent men that he later claimed were about to attack. Their testimony has been quashed. Why?"

Cherry hadn't heard those versions of events. She only saw one official press release. Would the president of a country award an honor … she thought of the men who had hunted her uncle for years. They had been given medals.

"Eat." Captain Amanow finished his soup and smiled at her. "We have quite a long journey ahead of us."

GU PENG HURRIED TO THE suite where the Brothers held the Knight, her walking stick tapping out a quicker rhythm than usual. The Freedom Stone was so close, she could feel its energy. If she could get just one step ahead of the Knights, she might convince Jacob Stearne to help. If she couldn't persuade him, perhaps his girlfriend could be persuaded. She didn't want to think about other methods. If there was one person she never wanted to become, it was the tank driver who crushed Gu Tong.

Still, in the long and documented history between the five factions, the Brotherhood had been successful only when resorting to violence. That fact had made her insist the Brothers train like soldiers. It would be best if they never resorted to violence, but also wise if they were prepared for any situation.

Peng knocked on the suite's door. A Brother let her in and showed her to the dining area. A bloodied and beaten Knight was tied to a chair at one end of the table. One eye was swollen, his nose broken.

Peng gasped and tossed her walking stick aside. "Ice, at once. Who do this thing?"

"Not us," Danny quickly responded. Fiona, standing behind him, ran for ice. "Jacob Stearne did this with his elbow."

Peng met Danny's gaze with one eyebrow raised. "Untie him. Least we do. Treat him guest not prisoner."

Danny said, "He was quite violent when—"

"Are your guests allowed to leave?" the Knight asked in a thick accent.

"You speak English?" she asked. "I Gu Peng. He my associate, Danny. We speak of universal brightness. We illuminate whole universe.

We not animals. You go free when we render aid."

The man scoffed, his swollen eye taking in Gu Peng from head to toe. "Does this first aid involve knives? Needles? Something barbaric? We have been warned about you."

Fiona returned with ice wrapped in a towel. She applied it to the Knight's swollen eye. He batted it away. The ice clattered across the stone floor. Without hesitation, the young woman dropped to her knees and picked up each cube.

"We not harm you," Peng said. "Have one question for you. Why girl? Why no Jacob Stearne? Why no take his fiancé?"

The Knight spat on her.

Danny ran for a washcloth, wetted it, and ran back. Peng smiled at him as she accepted the cloth and wiped her blouse clean.

"This mean you not know?" Peng heard herself using someone else's voice. As if she'd channeled some long dead warlord.

"Her name is Cherry Crocker," Danny said. "She is descended from a nineteenth century railroad tycoon on her father's side."

Peng admired his cunning approach, to propose something to see if their adversary would correct them. It was almost impossible for some people to keep secrets. Especially when they could establish themselves as superior in knowledge by revealing it. She replied to Danny, "You think was old-fashion kidnapping? Have esteem Knight run low on cash?"

The Knight's irritation rose. But he didn't speak.

Fiona offered him the ice and towel again. This time he took it and held it to his face.

"After years of corruption and mismanagement under the Guardian, what else could it be?" Danny asked.

"You are fools." The Knight tried to spit on her again.

Peng had learned to twist aside quickly. The spittle flew past her.

The Knight began chewing on something, his jaw working in circles. Inside his mouth, the tongue worked hard enough to see it pushing against his cheeks. Peng puzzled at this odd movement for a moment. Then realized what it was.

She could let him go on. The man certainly deserved his fate. One could reason that all the Knights deserved such a fate. But then, that was what separated the Brotherhood from the Knights. Caring about others.

"Open jaw!" She grabbed his head with one hand and his chin with the other. "Push towel over tongue!"

Danny didn't understand but grabbed a spoon from the dining table and pushed it into the Knight's mouth.

"Force mouth open!" Peng shouted as they struggled with the Knight.

Again, Danny complied without fully understanding. Then they saw the flash of something white inside the Knight's cheek. Danny leveraged the spoon harder. The man gagged.

Peng shoved her fingers inside his mouth. Ignoring his attempts to bite her hand, she extracted the small object and held it up. As she suspected: a cyanide pill hidden in a false molar. An old trick among spies. And a demonstration of the Knights' resolve.

"The world be sadder place without you energy." She patted the Knight's shoulder and stepped back and gestured to the door. "You free to go. Keep ice."

CHAPTER 13

MERCURY POINTED AT PROFESSOR RAFAEL Tum. *I saw that look on your face, dawg. You thought the old man was hitting that shit. Admit it. Dude, you should be ashamed of yourself for thinking like that. Ol' Rafael and Cherry were economizing cuz they're family, that's all. Cannot believe you and your filthy mind.*

Keeping my eyes on the road, I said, *You thought the same thing.*

Mercury said, *Did not. But it don't matter. You gonna explain to him what you're doing or you gonna let him worry like that?*

I said, *Isn't he one of the meek? Since when do you care about them? You told me to leave them alone.*

Mercury said, *Yeah. Well. See. Seven-Death asked me to do him a solid and look out for the guy.*

I said, *You're kidding, right?*

Mercury said, *I may owe some money to the Mayan gods. But, c'mon, dude. Just look at the man. He needs your help.*

"I told you, I'll get her back," I said, glancing over my shoulder. "I have methods."

Rafael didn't say anything. He sat in the back seat, his nose against the window of our little rental car.

"I don't get it," Jenny said. "Why did they take her?"

I had two theories, and neither were the kind of thing I wanted to discuss in front of her uncle.

It was late afternoon when we arrived back in El Remate. We all saw the well-dressed woman at the same time. A line of people snaked up to the back of a truck, where she was handing out bags of food. I said, "Is that Carlotta, the grumpy old lady from Hidalgo's dig?"

Jenny said, "I think so."

From the back seat, Rafael's pained voice said, "She touched the Freedom Stone."

We didn't want to know what that meant, so we didn't ask. We were modern, science-based people who didn't believe in magic stones. A few minutes later, we pulled into the hotel parking lot. Cops still combed the grounds. We trudged through the open-air lobby and out to the restaurant. If there was a clue left, the cops had picked it over. Still, we looked. A cop lifted a spot of blood where I had leveled the Knight who'd tried to ambush me. The cop tucked it in an evidence bag.

We went to Rafael's room, where we saw three cops inspecting every surface with tweezers and magnifying lenses. Rafael looked at me with an expectant gaze. As in, next idea?

Mercury nudged me. *You thought you'd come back to the scene of the crime, find a clue to Mr. Baldy's lair, and be on your way, huh, homie?*

I said, *That was one possibility.*

Mercury said, *And you ain't got no other possibilities. You should tell the ol' man you done run outta methods.*

I said, *But you're going to help me, right?*

Mercury said, *Forty-eight hours ago, you promised to tell Jenny all about me. You spent most of the next day walking through a jungle and not one word about the Capitoline Triad, or the Dii Consentes, or the holy messenger of the whole damn pantheon. And now you ask for help? Go on now, she's standing right there. Say something.*

I faced Jenny. She looked up at me expectantly. I said, "Jenny, uh, you're an atheist, right?"

She said, "That's not going to be a problem, is it?"

I said, "Not at all. I just thought we could have a conversation about the mysteries of life sometime."

"Now?" Her tone of voice sounded agitated.

Rafael gave me a curious once-over.

I said, "Well, sometimes there are circumstances … in which the reality we know is …"

Over her shoulder, I saw the tall, thin guy with long auburn hair gelled back. He hovered near the corner of a building, watching us from behind the broad leaves of a banana tree.

"I'll be right back," I said.

I strode over to him at a speed that would make any retreat on his part awkward as hell. He looked behind him, then to the side, as if considering a duck-and-run. Out of options, he straightened and stepped onto the path.

"I've seen you and the Chinese lady all over the grounds today," I said. I stuck out a hand. "Jacob Stearne."

"Danny," he said and shook.

"Did you see the guys who tried to jump us?"

"I saw one of them." He hesitated a moment, then lifted his chin as if he thought of something. Like a new tactic. "And I know where he went."

It took me all of two seconds to reconsider who the guy was and why he'd been hanging around. "You're not with the Knights of Mithras."

He took a long moment to gather up his response. "I am one of a small band who knows how dangerous and misguided the Knights are."

"They kidnapped a friend of mine," I said. "Would you mind telling me where they went?"

Danny's gaze snapped to the police emerging from Rafael's room. "Have you told them about the kidnapping?"

"No."

He waited for me to elaborate. I stood still.

"Wise," Danny said after a moment. "They are untrained for the ruthlessness of the Knights. Involving them would cost innocent lives. Come with me and I'll show you where they went."

I grabbed his arm as he turned to walk away. "Not happening. You tell me where they are, and I'll take care of it."

"Then we are at an impasse. I have trained for years in dealing with them." His words didn't match his posture.

I'd seen men prepare to face death. Everyone has a certain amount of fear. The seasoned veterans show it in the form of readiness. They check their gear, go over their role, look you in the eye to see if they can count on you. The untested new kids straight from Basic talk big but their eyes quiver. Danny was closer to boot camp than veteran, but he didn't know it yet.

"You aren't going with me," I said in my master sergeant voice.

He took a deep breath. "We are allies. We each need the other. I will go with you. I'm not negotiating."

Jenny and Rafael joined us for the last sentence. They looked at me. I explained the situation. For some bizarre reason, they agreed with Danny. Everyone wanted to go. As if taking on thirty-odd heavily armed killers was something in their wheelhouse. There ought to be a law against James Bond movies. Everyone thinks they can storm the castle and live to see the credits roll.

But Danny was my ticket to finding Mr. Baldy, the man who had executed fifteen civilians. Mr. Baldy was going to pay for his crimes.

I put my foot down. I'd take Danny and no one else, only because I didn't know the guy well enough to care if he lived or died. He didn't flinch at that. Rafael and Jenny would stay another night at the hotel. We would leave at zero-dark-thirty.

"What time is that, exactly?" Danny asked.

"It's not an actual clock time. It's any time I think their defenses will be at their lowest point."

I kept him with me. If we were going to war together, I didn't want to let him out of my sight. A text, a call, a hand signal would be enough to set a trap for me. Danny understood my concerns and didn't complain.

When we got to our room, Jenny got enough separation from Danny to whisper. "You want me to keep an eye on the professor?"

"This guy could be leading me into a trap," I said, nodding at Danny. "I don't know who to trust. They could be working together. If anything looks funny back here, call me."

She didn't like her assignment, but she recognized the necessity of it. She said, "You do your thing and I'll do mine. Balance."

I didn't know if that qualified for yin-yang or duality, or whatever, but I liked her line of thinking. I smiled. She smiled. We kissed quickly.

I unboxed the ammo I'd picked up at the hunting store next to the car rental in Flores. I reloaded my spent magazine and put the remaining box of bullets in my pocket. I attached my suppressor and checked the action. I had ten handheld Sabel Darts, each the size of a rifle bullet. The clever injectors deliver a non-lethal dose of inland Taipan snake venom that causes instant flaccid paralysis and a secondary dose of powerful sleep medication. Anyone stabbed with a dart is paralyzed long enough to fall asleep for several hours. On a night raid, they were the best weapon available. No gunshots, no cries in pain, just the quiet slump of a body falling asleep. I grabbed my Sabel Visor, promised Rafael I'd bring his niece back, and gave my girl another kiss.

Danny retrieved a pistol and a GPS unit from his room under my watchful eye. We got in my rental and he gave me directions. He'd tagged one of the Knights I'd knocked unconscious with a GPS tracker. Clever enough, but being a civilian version, the accuracy was only within twenty-five feet. That could get him killed. The units Sabel Security used were much more accurate, much smaller, and had exceptional battery life. But I didn't have any—because I'd quit.

Mercury said, *Another reason you should go back to Pia-Caesar-Sabel, yo.*

I said, *And get shoved out on a cold and lonely cliff again? No thank you.*

Mercury said, *Hey now, I take care of my homeboys. You saved everyone in Odessa. You got a medal in Paris. You made it out of Mumbai. Nothing bad happened in Spain. What do I gotta do to make you believe?*

I tuned him out and concentrated on the driving. We were heading due north. Through Tikal and into Uaxactun. I was going back toward Hidalgo's dig with a man I didn't know from Apollo. I had a bad feeling about this.

CHAPTER 14

WE DROVE THE RENTAL TO the end of a farm road three miles northwest of Uaxactun, arriving just after 0200. The whole drive, Danny assured me he had mad skills. I listened and asked questions and tested his knowledge of certain situations. He had a good grasp of tactics and fighting. His bravado told me he was young and scared. Lots of quality training that had never faced a real threat. I admired his enthusiasm, it reminded me of the first day my boots hit the ground in a combat theater.

He gave me an overview of his band of merry men, the Brotherhood of Claritas. He said, "Ours is a simple cause, we quietly advocate for good."

I said, "Hundred bucks says the other guys say the exact same thing."

My snark earned me some side-eye from the boy. Then he continued with his story. I zoned out while he droned on about brightness and light. They considered themselves the defenders of freedom. The Brotherhood had liberated societies since the dawn of time. According to Danny, they'd kept the early Indus Valley and Egyptian societies democratic, but they'd been suffering setbacks lately. Authoritarians were gaining ground the world over. They had their sights set on freeing China next. Which was nice.

Mercury leaned to my ear from the back seat. *It's pronounced CLAIRE-it-toss, homie. Not Claw-REET-ass like some crackerjack town in California. They've been around since the beginning of civilization, always trying to help the meek. They thought they were helping the meek when they collapsed the Mesopotamia.*

I said, *Can I trust them?*

Mercury said, *Why would you trust people who want to help others?*

Talk about your basic losers.

I said, *Trajan helped others. He's considered the greatest emperor of all time. Under his reign, Rome's borders extended farther out than ever before. And he was a great philanthropist. He instituted a social welfare program called Cura Annonae, after the goddess Annona. It provided basic income in the form of grain.*

Mercury patted my head. *Aw, ain't that cute? You've been reading again. You forget who he took that grain from to give to the Romans.*

I turned that one over in my head. It had to come from somewhere. Gaul? Hispania? Dalmatia? Taxing the poor to feed the rich. Guess it's been going on for a long time.

Mercury said, *Back to the question: can you trust a guy who claims he does good?*

I trusted Danny as much as a stray dog. They're both nice and in need of positive reinforcement, but I didn't have time for house training.

Besides, for all I knew, Danny was leading me into a trap.

I parked the rental as far into the weeds as I could get it. While Danny checked his GPS in the passenger seat, I jabbed him with a Sabel Dart. He slumped in place. I let the seatback down for him because tall guys don't do well cramped in small cars for hours on end. I'm nice like that.

I grabbed his GPS unit and headed into the trees.

A mile into the woods, I found a trail that led in the general direction of the Knight's position. I circled the area by a quarter mile and found no guards. My second circle spiraled inwards by two hundred yards. This time, I came across four clearings with the distinct look of recent campers. There were holes where stakes once held tent lines. Smoothed soil where tent floors or sleeping bags once lay. A large number of people had cleared out. To a better spot a hundred yards away, or out of the region?

I moved on until I found one guy guarding the only trail leading to the center camp. A single sentry was light for a platoon as big as theirs.

On my third circle, I began to suspect a trap. What kind wasn't clear. But the encampment wasn't big enough for thirty men. There was one large unoccupied tent in the center and three others nearby. One of the tents had four horizontal heat-signatures. Presumably four Knights sleeping. Another had two. With one man on watch, that gave me a total of seven. They wouldn't have twenty-five on patrol. The Toyota pickups that attacked us had carried fourteen. Something was off.

Stearne's Law: *Paranoia is the result of acute situational awareness.* In my line of work, you know you're doing things right when everyone is trying to kill you. But no one was trying to kill me yet. I checked the forest behind me. And to the left, then right. I checked the tree branches high above me. Nothing. Not even a monkey. Still, my skin itched as if there were someone about to jump me.

If it were a trap, it would have to be one hell of an elaborate one. They could've killed or captured me at the Flores airport. I was outnumbered and outgunned. But they left me standing there like it was an insult. Instead of taking me and torturing the location out of me, they took the least likely to know. Then I thought about it from their point. Cherry was also the most likely to crack under pressure. Anyone could look me up and know I've been trained to resist enhanced interrogation. Jenny had been a US Navy officer. Rafael Tum must've been a serious dude thirty years ago. He still had the kind of toughness I'd seen in SEALS. Not as tough as Rangers, but close.

Crawling back carefully to my starting point, I searched for the lone sentry at the head of the trail. He had left. I followed the heat in his footprints and decided he'd gone to patrol the area. As silent as I moved, there were so many bugs, birds, and animals in the jungle, he would've sensed a disturbance and gone to investigate. Which meant he was a professional. And he was on watch alone.

That also meant the camp was unguarded. I went back, doing another circle in case I missed something. Zig-zagging my way through the trees, I came to the side of the tent with two sleeping bodies. I crouched and listened. No whispered radio commands. No signs of people faking sleep. The two guys inside were snoring quietly in a syncopated rhythm. When you sleep, your heart rate and breathing slow. You can fake it for a while, but not five minutes. Which is how long I waited. There was no need to rush.

Being inside a tent was a vulnerable position. Only one way out. Which meant, if I went in, I would be committed. If it was a trap, I was done. If it wasn't, then this camp was not where the Knights were holding Cherry. Maybe a decoy camp, which brought me back to thinking it was a trap. But not a good one. There was only one guy on watch and six more asleep. I scratched my head.

The fact that it didn't add up didn't reduce the danger. There was only one way to find out if they were holding Cherry in either tent.

When I was satisfied they were definitely asleep, I greased the zipper to quiet my pull and slowly opened it.

Crouch-walking my way in, I stabbed each guy with a Sabel Dart, then waited. No one moved outside. No footsteps approached. No communication devices squawked. I checked their faces. Both were men. Neither of them was Cherry.

I crept to the next tent. I repeated the same cautious approach. I quickly stabbed darts in three men, then held my pistol to the nose of the fourth. He had a swollen eye and a broken nose.

He was a sound sleeper. I nudged him three times before he awoke. His eyes crossed when they focused on the long silencer. Slowly, his gaze rose to meet mine. He hadn't seen me when I knocked him unconscious, but he recognized me anyway. These guys had done their homework.

"Danny sends his greetings," I said. "He couldn't make it in person, but he's with you in the spirit of the brightness. Whatever the fuck that means. So, listen up. I've got one simple question for you, then I'm on my way. Where is Cherry?"

He resigned himself to his fate. His eyes closed as he said a silent prayer, then opened again with ferocity. He managed to cry out a warning as he took a swing at me. Lying on your side is not a good launching point for a punch. I stabbed him with a dart.

So far, the trap had failed to materialize. Which meant I was standing in a residual camp. Maybe the Batmobile they hired to exit the region was short seven seats.

I trotted out into the dark, found an ambush point, and waited for the lone watchman to return. He did. At a gallop. Sad when you think about it. All that professionalism while on duty and he let his instinct to rescue his friends rule his temperament. He never saw me. Ran right past the tree I was using for cover and straight into the Sabel Dart I held in his path.

That freed me up to wander the camp looking for clues. I found their lighting system, three solar-charged LEDs without much juice left. I got a look at the outside of the tents before the lights went out. Under a tarp, a stack of clean shovels, and a couple dirty ones stood in a staging area. A well-used wheelbarrow filled with fresh 2x4s waited for someone. Several worn and dirty work gloves. These boys had been digging for treasure. Since one could find ancient Mayan pottery by kicking over a rock in this region, the fact there wasn't any stacked up around the tools told me they were looking for my alabaster albatross.

I pondered their chances of finding it. Either I was totally insane and they would find the thing leaning against a tree where I left it while hallucinating like a hippie on acid—or Seven-Death had my back. And that is the eternal question of faith. Do you believe?

Next up, I went to the big tent, where a central LED lit up the space like daylight. This had been the boss's headquarters. It was big enough to stand in. In one corner was a plastic chest of drawers. At the far end stood a small table with two chairs. Only the boss gets to eat indoors. Mr. Baldy—the man who executed professors and graduate students—had been here. I inspected the area more closely, my ears vigilant for a noise outside. That trap I feared could still come down on my head at any moment.

Pieces of smooth rope lay in the corner. Nice rope, like you'd use for something indoors. And short, like you'd use to tie a woman's hands. Considerate of the Knights not to tie her up with zip ties. I found a couple strands of long black hair. Footprints led outside at even strides. Three pairs of men's shoes, one smaller and therefore most likely Cherry's. The plastic drawers smelled of gun oil. In one was a receipt for .22LR ammunition from a store in Winnetka, Illinois. The kind used in a Volquartsen Scorpion. A dab of oil had kept it stuck to the back of the flimsy drawer when Mr. Baldy cleared out. I took a picture of it.

I heard running footsteps closing in fast. Too fast to do anything about the lights. I crouched behind the plastic drawers, hoping it would cover my shadow on the outside.

The runner came straight to the tent. I'd left the flap open in case of emergency. A boy, maybe fifteen or so, ran in. His head swiveled in every direction until he saw me rise from the shadows with my 9 mil trained on his forehead. He gulped.

"Where did they take the girl?" I asked.

The boy lacked the dedication of the other Knights. He broke out in a sweat. He trembled.

I grabbed his shirt and pulled him close, the barrel digging into his skin. "Where did they take the girl?"

"Joe Griffith."

His accent was so thick, it was hard to tell if I heard him right. "Joe Griffith?"

He nodded vigorously, rubbing skin off his forehead on the silencer.

"Where can I find Joe Griffith?"

His eyes fluttered for a moment while he decided what to do. The question that comes to people's mind when you hold a Glock to their head is, *If I tell him, will he kill me anyway?* The answer is almost always, *Yes.* Except, I'm not that guy. The kid sensed that.

With a shaky voice, he said, "Chicago."

CHAPTER 15

I STORMED INTO THE RESTAURANT'S palapa overlooking the lake, hoping they'd leave me alone. They didn't. They followed me in, all complaining at the same time. Danny had woken up a few miles outside of El Remate and had been yelling at me ever since. Fiona-the-blonde, who'd saved Jenny by stepping on a Knight's wrist, voiced her displeasure that I'd stopped her man from proving himself. Professor Tum was beside himself with grief. He had anticipated the Hero of Paris would come home with someone who was no longer in the country. The pressure to perform miracles made me feel as if I'd plunged deep into the darkest ocean depths.

Jenny grabbed my hand and squeezed her support for me through it. I gave her an appreciative smile.

"I get it," I snapped over my shoulder as my entourage harangued me to the table. "I'm a big disappointment. Well, I'm a hungry disappointment and I'm going to eat."

"I told you, I know how to read the Knights." Danny took the chair opposite me. Fiona sat next to him. "I could've told you what they're digging for out there."

Danny glanced at Rafael, realizing too late how it hurt the old man to hear about dirty shovels. Rafael fell into the chair to my left. Jenny took the chair to my right, her empathetic gaze on Rafael Tum.

"Don't listen to the kid," I said to Rafael. "She's alive and well. They're treating her nicely."

"They kidnapped her right in front of you," Danny said. "You call that nice?"

His voice still wavered. Pre-mission anxiety still ate at him even though I'd spared him the indignity of peeing his pants.

"There were four sets of footprints exiting the main tent." I tried to keep my voice from rising to a shout. "Three man-sized shoes over top of a smaller set. What does that tell you?"

Danny knew what it meant. So did Jenny. Their gazes dropped to the table.

Fiona didn't. She asked, "I don't get it. How can you tell they were a woman's footprints if three men walked on top of them?"

"People don't have the same stride. There was one small print every third or fourth stride, between the treads in larger sizes. They covered up her first and second strides. Her third and fourth were clear."

Fiona said, "You say that as if it's important."

Jenny put a hand on mine.

Before I could explain, Rafael spoke up. "She led the others. The men followed. That meant they treated her with a little respect. She may have been at gunpoint, but with the ropes off and no sign of struggle, it's more likely she went willingly."

Everyone leaned back and thought about why Cherry would go with them.

Danny and Fiona put their heads together and whispered. The only part I could hear was at the end when Fiona said, "...be on the winning side."

Without the first part of the sentence, it didn't make sense. I tried to imagine what the first part might've been and couldn't come up with anything good. I didn't like it, but I couldn't put why into words.

"They enticed Cherry?" Jenny offered. "Or they threatened to hurt you?"

"No enticement would lead her astray." Rafael cursed in Mayan. We could tell because curses have the same tone of voice in any language. "She fled when they came to Hidalgo's dig because she recognized them as dangerous. The only reason she would accommodate them was to protect me."

He turned his gaze to the lake. We watched him, knowing there was nothing we could do to console him.

"Then what were they digging for out there in the middle of

nowhere?" Danny asked, his eyes fixed on me.

"They wouldn't be the first Mayan looters in the Petén Department." I wasn't sure if I trusted him with more information than that. He hadn't mentioned the Stone, only that he knew about the Knights. "What's your interest in the Knights?"

"They are an ancient society." Danny pursed his lips as if deciding what and how much to tell. "Benito Mussolini was a Protector of the Knights. So were Ivan the Terrible and Napoleon. The Knights favor centralized power and strong leaders."

Secret societies, ancient myths, sacred stones. Holy Jupiter. I closed my eyes and wondered if I'd fallen into a terrible Dan Brown novel. Nah. It had to be real—it was too crazy for fiction.

"Fascists." Jenny let that word escape, then glanced around the table to apologize for interrupting.

"A modern term for an ancient practice," Danny said. "Before fascists there were kings. Before kings there were chiefs. They see themselves as the guardians of civilization."

"And what do you see?" I asked.

Danny turned a serious gaze my way. "The same as you—murderers."

"And what about the Brotherhood of Claritas?" I asked. "What are you after?"

Jenny tried to give me a warning glance. She didn't like my direct approach. She wanted me to yin my yang. Or whatever. She was right, but it was too late.

Danny took a few seconds to answer. "We do our best to protect the common people from the Knights."

"So, you're the good guys." I couldn't keep the cynicism out of my voice. "And I'm supposed to take your word for it?"

"I tried to help you." Danny looked perplexed.

"Look, whatever love-hate relationship you have with these guys is not my problem."

I didn't like where this whole Yucatán trip was heading. Ever deeper into something that had nothing to do with me. Danny caught my drift.

I faced Rafael. "What's your deal? Why did you and Cherry come to me anyway? She said you knew those guys were coming. That means you planned to be at my campsite when they arrived. Instead of warning the others, you came to me for protection. Why?"

"I did warn Hidalgo." He closed his eyes and shook his head. "There are people who study such things and think these are just old tales told by uneducated Mayans to scare their children. Some of those old tales carry truth. How many medicines are derived from ancient remedies? Aspirin, penicillin, morphine. Do the academics believe such things? No, it's all mythology to them. Not even Cherry believed me. I admit, it sounds outlandish. But that night, I began to doubt myself. I packed enough of our belongings in easy-to-carry packs just in case my fears were realized and went to visit you. Not to seek your protection. Though when my nightmare proved true, I was glad you were there. I appreciate all you have done."

What he didn't say felt like a city bus sitting on my shoulders. He still needed my protection. He needed my help to rescue his niece.

Jenny waited for me to say the words. She was ready to go. She believed in me. She wanted a cause to champion. She wanted to save Cherry.

Danny waited for an invitation. But he wasn't getting one no matter what. I didn't know why I trusted Rafael Tum, much less Danny. Come to think of it, I didn't even know Danny's last name. I'd introduced myself a few hours earlier by my whole name. He'd only responded with his first name. I hadn't even asked him for ID.

Just as I was about to open my mouth to interrogate the boy, my lost god took a knee between us.

Mercury said, *Need I remind you, home slice, that you've got a business that isn't running and your first client, Mikhail Yeschenko, is wondering why you didn't call at 0500 yesterday.*

I said, *Yesterday? Wait, did I blow off the most dangerous oligarch in all of Russia?*

Mercury said, *Look at your phone app.*

I did. There was a reminder blinking away. Twenty-six hours overdue. Damn.

I said, *What should I do?*

Mercury said, *Tell these losers to pick up the check. Then start dialing Mikhail-Caesar-Yeschenko for an advance while you drive to the nearest airport and get started finding Yuri Belenov.*

I said, *I thought you wanted me to help Rafael and Cherry.*

Mercury said, *You can't do that without any money—and guess what you just ran out of, bro.*

The hotel manager took a knee on my other side. "Señor, your credit card was declined. Do you have another we could try?"

Jenny reached into her purse. She hadn't kept a job during her RTS recovery. She didn't have any cash of her own. Which meant, she was going to use Dad's credit card. Since the guy called me a gold digger and a loser, I couldn't let her charge the revolution to him.

I waved her off.

"I'll call the bank and get it fixed," I said to the manager, who scurried away.

"My good man," Rafael said, his voice sounding suddenly frail, "would you be so kind as to help me rescue my niece from Chicago?"

In a strange harmonic voice, I heard myself say, "Absolutely."

Except that I had intended to add the word "not" to the end, but halfway through the second syllable I realized the harmony had come from Jenny speaking in unison with me. I glanced her way. She smiled, convinced we were thinking on the same wavelength. My face felt like it was forming a "WTF are you thinking?" expression when I pulled it together and decided this was not the right time to yang at her yin.

Or whatever.

"I'll come too," Danny said. He drained a glass of orange juice I hoped he was paying for.

"I gotta make a call," I said and pushed back.

I found a quiet place while the other four started planning my death. Not that they knew that's what they were doing—but it was. One soldier, two amateur do-gooders from the Brotherhood of Brightness, a failed revolutionary long past his expiration date, and a former naval officer who'd spent her career plucking objects from the sea floor were going to take on an ancient order of warriors armed to the teeth? No intel, no support, no recon, no communications system? And I couldn't even pay the hotel bill.

I dialed Yeschenko's number.

He answered, "Jacob, how is Guatemala?"

"How did you—"

"Internet news, amazing, no? Two days ago, I search Jacob Stearne, I get nothing but you and French president, *Geroy Parizha*. Big smiles as if he cared about you. I know him. He does not care about you. But yesterday, when my old friend—who still owes me for emptying out six shell companies—forgets our appointment, I search and what do I get? Many things about 'material witness' and 'mass murder of archeologists.' Jacob, do you murder archeologist again?"

"Mikhail, I never murdered any … Wait, Ms. Sabel emptied those shell companies. You're not suggesting I need to pay you back for—"

"Of course you pay me back. That was our call yesterday, yes? Twenty-eight million dollars US. You bring Yuri Belenov back and I lower by one million. That is deal. Yes?"

"Uh. No. I don't have—"

"Of course you don't have now. But you find. Maybe you find in Pia Sabel's spare change jar. But you find. You value your life, my friend. You value your upcoming marriage—congratulations, by the way. I'm hurt I've not received invitation yet. But I'm sure you send soon. Yes? Good talk with you, Jacob. Good to clear air, as you Americans say."

"Wait, Mikhail, in order to find Yuri, I need a small advance on … shit." I was talking to dead air.

I turned around. Mercury stood directly in front of me.

I said, *What in the name of Hecate was that?*

Now you with me, homes? Mercury asked. *You got no time to be fooling around with Losers of Claritas. You got to find Yuri. He might have twenty-seven million. He stole a lot more than that from a hedge fund last week.*

I felt someone touch my arm. I turned to find the Chinese lady. Up close and personal, she was strikingly handsome. Her wrinkles looked wise and her un-dyed gray hair gave her a dignified air. Her eyes sparkled as her smile swept across perfect teeth.

"I take care hotel bill," she said. She bowed at the waist and took my hand in hers as she rose. "Gu Peng. It pleasure meet you, Jacob. We go now?"

"Hold up, uh … go where?"

Her face fell to disappointment the way my math teacher's used to do when I shot my hand in the air but had the wrong answer. She said, "Chicago."

CHAPTER 16

DURING MY SABEL SECURITY CAREER, I'd been pampered so much, I'd forgotten what a middle seat in coach felt like. I was still stretching out kinks when we left Customs in Chicago.

Miguel Rodriguez, my best friend and coworker at Sabel Security, not to mention my best partner through five of my eight combat tours, waited for us wearing a chauffeur's cap. At six-five, 220 pounds, he's easy to pick out of a crowd. He held a cardboard sign that read, "Not You." He quickly separated Jenny and me from Gu Peng's herd and ushered us to a limousine outside before the Brothers noticed. He handed the cap to the driver and got in back with us.

"Pia sends her regards," Miguel said after the dividing glass went up.

"She sent you to ask me back?"

"She was on her way here when I talked her into sending me alone." He waited a beat. "You know we need you. You know that door is open. But. You have to do your thing."

I waited my own beat. "Any chance you'll join me?"

"No," he said.

With a withering glance, he let me know leaving Sabel was a big mistake.

"Where are you taking us?" Jenny asked.

"To the Drake Hotel," he said. "I brought gifts."

"We're helping some friends," Jenny said. "They're expecting us at the Hampton Inn, Skokie. Could you drop us there?"

"No."

I gave her a slow side-eye. We'd argued about helping the Brotherhood during the flight back. I saw undisciplined amateurs likely to get us killed. She saw freedom fighters. Jenny had fallen under Gu Peng's spell after already being under Rafael Tum's. I'd taken the plane ticket because I didn't know how else we'd get back to the States given that my credit card was maxed out.

In the end, I committed to nothing after the free ride. Outside of wanting to track down and kill Mr. Baldy, I wasn't interested in the Brotherhood's mission. I'd saved the world a few times and didn't find it all that rewarding. People still cut me off for parking spaces at the grocery store.

Miguel said, "I read about the archeologists. I hear you're a wanted man. Again."

"Nah. I cleared that up with the authorities."

He nodded as if he knew something I didn't. Then he said, "The gifts are in your suite at the Drake. They'll help you with Gu Peng or Mikhail Yeschenko, whichever way you're going."

"How do you know about Ms. Gu?" Jenny squeaked with surprise.

I held up my Sabel Satellite phone. "Welcome to my world. Not only did Ms. Sabel let me keep my old company phone, she gave you one in case I dumped mine. She can track everything we do whenever she wants."

Jenny shriveled into her seat, a little creeped out by her old friend's Big Sister-ish behavior. She looked at Miguel.

He shrugged and said, "Not directly. Pia owns an international conglomerate. She doesn't have that kind of time. I monitor Jacob's penchant for getting into trouble. I told her you could use some help. She wants to help. That reminds me—you left this on the *Numina*."

Miguel held up my Centurion card, then slapped it in my hand. An American Express card issued by invitation only. It's black, made of titanium, and has no spending limit. At all. It also bills directly to Sabel Security. Using it would put me in her debt. I said, "I will never, ever accept help from Ms. Sabel."

"Never say never," they said in unison.

"How is she?" Jenny asked.

"Pia's patience is wearing thin," Miguel said. "She's dealing with the stuff her dad used to do and it pisses her off, makes her edgy."

"What do you mean?"

"People want her money and time. Invest in this, give to that. Everyone she meets wants something from her."

"She'd rather play soccer." Jenny puffed air in sympathy. "She was on the verge of being the greatest of all time."

Jenny looked at me and the Centurion card. I held it in my palm like a black widow. Miguel's face told me he would consider it a personal insult if I handed it back. I shoved it in my pocket. I didn't have to use it.

My phone vibrated with texts from Ms. Gu sent to both Jenny and me. She wondered where we went. I texted back, "Ran into an old friend."

The driver dropped us at the Drake. We rode the elevator to a suite with a view of Lake Michigan. Aluminum suitcases stood in a neat line in front of the coffee table. Technically, Ms. Sabel wasn't asking me to come back. She was sending me a reminder of how good the accommodations would be if I stayed.

While I started opening the aluminum cases like a kid diving under the Christmas tree, Miguel gave us some intel on our new playmates.

"Gu Peng is an internationally renowned artist," he said. "Her sculptures are on display from the Hirschhorn to the Guggenheim Bilboa. Patrons flock to her studio in Vancouver. Back in '89, she lost her husband in Tiananmen Square. China labeled her an enemy of the state. Same as you."

That got Jenny's attention. She looked to me for an explanation. We'd only been dating a few months. I hadn't had time to tell her about every government that considered me a subversive. I shrugged.

"Did you find anything about the Brotherhood of Claritas?" Jenny asked.

Miguel's blank look told us he hadn't monitored everything. We left it alone.

I checked the contents of one suitcase. Encrypted comm links for ten people. The next case held five H&K MP7 rifles. The next, rounds of ammunition for the rifles plus high capacity magazines for my Glock. Five Sabel Armor units, liquid Kevlar protection from the knee to the throat, waited in one case. They're flexible and light yet highly effective. The next held a hundred Sabel Darts. Another held a pair of drones with infrared, thermal, and 3D room mapping software. From outside a window, it could give you a fair 3D model of a room's furniture and inhabitants. Great for dramatic entries with 9 mils blazing. There was a monocular in another case with binoculars and Sabel Visors. I checked out the monocular.

Miguel took it out of my hand, pointed it at the window, then motioned for me to look through the lens.

"The range in the view finder," he said, "indicates how far out the built-in laser will heat the air to form a mirror. Works like a mirage. Let's you see around corners. It's like an invisible periscope."

I checked it out, adjusting the range to twelve feet. Looking into it gave me the same perspective as sticking my head out the window and looking straight left. There was a bit of heat shimmer, like looking down a road in the desert. The laser was superheating a small patch of air to make it reflective. I rotated a ring on the outside and was looking straight down instead of left. I moved the range out and kept extending my view. It maxed out at a hundred meters. In theory, I could see around the corner of a building at the far end of a football field.

Mercury pulled the monocular periscope away from my eye. *I know what you're thinking, homie. You're thinking you could actually rescue Cherry Crocker, get the reward, and then go find Yuri Belenov. But that's a bad idea. You—*

I said, *What reward?*

Mercury said, *You don't know her daddy's rich? Nob Hill people in San Francisco. They don't even know she's missing. Probably ain't no reward, come to think of it. Let's keep focused here. Yuri Belenov ripped a couple million from an Asian defense contractor yesterday. That's on top of the thirty million he took from hedge funds last week. See, whatcha gotta do is shake down Yuri for thirty million, pay off Yeschenko, use the rest to fund Stearne Security and—zoom—you're on your way to becoming a Caesar. Finally. It's been a long painful wait, ya feel me?*

I said, *That's not a bad idea.*

Jenny and Miguel stared blankly at me as if waiting for me to say something.

I said, "Going after Mr. Baldy, I mean."

"After we rescue Cherry?" Jenny said with a death ray in her eyes.

I began to understand yin and yang. Or whatever. We had balanced goals: she wanted to save Cherry; and I wanted to kill Mr. Baldy. But I couldn't tell her that last part. Jenny never condoned vigilantism.

"Right." I gave her my that-part's-obvious shrug. "Of course."

Mercury tossed his hands in the air. *Dude, you are SO whipped. And it's only been four days, not a week like I gave you. It's embarrassing.*

I said, *She's good for me. We balance each other. We have yin or yang. Or whatever.*

Mercury made a whipping noise, *Whtt-tssh.*

"Just so we're clear." I gave Jenny the putting-my-foot-down stare. "I'm not getting involved in this Brotherhood thing. I don't know what Gu Peng wants, but I'm not a benevolent society. I have a contract to find Yuri Belenov." Jenny scowled at me, so I added, "Um, I mean, right after we rescue Cherry. Of course. OK?"

Mercury said, *Oh yeah. Totally whipped.*

CHAPTER 17

Dusk descended on us like a blanket. I kept my big binoculars trained on the shores of Lake Michigan in Winnetka, Illinois. According to property records, the billionaire vulture capitalist, Joe Griffith had a property somewhere near here. Jenny piloted our two-person sailboat—courtesy of Ms. Sabel's Centurion Card—and kept shouting things like, "ready about" and "lee ho" before the big aluminum beam would come at my head like a batter taking a swing at me. I'd felt safer in Kabul. Farm boys from Iowa have no business on a sailboat. Eventually, I got into the rhythm of ducking and switching sides.

Before we left the dock, she'd explained all about "beating" and "no-go zones" and "close hauled," which she'd learned during her Naval Academy training. It meant nothing to me. She gave up after a few minutes, put a life jacket and helmet on me, and told me to duck to the other side whenever she yelled. She was right, we did balance each other.

All that ducking and repositioning made it hard to get a solid look at the shoreline.

After a while, I gave up and checked the tablet. My drone zipped along a pre-programmed route at three thousand feet, taking 8K footage of every house along the way. I scrolled through the online recording of its path. After ten minutes of scrolling, I found the house.

"How do you know?" Jenny asked.

"Because none of the other sprawling mansions have bulwarks and armed guards. I'm not talking Tasers; these are Smith & Wesson guys."

"How many?"

"I'll get a count when we get back and can study the footage. More than I expected."

I zoomed in on a couple faces. They weren't the Knights from Guatemala. These guys wore uniforms and looked pudgy. That meant this Griffith guy had his own security.

I zoomed in for a look at the roof before it got too dark. Then I dropped the drone to see if I could get a look in the windows. It was tight. The property had a lot of trees. Sabel drones make less noise than most but moving enough air to hover creates noise no matter how good the craft. Noise could give away my inspection, which would destroy my element of surprise. To see between the budding trees, still somewhat bare in early March, I kept it out over the lake and zoomed in.

Most of the upstairs windows had drawn curtains. In one room that didn't, a woman crossed the space with a towel around her body and another around her hair. Then she was gone. The opening between curtains was narrow and her appearance fleeting, so I couldn't tell much about her.

In another barely visible gap, someone's feet protruded from a recliner. Judging from the flickering colors lighting up the room, he was watching TV. I had the drone take laser scans of the room interiors for later rendering.

I changed the angle and altitude to the ground floor. A spacious living room overlooked the patio, beach, and dock. The windows were wide open. The room was empty, which told me nothing other than Griffith's taste in decorating leaned toward Louis XIV-Extra.

From the large stone patio outside the living room, designer bushes framed a stone staircase that led down to the beach. Empty lounge chairs lined both sides of a long dock. No boats. No boathouse. Those were kept elsewhere to preserve the view.

Lights came on around the property. A security patrol swept the patio near the living room's twenty-foot windows.

Below them, Danny strolled along the beach holding hands with Fiona. They were far from the water's edge, violating Illinois' feet-wet-beach-access rule. If you're feet aren't wet, you're trespassing. They turned and trotted up the stone steps to eye-level with the house. Clearly casing the property. I wanted to scream.

"Do you have Danny's cell number?" I asked.

"Why?" Jenny asked.

"He's walking on the beach in front of Joe Griffith's house," I said.

"Oh, good. He'll get an up-close look at the property."

"No, he'll get whacked on the head and dragged to the local police station. The idiot's going to blow our cover."

Jenny had taken us up the coast from the house and announced we would be turning around. This time with the wind at our backs. And that meant we wouldn't have to tack. Which was a good thing for surveillance.

She made the maneuver and I ducked the beam but not enough. It banged off my helmet.

"That's why I made you wear that thing," Jenny said.

I looked at her with a mixture of humiliation and loathing. Next time we rent a boat, it'll have a motor and no sails. Hopefully, the Navy taught her how to operate those.

The time it took to maneuver took my focus off Danny's escapade. When I searched the drone's feed for him, he was gone.

I sent my drone down to ten feet above the water and switched to thermal view. That made it easy to find them. They were on the patio, being held at gunpoint by two guards.

"Damn it," I said. "Did I tell them stay at the hotel? Did I tell them not to follow us? Was I not clear?"

"They're trying to help. What's wrong with that?"

"They got caught. Now Griffith's security team will be on high alert."

"Chill," she said. "They did what they thought best."

"A security outfit like that will identify them. They endanger Cherry Crocker's life doing that. They have no discipline, no respect for orders."

"You didn't give them orders." Jenny strained to see the pair as we approached the house. "We have to help them."

"Not without giving up on Cherry's rescue. They chose this option against my order to stay at the hotel."

I lifted the drone higher and out over water to keep the noise down. I scanned the beach for any signs indicating the Brothers had intentionally crossed onto private property. Stone walls marched along Griffith's property line down into the water and out into the lake. Shiny new signs were posted every ten feet along the wall. Willful trespassing. They were screwed.

"Take us back," I said. "Peng has to get her people under control. Hopefully, their planned excuse of being lost in love will get them a pass from the cops."

"Cops?" Jenny asked.

"Pulling in the driveway now. That was quick."

"You have to help them. What can we do?" she asked.

I thought it would be a simple mission like the camp in Guatemala. That was when I thought Griffith was just a guy who lived in a house. Then I saw his Colonial Revival mega-mansion designed to survive the apocalypse. Getting Cherry out would be next to impossible. Saving Mr. Wunderkind added a level of complication I couldn't begin to calculate.

I said, "Choose between saving Cherry and saving the Brothers."

"Cherry," she said with a sigh.

We sailed back to the boat rental in the dark without another word.

CHAPTER 18

WITH THE TABLET CONNECTED TO my suite's flat screen, I could see more detail from the drone recording. Like so many modern mansions, the house was not built for a view or any family purpose. It was more like a commercial building, meant to enclose as many square feet of space as possible. The front, back, and sides of the top floor had gabled windows set in a steep sloped shingle roof. But that was for show. The actual roof was flat and held the air conditioning, a series of vents and chimneys, and a solar panel array. The diameter of one vent scared me. It was too big for the gas-fired fireplaces. Too big for oil or coal heat. It wasn't even a vent. It was a smokestack.

The house filled the multi-acre lot from side to side but allowed for a sweeping driveway circle in front and the massive patio out back. There was no garage. I found that odd. I kept looking at the place and noticed a walkway and gate from the neighboring lot. On closer inspection, the house due north was small and old for Winnetka's waterfront. But the eight-car garage that dwarfed it looked much newer. A narrow stone path led from the garage directly to the big house. My guess: security, staff, and chauffeurs were kept in the smaller residence. Wealthy people like their privacy.

There were several free-standing granite block walls along each entrance to the house. To anyone arriving or exiting the house, they looked like decorative walls meant to impress with their scale and bulk. Walking past them would be like walking past giant hedgerows made of granite. I knew their real purpose.

The upstairs windows looked normal from the street. Zooming in showed two-inch thick glass with that unmistakable green tint that comes from laminating several layers. Hard thick glass was sandwiched between thick layers of soft plastic. The hard glass provides rigidity while the plastic allows flexibility. Combined, bullets bounce off like rain drops. A .50 cal machine gun wouldn't penetrate it. Snipers need not apply.

My laptop dinged when it completed rendering the room scans. The lasers went in the open windows and bounced off any surfaces, measuring the nanosecond delays to find the distances between objects inside. It was far from perfect. It was limited to what it could see through the narrow slit. It was like a pie slice. But it gave me the approximate depth of the two rooms facing the lake. They were big, but not half the depth of the house. Most houses have a hall in the middle with rooms off either side. This one had to have at least two hallways. Maybe four.

The place also had a basement and a finished attic, altogether four floors of living space, which made me wonder how many people lived there. Then I recalled Ms. Sabel telling me how she once wandered her extra-huge mansion and found a room she'd never been in being cleaned by an employee she'd never met. The mega-rich live in a surreal world.

Joe Griffith thought his surreal world was impenetrable.

And that worked to my advantage.

I measured out the probable rooms. If he had a home theater in the center upstairs, what was below it on the ground floor, a ballroom? Then what occupied the center in the basement? A safe room? No, a wine bar outfitted in brick that could double as a bomb shelter. Maybe an indoor swimming pool. At that point, I was speculating.

I started looking at the video from the upstairs rooms. First, the feet on the La-Z-Boy were clad in Ferragamo shoes. As best the 3D scanner could tell, the room was twenty-four feet deep and probably twice that long. It had a king-sized bed several feet from the chair. Even in a monster-mansion, a bedroom that big had to be the master. Rich guys never give their guests that much space for fear they'd never leave.

Scrolling ahead on the video, I came to the woman in the towel. I paused it when I heard someone at my suite's door. My Glock found its way into my hand and slid low by my hip. Habit.

Jenny waltzed in with Rafael Tum, Gu Peng, Danny, Fiona-the-blonde, a guy named Mark and another guy whose name I didn't know.

Peng rested on her walking stick in the foyer and looked around the expensive suite.

"Don't worry about it," I said when her gaze fell to me. "You're not paying for it. It's a gift from Pia Sabel."

Peng held my gaze without saying anything. Which was a bit unnerving and made me regret my outburst.

Rafael did that thing where he dropped into a cross-legged position. This time, he was on the coffee table, just to my right. He was the kind of old man who could get comfortable on broken glass. He pointed at the screen. "Cherry."

He was right—the woman in the towel was his niece. I hadn't recognized her earlier because, last time I saw her, she'd had a layer of archeologist-dirt on her. Even after we'd cleaned up in El Remate, she still looked more like a camper from the back woods than a wealthy Winnetka housewife.

The others swarmed around the couch to look at the screen. I scrolled forward and back. We had only a few seconds of her crossing the visible space. It appeared she had showered and was going to change. Her eyes were downcast at something below her waist, a yard or two in front of her.

I pulled up the 3D rendering of the room. My view of Cherry's room was an even narrower slice than the master bedroom, but it was clearly another bedroom. From where she stood, she was looking at the foot of the bed where a hope chest or a sitting bench appeared to be. Clothes laid out for her?

"We have to go in," Danny said. He and Fiona and the other guys looked like recent college grads. Early-twenties at best.

"We?" I asked.

"Yes, we," Danny snapped. He pointed at his cadets. "We trained for this. We know what we're doing."

"Is that how you wound up in police custody?"

"That was an accident." He sounded like a kid pleading its-not-my-fault. "We pushed too far, that's all."

"It was a colossal failure to follow orders. You were lucky they didn't shoot you on sight. They were—"

Rafael rose on the coffee table, his hands rising straight out from his sides. Our attention went to him.

"Might we turn the conversation to helping Cherry?" he asked.

"I have a plan." I used my Master Sergeant voice. Everyone turned to me. "It involves me and one other person in a boat. No one else."

"We've been there," Fiona pushed up to me. "Up close. Not from three hundred yards away."

"How many guards were on duty?" I asked. "Were you able to count them from the back seat of the squad car?"

She whimpered away.

"I don't need to listen to this," Danny said. "We found a weakness in their defense. We have a plan too."

Jenny moved to my side and put her hand on my back. To the others, it looked supportive. To me, it felt like she wanted me to calm down and reconsider. Her yin wanted to balance my yang. Or whatever. She was right though; reason was better than escalation. She made me realize that Danny was acting out after being humiliated by Griffith's security.

"Look," I said. I backed up the video to the overhead view and pointed at the screen. "You guys are thinking, 'swashbuckling rescue, what fun.' In your minds, you'll take down the guards, storm the castle, rescue the princess—just like Tom Cruise in *Mission Impossible XXVII*. Well, no matter how you fantasize the scenario, reality defines your fate. In the real world, this place was built to repel a ground assault."

I pointed at the free-standing walls. "See these four-foot-thick stone walls? That's anti-tank armor. If the FBI served a search warrant with a bulldozer, they wouldn't get in before the servers were wiped clean and the documents shredded. Think you can sneak in on foot? This is where their guards wait for people. These walls turn the walkway into the guards' shooting gallery. They have the same arrangement facing the beach. The windows on both floors are bulletproof. You'll need a howitzer to breach the home. So tell me, Rambo, how are you planning to get in the building?"

Danny's eyes fell to the carpet.

"He's right," Mark said. "That is a fortress."

Rafael, still standing on the coffee table, jumped down and turned to me. "Perhaps you could use some help from these energetic young people. Their intentions are noble."

Only because he was a likable old man did I consider his request. They could provide a diversion. Maybe blow up the service house next door. Keep the guards busy putting out a fire. But the guards were professionals. Before they put the fire out, they would eliminate the threat. Danny and his squad would die in seconds.

Or, I could let Danny do whatever he wanted. The security team would be exhausted after playing soccer with Danny's head. When they took their victory break, their defenses would be at an all-time low.

Nah. My mean streak didn't extend to using the young for cannon fodder.

I patted Rafael's shoulder and shook my head.

"Depends on how you want your niece to come back: riddled with bullets, decapitated, or cremated?" I pointed at the roof of the house. "A smokestack like that on a private residence? That's the kind you find at a crematorium. What are they burning?"

Rafael paled as his imagination drew a blank on alternative uses.

Peng crossed to me. "How you plan get in?"

"The easy way," I said.

CHAPTER 19

I REFUSED TO TELL THEM my plan. I couldn't. I didn't have one. Just a concept. But I made it sound like I didn't trust them. And that gained Rafael's blessing. Since it was his niece I was rescuing, no one could argue. Peng told her people to stand down with a glance. She gestured them toward the door.

Whether he was acting out or just pissed, Danny wanted to prove himself. He stepped in front of me. "The Knights have been our enemy for two thousand years. We've studied them and trained to fight them. You're not one of us. You have no idea what you're up against."

I stood still.

He turned to Peng. "Why listen to him? He's not in the Brotherhood."

Peng lowered her eyes.

Jenny slipped between Danny and me. "Why listen to him? He raided his first fortress back when you were playing with GI Joes. He took on an army of terrorists in Denmark, and vigilantes who were out to kill my mother in Washington, and a rogue faction of the Russian Army in Latvia. He's killed more men than you've ever met—"

"He gets the picture," I said. My arm gently pushed her aside. If she started listing the dead, I could end up sounding more like a serial killer and less like a hero.

Reason didn't work on Danny. His anger exploded. He rushed me using a standard Krav Maga technique. What goes well on a mat in a gym sometimes goes well in real life.

Not this time. His first encounter with a real street fighter was over before he knew it. As he lunged, I arced my arm inside his closest shoulder, my hand rising past his neck. From there, I extended my forearm, forcing his head to the left. Where your head goes, your body follows. Redirected, his momentum carried him over my hip. He rolled off the couch and landed on the floor.

"The US Army teaches *Combatives* in Basic Training," I told him, aiming a finger-pistol at him. "It's about disabling, not killing. We have 9 mils for that. So do Griffith's men."

The look in his eye told me he was about to jump up and try again. As he lunged for me, I put him in a headlock.

I pressed my thumb hard into his atlas bone. It's the one that connects the spine to the skull. I said, "That bone is the weakest link in your spinal column. One directed blow there and you'll never move an arm or leg again. I learned that one at Ranger School—after Basic Training."

I spun him around, pushed him three feet away, and extended a hand as a peace offering. He stared at me with hatred.

As he panted, I looked for a way out. I said, "I admire your energy. If I had time to work on something, I'd include you. But I don't."

"Give me more detail about your plan and we'll take care of Cherry." Danny sneered. "You can go back to doing whatever it is you do."

"Listen, kid," I said. "There isn't a magic plan. It's a series of options and opportunities. A thousand of them. One wrong choice and you come home in a box."

Peng tugged his arm. Danny glanced at his friends. Their shoulders drooped as they turned toward the door and filed out.

Rafael hung back, holding the door for the others. He gave me a soulful look, his eyes asking if I'd bring Cherry back.

I asked, "When are you going to tell me what's in my alabaster box?"

"Bring her home," he said. "I beg of you."

He turned and walked out.

The instant the door clacked shut, Jenny said, "What the hell is wrong with you? Is that how you treat people?"

"Danny?" I faced her, a little surprised by the heat in her delivery. "He's young, impatient, and untrained."

"So were you once." She stuck out her jaw. "They want to help, to feel useful. You could give them something. You didn't need to humiliate Danny like that."

"As a Navy officer, did you have to write letters home to grieving parents? Are you ready to write a letter to Danny's mom that says, 'We gave him a role in a dangerous mission when we knew he was ill-prepared and untrained?'"

"There are plenty of things they could do that would keep him out of danger."

"Like what?"

She flopped her arms. "I don't know. Keep watch at the street. Check the beach for patrols."

"Did you notice how quickly the cops arrived when Danny got caught? Those guys didn't come from the station. They came from the open end of the cul-de-sac. What does that tell you?"

She crossed her arms and huffed without lightening her glare. "The cops are part of his security team."

"He's a big deal to the locals. They're not going to let a stranger wander the hood with eyes on Griffith's front gate."

"Well, think of something. Get creative."

"No. It's not a discussion."

"Since when do you get to decide?" She hurled her questions at me. "Aren't we a partnership? Shouldn't we work things out together?"

"What?" I felt the lid on my anger management system fly off. "We don't 'work things out' when we're talking about getting innocent people arrested or killed. I'm the only person in the room who has actual combat experience. The Brothers have no discipline and don't follow orders."

"You just want to be the lone hero again. That's why it's always you and nobody else."

"Maybe I'm sick of being shoved out into the cold, alone." I tried to keep my voice down. "There's nothing I'd love more than to go in there with a Ranger platoon. I'd settle for SEALs. If I could, I'd bring Pia Sabel and the old crew. But those aren't options. It comes down to me because of the odds. If Danny tries it there's a hundred percent chance he will die or wind up in jail. If I go in there, there's a fifty-fifty chance I can grab Cherry and get to the dock. There are no other viable options. I'm the only one who can do it."

"Why do it at all then?" she barked.

"He who can, must."

"What?"

"When you're the only one who can, you must." I tried to exhale some of my anger. "I'm not discussing it anymore."

"Shutting down?" Her nostrils flared. "That's your answer? Isn't that what ended your decorated military career?"

"Don't you dare bring up my service record." I found myself shaking a finger at her. "You don't know anything about it."

"My mother wouldn't tell me why she was against our engagement. So I asked Pia. She told me everything."

She may as well have hit me with a water cannon. I staggered back a couple steps. Air wouldn't fill my lungs. I couldn't speak.

Ms. Sabel shared my psychiatric evals with her? I had trusted Ms. Sabel with that story. She shared her problems with me. We were like siblings. We were honest about everything. She even tried to believe in Mercury. It didn't go well, but she tried. How could she violate that trust without asking me first?

Mercury patted my shoulder. *Dude, women talk about everything.*

I said, *Could you give me a minute? I don't want to talk to you right now.*

Mercury said, *Could you imagine if men were like that? Doing stuff like sharing their feelings instead of going violent? Ew, yuck.*

I said, *Just go away.*

Mercury said, *There'd never be another war. And then where would the world be? B-O-R-I-N-G.*

I said, *My fiancé just told me she knows I'm a stark raving lunatic. The last thing I need is a mythical god chatting in my ear.*

Mercury said, *And that's where you'd be dead wrong, homes. This is your opportunity. Now is the perfect time to tell her the Dii Consentes has blessed your planned nuptials. We're looking forward to having her in the family. G'on now, tell her.*

Jenny's head was tilted. "Is it true? You have psychotic episodes?"

"Is that what Ms. Sabel told you?"

"That was my mother's take." She bit her thumb. "When I asked Pia, she told me something really crazy. Which was shocking because everyone knows she's nuts."

My mouth hung open. I couldn't find words. After I dragged her mother through the desert, past armed patrols hunting her down, that's the thanks I get? And Ms. Sabel? Who thought she was nuts? My mind reeled.

Mercury said, *Oh, you be getting your first taste of ungrateful mortals and you're hurt? Welcome to the world of the gods, brutha. Just this morning, a guy prayed for salvation when his car flipped through the air. Jesus grabbed the guy's ankle. Landed him safely on a sand dune, saved his life. All the bastard could say was, "Whoa, totally rad." But, whatcha expect from a stoner in Malibu?*

"I'm one hundred percent sane." I glared at Jenny. "And this is not a debate. My neck—my risk."

"Not a debate?" She stamped her foot. "I'm asking you to consider something outside the box and you're not even going to discuss it?"

How do you discuss whether some snot-nosed kid should live with a humiliation he'll forget in a week or die at the hands of trained assassins? She was making the same mistake the Brotherhood was making: grossly underestimating the firepower prowling Griffith's property?

Or was there something else going on with the Brotherhood? Why did Gu Peng stand there like a statue while Danny and I got physical? Was she giving him some kind of test? A rite of passage to strengthen the Brothers? Who the hell were they anyway? Danny's explanation sounded like something not even Diana Gabaldon would make up.

Could I create a role for the Brotherhood to play? They had helped when the Knights attacked us at the hotel. And Danny had led me to an encampment through a bit of cunning. But his amateurish fiasco earlier in the afternoon was a huge liability. If he did something like that under fire, we could all die. No. Not worth it.

"I've considered it from every angle," I said. "There is no role for the Brotherhood."

Jenny tightened her lips. She snatched her jacket off the back of the chair and stormed out.

CHAPTER 20

CHERRY TOOK ANOTHER LOOK IN the full-length mirror. Alexander McQueen sure knew how to make a tasteful-yet-sexy minidress. Black with white flowers embroidered on the right, it flowed like water when she twisted. She looked great. The pumps were a perfect match. And everything fit like a glove. Whoever "The Guardian" was, he knew how to pamper women.

She took a deep breath. That wouldn't change anything.

Captain Amanow knocked on her door. He offered a hand, which she refused. Unfazed, he escorted her down the grand staircase and showed her to the drawing room. At the far end, a fire roared in front of two wingbacks. A pair of legs extended from one, the owner's face remained obscured by the chair back. Amanow stopped ten feet away. Cherry marched forward.

The Guardian rose and greeted her with outstretched arms. He said, "My goodness, Cherry, you're even more beautiful tonight than you were at your debutante ball."

She remembered Joe Griffith from that horrid night. He was one of the many old men leering at her barely concealed breasts while her shoulders froze in the white strapless ball gown. It was the night the rift first opened between Cherry and her mother.

She scoffed. "I should've recognized your foul stench when I first arrived."

"And still every bit as charming." He looked beyond her shoulder. "You may go now, Captain."

Amanow said, "I thought it best—"

"You're done for the day," Griffith snapped. "I'll call if you're needed."

She glanced back in time to see Amanow steaming in anger. The man gave a deep bow from which he rose and glared at Griffith and retreated and closed the double doors behind him.

She faced Griffith. "You keep a tight leash on your assassins."

Griffith looked her over slowly. "Aperitif? Of course you will. Gimlets, I think."

He pressed a button on the side table and ordered, then he waved a hand at the chair facing his.

Cherry thought about spitting on him but wanted to know where all his subterfuge led. She took the chair. "Are you going to explain why you've not turned Amanow over to the police?"

"What on earth for, dear girl?"

"Girl? Really? Remind me—what century is this?"

"Ah, yes. He told me you held him responsible for the murders Jacob Stearne committed. You know about—"

"Don't try to gaslight me. I was there when Amanow arrived. Uncle Rafael warned me the Knights of Mithras would come. I saw them rounding up everyone at gunpoint. I was terrified. If Jacob Stearne killed those people, why did Amanow let him? He had forty armed men in that camp."

Griffith leaned back in his chair and stroked his chin while he thought. "All right, I'll admit they are a problem. And for the record, there are thirty-two. They were not my choice. Tradition holds that the Protector chooses the Knights, not the Guardian. For this round, the Protector chose a chapter from Turkmenistan. I'd have preferred more civilized Knights, maybe Norwegians or Scots. My orders to them did not include bloodshed. That's a cultural distinction I hadn't anticipated."

"Nonetheless, fifteen of my colleagues are dead."

"Regrettable, no doubt. And ineffective. But it's done and doesn't matter now. Life and death balance each other. A death here and there makes no difference in the grand scheme of things. The mission must continue for the preservation of civilization. And that's where you come in, Cherry."

She wanted to scream when he dropped the weight of civilization on her shoulders. Instead, she closed her eyes and thought of how Uncle Rafael would handle this man. With calm, calculated observation. He would listen without comment.

A servant appeared with a silver tray of green drinks in martini glasses. He served Griffith first. Cherry took hers, said thank you, and watched him disappear without a sound.

She said, "OK, I'm listening. What about civilization?"

"Why did some Mayan cities collapse and not others?"

"Drought is the prevailing theory."

"A drought that destroyed Calakmul but not Chichen Itza, a hundred miles away?" Griffith dismissed her idea with a backhanded wave. "The Poison Stone is real. You know it and so does Rafael Tum. It destroyed Mesopotamia. It ruined Egypt. It brought down Rome. And it wreaked havoc on the Maya."

"Poison Stone, Freedom Stone, Balance Stone," she taunted. "Fairy tales."

"If it's a fairy tale, why did your beloved uncle follow Jacob Stearne into the rain forest?"

It was a good question. One she'd been asking ever since Amanow and his murderous thugs showed up. Uncle Rafael knew they were coming yet left her behind with little more than a warning. Had he miscalculated their violence? Or had he fled for his life? Answers she would find later. She would show this man nothing.

"I see your proud Indian heritage won't let you divulge your thoughts," he said.

"Indians live in India." She glared at him.

"Mestizo, Latina, whatever." He dismissed her a second time with a wave of his hand.

She hated that her mother married into San Francisco society, then spent the rest of her life groveling to earn their acceptance. They handed her empty glasses at her own cocktail parties, asked her to bring fresh towels at the country club, and asked her to pronounce her name again. She'd politely correct them: *No. Not cerveza. Cereza. It means cherry in Spanish.* Her mother should've told them all to drop dead, Joe Griffith first among them. The reason she'd been the only brown person at her debutante ball was to help her mother become one of them. Even though the Crocker family was older and wealthier than any other in San Francisco society, they never accepted Cereza Tum Crocker. Cherry wasn't going to suck up to them only to suffer the same fate.

"Mayan," she said. "Unfortunately, only half. My mother made the mistake of marrying into a white family."

"Very well. Mayan then." Griffith chuckled as if it were cute. "Did your *Mayan* uncle tell you about the ancient society he's involved in?"

"What my family discusses is none of your business. Why am I here?"

He clasped his hands and leaned forward. "At the time of the American Revolution, the world's population was well under a billion. Today, we're nearing eight billion. The time for allowing cities and states to rule by acclamation is long gone. Look at China. They've dealt with a huge population for years. They went from the Stone Age to modernity in the space of two generations. They had no time for debate and council. They needed and benefitted from strong, decisive leadership. There are many of us who've worked hard to bring that same leadership to other countries. Culturally appropriate leadership, of course. We've done a great deal to prepare the world for the next step in civilization."

Cherry waited through his dramatic pause while suppressing her shock. She rolled her hand. "And?"

"Jacob Stearne has no idea what he found. Your uncle does. That box can unleash pure anarchy on this world. We could end up like the Mayans. We have to find it and secure it."

"What do you want from me?" she asked.

"Somewhere on your journey, Jacob Stearne hid the Poison Stone. Your dear uncle refused to retrieve it. We need you to help us find it."

JENNY'S FURY STRAINED HER MUSCLES as she strode through the lobby's labyrinth of hallways. With her eyes fixed on the gold-and-red patterns in the carpet, she saw nothing else around her. Was she making a mistake marrying Jacob? Her domineering father never let her mother make a single decision. Everything the family did was on his whim. Her mother had been a respected admiral before President Williams picked her as his vice president. Everyone else saw Anne Wilkes as a smart, capable leader. Why didn't Bobby Jenkins understand his wife could make rational decisions? Dad controlled everything within reach. Jenny found herself constantly trying to win his approval and never getting it. Nothing was good enough to please him. He even tried to control where Jenny went to college by claiming he would only pay for Stanford. Jenny chose the Naval Academy. She'd stood up to her father and proved she could make her own decisions.

"Jenny?" The voice came from across the lobby.

Jenny looked around. It was late and there were few people in the usually busy space.

Gu Peng waved a hand from a corner of the room, catching Jenny's attention. Peng sat with perfect posture, as if she were waiting for the queen. Jenny crossed the space.

"What are you doing here?" Jenny asked. She slid onto the small divan next to the older woman.

"Mother of light bless you," Peng said. She reached out and cupped Jenny's cheek with her palm. "But anger not best color on you. What trouble you, dear?"

Jenny found the touch comforting, calming. "I'm ashamed of how Jacob treated you. I told him to change his mind. We got into a fight."

"You want him do what you tell him?" Peng rested her walking stick against the edge of her seat and folded her hands in her lap.

"Yes. Just once."

"Why you so angry at him? He want me do as he say. You want him do as you say. It same thing. He want power over me. You want power over him. That give you power over me."

Jenny felt herself lean back. The old lady's expression was flat, not judgmental, not superior, just stating a fact.

"Yeah," Jenny said. "I hadn't thought of it like that. Still—"

"Brotherhood of Claritas over three thousand year old." Peng's gaze swept the grand space around them. "In all time, Council always elect woman to lead."

"That can't be."

"It can be—and there reason for it."

"What?" Jenny asked.

"Once in great while, pride of lion need male for strength, aggression, and violence. He defend pride from outside threat. Rest of time, he not do anything. Women run whole operation. They provide food, raise young. Women decide who is and who is not member of pride, including who is lion king."

Jenny had a feeling she knew where the conversation was heading.

"So why we call ourself Brotherhood?" Peng asked.

Jenny shrugged.

"Marketing." Peng laughed and pushed Jenny's knee. "We lioness. Let men strut and demand and threaten. Let men throw each other to floor. Young lion challenge lion king. Many time lose, one day win. No matter. We choose who is and who is not Brother. In that way, we choose who throw who to floor. And who is lion king."

Jenny nodded along with her new friend.

"It not good feminist," Peng said, "to call ourself Brotherhood. But would Danny join Sisterhood? Jacob?"

"Not in a million years." Jenny laughed. "Marketing. I like that."

"Danny more capable than Jacob know." Peng looked to the ceiling. "You fight for him. Thank you. I notice how you place hand on Jacob back. You steer him to right place. You light his way. Jacob in darkness, he not see. Danny deserve chance to prove himself. But there be another day. Another chance."

"That's what Jacob said." Jenny twisted to face Peng directly. "Are you saying I should give up?"

"Ah. You want win. Quick win is false victory." The old woman patted Jenny's knee. "Goal not win argument. Goal win lifetime together. Find harmony. Find balance."

Jenny thought about her parents. They had fought. In third grade, her carefully staged fairytale world of privilege and luxury was blown up by their divorce. Overnight, she was thrown from her stable, comfortable world into shouting and crying and being forced to take sides. Too young to understand the dynamics, she could still see their posture and hear their tones. Her mother challenged her father head-on. He stiffened and met the challenge with rising rage. They spiraled out of control. Peng was right. They were trying to win. To gain power over each other. In the end, everyone lost.

"You go through big life-transition," Peng touched her forearm. "Transition very scary time. Baptism, bris, *man yue,* confirmation, bat mitzvah all ritual to help you leave old monster from childhood behind. They prepare you for new monster ahead. Now you face big transition— marriage. You leave one stage and walk into fog forest. Unknown world. You worry about many thing. Will I be safe? Will I be accept? Will I have power? Will I have respect?"

Jenny felt her anger slipping away under Peng's analysis. She was afraid of the future. Afraid her future would parallel her parents. Ironically, she had taken the same position her father had, immovable. She didn't want to become her father. She said, "Not all transitions go well."

"No." Peng's eyes filled and she looked away. "It not mean we have no courage."

Jenny watched in silence as the grand lady composed herself. Jenny wanted to reach out, to say something, to console her, but something told her Peng's pain went far beyond Jenny's life experience. She sat still.

Peng produced a tissue from a hidden pocket, sniffled, wiped her eyes, and gave Jenny a smile.

"Thank you," Jenny squeezed the old lady's hand. "I'll make up with Jacob. How can I repay you for the advice?"

"It nothing, child." Peng shrugged. "Maybe one day, you join Brotherhood. Bring freedom to people."

"I would like that," Jenny said.

Peng swept the carpet with her shoe. "Maybe you answer question, help me. Jacob confide secret with you?"

"Oh yes, he tells me everything."

"Did he say where he hide Freedom Stone?"

CHAPTER 21

I JUMPED OUT OF A perfectly good airplane at 0250 hours and hurtled toward a dark mansion on a black lake along an unlit shoreline. It took sixty seconds to free fall the first ten thousand feet. For the next three minutes after that, I maneuvered my chute through a light breeze toward an easy landing on Griffith's expansive roof. Thanks to endless Ranger training, I could do it in my sleep.

While I floated down, the image of Hidalgo's head shattering across the plaza popped into my mind. The innocent archeologists cried out for justice. For their sakes and untold numbers of others, I vowed to track down and kill Mr. Baldy. Based on what I saw in his Guatemalan camp, he must've brought Cherry here. I could only hope he was still on the premises.

Griffith's roof was the one area where my surveillance exposed a gap in their security. One access door with one sensor. No cameras. No one expects an assault from above. Not the Taliban, not ISIS, not the Qatari … Wait. Forget that last one. I'm not supposed to talk about that mission until 2042.

Off the coast, Jenny's infrared beacon, visible only to me, blinked with a steady cadence. I added her reliability to the list of things I adored about her. After our fight, she came back to the suite and apologized. Then she rifled through my backpack, pulled the clay-covered altar I'd been carrying around in place of the alabaster albatross, and questioned me about where I left the real one. Which led to another fight. Why did I hide the stone without telling her? To protect her, I'd said. I learned a valuable lesson. Never protect her without discussing it first. I apologized for that oversight. We achieved balance, or maybe yin-yang.

Or whatever. We were back on the Highway of Love, and that's all that mattered in the end.

We went ahead with the mission in good spirits.

I checked my comm link. "Jenny, you look just as beautiful in the dark as you do in the light."

"That better be a compliment," she said.

A boat ran up the coast, heading toward Jenny. Before reaching her, it arced toward Griffith's dock. Half a mile east, another boat lay at anchor. Everything else was dark.

"Is that a security detail from Griffith's people?" I asked. "Kinda late for a shore patrol. If it is, you should back off another half mile."

"Checking," she said. Over the comm link, I heard her goose the motor enough to move quietly.

I flared and ran across the angled solar panels to deaden the thump of landing. It worked well except the chute caught on a corner. I struggled with it for a few seconds before deciding to abandon the rig.

The access door was full-sized sheet metal with a standard wireless sensor. Using my Sabel phone to mimic the sensor's signal, I used a slide hammer to remove the lock mechanism and open the door. The stairwell went down only one floor. Pulling the lower door open a crack, I used the monocular periscope to look around the space. A windowless attic, it held several desks and monitors in a narrow corridor. A wall separated the rest of the space. Along that wall were two doors. No lights seeped beneath them, but a sound came from the other side. I listened closely.

Snoring.

I risked a peek inside, quietly turning the knob to give an inch. The thermal setting on my visor revealed several bodies prone. A makeshift bunkhouse. The Knights? I quickly pulled the door shut again.

Mercury tapped my shoulder, scaring the crap out of me. *Always nice to know you got the enemy in front and behind you, right homie? Don't be making the same mistake Consul Paullus made at Cannae.*

You mean Hannibal's famous double envelopment move that wiped out the Roman army in 216 BCE? I asked. *Never heard of it.*

Mercury said, *Nobody likes a smartass.*

I said, *How about telling me something useful. Are all the Knights in there?*

Mercury said, *Only twelve. You left eight in the jungle. The rest are across the way in that service house. Basement. Griffith was too cheap to spring for a motel.*

I said, *Tell me the truth—do I have a chance of surviving this?*

Mercury said, *With your techno-gizmos and my brains, absolutely, dawg! Probably.*

Filled with confidence, I looked for and found the next stair well. It was a tight, unadorned service well wrapped around a small elevator. I could tell it was the service stair because it smelled of garbage. The rotting remains of dinners and parties had exited the building down these steps. Some had spilled.

The house was silent. Not even the heating system made noise. I crept down the next flight to the bedroom level and creaked open the door. A dark hallway lined with excess furniture, empty cabinets, nightstands, and end tables. Cherry's room was lakeside, to the left down a different corridor. I stepped into the passageway and heard the floor creak under my weight. I stopped and tested it.

I was in the service hallway where they'd cheaped out on the flooring. I moved to the edge where the joists held more of my weight and made my way down the hall. I came to a junction with the passageway to the owner's wing. The carpeting was much nicer. To my right, a grand staircase led to the ground floor and a foyer the size of my home.

From my position, I could see plenty of empty space down the main corridor in both directions. I tried to orient myself in the building. Cherry's room had to be one more left turn and down at the end of the hall.

Jenny's voice came over the comm link. "You're not going to like this."

"What?" I whispered.

"That boat. Not security. Danny and three others just tied up at Griffith's dock. They're armed with saps and bats. They're running up the pier toward the house."

I silently cursed the chaotic anarchists and their undisciplined methods. I said, "And the second boat?"

"Not sure. No lights, no movement. Strange place to anchor."

It was odd. She and I both knew it. Did Danny bring backup? Or a getaway boat in case his sank? It would be the smart move. It could also be Griffith's men. Or the local marine cops. Or drunken fishermen who gave up trying to find a port in the dark. The last thing I wanted to do was ask more questions in the dead quiet around me. I left it to Jenny to figure out.

The silence didn't last long. An alarm rang. Not loud on the owner's level, but distinct. I backed up to the door and listened for the Knights. I'd counted eight security guards on the day shift. During my descent from above, I'd only spotted two men making rounds, which led me to believe there were four to six overnight.

Thanks to Danny, they were now all alert and calling for backup. There could be five to fifteen more men deployed in minutes. Add twenty-four more if they wanted to roust the Knights.

Light burst from underneath a nearby door. Someone stirred inside. The room didn't face the lake, so it couldn't be Griffith. I slid behind a bookshelf and flattened against the wall. The door opened and Mr. Baldy, the man who assassinated Hidalgo, stepped out dressed in black jeans, t-shirt, and jacket. Two Knights flanked him. He carried his Scorpion at his thigh and strode confidently to the grand staircase. No silencer attached this time. For a split second, as he rounded the top of the stairs, his gaze was level with mine. He didn't see me.

It was all I could do not to pull my pistol and end his miserable life. But I couldn't. Not yet. The odd sounds I picked up in Jenny's comm link told me she had come closer to shore hoping to help Danny. And that put more lives at risk: hers, Danny's, and whoever else he brought. I took a deep breath. Griffith's regular guards would merely beat up Danny. Mr. Baldy would kill him without a second thought.

Decision time: kill the mission or use the diversion to rescue Cherry? As I'd told Danny, a mission wasn't a plan, it was a series of options and opportunities. His diversion made my escape nearly impossible, but there was another option. It would depend on Joe Griffith's next move.

"They split up," Jenny said. "Two of the Brothers have their hands up. Flashlights are on them."

I turned away from the main hallway and spoke quietly and firmly. "Jenny, if you can see that, you're too close. Get out on the lake. Get out of there. Now."

"We can't leave them here." Jenny's voice echoed the anger from our first fight earlier in the evening.

Why not? I wanted to ask. The idiot was a walking disaster. Did Jenny want to defect to their losing side? But the house was too quiet to voice that argument.

There was nothing I could do for Danny. I would go ahead with my option for Cherry as soon as I determined what Joe Griffith's next move would be.

"Wait," Jenny said. "It's going to be OK. Danny's rushing the guards with bats."

Another statement I couldn't argue without alerting the house to my presence. I knew the next scene before it unfolded. Unlike the movies, when a security team discovers a threat, the secondary team immediately protects the perimeter executing a disciplined, orderly plan. That way, no one gets the jump on them.

Jenny read directly from the script I'd predicted in my head. "Oh no! Two more guards just came out of nowhere."

I heard feet hitting the attic floor above my head. Mr. Baldy had called up the reserves.

"Jenny," I whispered as loud as I dared. "Get out of there. Now! Circle out a couple miles, then come back for me half a mile south of here. They will search the beach any second."

I heard her motor in the background speed up, then slow down.

"Damn it," she said. "Sorry, Jacob. That anchored boat was Griffith's. They've cut me off and are aiming guns at me. They're boarding."

Through her comm link, I heard shouting. Then I heard feet rushing as she was boarded.

"GET YOUR HANDS UP, PALMS OUT." The voice came through her comm link louder than hers. "PUT THE GUN DOWN. PUT IT DOWN NOW, LADY."

CHAPTER 22

THE SOUND OF POUNDING FEET came down the stairs from the attic bunkhouse. The Knights were on the move. I crammed myself into an armoire just as they spilled out onto the second floor. I couldn't get the door closed. I had to hook it with a finger and pray they didn't inspect it as they ran by. All twelve marched directly to the grand staircase and proceeded down. As soon as the last man disappeared around the corner, I fell out of the armoire with a loud thump. Their tromping feet drowned it out.

I ran back to the roof. Griffith's property was the local guards' territory. The Knights would be used for a sweep once they'd coordinated with Mr. Baldy.

Using the monocular, I scanned the grounds to get an idea of what they would do next.

Twelve Knights formed up in three rows of four on the patio between the lake and the mansion. The other twelve remained in reserve. A small blessing. Mr. Baldy and a uniformed guard discussed something at the head of the formation. A moment later, two groups of guards emerged from the surrounding trees. Jenny and Danny were held by three guards. Fiona, Mark, and another Brother stood battered and bruised next to two more.

At least Danny had shown the discipline not to tangle with a superior force. His companions had made the mistake of trying to fight their way out.

I heard Jenny's heartbeat in my comm link. It took a minute to realize why. She'd stuck her comm link's ear bud in her bra to keep comms open. Smart move.

The leader of the guards pointed toward the house. Danny and Jenny were led away, looking dejected. The other three were led off in the opposite direction. I tried to follow Jenny's group. They disappeared into the house right away. Fiona and the others marched around the south side and out to the front. I looked for cop cars but didn't see any. They kept going across the front walkway and around to the neighboring house. Breaking up the Brothers into two groups didn't make sense to me.

From my perch high above, I could hear Mr. Baldy giving orders to the Knights. They marched to the lake and began a professional and effective sweep of the property. Calculating their possible patterns, I figured they would comb the beach, up to the patio, then fan out on both sides until a smaller number of them reached the front. They would then come in all the entrances at the same time and push any intruders to the roof. In short, they would eventually find me. It was unavoidable. The armoire I'd used once would be inspected as they conducted a floor-by-floor, room-by-room search.

Mercury had given me a warning. He reminded me of Consul Paullus' horrific defeat. Hannibal surrounded Paullus in the same way Mr. Baldy was in the process of surrounding me. Paullus was killed in the battle but he wasn't to blame. His co-consul, Gaius Terentius Varro, engaged Hannibal prematurely, against Paullus's orders. Which was exactly the situation Danny put me in. And Jenny had been caught up in his fiasco.

Now I had to rescue Jenny—while little rebel Danny tagged along. Rescuing one person is a problem to be solved. Rescuing two is exponentially harder. The fact that Danny would pitch a fit like a five-year-old being forced to eat broccoli unless we also rescued his Brothers—in another building—would escalate the problem into infinity.

The first thing to do was to get back to the level where they were holding Cherry and look for options and opportunities. I made my way back down to the second level and listened. The Knights were doing the search as predicted. One man searched a room while another covered him. Separated like that, the option of taking out one of them went out the window. Which left only one option I could think of.

I had to stick to the original mission. The only way to save Jenny was to rescue Cherry first.

With any luck, that would send the Knights into a frenzy to find Cherry, leaving more opportunity to find Jenny and the Brothers.

Moving silently down the hall, I counted steps to measure out which room would be the one where I'd seen her in the video. I counted off doors and opened one slowly. One of Griffith's uniformed guards stood at the window, looking outside. He heard me as I ran across the room, my Sabel Dart in my hand. He raised a defensive arm but collapsed instantly. The dart works quite well in the forearm.

Looking around the room, I realized I'd miscounted steps. I was in Joe Griffith's master bedroom. He was nowhere to be seen. No doubt the guards had put him in a safe room at the first sign of trouble. I dragged the sleeping guard into the bathroom and stole his uniform. He didn't have my shoulders, but I wriggled into it anyway. I propped him up on the toilet and closed the door.

I checked myself in the mirror. I wore the uniform better than the guy I stole it from. But would I pass inspection? The Knights had the run of the house. I could only hope they didn't know the guards by name yet. I exited quickly.

Recalibrating my steps, I tried the next room down the hall. No Cherry. No rumpled sheets. No indentation in the chairs. Two towels lay on the sitting bench at the foot of the bed. On the floor were some price tags, one for a dress that cost more than my kitchen remodel. Nothing in the walk-in closet but an echo, nothing in the other walk-in closet either. Nothing under the bed. No phone, no charger, no means of communication. No purse.

On the bathroom floor lay Cherry's shorts and shirt from Guatemala and a small generic-looking makeup kit on the counter. She had been in the room at some point, but they had moved her elsewhere. In the convention hall of a house, she could be anywhere.

All my options and opportunities were gone. Where were they holding her?

I heard the Knights marching to the second floor. They would search this wing shortly.

I ran back to the master and waited for a knock. A Knight threw the door open and strode in. No knocking involved. His partner waited in the hall outside. He looked me over.

"Did you find them?" I asked.

He circled me, his stare going up and down. I twisted halfway, then repositioned myself to face him.

"You don't speak English?" I asked.

"I speak English good." He frowned. "You here whole time?"

I flopped my hands. "I would never leave my post."

He scratched his scruffy beard and looked out at his friend in the hall. The guy outside shrugged and said something in their native language. The man nearest me looked over his shoulder at me as if I were a mosquito, more annoying than threatening. He tracked around to the bathroom and checked inside. The toilet was in a second compartment, hidden behind a wall with its own door. I'd left the door open. The darted guard could have slumped his way off the porcelain throne and be visible. I couldn't tell because the Knight stood in the way. He stood there a long time.

In my comm link, I heard Jenny say rather loudly, "You're putting us in a bedroom? If you're planning anything sick, I'll kick your—"

Someone slapped her. Not hard and not gently. A voice said, "Shut the fuck up. Don't get your hopes up, you're not going to be violated."

"Tell me the window has a view of the lake," Jenny said. "I want to send a Morse code message to the next passing boat."

The voice on her end said, "Lake's on the other side of the building. Now shut up."

My clever bride-to-be had just given me her relative position in the house.

In front of me, the Knight grunted, closed the bathroom door, and strode out into the hall.

CHAPTER 23

WITH MY EAR PRESSED TO the door, I listened while Knights checked the other rooms on my end. I heard them march back to the connecting corridor. I heard them say something in English and a woman's voice replied. Not loud enough to make out the words through the solid wood. When all the prowlers cleared the hall, I slipped out. It would only take a minute for them to figure out I'd tricked them.

I turned toward Cherry's door and found a beautiful woman in an expensive cocktail dress ahead of me. When she pressed her key to open Cherry's room, she sensed my presence. Our gazes met. It took us both a moment to recognize each other. I hadn't seen Cherry out of shorts and plaid flannel. She had never seen me in a stolen uniform. She looked to be on the verge of screaming in surprise.

I slapped a hand over her mouth and pushed her inside and kicked the door shut.

When I let go, we stared at each other for a moment. A small purse hung from her shoulder. Her black dress had white flowers embroidered on one side. She was stunning.

She said, "What are you doing here?"

"Rescuing you. Why are you dressed up like—"

"You can't rescue me right now." Her eyes darted around the room. "Could you come back later? Maybe in a couple hours?"

I was too stunned to speak at first. After a moment, I said, "That's not how rescues work. C'mon, let's go." I grabbed her wrist.

She yanked free with a look that was half angry, half scared. "No, really. I'm busy. I, uhm, have a meeting."

My eyebrows rose so high, they hurt my forehead. "Did you notice

Mr. Baldy is here?"

"Who?"

"The man who executed Hidalgo and fourteen of your friends."

"Oh, you mean Captain Amanow. Yes. That was unfortunate. Horrible, I mean. But I'm not ready to go." She stared at me with that look people get when they're telling you it's not raining, yet you're standing in the middle of a downpour. "I … I have to change. I can't go out in this."

With my mouth hanging open, I pointed to the bathroom where her shorts and shirt waited. She all but ran to them. I hooked a finger around her purse strap and slipped it off her shoulder as she walked by. She looked at me funny. I pointed to the shorts hoping to get her moving. She went in and closed the door.

In my earbud, I could hear Jenny giving Danny a piece of her mind about his foolish actions. Which meant the guards had left them alone for the time being. That eased my mind.

I opened Cherry's purse. Her phone was in there, fully charged.

Somewhere else in the house, Mr. Baldy was shouting in Turkmen. Boots tromped back up the grand staircase. They sounded like a herd of buffalo.

Cherry opened the bathroom door in her camp gear. She looked a lot better in the cocktail dress. I grabbed her wrist and pulled her to the hall door. It was like dragging an anchor.

"They're coming," I said. "We have to go. Now." When she didn't move, I said, "Your uncle begged me to come save you."

Pain covered her expression. Her face crinkled in a prelude to tears.

The pounding boots came closer.

There wasn't time for *why are you crying?* I stuck my shoulder into Cherry's ribcage and hoisted her up. Running out into the hall, I could hear the Knights coming from the center. Looking the other way, I saw a door with a small window in it. I ran for it, slid inside, closed the door, and set her down. I put a finger across her lips to keep her quiet.

Extracting her phone from her purse, I held it to her face to unlock it, then looked at the recent calls. Five calls went to her mother, lasting three to five minutes each. Two to her father, each lasting ten minutes.

The last in the series went to a San Francisco area code not in her contact list. It lasted over an hour. Given the time zones, they took place after midnight on the West Coast.

I gave her my soldier stare long enough to make her shiver. Then I softened and said, "Your uncle begged me to bring you back. You made eight calls, but none to him? You could tell him you're fine, wearing a small fortune in a cocktail dress, and have an urgent meeting coming up at four in the morning."

Her face slumped. Her gaze fell to the cement at our feet.

I waited for her to say something. Most people would explain their behavior after the silence dragged out long enough.

Instead, her nose crinkled. Her gaze rose to mine then darted around the space. "This place stinks."

We were in another service stair on the other side of the building. And it stank of garbage as much as the first. How much stuff did the staff spill in the stairwells? Or was it that no one ever cleaned it because the owner never came in here?

I turned my attention to the window. Intended to prevent one servant from crashing into another while carrying heirloom crystal, it worked well for me. My monocular periscope allowed me to see Mr. Baldy coming down the hall holding his Scorpion at the ready. Four Knights followed him. They burst into Cherry's room.

Jenny's voice hit my ear. "Jacob, can you hear me? I'm looking out the window and see the driveway below me. We're in a bedroom, but the door's locked from outside."

A quick mental review of my drone video told me she and Danny were on the other side of Mr. Baldy. Which could be the far end of this hallway or another one running parallel. That didn't narrow it down much.

But the locked-from-outside mention gave me an option. I turned the monocular to focus on the doorknobs up and down the passageway. They were odd looking. Lever handles set into large metal locks, the kind you see on secure facilities. Not the kind of knobs usually found in mansions.

With my focus elsewhere, Cherry slipped her purse out of my hand and fled down the stairs heading for the ground floor.

I could go after Cherry or Jenny.

"Your Highness," I called down as she rounded the landing below me. She stopped and looked up. I said, "Your rescue is leaving the station. Now or never."

She continued running down.

A mission is a series of options and opportunities. Cherry lost all of hers right then.

I pulled the door open and stepped out into the plush carpeting of the hall. I ran to Cherry's room with a dart held at the ready.

Mr. Baldy left one sentry outside and took the second inside with him. A smart tactical move. The sentry's mistake was keeping his back to the short end of the hall. He heard me coming but couldn't get all the way around with his pistol before the dart plunged into his neck. He crumpled to the floor. I snatched a magnetic card clipped to his belt.

I grabbed the handle to the open door and yanked it closed. As I did, I got a satisfying look at a shocked Mr. Baldy. I'd rather have shot him, but that would complicate rescuing Jenny alive. When the door slammed home, I yanked the handle upward and felt a rewarding click.

I'd seen handles like it in storage rooms. Only a magnetic key would open it from the outside. And every door on the second floor had these odd, industrial handles. Which meant that all the bedrooms could be locked from outside. Joe Griffith was one paranoid old man. His guest rooms doubled as jail cells.

CHAPTER 24

RUNNING BACK DOWN THE MAIN corridor, I found the service hall next to the grand staircase and slipped into a dark space behind my favorite armoire. It was beginning to feel like home. I thought about the layout of this odd house. There were at least two service stairwells. Why would Griffith want that? Maybe he wanted servants using different access points to reduce the noise of them trotting past the bedrooms at night. Or maybe he didn't want the staff hearing the anguished cries of his prisoners. I'd come down from the roof in a central stairwell. Cherry had disappeared in one on the southeast corner. If there was any symmetry in the floorplan, there could be another well on the northwest end.

I checked out the furniture-strewn corridor I was in. Sure enough, behind a grandfather clock was another hall leading off at a right angle. It ran behind the wall of the grand staircase in the center of the building.

Four more Knights pounded their way up from the ground floor. They were keeping to the formal areas, which meant the service access would buy me a little time. Not much though, since the Knights were pros.

At the far end of the hall was another formal hall with nice carpeting and a third stairwell with a windowed door. I used my monocular to see around the corner. A Knight pushed Danny ahead of him. They stopped at the third door. The Knight unlocked it, pushed Danny in, pulled the door shut, flipped the handle into the locked position, then left.

Through the comm, Jenny said, "Danny, are you all right?"

"Fine." His answer sounded angry.

I ran quietly to their door. Unlocking it with the stolen keycard, I was immediately driven backward by Jenny's bodyweight.

It took two steps to catch her momentum as she kissed my lips and cheek. I grabbed her arms and pushed her back far enough for my eyes to focus on her. We spoke at the same time.

"Are you all right?" I asked.

"My glorious hero," she said.

"Right, but are you hurt in any way?" While I like to be worshipped as much as the next hero, escaping alive was my top priority.

Danny stepped into the hall and looked both ways.

"I'm fine," Jenny said.

I looked over her shoulder at Danny. "Are you able to run?"

"I'm ready to fight," he said.

"Great. You ready to fight your way into that, Ephialtes?" I pointed toward the sound of Knights charging toward us from around the corner.

I waved toward the stairwell and pushed Jenny that way.

She didn't need an explanation. She saw the exit and ran for it. Danny and I followed. We closed the door quietly. I monitored the hall with my monocular.

Jenny whispered, "Why did you call him, what was it?"

"Ephialtes." Danny answered for me. "The man who betrayed Leonidas to the Persians at Thermopylae. His name came to mean 'nightmare' in Greek."

"At least the kid knows his military history," I said. "He gets credit for book learning."

Mercury stood next to me, peering out the window. *Homes, the boy is a nightmare, but somebody done warned you about helping the meek.*

I said, *I'm only doing this because you said there'd be a reward for saving Cherry. I was going to use that money to go find Yuri Belenov and settle my debts with Mikhail Yeschenko.*

Aw, ain't that sweet. Mercury smiled and tilted his head. *Lying to god with a straight face. Not just lying but looking me in the eye when you do it. That takes balls, mortal. Most people save their lies for when they be praying. Hands together, eyes closed, head down, that way. Y'know how they do it, "If you let me win the lottery just this once, I swear I'll give half to charity. Or ten percent. Maybe five." Stuff like that.*

I said, *I might not have been lying. I might've meant it. You don't know.*

Oh, I know, Mercury said. *I'm all-knowing. I know you better'n you know you, You want to save Cherry so her uncle will be grateful and sing your praises. And if the old man likes you, then Jenny will be happy and will sing your praises. Then the Brotherhood and the whole choir will sing your praises. Face it, dude, you're just like the gods—always craving adoration.*

I said, *OK, so I want to be respected. You got me. Now how do I get out of this?*

Mercury said, *Get to the kitchen before Hannibal surrounds you, Consul Paullus.*

Then he walked through the wall.

I rechecked my monocular. Mr. Baldy rounded the bend with a squad of his men behind him. That meant there was another squad coming from the other direction. Which meant they were coming down the service hall I'd just used. That escape route was out. And they were on to my tricks.

"Down," I nearly shouted at my companions.

They lost no time in jogging down the stairs. I tried locking the door from the inside, but the latches weren't rigged that way. The cement well doubled as a fire escape, always open. I left it and followed the other two.

Danny reached for the door on the ground floor. I grabbed his hand just in time and pulled him back. I pointed down another flight. We ran down to the basement just as Mr. Baldy opened the door on the second floor.

He fired three shots at random down the cement well. Ricochets pinged around us. They were as dangerous to him as they were to us. He waited a second, then came sprinting down.

I took up a position on the last landing, basement level, and waited for him to come into view. Pistols are not accurate weapons, especially in tight confines under stress and in a dimly lit well. Yet I figured I was better than Mr. Baldy and had a 9 mil instead of a .22.

He sensed my tactic and came into view in a crouch, leading with his Scorpion. I made a bigger target than he, so I bolted.

Danny and Jenny were in a staging area backlit by industrial nightlights. Two large tables with surfaces of butcher block separated us from an industrial kitchen. Griffith liked to throw big parties. And lock his guests up. And have defenses to stop an army from breaching his doors. What in the name of Mars was Griffith into? Or have modern American billionaires become like Roman Emperors—the less you know the better?

I nodded at Danny. He grabbed one end and I got the other. We shoved a heavy table against the stairwell door. We grabbed the second table and set it on its side on top of the first, using the heavy wood to block the window. Then we looked for an exit.

Knowing we were belowground, I thought there had to be a loading elevator or some way to bring in supplies. While we searched for it, I sensed someone in a robe standing in the shadow. I aimed my pistol at her. She gasped and stepped into the light with her hands up. A live-in maid or cook; she was on the far side of middle aged, Latina, and trembling.

I put my gun away. "Where is the exit?"

She looked at Jenny, then Danny.

Jenny asked her in Spanish and got an answer. Jenny said, "There's a long corridor in the pantry."

"Ask her to show us," I said.

Jenny convinced the lady to help. Our reluctant guide started off through a warren of kitchen and prep areas. She talked a mile a minute to Jenny but walked like a turtle. We passed a room with a heavy steel door, sealed with a large padlock. When I asked what was behind it, the lady reported no one was allowed inside. I ran the building's floor plan through my head and estimated it was below the smokestacks.

Behind us, we heard the tables crashing to the floor. Our barricade was down. Shouts and flashlight beams bounced around two rooms away.

We rushed our new friend, who picked up the pace. Eventually, we came to what was more of a warehouse than a pantry. At one end was a long, wide underground passage leading to the service house next door. Deliveries were made there, then trusted staff dragged the goods through this tunnel to the main house. Griffith didn't want delivery people near his castle for fear of a surprise attack.

Jenny gave our guide a hug and thanked her and asked her not to tell the bad men about us. Not much chance, but our best hope.

I closed the entry door, slipped my Sabel Visor on, turned off the fluorescent overhead lights, grabbed Jenny's hand, and strode down the dark passage. The visor's mid-infrared mode gave me a small window of visibility. Something like a horror movie. Danny tagged along, holding Jenny's other hand.

"When we get to the other end of this thing," I said, "we're going to face twice as many men. I'm going to lay suppressing fire, you two are going to run for the dock and take the boat. You're not going to wait. You're not going—"

"I'm not leaving without my Brothers." Danny stopped, pulling back on our linked hands.

The Sabel Visor requires some light for amplification. There wasn't any. So all I could see of him was his thermal overlay. He was hot.

So was I.

"You've already put everyone at risk," I said. "You need to start taking orders from a veteran. You're getting out of this compound and getting out of here. I'll get your little friends out for you. Leave this to the grownups."

Jenny put her hands between us and shoved us apart. "Danny, haven't you figured it out yet? He's right. Leave it to him."

Behind us, back in the pantry, we heard the noise of the Knights. They hadn't found our passageway. Even if they did, as long as the maid didn't squeal on us, they couldn't investigate with full force. They'd have to split up. We had a chance. A slim one.

Of course, Mr. Baldy was the kind of guy who would shoot into empty space first and turn the lights on afterward.

"Did you find Cherry?" Danny asked.

"Yes," I said.

"Where is she?"

"Well. She had an appointment."

CHAPTER 25

I GRABBED DANNY AND JENNY by the arms and started marching them to the far end. It opened into a large shipping and receiving area with a platform elevator big enough for a truck. The top was sealed from the elements. At the back of the area was a wooden staircase. Next to that was an electrical breaker box.

The breakers were labeled neatly. I turned off the obvious ones: Underground Passage; Loading Dock; and Service Lift. With the visor, I owned the dark. Nothing else looked like it would shut off their communications. I pushed my companions against the wall and told them to stand still, then I crept up the stairs to a door on the ground floor. Opening it a quarter inch, I used my monocular to look around the room. It opened to a kitchen. No one was there.

I had the other two to join me. We tiptoed through the kitchen-dining room combination and into a room full of monitors. All the chairs were empty. Which was creepy. There should be guards. I counted three displays of six monitors each. Cables and computers were neatly installed for a clean and professional look. Beside each workstation were three red buttons. One for the main house, one for the service house I stood in, and one for the dock and beach. Which explained why they were so quick to catch the Brothers upon arrival.

We circled around the other way and found another room that looked like a break room. A Settlers of Catan game lay on a table next to warm coffee mugs. An open paperback rested on the arm of a chair. They'd just left.

A small gun safe stood open at the back of the room. I handed a Smith and Wesson to Danny. Using hand signals, I told him to guard the monitor room with his life. Jenny grabbed a Beretta. I positioned her by the front door.

I checked the monitors. It quickly became apparent why the house was empty. Everyone had been called into the search for us at the main house. They were scouring the grounds, going floor to floor, room to room, and bush to bush. A control screen listed thirty-three cameras. None in the service halls and none in the bedrooms. No wonder I'd gotten away with running around so much. I flipped through as many camera locations as I could.

Then I found Cherry. She sat at a conference table in her plaid flannel shirt. A wall-mounted big screen dominated one end. A professional video-conferencing mic sat in front of her. Checking out the monitor controls in front of me, I moved the camera to look at the screen she faced. A well-dressed man with a hint of Euro-fashion in his suit addressed her. They were deep in a conversation. The logo in the corner looked familiar. I zoomed in closer. *Cour Pénale Internationale* was written next to a graphic of the scales of justice surrounded by olive branches. A moment later, the name cycled to the English version, International Criminal Court.

Based in the Hague, Netherlands, they're responsible for trying war criminals and crimes against humanity. Why was Cherry talking to them from Griffith's house? He was harboring a mass murderer, Mr. Baldy. Was she turning him in?

I zoomed back out and panned the room. Off to one side of Cherry sat Griffith, dressed for success in a Kiton suit. His arms were crossed but his face appeared pleased. Mixed signals I couldn't figure out. He glanced at his watch, made a short call, then rose. He touched Cherry's shoulder in a familiar and friendly way. She gave him a glance I couldn't analyze because her back was to the camera. She returned to her video conference right away. She didn't appear angry or scared or anything. It was as if she were delivering an accounting report.

A few minutes later, movement on the monitor in the driveway caught my eye. The big iron gates swung open and three armored Ford Expeditions entered the grounds. They pulled up to the front walkway. Griffith and eight of his uniformed guards trotted from the house and climbed in. They drove away, into the dark unknown.

Somewhere in the house behind me, I heard kicking and muffled screaming. The kind of sound someone makes when trying to scream through a gag. I ran to where Danny stood. He'd heard it too. We both pointed to a closed door beyond the kitchen.

Jenny backed us up by covering the hallway.

Using hand signals again, I gave Danny orders. I would take point, he covered me from three feet back. I gave him my soldier stare until he nodded.

The door was not locked. I crouched—so Danny wouldn't accidentally shoot me in the back—and threw the door open. Two uniformed guards were wrestling Fiona-the-blonde. She was bound with rope from head to foot and gagged. They were holding her upright. Next to her was a large coffin-sized box made of heavy cardboard. Two more boxes lay next to the empty one.

I sprang forward, stabbing one guard with a dart while the other staggered back and aimed a pistol at me. Danny fired at the guy and missed. But he distracted the guard long enough for me to grab another dart and launch at him. The guard squeezed off a shot that buzzed my ear just as I hit his thigh with the dart.

The instant the two men were still, Danny pulled a serious knife out of his pocket and started cutting through Fiona's ropes. I opened the other coffin-boxes. In them were Mark and the other Brother, whose name I still didn't know, also bound and gagged. Mark thanked me for rescuing him. When he did, Fiona gave me an odd once-over without offering thanks.

I checked the rest of the house. With any luck, the walls would muffle the guard's pistol shot to anyone outside. But inside was another story. I sent Jenny to watch the screens for signs of guards coming this way or Cherry in trouble.

After clearing the attic and the second level, I returned to Danny. He was freeing the last of his companions.

I nodded at the cardboard boxes. "What were those for?"

"The crematorium," Mark said.

Danny looked at the boxes as if seeing them for the first time. In that instant, the depth of his misguided adventure sank in. He looked at me, colorless and wide-eyed.

I felt Jenny at my side.

I said, "Get your crew through the hedge on the north side, go around the neighbor's house, make your way to the beach. By then, I'll have a diversion that should clear the dock. Get in your boat and for the love of Minerva, get out of here."

This time, he followed orders. He and his Brothers filed past me.

I turned to Jenny. "Follow them. Take your boat two houses south of here. I'll be on the beach in ten minutes."

"Where are you going?" Jenny asked.

"I know where Cherry is."

"She turned down the rescue," Jenny said. "Maybe she doesn't need to be saved."

"I promised the old man I'd bring her back." I kissed her forehead, then turned her around. "And I'm the one who can, so I have to."

She said, "'He who can, must?' I don't like that expression."

CHAPTER 26

THE FIRST TIME I REVIEWED the videos of Griffith's stronghold, I had figured out most of the floor plan. The bedrooms and living areas were easy to guess and confirm. What remained a mystery was the center of the building—until I saw Cherry in the video conference room. On the ground floor, Griffith had a grand salon. Larger than a living room, it could host cocktails for well over a hundred. Upstairs, he had a gym and private living rooms and a theater. I'd guessed the basement held a massive wine and cigar bar. Maybe a man cave the size of a nightclub.

But after seeing Cherry, I realized the basement was the nerve center. While it held a kitchen, laundry and serving area the size of any other mansion, it also hosted the crematorium. Maybe there were torture chambers and interrogation rooms nearby. Even with that space accounted for, there was a large gap in square footage.

I figured it had to be a secure communications area. It would be surrounded by a Faraday cage to block electromagnetic fields. No one could use a cellphone, recording device, or bounce signals through the room. It keeps your enemies from listening to your phone calls. Sabel Security had several such secure rooms. So did the CIA, NSA, West Wing, and virtually every embassy in the world.

Why would a hedge fund manager need one? And why would a hedge fund manager have a secure link to the ICC? Especially since that group should charge him with crimes against humanity for his association with Mr. Baldy.

There was an alarm for each camera on the security system. I clicked the one for the front gate. The Knights were drawn forward, away from the dock and beach. I waited until I saw Danny and his crew sprinting down the dock and zipping away in their powerboat. Jenny followed them out into the darkness of Lake Michigan. Then I slammed the red panic button to draw the Knights to where I stood. Once I saw them on the move in the monitors, I ran to the breaker box and flipped everything off.

I switched on my Sabel Visor and flew down the wooden stairs into the pitch-black basement. From there, I ran down the underground tunnel. Before I arrived at the other end, I stopped to catch my breath and quiet my approach. Thinking like my adversary, I figured Mr. Baldy would split his forces. Twelve remained at the main building while the rest surrounded the service house.

The pantry was silent, but all the lights were on. Repeating the breaker box trick would draw more attention than I needed. I crept along, doing my best not to clatter pots and pans to the floor. I passed the crematorium and found myself in a dead end.

In a quiet place, footfalls are noisy. So is the cloth of your pantlegs rubbing against each other as you take a step. One of the many reasons I wear tight pants. The noise coming toward me swished like someone trying to keep their pants from rubbing. I holstered my Glock and readied a dart and flattened against a wall.

No footfalls, just the approaching swish-swish, which then went in another direction. I rounded the corner carefully and moved silently down a dark passageway. In front of me was a lone figure, walking with the confidence of an officer. He was a silhouette backlit by a brighter area beyond. He turned a corner and disappeared into the brighter area.

I stumbled over something. Checking around, I found god lounging on the floor as if he were on a throne eating grapes.

Mercury said, *You know, homeboy, they got twenty-four guys looking for you. When's your luck gonna run out?*

I said, *I was hoping you were handling that for me.*

Mercury said, *Do I look like the god of invisibility to you?*

I said, *Could you give me a hint about how to stay alive?*

Mercury mocked my voice, *Could you gimme a hint... How about you give Jenny a hint about how you always win against impossible odds? Here I am, saving your ass every day and what do you tell her about me? Nothing. That's disrespectful, ya feel me?*

Irritating as it was, he had a point. I'd been less than appreciative lately. I said, *Look, soon as we get back, I'll tell her a little bit at a time. If I tell her everything all at once, she'll freak out and run away. I'll warm her up. One step at a time. Whaddya say?*

Mercury popped up and grabbed my shoulder. *OK, but this is the last freebie, bro. Yeah, I see you nodding like you just got away with lying to me again. I swear I go too easy on you. So here's the deal. You looked over the screens back in the guard shack, but you never saw Mr. Baldy. Why? Because he's around the next corner, personally guarding the secure communications room and getting ready to pop a .22LR through your skull.*

He was telling me something I'd already thought about, so it wasn't like divine help, but I hadn't been grateful lately, so I figured I'd play him. I said, *Thanks, now that's useful. You really are the one and only messenger. Say, what is she doing in there, anyway?*

Mercury said, *I'll tell you a little bit at time. If I tell you everything all at once ...*

He laughed as he faded out of existence on our plane.

The trouble with gods is they're so omniscient all the time. You can't get away with anything.

Moving closer to the corner my quarry had rounded, I pulled up. I was in a wide passageway that spilled into a larger room. The light had an orange hue that came from fifteen feet deeper in the space. I sensed the presence of someone else. Maybe it was the electrical impulses humans give off. Maybe it was divine intervention, maybe it was Stearne's Law, but I felt like he was three feet away, waiting for me to come around the corner.

I considered the logistics. The report from a pistol would draw ten to fifteen armed men into this confined space. If I killed Mr. Baldy, it would be my last living act. I readied a dart. Once he was incapacitated, I could strangle him quietly.

I readied to launch myself and whispered, "Captain."

The sound of half a swish came from around the corner. Then silence. Mr. Baldy wasn't falling for the old ruse. I wanted him to sneak a peek around the corner so I could jam a dart in his eye. He wanted me to peek around the corner so he could put a bullet in my forehead. I knew if I didn't move, he would have to investigate. He was a professional, so I knew how he would do it. I readied my back foot for a leap forward.

The swishing sound resumed, this time I could track it. He was making an arc, swinging wide out of my visual range, to come around the corner five feet back from it. That way he could see me before I could reach him.

I calculated the steps and waited until he was two steps short of where he would see me. I launched out of my stance like I was rushing the quarterback. He was farther back in the room than I'd anticipated. That meant I'd have to take more steps to sack him.

Mr. Baldy had his Scorpion up and ready for my attack. His eye lay directly behind the iron sights. His arm steady. He took his time to find my center mass and squeezed the trigger. It hurt like hell. But the Sabel Armor did what liquid metal armor is supposed to do. It dissipated the energy over a wide area of my chest, preventing it from penetrating my flesh. I staggered a step but kept going.

Mr. Baldy hadn't expected that. He looked at his pistol in disbelief.

I raised the dart and pounded it into his neck. He twisted a clumsy but effective right hook that threw me to the floor. I scrambled to my feet and looked at the Sabel Dart. The needle was bent in half. I looked at Mr. Baldy. He had a metal earring bleeding in his ear.

Damn. What are the odds of hitting something as small as an earring?

I reached for another dart, but Mr. Baldy had his pistol raised. This time he was going for the headshot. I ducked and rolled and somersaulted into his shins. He jumped in the air before I connected and landed on my rolling body. The unstable landing tossed him on his butt.

Getting up as he went down, I slammed my heel into his face. Unfazed, he recovered and raised his pistol, this time looking for my thigh. I grabbed the last dart in my pocket and yanked. In my haste, it went sideways and caught in my pocket. Mr. Baldy fired again.

Few people had seen the non-Newtonian liquid armor in the heat of battle. With a second bullet deflected, Mr. Baldy's eyes lit up with recognition of why I was still alive. He quickly raised his aim to my face.

I dropped my knees onto his torso as I swatted his arm away. The pistol fired another round harmlessly to the left. My body weight falling into his abdomen pushed the air out of his lungs. That gave me time to retrieve my last dart, but not enough time to stop his legs from spinning around, encircling me, and scissoring the life out of me.

My arm was pinned to my side. He squeezed with all his might. Trying to free the dart and the hand that held it proved nearly impossible. I slammed my left hand to his face and felt his orbital socket crack. I gave him another, which only doubled his intent to squeeze the life out of me. Then I remembered one of the hundreds of training sessions I went through that dealt with scissor locks. I leaned back, used one leg to push off the floor, which flopped Mr. Baldy over like a pancake. He was facedown with my butt on top of his and me pulling back on his left leg. I reached blindly behind me and jabbed him with a dart.

He went limp.

I stood, gasped for air, pulled my pistol, and aimed.

At that moment, a door opened in an orange wall. Cherry stepped out. Her eyes fell to Mr. Baldy. Then rose to me. I holstered my 9 mil. Killing an unconscious man doesn't qualify as self-defense. Given her odd behavior, I didn't think Cherry was going to lie for me if I capped Mr. Baldy. Which pissed me off. This was the moment I'd been working toward for days and I was denied.

"Did you kill Captain Amanow?" she shrieked.

"He's resting." I held up the dart and explained it. The look of horror on her face didn't relax at all.

"You called him Captain?" I asked. "Tell me you were reporting him for the execution of the number one expert in Mayan culture."

"Number two," she said. "Uncle Rafael is the number one."

"Why you were calling the ICC?"

She looked shocked that I knew about her call.

"Will you at least call the local cops? He's holding the murder weapon in his hands."

Cherry examined the Scorpion. They're stainless steel with anodized black grips. Mr. Baldy chose the long barrel, giving it an extra sinister look. She shivered.

Voices rolled in from the kitchen.

Cherry pulled herself together and faced me. "How did you get in the secure area?"

"Turns out, it's not all that secure. What was the call about?" I took her elbow and marched her toward the exit at the opposite end.

"I can't tell you." She pulled out of my grip. "Look, I appreciate your concern, but I'm fine. I have a car waiting. I'll go straight to the hotel and speak to Uncle Rafael."

She might as well have slapped me. I stopped in my tracks. She gave me a look, then resumed her march to a small elevator. She pressed the button.

Behind me, boots clomped ever closer.

I bolted down the service hall and up the stinky stairwell.

When I got to the ground floor, I ran out the south exit. A Knight saw me and gave chase, calling to his friends. I bounded the fence into the neighbor's yard and crossed that. The Knights hesitated, unsure if their orders included involving innocent civilians. They didn't hesitate long. A bullet buzzed my ear. I zigzagged through the wooded area. Bark snapped off a tree trunk near my head.

At the end of the first property, I leapt a smaller fence, then ran down the wooden dock to where Jenny waited in her boat. She'd kept the motor running. Behind me, the Knights came at full gallop.

Jenny pulled away as I jumped. As soon as I landed, she cranked it up to full throttle and began evasive maneuvers.

I dug out my phone and called mild-mannered Professor Tum. As soon as he picked up, I yelled, "Meet me at the Drake. Be ready to tell me everything you've left out."

CHAPTER 27

Storming into the Drake's lobby through the labyrinthine lakeside entry, I found Mercury striding alongside me.

Mercury said, *You see how you got into the mess, right homie? Jenny wanted you to save the day for Peng and Rafael. And you wanted to be Jenny's hero.*

I said, *I try to help people, that's all.*

Mercury said, *For your own glory, not for the good of the Dii Consentes. If you keep fighting vainglorious battles, there ain't nothing any god can do you. That's how Hercules died, bro. Now, you need to be thinking big. Like how you gonna get twenty-eight million out of Yuri Belenov.*

I said, *Why don't you tell me something useful? Why not tell me what in Jupiter's name is going on here? And don't start with tossing the Poison Stone back in the ocean. We're past that. Tell me why Danny wanted to go after Griffith so badly. Tell me why Cherry doesn't care who killed her friends anymore.*

Jenny kept pace to my left. She looked at me funny. "What are you mumbling about? Whose friends?"

"Just working stuff out in my head, that's all."

Across from the concierge, Rafael Tum and Gu Peng sat on a gold loveseat, their expectant eyes watched me approach. No sign of Danny or Cherry or anyone else from Griffith's crib. I nodded toward the elevators. They followed. Jenny gave them a polite nod, but she sensed how pissed I was and wisely decided not to yin while I was yanging. Or whatever.

We rode in silence to my floor and entered the suite.

I pointed to an overstuffed couch facing two overstuffed chairs. They sat. Jenny took one of the chairs. I put a foot on the coffee table between us.

I pointed at Rafael. "What did the Maya think that stone was?"

"A weapon," he said.

I rolled my hand.

"Maya history is divided into three main periods: Preclassic, Classic, and Postclassic," Rafael said. "The earliest Mayans tamed the rain forest three thousand years before Christ. By 700 BCE, Mayans were building large cities like Nakbe. By 350 BCE, Tikal and El Mirador were thriving, erecting stelae and monuments covered in logosyllabic writing. Cities as big as Rome cropped up throughout Mesoamerica.

"By the time of Christ, Tikal's reign as the most powerful city was challenged by Calakmul, Palanque, and others. Wars and treaties followed. Then we enter the Classic period when the Maya flourished. As Rome descended into chaos, the Maya entered into elaborate trade pacts, built great roads, wrote detailed codices, and erected monumental pyramids. The codices detailed the extensive research of the Maya in mathematics, advanced astronomy, history, medicine, and religious practices. Their scientific examination of the heavens exceeded the Europeans by hundreds of years.

"With success came increased rivalries. In 378 CE, a man from Teotihuacan named Fire is Born walked into Tikal. That same day, Tikal's long-time king, Jaguar Paw, died. From then on, Tikal was allied with Teotihuacan. We can figure out what happened. From their glyphs we know of wars and threats and clashes that aligned various Mayan city-states over the centuries.

"Science and education also prospered. The Mayans developed the Long Count calendar whose accuracy remained unmatched by Europeans until Simon Newcomb correctly calculated obliquity in 1895."

"Hold up," I said. "Obliquity?"

"Axial tilt." Rafael looked at me like I'd forgotten my homework for a moment, then relaxed and softened to sympathy-for-the-dumb. "The Earth's axis is tilted from the orbital plane, giving us summer, winter, fall, and spring. The tilt, or obliquity, is not constant. It wobbles on a forty-thousand-year basis. The Mayans accounted for the wobble and could map star and planet positions tens of thousands of years into the future or as far into the past."

"Oh, yeah. Heard something about that."

He nodded kindly and continued. "They understood and used the concept of zero in their mathematics. Something Europeans didn't manage until the Arabs taught them algebra. If the Maya had harnessed the wheel for travel, we very well could've ended up in a Mayan-centric world today."

I contemplated that scenario for a moment. Human sacrifice atop the Statue of Liberty? Give me your huddled masses, we need to extract some beating hearts? He sensed the direction of my thinking.

"Ritual sacrifice was what rulers did in many ancient societies, like the Celtics and Sumerians. Mayan rulers would cut themselves, letting their blood flow into bowls to appease the gods in time of crisis, or to demonstrate their commitment to their community. It was an act of solidarity, like blood-brother rituals among modern boys. A statement that says, 'I'm willing to bleed for you.' The highest honor was to be sacrificed for the good of all. Not unlike Jesus." He gave me a retina-piercing stare. "Today, soldiers are willing to die defending their country. Back then Mayans were willing to die defending their communities from forces, physical or mystical."

I squirmed. "OK. What's all this got to do with my alabaster albatross?"

"By 750, the collapse was beginning. Something happened to specific cities that wiped them out. After booming for fifteen hundred years, in the space of two generations, millions of people, spanning a thousand miles stretching from Mexico City to Honduras, abandoned their authoritarian rulers and returned to village life. Palenque, Copán, Tikal, and Calakmul were abandoned while other cities such as Chichen Itza, Uxmal, and Coba thrived until the arrival of the Spanish. The cities that survived were ruled by councils rather than kings."

"And the weapon part?" I asked.

"There are obscure oral histories about the collapse that are quite different from the academic theories. The legends speak of a box containing the Enemy Stone or Poison Stone. In some stories, it is called the Freedom Stone. It was a secret weapon. One so secret, they never committed it to stelae or wrote about it in books. The city that possessed it would give it as a 'gift' to their enemy. Within days, the king would go mad or abdicate or simply disappear."

Jenny held up a hand as if she were in class, then realized it was unnecessary and asked her question. "Why only the cities with kings? How did the other cities survive?"

"Monarchy, dictatorship, authoritarian is fragile thing," Gu Peng said. "Single point failure. If king fall, city fall. Not work in democratic city, power share by council."

I expanded on her thought, "If you take out one council member, another continues the fight."

Rafael gave me an approving nod.

Jenny looked confused. "Then the winners should've been invincible. It shouldn't have brought down the entire civilization."

"When the US bombed Hiroshima," Rafael said, "the atomic bomb was a monumental secret. Only a few people knew what could cause so much devastation. When they bombed Nagasaki, everyone knew. They didn't know the specifics, but everyone knew the Americans had something powerful. The race to steal the plans began at that moment. And the same thing happened among the Maya. The danger of the Stone preceded the arrival of the box.

"We don't know who had it first or last, but if Tikal used it against a lesser city, then tried to use it against the king of Calakmul, instead of opening the box, presumably the king would keep it and throw back at Tikal's ambassadors. It would have a reverse effect. Or, if you had it, you could force any captured enemies to touch it."

"So the short version is," I said, "the box I've been dragging around led to the destruction of an entire civilization."

He shrugged. "If you believe the legends."

"Before the Mayans," I said, "the Romans had it. In the hundred years before sending this box to the edge of the world, they went through Emperors like tissue paper. Someone was doing the same thing there. It led to the downfall of Rome. Theodosius was the first successful emperor for decades. He reigned for fifteen years. But he consolidated power, dislodging four co-emperors. About that time, the cult of Mithras was all the rage in the military. Were they the same Knights?"

"We presume so," Rafael said.

"I'm guessing Theodosius used the Stone to help him. When he died, Stilicho got rid of it because he knew it could be used against him. So, what the hell is it?"

"For thousands of years," Rafael said, "people without the benefit of science had no idea why people who worked with mercury went mad. They only knew the result. Whatever is in that box was beyond their ability to describe. Between the five factions, we've come to believe—"

"Five factions?" I asked.

"Yes, the Brotherhood—" he nodded at Peng "—the Knights; my group, the Keepers; and two others, who we believe are dormant. As I was saying, the few scholars who've researched the Stones have formed some ideas. The primary concept is that they were large fragments of a meteorite. Just as we believe the building blocks of life came to Earth on a meteorite, many believe the Stones—"

"Wait a second," Jenny interrupted. "Did you say 'stones' plural?"

Rafael looked like he wanted to take back his words. He regrouped and said, "Yes, there are seven individual stones known to have existed at one time. But let us remain focused on the Freedom Stone for now. The experts who've studied the legends believe it may have a different type of magnetism from the simple North-South polarity of the Earth's iron core. There were references to extraordinary properties in an ancient Sumerian text, in some Roman scientific treatises, and the Mayan legends. Some have posited that the Stone may have a swirling form of polarity, one that changes the electrical signals of human synapses. Unfortunately, those references are mired in mysticism and prove difficult to relate in modern terms. The Keepers would relish the opportunity to study it should the current owner be so inclined."

"You mean me?" I asked. "I offered it to you once. You turned it down."

"You might be in possession of it," he said quietly. "But the Knights and the Brotherhood are challenging your ownership."

"Do you hear yourselves?" Jenny asked. "You're talking about who owns a magic rock. Really? This is all some mumbo jumbo from the days when they used to burn women as witches. Get serious."

"Very serious," Peng said. "Brotherhood use it, bring down repressive regime. Called Freedom Stone for good reason."

Rafael shrugged. "Sometimes myths are fairy tales, sometimes they hold a kernel of truth. The wise reserve judgement. To Peng's point, you saw what happened to Carlotta when she touched it. She transformed from an authoritarian to an altruist overnight. Cause or coincidence?"

I fell back in the open chair while I contemplated that. We sat in silence.

"Random," Jenny said after the silence grew uncomfortable. "Coincidence. A single event is not scientific evidence."

"What is of no consequence," Rafael said, "is the science of the Stone. What matters—"

"Is what people believe," I said. "You mentioned that."

"A doctor once told me," Jenny said, "the most powerful drug is a placebo. You tell someone what it does, and if they believe you, it works a shocking number of times."

Peng and Rafael stared at me, as if they were waiting for something. I pointed at Peng. "Your Brothers act like they're helping us. But they haven't been from the beginning. You're after the Freedom Stone. Why don't you just ask me to give it to you?"

"We not fool." She stared at me. "You hid Stone. You not talk of it."

"What makes you think he hid the stone?" Jenny asked.

I knew the answer, but I let Peng explain it.

"Strap on his shoulder not dig in so much when he leave forest as when he went. His pack much lighter now. Knights of Mithras know this too. They leave him El Remate, take Cherry instead."

"Why do you want it?" I asked.

Gu Peng turned to me with a piercing stare. "To free China."

CHAPTER 28

JENNY LEANED BACK WITH AN expression of enlightenment as if someone had told her the meaning of life. Her gaze connected with Peng. My fiancé finally found a cause to champion: liberating China.

I asked, "What do the Knights want it for?"

Someone knocked on the door. I looked at my guests as I reached for my pistol. Cautious to the end, I checked the peephole. It was Cherry. She wore blue jeans, a flowery print blouse under a light jacket—and a nervous expression. She patted beads of sweat off her brow.

I slipped the pistol back in the holster at the small of my back and opened the door. I pointed to the comfy chair.

Silently, with her shoulders drooped, she marched to her assigned seat.

I leaned against the wall next to the couch and faced her with my arms crossed. "Time to explain why you buddied up to Griffith."

She gave her uncle a contrite glance. He opened his hands, palms up, inviting her explanation.

Cherry looked at me. "You figured out Uncle Rafael was a rebel. In 1982, the dictatorship of Ríos Montt accused him of masterminding the murder of fifty-five civilians. It was a lie. Montt was convicted of crimes against humanity in 2013. But the false charges against my uncle remained filed in the International Criminal Court in the Hague for nearly forty years. They prevent him from visiting his sister in the USA. He's here today under a false passport."

Rafael sat still, emotionless, as if he were waiting in a doctor's office.

"What you do, child?" Peng asked. There was an edge in her voice that drew everyone's gaze.

"My father has business dealings with the US government. He can't associate with my uncle. They had to cut off all contact years ago. My mother's been beside herself for years. She wouldn't speak of him. I didn't even know what happened until I decided to study my mother's people, the Maya."

"What you do?" Peng asked with an even sharper edge.

I pushed off the wall. "Griffith arranged your conversation with the ICC to get the charges dropped?"

Near tears, Cherry could only nod.

"Why Guardian of Knight do this for you?" Peng rose, her face red.

Cherry said, "I told him where I saw Jacob hiding the stone."

Peng leapt at Rafael's niece. Jenny scrambled to her feet to intercept the old lady. She held Peng's wrists while the older woman's fingers clawed the air. Peng's face turned demonic.

"It's just a myth," Jenny said to Peng. "Just a stupid rock. Hidalgo said it was a fake."

Peng looked at Jenny as a fanatic would look at a heretic. "It freedom for my people."

I glanced at the professor. Unmoved through it all, he stared at his niece. I wondered what he was thinking because nothing showed on his face or in his posture.

Peng reached an accusing finger at Cherry. Jenny pulled it down and shook her head. She nodded toward the bedroom. Peng took a deep breath and silently agreed to go in the other room. Jenny closed the door behind them. They started talking, Jenny in calm tones, Peng in angry ones.

"It's a fake, right Uncle Rafael?" Cherry asked.

He shrugged. His expression remained unreadable. "The glyphs match the legends. If anything is true, it is the Freedom Stone."

He may as well have dropped an anvil in her lap. She sank her elbows to her knees and held her head in her hands.

We sat in silence, each contemplating Cherry's betrayal.

Jenny stepped out of the bedroom; Peng waited behind her in the doorway. "Griffith left in a hurry. Where did he go?"

"To Guatemala," Cherry answered. "I had a satellite phone with me when I saw Jacob that night. In case I got lost. He pulled the coordinates from it."

"I ranged a long way from where you and I met up," I said. "He'd have to cover twenty square miles."

Cherry let out a long and heavy sigh. "He's going to use LiDAR."

Mercury tapped me on the shoulder. *Dude, what the fuck is LiDAR?*

I said, *Could you watch your language? The god of eloquence should have ... forget it. LiDAR means light detection and ranging. Lasers measure the distance from an airplane to the ground and back. Because they can reflect hundreds of thousands of beams per second, they get a clear 3D picture of everything. They take the data back to the lab and use a thousand computers to sort out leaves from rocks from man-made structures. That's how they've found thousands of Mayan ruins.*

Mercury yanked me around to face him. *Say what? You mortals can see through trees now? Is nothing sacred? And these guys are going to find Seven-Death's crib because of you?*

I said, *Me? You told me to hide it there.*

Mercury said, *How was I supposed to know you idiot humans worked up some newfangled magic to find a temple what's been hid for a thousand years? Oh, brother this is bad. He's going to bust out an oozing pox on your face. You're going to look like maggot food, yo.*

Jenny's eyes were searching mine. She said, "Did you hear me?"

"Sorry, my mind is stuck on how Cherry morphed into Judas but no one seems to care."

"You have to take Peng there so she can retrieve the Freedom Stone and use it to save China."

Mercury dug his bony fingers into my shoulder and hissed, *Don't you dare, homeboy. You're going down the same path as Hercules. He thought he was so smart going out and killing the centaur Nessus with arrows dipped in the poisonous blood of the hydra. As he died, Nessus gave his tunic to Hercules's girlfriend and told her it worked as a love potion. Later, when Hercules was taking her for granted, she gave him the tunic. It was still covered in the hydra's poison-blood and it killed the man. Ya see what I'm saying?*

I said, *No.*

Mercury's nostrils flared, his eyes wide and slinging daggers. *Dude, what kills you is when you think you're the shit. When you think China's future is your call. When you run off to be the hero to impress your girlfriend. Homes, I'm telling you, leave the Knights of Mithras alone. Leave the Brotherhood of Claritas alone. Leave the Poison Stone where it is.*

I said, *LiDAR can lead the Knights to it. I can retrieve it before they get there. Seven-Death's temple will remain hidden. And I can give the Stone to the Brotherhood. Everybody wins.*

Mercury said, *What makes you think the Brotherhood is more deserving than the Knights? You know how many people died freeing China in the last ten thousand years? And where did it get them? No, homie. I'm telling you, anything you do with that Stone, you be doing for your own glory. And that's how Hercules died.*

I focused on Jenny's eyes. "I thought you didn't believe in the Stone."

"I believe in symbols. I salute the American flag. I love the Statue of Liberty. If this is a symbol that can free China, I don't care if it's a lump of coal or a magic meteorite. Think about it, Jacob. This is something we can do. This is a once-in-a-lifetime opportunity to do something great. We can earn our own reputations. Nothing to do with my dad. Nothing to do with my mom. Nothing to do with Pia Sabel. This is us overturning a dictatorship—and saving the day."

I didn't know what to say. So I didn't say anything. Her eyes searched mine.

After a moment, she said, "If we can free China, don't we have to? Didn't you say, 'He who can, must?'"

CHAPTER 29

Captain Amanow scratched at his wig. As much as he hated wearing a disguise while sitting in the Drake Hotel's lobby, he hated Jacob Stearne even more. Amanow had come so far in life. From the poverty-stricken shores of the Caspian to the halls of British education, he now stood on the brink of becoming one of the elite. He had no intention of ever returning to the filth and squalor of his youth. The Protector had helped him, guided him, and urged him on. He would not let the Protector down. His mission would not be compromised by the likes of Jacob Stearne.

His stellar military career in Turkmenistan had been ridiculed by Joe Griffith's guards after waking him from Stearne's poison. The guards had disrespected his Knights. They'd laughed at him. They'd deserved his wrath. They'd brought it on themselves. Amanow only wished he could see the arrogant Guardian's face when he returned to find his remaining guards lined up in cardboard boxes awaiting cremation.

The call came in. Amanow glanced around the lobby before he pressed his earbud to answer.

Joe Griffith wasted no time on pleasantries. "I gave you orders not to kill anyone in my house."

"This is so," he replied.

"Yet the security camera outside the Orange Room shows you firing a weapon at Jacob Stearne."

"This is true."

"And still he got the better of you!" Griffith's voice thundered through the phone. "You cannot kill him in America. He is a hero. They'll soon forget about him, but right now, he's still a hero. Killing him, even wounding him, will bring down an investigation that can unravel decades of work. You cannot jeopardize our mission when we are so close to success."

Amanow kept his reply in check. The late morning traffic circulating through the hotel lobby was thick. He said, "You ordered me to spare him in Guatemala. That has proven ineffective. Had you listened—"

"Don't take that tone with me," Griffith barked. "He would never talk. At least now we have two options to pursue instead of another failure by you and your murderous Knights. You must take responsibility for this series of failures. You must own letting Stearne slip through your fingers a second time. You had superior numbers and still you failed."

Griffith continued to berate him, but Amanow's attention turned to a striking couple marching through the Drake's revolving door. A man as big as a bear with the dark-auburn skin of a Native American walked beside a tall, strong woman who had the silky confidence of a tiger. They passed the registration desk without a glance. The big man wore jeans and a denim shirt under a long leather jacket. Beneath the leather rode a holstered Glock 18C, just like Jacob Stearne's. The woman wore a decadent, stretchy athletic outfit popular with American women in the gym. An open duster covered her without concealing the pistol strapped to her thigh.

The big man's gaze absorbed everything in the lobby from the speck of lint beneath a potted fern to the dot of dust just settling on the magnificent chandeliers overhead. The woman's eyes snapped like lasers from one person to the next, as if reading barcodes on their noses. When she turned her electric stare to him, Amanow shivered. They never broke their pace. They marched to the elevators and parked themselves there for a second while waiting for one to open. Amanow realized a short, wiry man of Indian descent had slipped past him and now waited with the taller two. The woman's gaze wheeled back to Amanow.

He looked down at his phone. While Griffith's diatribe continued in his ear, he searched for images of Pia Sabel.

"For these reasons," Griffith said, "I intend to ask the Protector to replace your contingent of Knights."

The elevator dinged; the three got on. When they turned in the small space, the woman's piercing gray-green eyes bore through Amanow as the doors closed.

"We will come back to the Protector in a moment," Amanow said. "Just now, I have identified Pia Sabel and two of her top lieutenants entering the hotel. No doubt they are to meet with Jacob Stearne."

"That's a serious problem."

"Perhaps," Amanow said. "Perhaps not. Does she have a position on the Poison Stone? Is she aligned with the Brotherhood or the Keepers?"

"She's never been on any list," Griffith said with a concerned grumble in his voice. "Certainly not on ours."

"Respectfully, I submit it is time for the Guardian to do his job. If this American woman has no allegiance, it is your charge to propose one. Rather than cast about for scapegoats and lay blame for your passive and ineffective methods, you must contact her and entreat her. If nothing else, stop her from aiding the Brotherhood."

Griffith stammered before finding his tongue. "Now you listen here, you—"

"No, it is you who will listen. The Protector heard my report twenty minutes ago. I explained to him how your intelligence failed to prepare us for such simple matters as Stearne's sleeping darts. Your briefing on your property failed to reveal extensive passages for servants. He was gravely concerned that your detachment from the working class cost us an opportunity of great value. He will remind you that the role of the Guardian is not to order the Knights about as waiters in a café, but to guard our ability to operate. And, might I remind you, the Knights operate at the Protector's direction."

"You spoke to him?"

"And he is not happy with either of us, Mr. Griffith. He reminded me the mission culminates soon. In a matter of days, the leaders of the free world are to gather on a mountain in Germany. There will be no second chance should we fail. He believes your reliance on LiDAR will take too long. He approved my plan. I assure you; it is both aggressive and effective. He gave us one last chance to work together. He insists we return with the Poison Stone or face our fates—together."

Griffith was silent for a long time. Amanow let him breathe and think.

Humility is an attribute that takes time for the arrogant to internalize. He was willing to let Griffith take all the time he needed, provided he could count it in seconds not minutes. He heard Griffith take the penitent breath that presaged submission.

Griffith said, "Does your plan involve killing Jacob Stearne or any other American?"

"Those who oppose the rule of the Knights control their fates. We will neutralize resistance by any means we deem effective."

CHAPTER 30

JENNY AND PENG TALKED ALL the way through my nap. I'd been awake for most of the previous seventy-two hours. In my view, I deserved a little peace and quiet. Not in theirs. They held an excited war council with Rafael, Danny, Fiona, Mark, and the guy whose name I still didn't know, in the suite's living room. While the walls were thick and the bed was soft, they kept getting excited and raising me from my near-coma to that almost-cognizant stage just before awakening. Their voices would rise to a crescendo about some place in Germany, then sink after I'd groan.

Eventually, I gave up on trying to sleep. I showered and slurped a pot of coffee and ate a bagel before joining the others.

"Catch me up," I said. "I recover the Whatever-it's-called Stone and give it to you. Some period of time later, freedom rings in China. What happens in between?"

Jenny perked up. "We take it to Garmisch, Germany for the G20 Summit and give it to the Chinese president."

"And we walk past an army of German guards, then walk through an army of Chinese guards, then sneak past the president's staff, and say, 'wanna pet my rock?'"

Everyone looked in different directions at once. Guess they hadn't visualized the endgame. They planned themselves right up to the city gates and stopped there. As we learned in Iraq, the siege is the easy part. What comes after is the problem.

I tossed up my hands. "Even if you do get someone to touch it—and the magic works—Zhongnanhai is full of people who'll take over instantly if something happens to the president."

"We have Brother standby in Zhongnanhai," Peng said.

That shocked me. China's equivalent of the White House, Congress, and the Supreme Court work from one convenient location: Zhongnanhai. To have an operative there—one high up enough to have a shot at taking over—was the goal of every major country in the world. I'd judged the Brotherhood by their young and inexperienced warriors. Now I realized they were far more formidable than Peng had led me to believe. Hers was a strategy clever enough to make Sun Tzu proud.

I looked up the G20 location. The meetings would be held at a shiny steel-and-glass science center perched high above the tree line on the largest, sharpest hunk of limestone I'd ever seen. The tallest point in Germany, the website said.

Mercury leaned over my shoulder. *That rock formed in the Mesozoic era, homie. The most boring epoch in the creation of the universe. Nothing but brainless reptiles everywhere ya went. But no big deal for me. I was in god college back then. Part-TAY every night, y'know what I'm saying?*

I said, *When you say things like that, I start to think people are right to call me crazy.*

Mercury said, *Whoa, dude. No one calls you crazy to your face. Chill. Just imagined you'd be interested in my life for once. What was I thinking? Y'know, when people pray, they never ask how's it going for the god they're praying to. It's always about them. Can you do this? Can you help with that? No one asks, Hey, how you doing, Mr. M?*

"There are some gaps in the plan," Jenny said. "We thought you might have some ideas."

"I do have ideas." I checked Danny. "I'm a former Ranger who graduated Ranger school with honors. Our motto is *Sua Sponte,* of their own accord. But you're not, so that means the only way this is going to work is for everyone to follow orders. If I tell people to sit down and shut up, they sit down and shut up. Anything I'm involved in has to run with military precision."

"Yes, sir." Danny spread his hands wide and bowed a little. "I've learned."

"Next, I need to know … wait a second, where is Cherry?" I turned to the charming professor.

"She was in need of rest," he said and nodded toward the spare bedroom.

"Ms. Sabel's generosity extends to traitors now?" I asked the room.

"I offered it to her," Jenny said quickly.

"Any anger you feel toward my innocent niece should be directed to me," Rafael said. "It is I she fought for. Against my wishes, and without my knowledge or agreement, yet with the best of intentions."

"About that." I gave him my soldier stare. He didn't flinch. "Why are you here?"

"Ms. Gu's plight is most interesting." He nodded to the old lady. "If I can be of assistance, I offer aid without reservation. If not, I am content to observe history in the making."

"And your disloyal-on-your-behalf niece?"

"Undoubtedly, she will speak for herself, but I imagine she feels as I do. If either of us could be of any use, your wish is our command."

Given the look on Jenny's face, sending them packing wasn't an option. This was one of those times we were going to yin and not yang. Or whatever. I considered options. On every mission I'd been on, there had always been a shortage of cannon fodder. If an opportunity came up where I could repay Cherry's treachery in kind, I'd happily toss her in.

"All right," I said. "We need to get back to the Yucatán."

Again, everyone's gaze wandered off as if I'd made a pope-joke to the Pope.

Peng glanced at Jenny, then spoke. "I hope you give Freedom Stone when we arrive Chicago."

"Why did you think that?" I asked.

"She thought you'd given it to the Knights," Rafael said. "And that you'd get it back when you saved Cherry."

What she really thought was that Danny would get it back. That's why they were looking for Griffith. Peng thought I'd sold them out. Danny's crazy dash made sense in that light. But something was off about his behavior on the property. Something ticked in the back of my head. There was some kind of deception going on, but I couldn't see it. Maybe I suspected everyone after Cherry's behavior. Stearne's Law:

Paranoia is the result of acute situational awareness. Everyone really is trying to kill you.

Peng waited until I looked her way, then she said, "Take all my saving get here."

That statement caught me up. That was the last clue I needed to figure out the problem. Everybody's down for the revolution until somebody has to pick up the check.

Jenny had her eye on me. She wouldn't ask her dad for money unless I agreed. Which was a good thing in a marriage. Solidarity. Unity. All that. But her dad would never fund this operation in a million years given that he hated revolutionaries of any stripe. He was the kind of guy people rebelled against. And that meant we would have to lie to him. Not happening. I couldn't start my marriage by lying to my father-in-law. Even if it was for a good cause.

That's when the door opened. Someone with a key clacked it open, causing me to jump into defensive mode. I leapt to my feet, 9 mil drawn, before the others realized what was going on.

Without the slightest concern, Dhanpal, a former Navy SEAL and one of Ms. Sabel's inner circle of trusted personal bodyguards, walked in and nodded at my pistol as if it were a banana. Behind him, the unmistakable silhouette of Pia Sabel followed, her duster flowing from her shoulders like a cape. Our eyes met. We both flinched like ex-lovers seeing each other again for the first time after a nasty split. She stopped, still in the foyer.

Miguel Rodriguez brought up the rear and closed the door. He saw our awkward encounter and waited patiently.

Whatever prepared statement Ms. Sabel had in her head refused to come out her mouth.

I wasn't in any better shape. The last time I spoke to her, I was stepping onto her $20 million luxury chopper for a free ride to the Yucatán and telling her I would never work for her again. She'd taken it like a gut punch. I felt like a heel.

Mercury tapped my shoulder. *Now's your chance to patch things up with Pia-Caesar-Sabel, homie.*

I said, *Nothing to patch. It's over. I'm never going back.*

Mercury said, *OK, let's pretend you didn't have a Russian oligarch hit you up for twenty-eight million bucks three days ago. Let's pretend you can continue breathing for six more days without sending him a check. Let's pretend you're not about to do something earth-shatteringly stupid, like get yourself killed while freeing flipping CHINA. And then let's think about how you could use this situation to get even with Pia-Caesar-Sabel.*

Even though I knew Mercury had an ulterior motive for his suggestion, the idea of turning the tables had a certain appeal. Maybe I could use her to achieve my goals. That would be a twist.

I smiled at her and spread my arms wide. "Welcome to the People's Liberation Army, Version 2.0."

A skeptical expression crossed her face.

Dhanpal and Miguel leaned against the wall, arms folded, with faces that said, *Can't wait to hear this bullshit.*

Before I could think up a good one, Peng crossed to her. In a sharp voice, the old woman asked, "What you do here?"

"Pia Sabel," Ms. Sabel said and extended a hand to Peng.

"We not need tycoon." Peng turned her back on Ms. Sabel's hand. "Too many in world today. All are same person, look out for each other. Not trusting. Not reliable. Exploiting everything. Not helping common people. No thank you."

Gu Peng grew three feet taller in my eyes. No one ever stood up to Ms. Sabel like that. The old lady just saved me from having to turn down whatever help was about to be offered, and with it, any conditions that might go along.

"I'm not here to join your operation," Ms. Sabel said. "I was on my way to spend a few days at Chan Chich, a little resort in Belize. I was in town and wanted to catch up with Jenny while we had a chance."

Everyone in the room looked up Chan Chich on their phones at the same time. Chan Chich is an eco-tourist resort of the first order. Deep in the jungle of Belize, it sits near the borders of Guatemala and Mexico. Coincidentally, it's not far from where I left my alabaster albatross.

Mr. Baldy was smart. He would leave a few people on the trail from the Mexico side, near the trail from Hidalgo's dig. He'd leave a few on the Guatemalan side, near Uaxactun. They would follow me to my destination, then take the Stone. Ms. Sabel had found a place equally close to either route but unknown to Mr. Baldy.

As usual, Pia Sabel was ten moves ahead of me. No matter what else I thought about her, she is a brilliant strategist. Her choice of destination sealed a proposal no one had made yet.

After checking it out, everyone in the room caught up with me. They understood why Ms. Sabel was heading there. Including the leader of the Brotherhood.

Peng said, "Your light shine strong and clean. You mean well. But money always find power—power always find money."

"You don't know her," Jenny pleaded with Peng. "You can trust—"

"I understand," Ms. Sabel interrupted. "My company has many ventures in China. You have a right to be concerned about my allegiance. I'm not offering to get involved."

"What you do here?" Peng re-asked her original question.

"I came to offer Jenny a spa day with me at Chan Chich." She left a dramatic pause. "Of course, everyone's invited. There's plenty of room on my jet. And for privacy, I booked the whole resort for a week."

CHAPTER 31

BY LATE AFTERNOON THE NEXT day, I was jogging through the jungle on the western side of Belize with a stone altar in my backpack. My heading was due west, toward Guatemala and a long-forgotten temple hidden in its trees. I checked my pace to keep a steady five miles per hour. Thirty miles out and thirty miles back gave me twelve hours of jogging. A little run that could qualify as an ultramarathon.

What would ensure my survival was the training I'd received in Ranger School. They taught me an important factor: you can go farther and endure more—if you want to. It's mostly in your head. Mother Nature has your brain wired to conserve energy as soon as you burn off forty percent. You want to stop and rest when you still have sixty percent left in your tank. Humans are capable of considerable feats of strength and endurance. I knew I could make this run. And I knew Danny would give up if he tried to follow me.

One adversary I couldn't anticipate was Mr. Baldy. From the beginning, he appeared to have a religious fanaticism that might equal Ranger Training. I'd gotten the better of the Knights on a couple occasions, but that wasn't because they were dumb or incompetent. None of my wins were due to superior tactics. I had survived by pure luck.

The Knights had not expected young, dumb Danny to have planted a tracker on them. No one would have guessed Griffith forgot he had obscure passages throughout his house. The Knights had anticipated our moves at El Remate. If their pontoon boat had one extra horsepower, we could've died there. The only thing I had going for me on this trip was the unexpected starting point at Chan Chich.

Which was not a bad resort as exclusive eco-resorts go.

Ms. Sabel's end-run around me went without a whimper of protest. Peng's concerns about money, power, and plutocracy faded once she stepped into a bubbling spa. Danny and his squad downed the free-on-arrival daiquiris like hummingbirds at a feeder. I should be grateful. It was generous of Ms. Sabel to bail out the Free China Movement when we'd run out of cash. Unfunded revolutions are sad affairs.

She was nice enough not to make me thank her. Jenny did that. To spare me further humiliation, she thanked Ms. Sabel all the way south on Sabel One. Jenny smoothed all my rough edges. For a second, I wondered if that was order or chaos, yin or yang. Or whatever. She was right, she balanced me.

As the clouds assembled and darkened the afternoon sky, I was running my shoes off. Everyone else scheduled hot stone massages and ate locally sourced salads and went on birdwatching tours. There were probably yoga sessions.

The sky grew darker every mile. Thunder rolled in the distance and the wind picked up. It didn't get to be a rain forest by accident.

Jogging cross-country through the jungle is not that hard. Since little sunlight penetrates the canopy, there isn't a great deal of ground cover. There are game trails through the thickest spots. Most of the time, it's a matter of hopping fallen branches and saplings and stepping lightly in case your foot slides in mud or decaying leaves.

Mercury swung through the branches like Tarzan. Only Tarzan used vines while Mercury defied physics with the tiny wings on his helmet.

Mercury floated down to ground level. *S'gonna rain, bro. That'll slow up your arrival time. And that means the Knights of Mithras could catch up with you. Then whatcha gonna do?*

I said, *As long as I get there and get back before they can process their LiDAR readings, they'll never catch me.*

Mercury said, *What if they use old-fashioned methods? Like, they post scouts at all compass points.*

That was what I expected Mr. Baldy to do. Fix a few people to the obvious trails and have his main force deployed in a circle around Cherry's last known coordinates. I'd mapped out a route that kept me a mile north of that point. Then I would use the standard double-back trick.

Go beyond your destination, turn around, and come back. If someone's following you, you meet them head-on.

I asked, *How can I avoid the Knights?*

Mercury said, *You can figure that out for your own self, boy. The night you hid it, you were only gone twenty minutes. Cherry found you a mile from the campsite, so they know you were within a mile of that spot. You draw a circle with a one-mile radius, and you have 3.14 square miles to search. That means the circumference is a circle 6.28 miles around. If Mr. Baldy puts four men on the northern trail and four on the southern trail, he still has twenty-four left to scout that circle. Those men would be 1,380 feet apart, roughly a quarter mile. Not within visual range, so you're good to sneak between them—provided you see them first.*

He was right, I could've worked that out for myself. I went to high school. I know $C = \pi d$. But it was nice of him to do the math for me. Sometimes he's OK to have around.

I kept up my pace, jumping an iguana the size of a dachshund. I was surprised. So was the lizard.

As the afternoon turned to evening, what little sunshine I had disappeared. I put on my Sabel Visor. Lightning strikes grew closer and more frequent. The wind whipped the treetops high overhead. The canopy protected me for the time being.

Stopping to check my position against the map, I listened to the forest around me. My tours of duty involved mountains and valleys where you could find a vantage point and see great distances. Dust plumes and heat signatures gave away enemy positions far in advance. The jungle was a different experience. Even with my visor, visibility wasn't far. Thirty yards at best due to tree density. My skin crawled. Something felt off. As if the Knights were watching me already.

Stearne's Law.

I resumed my run.

Mercury said, *So tell me homeboy, why you helping the Brotherhood of Claritas instead of the paying gig for Yeschenko?*

I said, *Because Peng wants to liberate China. Did you see how people reacted to meeting the Hero of Paris? Imagine how many will hire*

Stearne Security when I'm on every news site in the world as the Liberator of China.

Mercury said, *You're going it alone? Then it's gonna be more like, the man who died pointlessly trying to assassinate China's General Secretary. You get in there, hand him the Poison Stone, his people shoot you dead. No medals. No pictures on websites. No more brain function. Just me—guiding you to the underworld.*

I said, *We'll see.*

Mercury said, *Why not help the Knights instead? At least they have enough money to get where they're going. And they're in favor of law and order.*

I said, *Mr. Baldy murdered fifteen innocent people.*

Mercury said, *That's nothing. Vulcan wiped out over eleven hundred Pompeiians when he lit Vesuvius. And he's got nothing on Neptune, who wiped out millions in the Yangtze floods of—*

I said, *The Knights are evil. At least the Brotherhood has good intentions. So, I'm helping them. To do that, I need to get that box and get out of here before the Knights find it and destroy our freedoms.*

Thunder barreled overhead. I kept my pace as a gentle rain started falling. Rain created a problem for thermal imaging. A large FLIR system, the kind found on boats and trucks, weighs forty pounds, and can see through rain. But the lightweight cameras mounted on the Sabel Visor are fair-weather friends. A similar situation occurs with infrared systems. Sabel Visors have a third system of amplified light. I could see well enough until lightning struck nearby, then everything was blown out for a second until the system recovered.

A tribe of spider monkeys swung through my path. I listened to their effortless movements to test my hearing in the rain. The sound of fat raindrops hitting large leaves drowned out a lot of other sounds. I stepped on a branch just to gauge the decibels. Noise was severely dampened. My skin itched again. I kept running.

Mercury kept talking. He filled my head with odd bits of Roman history. Most of which was salacious gossip about other gods. While I had no interest in it, there was little else to do for the last ten miles.

I slowed as I came within three miles of my destination. My double-back trick didn't turn up anyone following me.

After a short search, I found a clearing and launched my drone above the treetops. The rain was steady and threw off the cameras. I maintained a grid pattern and found a small herd of deer. Little else showed up despite the Yucatán having plenty of night creatures. When I'd completed the grid, I plotted a path to reach Seven-Death's temple. I flew the drone over it several times.

Just when I was confident I was alone, I found something. A heat signature as big as a small deer in the area but obscured by a ton of trees. It might be a man or a larger animal. I couldn't bring my drone in too close because the noise would give it away. I plotted a course around the thing and recovered my drone.

It landed in the clearing. I trotted out to get it. I could hear the motors running after I shut them down. I double-checked. The motors were off. I looked up. A drone floated overhead. Not mine.

Damn.

I grabbed my drone and ran back for the cover of the trees. The Knights had similar hardware advantages. I could only hope they had the same problem with rain. Finding a thicket of palms, I drove myself in and pushed through the length of it until I couldn't hear the drone anymore. I waited and listened.

Mercury had raised a good question: What did they have planned?

Which was a great question to ask of an omnipotent deity. I looked around. No Mercury. A fair-weather god if there ever was one.

It was now or never. Now that they found me this close, they could stumble on it as easily as follow me to it. A careful search by a full platoon would turn up a toothpick. Could I run in, run out, and stay ahead of them? Waiting would only bring their drone around again. The longer I waited, the worse my chances became.

Which left me one option.

CHAPTER 32

PIA SABEL CLICKED OFF HER call and stretched out on the massage table, her earbud still in her ear. The masseuse adjusted the towel covering her butt and spread oil on her bare back. She contemplated deleting all the waiting emails and voicemails. It seemed like work never left her, even in remote Belize.

She turned her head to the side as Danny's blonde friend climbed on the table next to her. She couldn't remember the young woman's name.

A call came in. Pia sent it to voicemail.

"Wow, you're buff," the blonde said. "I mean, I mean, big, uhm … tall. And muscular. Or, uh, strong. In a good way. Like Dafne Schippers. Or, I mean, Dafne Schippers is like—"

"Stop."

"OK." The girl blushed full red but exhaled, relieved to be pulled out of her downward spiral into awkwardness. The masseuse centered the towel over the blonde's butt, then rubbed oil on her back.

"I apologize," Pia said softly. "We were introduced, but I forgot your name."

"Fiona. It's OK. You met us all at once and you were focused on Jacob."

"Nice to meet you, Fiona." Pia glanced at the emails on her phone while she spoke. "I find your dedication to Ms. Gu's cause admirable."

"Isn't Jacob engaged? Not that I'm insinuating anything about you being here and offering all the—"

"Yes, they're engaged and no, I didn't show up to break them up. I'm not romantically interested in Jacob. Or Jenny."

Pia watched Fiona's mouth open and close as words formed in her head but mercifully stopped before she voiced them. In Pia's experience, people who were mired in awkward overtures wanted something from her but were afraid to ask.

Another call came in. Pia sent it to voicemail. Just more people wanting to sell her a company or two. She thought of her father and how he told her, *You can't give people help. It makes them feel diminished, inferior. If they aren't bold enough to ask for your help, they'll blame you for every failure. Give them space, let them explain what they need, then they'll be invested in the outcome and work ten times harder to prove themselves.*

Pia said, "Jacob is a good friend and recently I treated him badly. This trip is just to prove I'm there for him if he needs me."

"You were never romantically—"

"No." Pia regretted her sharp tone. "We're like siblings. He's the brother I never had. Why?"

"Danny and I were like that. But then, something sparked and we … well, we work well together. He means everything to me now."

"I'll stay clear."

"Oh, that's not what I meant at all."

Pia smiled. Another call buzzed her phone. Fiona watched Pia's hand. Pia sent the call to voicemail.

"Your phone never stops ringing," Fiona said. "Are people always after you for something?"

"The curse and blessing of wealth is that everyone wants you to help them. Business deals, charities, personal problems. The blessing is that you're offered tremendous opportunities to do great things. The curse is that some turn out to be complete frauds. The difficulty lies in deciding which is which."

Fiona nodded. "How can you tell?"

"I listen to every proposal, make my best guess, and, if I like it, dive in. If it turns out badly, I'll quit as soon as it becomes apparent and move on to the next opportunity. In time, the good deals outnumber the bad. The sad part is when people talk a lot but never get around to asking for what they need."

Fiona nodded. She closed her eyes to savor the fingers working on her back.

"What do you need, Fiona?" Pia asked.

Fiona's eyes blew open. "Oh, I don't want any—"

"The spa had openings all day today, yet you chose this odd after-dinner time slot. Did Peng send you or did you choose it on your own?" Pia waited, but Fiona couldn't find an answer. "The Brotherhood ran out of money in Chicago. You left a dozen of your Brothers in Guatemala for lack of funds. You're planning the overthrow of a powerful leader, but you're in Belize as a guest of a woman you've only read about. You need help. This is your chance, Fiona. Tell me what you need."

Fiona choked. "I … I just wanted to ask if you knew what the Knights want. You know our plan. Do you know theirs?"

"If they were interested in my help, they would reach out to me. They haven't."

Fiona blinked several times, uncertainty covering her expression.

Miguel stepped into the massage room. He held up his phone. "Sorry to interrupt, Pia. There's a guy who's been trying to reach you all day. I vetted him. I think he has something that might interest you. If this is a good time, I'll forward his call."

Pia looked at Fiona and waited for her to say something.

The young woman's face clouded. Fiona pulled her towel tight around her and got up. She said, "I'll give you some privacy."

Fiona fled as if a tiger were chasing her.

"For the lack of a skilled messenger, the revolution was lost." Pia looked at Miguel. "Am I that intimidating?"

"Yes."

"I tried to give her the floor."

"You've been losing your patience lately. She wasn't ready. Some people need more time."

He was right. She felt that. She wanted to help everyone who needed it. But the pressure of people lining up to talk to her felt like a giant vise squeezing the life out of her.

Pia's phone buzzed. She sent it to voicemail. "Time is a luxury I don't have."

Miguel shrugged.

"OK," Pia said. "Forward the call, then ask Dhanpal to bring Peng in. I'd like to talk to her."

"Peng and Rafael have been swapping revolutionary stories all day," Miguel said.

"Are you implying a romantic entanglement?"

"At their age, more like nostalgic yarns of shared suffering."

"Don't underestimate their age," Pia said.

Miguel smiled and transferred the call as he walked out.

Pia waited for it to buzz in her hand, then answered. "This is Pia Sabel."

"Pia, Joe Griffith here. I don't know if you remember me—"

"Of course I remember you." Pia nestled into the face cradle as the masseuse worked her neck and scalp. "You brought my father several opportunities. We bought a non-lethal dart maker from you. Still one of our better investments. You sent nice flowers to his funeral. Why haven't I heard from you since?"

She knew damn well why he, like so many others, hadn't called in well over two years. No one in the business world had expected her to survive. How could a young woman, a soccer star, ever be as successful as her barrel-chested, hard-charging, deal-making, testosterone-fueled dad? A day after his death, there had been odds in Las Vegas as to when Sabel Industries would be dissolved. Not if, but when.

Pia listened while Griffith made a few preparing-to-speak breathing noises. She felt a certain satisfaction in letting him sweat.

"I, uh," he said, "haven't had anything … your dad, God rest his soul, only wanted the best deals, I presumed you were the same. So I waited for the right opportunity."

"I'm listening."

"Right now, there is a tremendous opportunity for someone like you." His voice picked up steam and confidence. "Assuming, of course, you care about the perilous future of civilization."

"Spare me the dramatics, Joe." Pia could almost read his mind. She knew he was thinking: *What a bitch.* She smiled.

"All over the world," he continued, "law and order is under attack. Terrorists threaten our way of life, our business operations. Watch the news in any country and you see attacks on the channels of global commerce. But very soon, things will come to a head. Many of us have been working behind the scenes to ensure a stable and consistent future. And we need your help."

"I'm flattered," Pia said. "Who is 'we' and what help do you need?"

"I'm glad you're interested. The details are something we should discuss in person. Are you free in the morning?"

"First, tell me about your threat." She paused a beat before going on. "I sense you're preparing to deny you intend to threaten me. Before you make that mistake, let me remind you of your last deal. When my father tried to negotiate the price for Sabel Darts, you threatened to expose a regrettable foreign transaction. Money laundering, some might have called it. I can hear you prepping that denial again. Let me assure you, Alan Sabel kept me in the loop in all his dealings. That's how I stepped into his shoes without missing a beat. My father said a thousand times, 'Make no enemies.' For that reason, I don't hold your previous dealings against you—heinous as they may have been. It simply informs me of how you do business. So, let's save some time and get to the heart of the matter. Tell me about your threat."

She heard him inhale, as she'd heard so many privileged alpha males do when cornered. She gave him time to process his situation.

"What makes you think it's not the same threat as last time?"

"Dad kept the audio recording of your calls and meetings. Since you didn't report him, that makes you an accessory to any crime that may have been committed. Since it happened on his watch, and I've amended all subsequent reporting, I'm clean. But these are all things you know."

"Yesss. You are your father's daughter." He took a deep breath. "I know where Jacob Stearne is—twenty miles north of Uaxactun."

Pia bit the inside of her cheek to stop herself from screaming her angst. It was an odious threat. Jacob was in mortal danger. She couldn't acknowledge that without losing leverage. "He left my employ last week."

"But not your heart."

This time she couldn't help herself. She took a deep breath. "Where would you like to meet?"

"I'm in Washington now. As I said earlier, how about tomorrow morning?"

"I'm not in DC. How about London the day after? White's in St. James?"

"The club the royals belong to? You can't get in, it's men only. Plus, they haven't taken new members in decades."

"They took one recently. And she wasn't a man. Shall we say six tomorrow evening?"

"Uh. Yes. Done."

They clicked off. Pia sensed someone standing opposite her masseuse. Leaning up on one elbow, she discovered Gu Peng.

"Your messenger is too young and inexperienced," Pia said. "You should've come yourself."

"Brotherhood not top-down like Sabel. Each Brother take her own initiative. Each person independent in thought, word, and deed."

Pia sat up, wrapping the towel around her, dismissing the masseuse with a nod. "Then help her. What does Fiona want from me?"

"Young people impressed by big money. Maybe she want you fund Brotherhood."

"And you? What do you want?"

"You have lot of light. Very strong." Peng cupped Pia's cheek in her palm. "Many color. Hard to read. All rich people come from same village, have same interest. Everything neat and orderly. Always under control. You never give up everything for love. People like Jenny and Jacob, they do anything for love."

Pia considered arguing. She didn't have the luxury of risking everything for love. One wrong move, the wrong post on social media, a bad choice of lovers, a confidence shared with the wrong person, could topple her company, leaving thousands unemployed. A burden she'd learned was lost on most people. Pia said, "OK, but what—"

"Nothing I want can be asked." Peng waved her off and turned for the exit where she met Dhanpal stepping in. They danced left and right. She stopped and turned back to Pia. "I hear you talk. You go London. You see with your eye, hear with your ear, what Knight of Mithras want. Then, you tell Gu Peng what you do."

"That's not how I work. I listen to what people need, evaluate how I can help, and do what I can."

"That is you?" Peng scoffed. "When my husband lay crushed beneath tank. When police take my daughter from my arms. Many people hold me, ask 'what can I do?' I cannot speak. My mind lost in pain. One man, I never know his name, he take me by shoulder, put me in car, drive me to river, lead me to boat, sail me to Vancouver. I alive today because he not ask. He not 'evaluate' how he can help." Peng clenched her fists. "He act."

The old woman pushed Dhanpal aside and disappeared.

The former SEAL raised a brow.

"Yes, yes. I'll act." Pia nodded as much to herself as Dhanpal. "But first, something's come up." She strode to the changing room, talking over her shoulder. "Get Danny and Fiona, all the Brothers. Jacob's in a lot more trouble than he realized."

CHAPTER 33

I RAN AT AN ANGLE to my destination, then turned and doubled back. No one followed me. And I'd given their drone the slip. Feeling a little more confident, I found the giant mound of Seven-Death's temple. I jogged the steep side to the tree-covered top.

The large stone stood unmolested, still gripped by tree roots. I pulled on the tree and the stone tilted up, just as it had before. A hole darker than the night beckoned me inside. I looked around and listened. Nothing.

Mercury materialized next to me, scaring the living wits out of me. *Yo, homie, you can't close that thing behind you.*

When my heart rate returned to normal, I said, *Don't sneak up on a guy like that. Why can't I close it?*

Mercury said, *Cause you can't open it from the inside.*

Great.

Rain collected on the broad, flat temple mound and flooded into the secret opening. It spilled down the steep and narrow steps. I recalled how slick the stones were when they were dry. And I remembered the pit of liquid mercury at the bottom. One wrong move and I was face down in a pool of poison. Why was I doing this? Because my bride-to-be needed a cause to champion: Freeing China. A noble endeavor if there was one.

I started down, touching the walls on both sides to steady myself. The treads were too narrow, the risers too deep. A stream of rainwater swirled around my ankles like a mountain stream. Four steps down, my right foot slid out from under me. My butt hit a riser while my hands grabbed at the walls. A move like that lower down, where there were no walls, could be instant death.

Mercury said, *Don't forget the pile of bones you saw at the bottom, brutha. But don't be worrying about that shit. Seven-Death is waiting for you. C'mon now.*

I said, *Is there an easier way in?*

Mercury said, *If there was, the Knights could use it to ambush you down there.*

A good point that served as a confidence builder. As more rain cascaded down the stones, I resumed my downward march. Carefully planting each foot before I put weight on it, I took one tread at a time. The stairway turned at each corner of the pyramid temple. A wild river of rain threatened my footing on every step.

The supporting walls disappeared when I entered the main chamber. The cavern was the size of a cathedral with the stairs being suspended in the middle, no handrails, no side support. Nothing to hang on to. And a hundred-foot drop on both sides. Either you stayed on the straight and narrow by faith, or you fell off and died.

That's when I heard men above me. The Knights had found the entrance.

Moving faster, I slid again. Both feet went out this time and my butt followed. Just before I fell to my death, I twisted my torso at the waist and grabbed hold of the stone steps with both hands. Scrambling to swing my feet back on the stairs, I nearly slid off the other side. Water splashed in my face. Voices echoed in the upper halls. A light flashed one turn above me in the previous hall.

Regaining my balance, I righted myself and waded down more stairs. I slipped again, this time in unison with one of the Knights far above me. I was getting used to the heart-stopping fear and clambered back into position quicker. I steadied my balance and focused. Like they taught me in Ranger School, you can always persevere if you want to. I moved carefully down the remaining steps and turned onto the landing as a strong light flickered into the chamber from above. They were anxious about the steps, keeping the light focused on where they were stepping. It helped them miss me.

But they caught sight of the lake of silver. They stared in awe as the lead man tried to determine what lay below. Being accompanied by gods the first time I'd seen it, I'd taken its other worldliness for granted. Seeing the Knight's beam fixed on it now, I realized how it would appear both wondrous and alarming to someone expecting only dirt. Then his flashlight found the pile of human bones stacked neatly in the corner. Their awe turned to horror. Their voices rose in volume and pitch. They were a little freaked out.

The rainwater spilled off the staircase and into a channel that disappeared into the wall at the side of the lake. It was as if the ancient Maya wanted the steps to be slippery. They were a crafty bunch with sophisticated fountains, sewers, and drainage ditches. They knew what they were doing.

When I reached the bottom, I couldn't see the steppingstones Seven-Death had walked me across the first time. Back then I just followed him. After a bit of inspection, I noticed little silver bumps. The mercury had tinted the stones, making them nearly invisible. I started across, using my visor instead of a light. The infrared worked well. I made it to the other side and stopped at the low entrance to the cave of knives. Where they had been lying on the floor the last time, their hilts were stuck in the wall now. To get through, I would have to crawl on my hands and knees, pushing the pack in front of me.

I checked out my pursuers. Three of them were carefully picking their way down the steps, still sixty feet above the lake. Dressed in the same black shorts and short-sleeved shirts as the first time I'd seen them, they glowed yellow in the thermal range. I could keep track of them down here. I turned around, slid my pack into the cave, and crouched.

Then I heard a scream and a thudding splash. An odd sound unlike anything I'd ever heard. I turned around.

Mercury leaned over my shoulder. *Ugly way to go, homie.*

I said, *What happened?*

Mercury said, *Thought you were all up on your high school science, bro. Hydrargyrum, liquid mercury, has twice the density of iron. Remember that YouTube video you watched when you were stoned where a guy floated an anvil in it?*

I said, *I wasn't stoned. I was ... bored.*

Mercury said, *OK, bored. One of the Knights just slipped and fell onto a liquid surface denser than iron.*

That thought messed with my head. How could a liquid be denser than iron?

Mercury said, *The unworthy have a bad habit of—*

I said, *Slipping on the steps. I remember.*

The next Knight in line dug out a flashlight and trained it on his fallen friend. For a moment, the two remaining guys stood still. It just got real for them. The beam flashed around the chamber, looking for me. They had rifles slung on their shoulders. They would be happy to shoot me and search the place alone. I backed into the cave of knives.

The Knight in back shoved the guy in front. They resumed their march for three steps. Then the second guy fell to his death. The third sat still for a long time. Three more men came down from above. He gave the newcomers a report just as a third man fell to his death. The remaining Knights stayed still again. They cupped hands over their ears, listening to their comm link in the echoing chamber.

Then they turned around and crawled back up, using their hands and knees.

I considered their strategy. Three dead; time to change tactics. They'd wait for me at the top. There was only one way out, according to Mercury. I'd have to deal with that later.

I crawled through the caves, pushing the fake stone in front of me. First the cave of knives, then the river of blood, the cold, and the others. When I made it to the end, the alabaster box waited for me. Seven-Death stood next to it, grinning like a proud papa, his feathery headdress floating as he nodded. He shook his stick, the attached skulls rattling his approval. I'd survived his gauntlet.

I said, *When I get back, I'm going to see a shrink.*

Mercury said, *Don't be such a drama queen, bro. There's nothing wrong with seeing Mayan gods and Roman gods hanging together. Diversity is all the rage these days.*

Especially when you're both low on believers, I said. *How do I get out of here? Tell me there's a back door.*

Mercury said, *Back door to where? You be halfway to the underworld down here. You gotta go back the way you came. You'll be fine. Just go up there and yell BOO! They'll run away.*

Mercury laughed.

Seven-Death took my false-altar and brushed the mud off the carvings.

I said, *Thanks for loaning it to me, but everybody figured it out.*

Mercury said, *That's not why he gave it to you. It picked up on your future. Check it out.*

The carvings on the smaller stone were different from what I remembered. But then, I didn't really look at it that close when I took it. I thought it was just a replacement weight. Turning on my phone-light because the infrared wasn't cutting it for the details, I saw a figure kneeling with his arms and hands bound behind his back. Much larger men wearing balaclavas surrounded him. One held a knife at the bound man's throat. Another man appeared to be taking the alabaster box containing the Freedom Stone. A reasonable person might argue the captive was me. A chiseled man in t-shirt and jeans.

Mercury said, *Don't worry about that side. Check out this here.*

I turned the altar to the other side. An image of Mercury flying above a city while throngs of people in the streets threw flowers in the air.

I said, *That picture was taken a long, long time ago.*

Seven-Death howled with laughter. Which he stifled as soon as Mercury gave him a nasty glare. Seven-Death pulled my alabaster box from thin air and wrapped it in the blanket and shoved it back in my backpack. He handed me the pack, and smiled, waiting with an expression like he expected me to leave.

I said to him, *Thanks for the hiding place. They're probably waiting up top to kill me and take the Freedom Stone, so I guess it was all in vain, but you did your part. So, thanks again.*

I tossed a glare at Mercury.

Mercury said, *Dude, would I let you spill your blood all over Seven-Death's nice temple? No way. I mean, who would clean it up? Don't worry. They were freaked by the silver lake that their boys bounced off. They're not hanging around at the entrance. You get up there, you'll see what I mean. You can figure it out.*

That didn't make me feel better. It felt like one of the tests the gods are always giving their best believers. But I crouched down and pushed my pack ahead of me through the caves and trotted across the stones in the silver lake. Floating in a corner of the lake were the bodies of three Knights of Mithras. I climbed the steps.

The rain was still flooding in but somehow, uphill was easier. I was on the balls of my feet where my toes could grip. When I got to the last bend, a bolt of lightning lit up the night sky above me. There were no silhouettes of men staring down at me. The Knights weren't waiting near the entrance.

I raised the rifle I'd been carrying, a H&K MP7, and carefully mounted the steps one by one.

Another bolt of lightning showed me their plan. The drone waited a thousand feet above the altar. It would follow me to a place where they could surround me. Smart. I waited for another bolt of lightning.

When it came, I put a bullet through the drone. Its shattered pieces fell from the sky.

CHAPTER 34

I CLIMBED OUT AND RIGHTED the tree, which put the stone back in place, and ran down the rain-drenched hill. When I reached the flat without hearing bullets whizzing past my head, I gave thanks and praise to Mercury. Then I zigged and zagged into a grove of young, head-high palm trees. As noisy as crashing through them was, it would be equally noisy if they followed me.

Halfway in, I took a knee and checked my map. Zig-zagging my way home would give them time to locate and track me down. It wouldn't take them long to determine a general direction from my twists and turns. They could average them out and figure Chan Chich was the only hint of civilization within fifty miles.

Having run through a city-block's worth of palms, I should've heard them following me. I didn't. And that worried me more.

The drumbeat of raindrops hitting the large leaves drowned out subtle noises. Still, I should hear pursuers. Unless they were really good hunters.

I gave it some thought. What could Mr. Baldy be doing? He and the Knights had located me a mile from the temple on my way in. That had been part of my intentional misdirection. If he looked there for my exit, he'd end up a mile north of me. But I couldn't count on that. My best bet was to make a run for it. I was tired, carrying a hundred pounds of rock, but in better shape. I could outrun them over time. Endurance was my strength, and therefore, my best bet.

I fixed the direction to Chan Chich in my head, took a deep breath, and ran. Crashing my way out of the palms, I stayed under the thickest part of the canopy. If Mr. Baldy had one drone, he could certainly have two. I ran at a steady, aggressive pace, reserving enough speed to burst forward should they get behind me.

They showed themselves after half a mile.

Off to my left, three black shadows jogged at my pace twenty yards away, parallel to my path. I turned abruptly right and picked up speed until I saw a second squad of runners.

I readied my rifle as I ran, then did a 180 degree turn and fired a whole magazine into the forest ahead of me. As I expected, the spray didn't hit anyone—too many trees—but it sent them scattering into the woods. I ran through the gap and spun around again. I fired a second magazine, leaving me only two more. Again, they scattered.

I took off in a straight line for home.

Calculating their speed and endurance, I realized I'd underestimated them. They had training and fitness equal to mine. They'd left Chicago at roughly the same time I had. That put them thirty miles from Seven-Death's undiscovered temple at the same time I left Chan Chich. Yet they established a perimeter and mapped out possible routes for ingress and egress in the time it took me to arrive. Which meant they were good. Very good.

They'd also made a smart bet on which way I was heading. They didn't need to form a giant circle, as Mercury and I had figured. They staked out three approaches to the area. More men patrolling smaller patches meant that while I was in the temple, some of Mr. Baldy's men were looking for signs of my approach. They'd found it.

And that meant there were more than the six men I'd seen and scared off. There were another fifteen trying to outflank me.

Could I reroute to Uaxactun? Not while carrying a hundred pounds. They'd gained on me because they were carrying a mere twenty pounds of water, ammunition, and weapons.

Why hadn't they shot me? It was the easiest solution to the problem. The only thing I could think of was they didn't want to damage the prize.

They were gaining on me again. The squad of three paralleled my left flank. I couldn't waste ammunition on another frontal assault.

Why parallel me? They wanted to herd me into a specific area. Probably an area where the surviving fifteen were running full speed to bring my run to an end. That would be something I had to avoid at all costs.

I cranked up my speed. The backpack swung back and forth with each stride. The shoulder pads dug into my shoulders; the weight rubbed sheets of skin off my back. I could endure this. I had to. Jenny wanted to free China.

The squad on my right tracked closer. They came within ten yards. Then five. They were pushing me left. Which meant the ambush site would be to the left. Unless they were counting on my contrarian streak pushing back. A false signal to get me to turn right.

A tossup. I turned left abruptly, running directly at the left flanking squad. I raised my rifle as if to fire at them.

They had to be the guys from the pontoon boat. They'd learned I don't always fire when I aim.

They raised their rifles. I was running straight into three barrels.

I turned hard right. The right-hand squad now close enough to grab me if they wanted.

A noise zoomed overhead. A big drone flew by with a long black tube hanging underneath it.

Both squads fired at me. I picked up speed again.

The drone dropped its payload. A large roll of something black, six feet wide, unfurled from the drone and fell into my path. I tried to stop but my feet were already on it. A slick surface. The drone dropped the end from the top and a large net fell around me. I crashed to the ground. It was plastic fencing. The kind my folks used to keep deer out of the fields back home.

It was thin and weak material, but it instantly entangled me. I struggled to rip through it. My rifle was caught sideways, my pack was tugging backwards, my feet were immobilized. It felt like a nightmare, struggling without traction, pushing and twisting and never getting free.

I let go of the rifle to use my hands. Moving as fast as I could, I easily ripped through the netting around my head and pulled it to the sides of my chest. I shrugged it off my backpack, but my legs were stuck.

It was too late. Four hands grabbed my left arm.

I reached for my rifle with my right but felt four strong hands grab my forearm and twist hard.

A second later, they took all my weapons: the darts, phone, visor, drone, pistol, rifle, and spare magazines. They never found the blade I keep in my belt buckle, not that it would be of any use against twenty Knights. Two rifle muzzles rose in front of me. Someone kicked the back of my knee. I dropped to the forest floor. The rain poured through my hair and ran down my face. More hands moved to the task of removing my backpack.

The prize was lost.

"Thank you, Jacob." Mr. Baldy stepped in front of me. Up close, he looked like the bad guy sent from central casting. He should have smoked a black cigar. It would've completed his look. Depending on which hat wardrobe put on him, he could fit into anything from a Western to a Nazi flick.

Ropes twisted around my upper and lower arms. Another went around my wrists with practiced efficiency.

As they trussed me up, I saw a small shadow flicker through the trees in the distance. A second later, two larger shadows flickered through the same distant space. I wondered how many Knights were still out there. Not that it mattered.

A thousand negotiations ran through my head. But I had no leverage. They had me. I was dead. It was only a matter of minutes.

I held my head high, looked him in the eye, and stayed still.

"You're not going to ask why I thank you?" He strode around me, rain dripping from his elbows. He drew his silver Scorpion. No silencer this time. Just the long, shiny barrel.

"I am grateful for your professionalism, Mr. Stearne." He smiled. "You proved a worthy, albeit stupid, adversary. I say stupid because you should have killed me in Chicago. That small oversight has now cost you your life. Before I dispatch you, I say thank you for not killing more of my men."

"I didn't kill any of your men."

"What happened in your chamber of horrors then?"

"The Mayans didn't build their stairs to code. Your Knights fell into a lake of liquid mercury."

Mr. Baldy frowned and tilted his head. He turned and spoke in his language to his men. There were several answers. Judging from the tones involved, they decided my story might be accurate.

"And yet you survived." Mr. Baldy sounded amused. "As I mentioned, Jacob, you have proven to be a most worthy adversary. Unlike that little troupe of women playing dress up and calling themselves Brothers. They will no doubt mourn your loss with many tears and wailing sobs. Without you, they are ultimately pathetic and hopeless. I wish I could see the look on Gu Peng's face when she hears you will no longer be available to aid her ridiculous cause. And the greatest shame of all: that you will not return to the accolades of that sad band of chaotic, undisciplined anarchists. Well, enough talk."

He raised the Scorpion and held it an inch from my forehead. His finger squeezed the trigger.

CHAPTER 35

AUTOMATIC WEAPONS FIRED FROM THREE directions at once. The muzzle flashes obscured the shooters, but I recognized the sound of Sabel Security's standard issue H&K MP7s. It had to be Ms. Sabel flanked by Miguel and Dhanpal.

Mr. Baldy and his Knights dove for cover. Some of his men returned fire. One picked up the Stone and tried to flee. He was felled a split second later.

Still bound, I rolled away from the Knights.

Mr. Baldy held a beautiful weapon for competitions and assassinations, but the wrong one for a firefight. He fired a couple suppression rounds before spotting me making my getaway. I squirmed around a tree. He blew a hole through it just over my shoulder. I rolled to the next tree. A hundred bullets buzzed the air between us. He went back to survival mode and returned fire.

Three people with night visors can hold off double or triple their number. The Knights began to understand what they were up against and split into squads to outflank Ms. Sabel. It was a great idea on paper. She used their maneuver to move into a defensive circle around me. The Stone lay nearby, within our reach and out of Mr. Baldy's.

Trees and leaves were shredded by high velocity armor piercing rounds. The Knights knew it was time to retreat. They formed a perimeter around Mr. Baldy and began exiting the battlespace.

They made it twenty yards. Miguel and Dhanpal swapped mags and laid down a relentless fusillade that pinned the Knights behind a rock formation. Then, suddenly, there was silence.

Which was followed seconds later by the counterattack. The Knights began spreading out, right and left. Strength in numbers.

Ms. Sabel sliced my bindings with quick, expert flicks.

I shook out my ankles and wrists to get the blood back in them, then I held out a hand for a weapon.

She held up her rifle, indicating it was the only weapon she'd brought. "Danny and his crew are twenty minutes behind us. They'll have something."

Using a tree for cover, she scanned for Knights.

The contents of my backpack lay on the forest floor ten yards away. The alabaster box had fallen open in the melee. The Stone lay on the blanket as if on display. Dhanpal ran from cover, scooped up the Freedom Stone with his bare hands and began to wrap it in the blanket. He stopped. For a second, he stared at the black glass embedded with gold flecks as if it were a newborn. Then he held it to his face and rubbed his cheek on the surface.

The Knights halted their attack. No one fired. We all stared at Dhanpal.

He wrapped the Stone in the blanket, laid it gently back in the box, and snapped the lid back on. He shoved it back into my backpack. Then he did something he'd never done before: He glared at me with intense hatred. He turned his scowl to Ms. Sabel and Miguel. Then he rose and jogged into the forest in the opposite direction of Chan Chich.

Mr. Baldy's voice floated through the darkness. "Allah has smiled upon you once more, Jacob Stearne. I missed my opportunity to kill you, but it is a small matter. You are about to endure the worst fate a soldier can ever face. What fate is worse than death for an international hero, Jacob?"

I said nothing.

He waited a beat. Then he said, "Defeat."

The Knights retreated. They pulled out with too many trees between us to stop them.

Ms. Sabel and Miguel looked at me. She said, "Are you hurt?"

"No."

"Then go back along the trail and meet Danny and the Brothers. They'll escort you back to the resort. We're going after Dhanpal."

Instantly, she and Miguel disappeared into the darkness.

I wanted desperately to follow, but she was right. Tactically, I'd be nothing but a liability. If they could recover our comrade, the battle would be a minor loss. If they could recover the Stone as well, it would be a draw. I had to leave it in their capable hands.

And that made me realize Mr. Baldy was also right. His words echoed in my ear. For a soldier, nothing is worse than defeat.

I started walking. And trying to imagine what I'd say to the Brothers and Jenny.

Mercury appeared next to me.

I said, *Go away. I don't want to hear it.*

Mercury said, *Hear what, homie? About how you got spanked by a mediocre soldier from Turkmenistan? I wouldn't bring that up. Nor would I bring up how you SHOULDA LEFT THE POISON STONE AT THE BOTTOM OF THE OCEAN, because I'm not that kind of vindictive, mean-spirited god. Now, I did hear about a dude who once took a whip to the moneychangers in the temple—*

I said, *Just leave me alone. I don't need any spiritual guidance right now.*

Mercury said, *Boy, you'd be dead wrong right there. Think about it— if I left you alone right now, you'd get all suicidal and shit.*

He had a point. I felt like Napoleon crossing the Berezina. The Frenchman went to Russia with half a million men. By the time he retreated to the river, he was down to 90,000. Only half that many made it home. One of the greatest defeats in the history of warfare. In the same way Napoleon disappointed France, I'd let Jenny down. And Peng and Rafael and Cherry and Danny—and why not throw in a billion Chinese while I'm at it?

Mercury said, *Hey, who told you to make up with Pia Sabel?*

I squinted at him. *Not going there.*

Mercury said, *She saved your ass back there. If you had her and Monster Slayer backing you up from the beginning, you—*

I said, *STOP! If you're so great, why didn't you tell me something useful when I needed help?*

Mercury said, *Why didn't you tell Jenny about me when you had the chance?*

I said, *Because you're not real. I'm totally off my rocker and having this conversation is proof.*

Mercury said, *What is with you, bro? I already done told you how to get ahead of this, but you didn't spend one minute reflecting on my hints.*

I said, *Told me what?*

Mercury said. *Why do the Knights of Mithras want it? What're they gonna do with it?*

How would knowing Mr. Baldy's plans help me? I didn't have the Stone. I wasn't going to hand it to Peng so she could save China. And that meant Peng would be disappointed. If Peng were disappointed, Jenny would be disappointed.

Mercury said, *There's probably something Freudian about you being afraid to disappoint women. Still, you gotta think about things here. You can't go around saving humanity without the right knowledge about stuff. Knowledge is what sets you apart from your average, everyday hero. You can't just save lives, you gotta save the right lives for the right reasons. That means you need to know stuff like: If the Brotherhood wants to free China, what do the Knights want?*

I said, *To subject China to ... I don't know. What?*

Mercury grabbed my arm to stop me. He looked into my eyes. *Dude. We've been over the god-rules before. We can't be spoon-feeding you this shit. The whole point to your life on Earth is to figure things out for yourselves. Like Holocaust, bad; acceptance, good; atom bombs, bad; medicine, good; prejudice, bad; loving the one true messenger—*

I said, *Yeah, I get it.*

Mercury said, *Bro, China is a dictatorship. If Peng's gonna turn a dictatorship into a democracy, the opposite is gonna be what?*

I said, *Turning democracies into dictatorships? What's that got to do with anything? You kept telling me to work for Yeschenko and leave the Brotherhood alone. Now you're telling me, what? Why can't you be clear?*

Mercury said, *You didn't want to work with Pia-Caesar-Sabel. You wanted to go it alone. Well, guess what homie? Look around you. You be alone.*

I looked around. I was alone in the middle of nowhere. I looked up and let the warm rain fall in my face.

Mercury said, *Because you wanted to go it alone, all you could handle would be finding Yuri Belenov for Mikhail Yeschenko. If you want to turn China into a democracy, you gonna need some help. You gonna need the Brotherhood. And even then, you're gonna be shorthanded. Ya feel me? You need Pia-Caesar-Sabel.*

His endless chatter felt like torture. Especially because it made sense. But I didn't want to hear any more. I was tired. Beat. Defeated. I had to figure out what to tell Jenny. I sat down under a tree.

I'd never felt so helpless before.

I once saved a hundred worshippers in a Paris cathedral. I saved an admiral from murderous vigilantes. I saved the world from a mad arms dealer. I did it alone. Sure, I had help getting around the world thanks to Ms. Sabel's jet. Sure, I had an unlimited expense account at Sabel Security. But when it came down to it, I faced destruction with no one else around me. And yet I managed to come back alive every time. Until now.

Defeat.

Half an hour later, I was still sitting under the tree when I heard people running in the forest. Shadows came through the trees to form a circle around me. Danny, Mark, Fiona, the guy whose name I still didn't know, and the rest of the Brotherhood materialized into view.

My shame was complete.

CHAPTER 36

JOE GRIFFITH ENTERED THE SUITE at the Lanesborough Hotel in London. It belonged to the Protector of the Knights of Mithras. The Ionic columns separating the foyer from the green room impressed him. He made a mental note to have solid marble columns installed in his foyer. If the Protector had something, Griffith wanted to have the same thing—only better.

Griffith's father had been a Guardian who was passed over for Protector when the Central Asian crowd showed up. Why the board of the Knights wanted to muddy their Anglo-Saxon lineage with a Georgian-born Protector baffled him. Griffith had been so disappointed that he'd joined the Keepers when he came of age and rose through their ranks. But in his heart, he'd always wanted to earn the title denied to his father.

In later years, he switched to the Knights because the Protector proved to be adept at manipulating connections despite his heritage.

The Protector had proven his value by pulling strings in every major country. He knew presidents and prime ministers and every diplomat worth bribing. Griffith had been impressed by the man's pull. And he profited handsomely.

At the same time, he'd been shocked and horrified at the man's unnecessary brutality. There are many ways to achieve one's goals. Griffith preferred financial leverage to this barbaric killing spree they were on. Violence poisons all connections eventually.

When the time was right, he would replace the filthy Turkmen and Georgians who'd overstayed their welcome among the Knights. He would return the Knights to civilized methods. That was a vow he'd made to his father on the old man's deathbed.

The butler, in tails and white gloves, coughed politely. Griffith stopped daydreaming and followed the man into the blue room. The walls, the upholstery, the carpet, all in differing shades of pale blue. Just like the color-coded rooms in the royal palaces nearby, Buckingham and Kensington.

A giant video screen stood to one side. A bright yellow chair faced it at a good distance.

The butler coughed again and pointed to a place on the floor next to the video screen. "Here, sir. Face the chair."

"Of course," Griffith took his position, standing at attention before the yellow chair.

The video screen flickered to life, visible in Griffith's peripheral vision. The butler stood in front of it, adjusting something with a remote control. The butler said, "Ah, there you are, Captain Amanow. Very good, sir. You can hear me?"

"Indeed," Amanow's voice was crisp.

Griffith stole a glance. The Knight stood at attention in what appeared to be a Yucatan hacienda, the faux limestone walls fashioned to look Mayan.

"Gentlemen," the butler said, "kindly remain standing until His Excellency, the Protector, arrives. Good day."

The butler closed the double doors at the far end as he exited.

Griffith considered chatting with Amanow to gauge the tension between them but decided against it. Better to let the Protector witness Griffith's superiority in the moment. Apparently, Amanow had the same thought. They waited ten minutes at least. The silence stretched until Griffith's knees began to demand movement. He knew the soldier in Amanow would endure the drill. Griffith resolved to best his adversary.

Behind him, a door opened, and the sound of the Protector's shuffling walk came to him. Griffith turned his head, considering if he should assist the limping older man, but recalled being told the powerful Protector hated any offering that diminished his standing.

The Protector's knuckle pushed Griffith's chin forward. A silent rebuke for not maintaining his posture.

The old man wobbled with the aid of a four-wheeled walker to the yellow chair and sat with a tired exhale. He rolled the walker to the side. Griffith noted the Protector did not look well. He wore a black military uniform festooned with medals under a thick robe of deep navy blue. His face had gone from light gray to nearly iridescent white. After a bout with skin cancer, the Protector had taken sun-avoidance to new extremes. Even that didn't explain the man's pallor. Griffith bowed and caught a glimpse of Amanow doing the same on screen.

"You were given a simple mission," the Protector said in his rough baritone. "It is time to deliver your progress report. Captain Amanow, have you succeeded?"

"I have," Amanow said. The pride in his voice spilled out in his words. "I am in possession of the Poison Stone now."

"Have you opened the box?" the Protector snapped.

"Not yet, Your Excellency. We have just returned—"

"Then you could have a sack of flour for all you know. Jacob Stearne is no fool. Have one of my Knights open it behind you while we talk. Have him hold it with his bare hands."

"We have one of Sabel's people," Amanow said. "He picked up the Stone and joined us. An Indian named Dhanpal. It worked to convert him to one of us."

"How do you know he is not a plant tracking your every move?"

Griffith desperately wanted to look at the screen to his right. He could only imagine the look on Amanow's face at being called out.

"We will test the Stone at once, Your Excellency." Amanow gave tersely whispered orders to someone off camera.

"Captain," the Protector said, "you have questioned the effectiveness of my chosen Guardian. State your accusations."

Amanow cleared his throat. "The Guardian's function is to provide critical intelligence about the mission and shield the Knights in the field from—"

"Do not tell me what I already know," the Protector snapped.

"My most sincere and humble apologies, Your Excellency," Amanow said. "The Guardian failed to inform us that Jacob Stearne left Hidalgo's camp before our arrival. Further, he failed to provide an accurate location for Stearne's exfiltration. His order to preserve Stearne's life, focusing instead on the young woman, proved disastrous in our exit from Guatemala. We could have easily killed Stearne and taken the girl to the location that day. Instead, we wasted five days clearing records at the International Court—"

"You knew where Stearne hid the Poison Stone on the first day and you failed to recover it?" the Protector asked.

"Not exactly. But we could have triangulated the location and conducted a search—"

"Ultimately, you required Stearne to retrieve it for you, did you not?" The Protector's voice grew louder. "Even if you located the temple, penetrating it proved disastrous. Stearne made it all the easier for you. And he did so because of the Guardian's efforts, is that correct?"

Amanow said, "Yes, Your Excellency."

"Continue with your next accusation, Captain."

"When under fire in Chicago, the Guardian failed to secure his own property with his security team. Amid the search, the Guardian fled the premises. When he called upon the Knights to defend his stronghold, he failed to tell us the extent of his hidden passages. Had we been so informed, Stearne would be a handful of ashes at this moment."

"Again, you raise the question: How would you have retrieved the Poison Stone?" the Protector asked. "Next."

Amanow stammered for a moment before taking a breath and continuing. "The Guardian proposed to use LiDAR to find Stearne's hiding place. He wasted days and still has nothing to show for it."

The Protector turned his pale face to Griffith and stared long and hard. Griffith could find nothing to say. The LiDAR map wouldn't be completed for another day. The engineer overpromised the processing time. This idea had indeed been a failure.

In a voice loud enough for Amanow to hear, Griffith said, "The honorable Knight is correct. My miscalculation of the delivery time would have cost us an extra twenty-four hours."

The Protector scowled and turned back to Amanow. "Anything else?"

"Yes, Your Excellency," Amanow said. "He refuses to share information on Stearne's current location."

Again, the Protector turned his cold eyes to Griffith and said nothing.

Griffith said, "I refuse to reveal information obtained from my asset for fear of exposing that person. Stearne is no longer of any concern. My asset will be extremely valuable to us in the next phase."

The Protector turned back to Amanow. "What do you propose as a corrective measure?"

"The Guardian has done nothing effective and has caused us many delays," Amanow said. "If you approve, I propose we dismiss the Guardian and I will assume his duties."

Griffith felt a cold shudder overtake him. He hadn't expected a Knight to be so bold. He tried to read the Protector's inscrutable face as the older man turned to stare him down.

Dismissal could be a blessing. He could go back to his hedge fund and be done with all this intrigue. In fact, if he'd known these superstitious Eurasian-rednecks believed in the stupid artifact, he would've avoided them and stayed with the equally august and ancient body of the Keepers. Connections and death-bed promises be damned.

Then again, Griffith considered what the word *dismissal* meant to these people. Educated as they were, their morals were decidedly medieval. In the Roman era, the ancient order chose rank by contest. Like gladiators, those aspiring to higher office fought for the honor. Losers were even executed on rare occasion. In this case, the Central Asians would insist he take his own life. Even if he were allowed to live, the Protector would destroy Griffith's empire.

Perhaps he should turn the tables and recommend dismissing Amanow. All Griffith's hard work was on the verge of paying off. The dumb bastard would get them all thrown in jail before it was over. But the Protector favored the brutal solution to every problem over anything requiring finesse.

"Indeed, I have failed you," Griffith said. "In one small detail that would not have cost us the mission. But that is a detail for you, and you alone, to judge. I will not question your decision. In my defense, I have a plan for completing the mission. One based on proven methods that I have reviewed with you. Captain Amanow pins all his hopes for the future on an unproven piece of rock. Without it, the Knights of Mithras have prevailed for centuries. Our only setback was a brief span of time after the Second World War. To leave everything we've worked so hard to achieve in the hands of a mere captain from Ashbagat would carry great risks. In twenty-four hours, I meet with Pia Sabel. Would a woman of her means meet with our good captain? In a matter of days, our well-trained but low-caste Knight expects heads of state to meet with him? My answer is to dismiss our presumptive captain and replace him with one of the other Knights."

Griffith didn't need to look. He could feel Amanow's hate and anger through the screen.

"Need I remind you," the Protector asked, "that I plucked Captain Amanow from obscurity, sent him to the finest schools, arranged for him to have the finest military training in the world? Of course not. You know I did these things because, even as a boy, Batyr exhibited no delusion of morality, no concern for personal safety, no weakness. He did as instructed without hesitation. He has always followed my orders. No one from any other chapter of the Knights has bested him. You, Mr. Griffith, came to me with the highest recommendations from the Keepers. You should know better than to diminish a man of his standing."

"My apologies, Your Excellency."

"Do you not believe in the Poison Stone?" the Protector asked with an edge in his voice.

"I believe in what has been proven. Would it not be the most prudent course of action?"

Instead of answering, the Protector pointed to the screen. "Step around and we shall see together. If the legend is true, you will work together. If it is false, you will be dismissed together, and I will take the meeting with Ms. Sabel."

The Protector had better connections than Pia Sabel. In fact, the Protector could have easily set the meetings for Griffith but had chosen not to. Why? When the old man clearly favored Amanow over him, why was Griffith suddenly the front man? Was the old man's illness worse than it looked? The Protector's threat shook him to his core. It was all he could do not to visibly tremble.

He took two steps forward and turned to face the screen. Amanow, a worried look on his face, had half-turned from the camera to watch a man at a table. The alabaster box lay open. The man extracted a stone, black as obsidian, the size of a large loaf of bread. He held it in his hands at an arm's length. He raised it to the sky, then lowered it to his face as if looking inside it. He kissed it, brushed it against his cheek, then gently replaced it in the box. He put the cover back on and pressed down until they all heard an audible click.

The Knight turned to Amanow and spoke in their language. The man spoke with a pleading tone, his face penitent.

Amanow's face first clouded with confusion, then shock, then horror as the Knight made his case.

The man who'd held the Poison Stone turned to the camera and spoke softly in English, "In all respect, most esteemed leaders, I must follow Allah. From today on, I am working for Islamic Charity Relief Fund to feed hungry and comfort sick."

Amanow pulled his silver pistol and shot the man in the forehead.

Griffith gasped, unable to hide his shock. Not even the worst gang lords of the ghetto summarily executed people in front of their bosses. He turned to face the Protector, unable to close his mouth.

"Consider the Poison Stone proven, Mr. Griffith," the Protector said.

CHAPTER 37

IT WAS LATE MORNING WHEN I returned to Chan Chich. The place was quiet since most of the Brotherhood was still a few miles behind me. They were nice. They never said a word. Not even Danny. So, I'd used my superior conditioning to run ahead of them. I wanted to face Jenny's disappointment alone.

She would be angry. And why not? I hadn't listened to her. She'd told me to include the Brotherhood and Ms. Sabel. I didn't and the result was failure. Not a great start to the marriage. If the wedding was still on. I mentally prepared for being dumped. Not for failing the mission as much as not listening to her. Who could blame her?

Mr. Baldy was right. I should've ignored Cherry's presence and killed him in Chicago.

When I reached the resort, I strode down the main stone path to the cottages. Each free-standing, hand-built cottage had been nestled into the jungle for privacy. It was hard to tell if Ms. Sabel picked this place to remind me how cushy things were in her employ or if the price and exclusivity were immaterial to her, but I appreciated it. The last thing I wanted was to have Jenny yelling at me in the thin-walled, sardine-packed kind of motel I could afford.

The wooden boards creaked with designer atmosphere when I mounted the steps to our cottage veranda.

Jenny looked up from a book on the far end. She jumped up when she saw me and ran to me. She wrapped her arms around me and squeezed as if I was the last lemon for lemonade. She buried her face in my shoulder and stayed there, hugging and holding me for a long time.

Then she said, "Thank god you're back. I was worried …"

She broke off when she started to choke up. Backing up, she covered her face, broke down in sobs, and fell onto the sofa. I eased in next to her and stroked her back. After a few deep breaths, she turned around and snuggled under my arm. We sat like that, facing the lush green jungle for a long time. A little stone path wandered through the bushes from the main lodge.

When she'd composed herself, she said, "I wished I'd gone with you."

"You'd have saved my life. Probably the mission." I waited a beat. "As it is, I tried to help the Brotherhood and failed. There's nothing more I can do here. We need to clear out."

Surprised, she looked up at me without a word.

"This whole thing is a fight between Peng and Mr. Baldy," I said. "We should've stayed out of it. If that guy and his Knights come to finish off the Brothers, we'll just get caught in the crossfire."

"You want to walk out on them? Now?" Jenny sat up, looking at me close enough to make me cross-eyed.

"I've seen Mr. Baldy and his Knights working like a finely-tuned military unit. They're good in combat. And there's twenty-eight of them and one of me. The Brotherhood has a whole different style of confrontation. I get that now. I didn't think it would work, but maybe it will. If they've been around since the dawn of time, it must work better than I thought. Whatever's going down between them is outside my skill set."

She searched my eyes. "That doesn't sound like you."

"How did we get involved in this thing anyway? Peng and the Brotherhood of Claritas had a plan long before you and I came along. I had a plan, too—to start Stearne Security. So far, all I've done is mess up Danny and Peng. I need to call Yeschenko and find Yuri Belenov."

As soon as the words left my mouth, I realized how bad they were. Jenny had put her faith in me for a reason. She believed helping Peng would establish us as a couple, separate from her mom the admiral, her dad the billionaire, and my former employer, Ms. Sabel. She was anxious to see us stand together.

I liked that concept. I liked that she had faith in me, even after this failure. But I didn't see how it could work. The concept was based on mythology. When the ancients encountered the unexplainable, they invented explanations. Your civilization collapsed? Could it be because your leaders were psychopathic narcissists? No, of course not. He went mad because of a magic rock. Somehow, I had to break it to Jenny that Peng wasn't going to free China. With or without the Freedom Stone.

Before I could find the right words, Rafael and Cherry came up the narrow path out of the rain forest. As he reached the veranda, he said, "We are delighted to see you safely returned."

Trust is important to me and I didn't trust Cherry. But her uncle was a welcome sight. They joined us, taking two chairs opposite our sofa. Cherry had the good sense to keep her mouth shut and her eyes averted.

"Why are you here?" I asked Rafael. "Shouldn't you be teaching at a university somewhere?"

He said, "I go where my skills may be of use."

"Do you believe in this Freedom Stone thing? And don't give me that stuff about what other people believe. I'm asking you."

Rafael sat perfectly still, staring at me while the women glanced back and forth between us. No one spoke.

Finally, the old man said, "Like everyone, I desperately want to believe in magic. But like Jenny, I believe only what is proven. I saw Carlotta's personality change after touching the Stone. Was that because of the Stone? Or was it because a lifetime of anger and meanness, so exhausting to maintain, finally snapped?"

Perfect. This guy was as vague as my used deity.

"What do the Knights of Mithras want with what they call the Poison Stone?" I asked.

After an awkward silence, Rafael cleared his throat and said, "It is their belief that the Poison Stone causes people to go mad. While we have judged Carlotta to be in a better place, no doubt her heirs believe she has gone quite mad. After all, she's giving away their inheritance. Anyone changing behavior from one extreme to the other is judged mad by those who knew them before. Consider, then, what would happen if an elected leader were to abruptly change her mind?"

I met his gaze. "They'd lose power."

"Or seize it?" Cherry offered.

"Are you telling me the Knights of Mithras are planning the same thing as the Brotherhood of Claritas? They're going to make people touch the Stone at the G20 Summit meeting?"

Rafael shrugged. Cherry nodded.

Mr. Baldy was driving me insane. If that box contained a means to turn democratically elected leaders into maniacal tyrants, the Knights could destroy the world as we know it. I couldn't imagine how that would work, but, as Rafael keeps reminding me, what matters is what people believe. And a lot of people put their faith in the contents of the alabaster box.

I turned to my second-hand god. *Earlier, he said the democratic Mayan cities survived the Stone. So why worry about it now?*

Mercury carried a plate of canapes and stood behind Rafael. *Dude, the bald guy didn't raise that army overnight. What was he thinking before you dragged the Stone out of the deep?*

I said, *He must've had a plan to kill certain people within the democratic leadership to create a power vacuum.*

Mercury said, *How about that? You ain't as dumb as Mars and Diana keep saying. And now that Mr. Baldy has the Stone?*

I said, *He creates the power vacuum and converts the leader. In one or two steps, a nice country like South Korea could wind up with a dictator controlled by the Knights.*

Mercury said, *And that's not your problem because you're too proud to ask for help?*

That stung.

The tapping of a walking stick on the path announced Gu Peng as she marched through the jungle to our clearing. Her face was downcast and angry. No one said a word to her; we just watched her approach. She stomped up the steps and crossed, stopping with a smack of her stick on the wood. She glared at me.

"I failed." I stood and faced her. "I'm sorry. There's nothing more I can do here."

"You turn down help from Brothers," she snapped. "You turn down help from Pia—"

"I thought you didn't want rich people," I said. My beloved gave me a nasty glare for interrupting the old lady. But it hadn't stopped Peng. She was still going.

"You not take any help. You not take any advice. You light no good. You light all darkness. You want all glory youself. You say you go only if everyone do as you say. Yes. And now, everyone do as you say." She stamped her walking stick. "You fail. Now you say nothing more?"

I looked her over. "Lady, I'm not interested in getting killed for a mythological rock. I'm not going to beat the Knights. I went up against them and now they have the Stone."

"You so proud," she said. "You let Knight beat you. You quit. No good to Brotherhood."

She turned and stormed away, pounding the stick into the boards as hard as she could.

Mercury appeared in front of me. *What'd I tell you, homes? You failed because you went alone. You succeeded in the Army. You succeeded with Sabel Security. You succeeded because you had a team. By yourself, you're not going to beat Mr. Baldy. Time to suck it up and talk to—*

I said, *I'm not going back to Ms. Sabel. She used me like a tissue and tossed me aside. I'm done.*

Mercury said, *You know that guy is a cold-blooded killer with plans to rule the world. If you patch things up with Pia-Caesar-Sabel you can take him down like a calf at a roping contest.*

I felt Jenny rise behind me. She stood at my side and slipped her arm around me. "We have to make this right."

CHAPTER 38

IT'S ONE THING WHEN GOD tells you to do something, it's a whole new level of "have to" when your fiancé tells you.

Everyone left me alone to think. I took a long, hot shower. Then I sat on the veranda, staring into the endless green thinking up ways to bring Mr. Baldy to justice. Jenny left me a note that read, *I know you'll think of something.* Then she had room service bring me a glass of lemonade. I sipped and thought.

There had been no sign of my delinquent deity for hours. Typical.

If I was going to stop this guy, I had to figure out how Mr. Baldy planned his attack. The G20 meeting was scheduled at a research center at the top of a huge mountain called Zugspitze. There were three ways in: train, helicopter, or on foot. The train ran through a tunnel and would be guarded by roving bands of security from several different nations. The helicopter approach would require special clearance to land. The international security people would be crawling all over the place. I knew some of those guys; they would never fall for the obvious ploys, like for a Knight embedded in a catering outfit. That only works in the movies.

I'd have to find Mr. Baldy's stronghold and storm it before the meeting started. Except, I didn't know where he would hole up before his assault on the G20 Summit. There were hundreds of hotels along the German-Austrian border. Thousands of private homes.

The next option was to figure out where we would attack and intercept him. Hiking in was a likely option. The trail was seven miles long with a mile-and-a-half elevation gain. Cliffs lined the route. The Knights had proved themselves fit enough to keep up with me through the Yucatán, so they could probably scale a mountain or two. Then I realized hiking couldn't work either. The meetings were held at the top of ski slopes. From the tree line to the buildings, the Knights would have to cross a mile of snow. No one could cross all that bright white undiscovered.

I could explain all this to the security people and make it their problem, but what would I tell them? A bunch of crazed Turkmen with a magic rock are coming. I may as well tell them about my friend Mercury, winged messenger of the Roman gods. Either way, they'd have me committed.

I didn't have enough people or drones to cover fifty square miles of rock and forest. That meant I needed Ms. Sabel and her resources. Which meant crawling back after refusing her many offers.

Mr. Baldy was right—defeat was worse than death.

I felt my chest tighten. How did I get into this? Why did everyone have such high expectations of me? You save the world a couple times, and everyone thinks you can leap tall buildings in a single bound. The pressure to solve this unsolvable problem made me feel like I was in a giant vise, having the life squeezed out of me.

I watched the leaves rustle. The endless sea of green was mesmerizing. I kept staring and sipping lemonade and thinking.

No matter what I thought, I kept coming back to my first conclusion: it was hopeless.

An unexpected sight stirred me from my thoughts. Ms. Sabel and Miguel carried a man slung from a pole stretched between their shoulders. They looked like game bearers from an old safari movie. They marched along the stone path and up the creaking steps and crossed to me. Their captive had the distinctive green Turkmen tattoo. He was awake, alert, and angry.

"Danny warned us about the cyanide capsule they keep in a false molar," Ms. Sabel said. "We took that first."

"No sign of Dhanpal," Miguel said. "Maybe he switched sides."

Neither of them said the Poison Stone had converted him. We were modern people of science and couldn't imagine that was the case. Silently ignoring the facts, we opted for believing he went undercover. Except that Dhanpal never went under cover.

They dropped the Knight with a thump. He groaned.

A small crowd of gawkers followed them to the clearing in front of the cottage, Danny in the lead. Peng at his arm. They kept their distance as if Ms. Sabel and Miguel were something to be feared. Good call. Jenny pushed through the Brothers and came up the steps.

"I thought of a few ways to get information out of him," Ms. Sabel said. She squatted next to him and looked him over. "I used Sabel Darts once. I knocked him out, then woke him up with smelling salts, then knocked him out again. It worked a little like truth serum."

She turned to face me, her back to her captive, and gave me a look that spoke volumes about what she was doing. She was giving me a shot at redemption. If I could get some critical information out of him, I'd be on the path to regaining my hero status.

Miguel untied the pole and pulled it from the Knight's hands and feet, then untied the gag.

The man exhaled with relief. I'd never been carried for miles hanging from a pole. I can't imagine it's comfy. He shrugged his shoulders and shook his legs. With his wrists and ankles still bound he wasn't going anywhere.

Jenny put her hands under the captive's shoulders and helped him to a chair.

Hate and anger spewed from his eyes. He took long deep breaths, imagining exactly how he would kill us all with each intake and promising himself it would happen with each exhale. Been there. Done that. Rarely works out. But it's a nice distraction.

"We're going to leave him to you." Ms. Sabel tossed me a knife. "I need a bath."

Miguel said, "Me too."

They turned and walked back toward their respective cottages. The crowd of onlookers respectfully parted for them, turning to watch the pair pass in awe and wonder. Carrying a hundred and seventy pounds of captured enemy dozens of miles was a feat of strength not lost on the Brotherhood.

Peng pivoted around her walking stick to give me a disapproving sneer. Her message was simple—why couldn't I be more like Ms. Sabel?

Peng was another relationship I needed Jenny to balance for me.

Rafael and his niece came forward as the rest of the crowd broke up and went back to whatever they were doing. Stopping below the veranda railing, he looked up at me. He said, "I cannot condone mistreatment of prisoners—"

"Hidalgo is dead. This man is complicit in mass murder." I casually tipped the knife point in the Knight's direction. "Don't you care about your brothers in academia?"

Jenny caught my disdain for Rafael's guidance. She tracked down the steps to where the old man was parked below me and took his elbow and tugged him away. He glared at me before nodding to Jenny and leaving.

As she walked away, Jenny pulled her phone. She texted me, "Feed him."

I didn't feel like showing any kindness to a Knight. They'd proved themselves ruthless in pursuit of their cause.

Then I considered what Jenny meant. I'd promised myself to give her ideas more consideration. It took a minute, but I understood.

I went inside the cottage, grabbed a menu and the room service phone. I tossed the menu on the small table in front of my captive. "I'm having the pork tacos. They're to die for, bro. What do you want?"

He stared at me instead of the menu.

I said, "OK, keep staring at me like that, motherfucker, and you're getting the vegan quinoa."

"Tacos," he said quickly.

I ordered for us, adding sopapillas and lemonade.

Repositioning the table and another chair, I made a cozy dining area for us. I sat and motioned for him to hold up his hands. When he did, I sliced through his bindings so fast it made him flinch. He examined his chafed wrists for knife marks. Not a scratch.

"You got a name?" I asked.

He gave me his soldier stare again. It was pretty good. This guy had stared down the barrel of some tense times. Then his gaze shifted to the knife. I picked it up and threw it hard into the door frame ten feet away. It drove in, point first, two inches deep. Anyone making a play for it would spend several seconds pulling it out. That rendered it useless to both of us. He calculated my gesture and relaxed just a little.

"I'll call you Phineas then." I tilted my head to see if he cared. All names in English sounded equally absurd to him, I guessed. "Well, Phineas, I'd appreciate it if you would keep my secret."

That got his attention. He turned his head in a skeptical expression.

"See, my friends think I escaped from you and Mr. Baldy." I pursed my lips and nodded. "You and I both know he could've killed me back there. It would be embarrassing if they knew he let me go. It would mean you guys aren't afraid of me—and I don't want that getting around. Ya feel me? So, what do you say, Phineas? Can I trust you to keep a lid on it?"

He leaned back as if I'd tossed a bucket of water on him. But he didn't speak.

Room service arrived with our food. Two guys laid out a white tablecloth and real silver. They swirled the plates into position like we were at the finest restaurant in Manhattan. They stole glances at Phineas's bound ankles but said nothing. They poured the lemonade and bowed and left.

Phineas stared at me as if eating food was beneath him.

"You haven't eaten in twenty-four hours," I said. I took a bite and munched. Excellent pork cooked Central American style, with tartness and sweet onions as opposed to Mexican style with spices. "Go ahead, it's not poisoned."

I smacked my lips and mmm'd to encourage him. What finally did the trick was inhaling through my nose. The scent was irresistible.

He took a tentative bite and loved it. He wolfed down everything on his plate.

"What's the deal between the Knights and the Brothers, anyway?" I asked. When he didn't answer, I said, "You guys know I'm not on either side, right? I'm stuck in the middle. Mr. Baldy tried to kill me to get that box. I found that a bit rude. And he tried to kill me when I went to rescue Cherry. Again, just plain rude. Otherwise, I'm with the Brothers because they asked nicely. Said they were going to use it to save the world."

Phineas kept quiet. He downed the lemonade in one go.

"I get it, you're not going to tell me anything. Fine. When you're done, you're free to go. See, I watched that bald guy execute fifteen people. The way I figure it, I could torture you, but what would be worse is sending you back to that homicidal maniac. So. You're free to walk away. Eat up, you'll need the energy."

He mopped up the honey with the last sopapilla on his plate then tossed his napkin on the table. A form of gauntlet to challenge my promise to free him.

I finished eating in silence. When I was satisfied, I retrieved the knife from the doorjamb. I knelt at his feet, put the knife in my left hand, looked up at him with a wry smile, shoved my pistol in his face, then sliced the bindings on his ankles.

He rose slowly, my pistol tracking his every move.

I rose with him and nodded to the exit. "Free to go, Phineas."

He watched me slip my pistol back in the holster at the small of my back. After a long moment, he said, "Zafar. Zafar Muhadow."

Reluctantly, he ambled across the veranda and down the steps and into the jungle and out of sight.

CHAPTER 39

"YOU WHAT?" MS. SABEL'S VOICE rarely rose to that volume.

I turned to Miguel in the poolside lounge chair on my right for support. He yakked on the phone with his sister in Navajo, talking a mile a minute without looking up. Most of the time I counted on him to back me up in arguments. This time, he chatted away like a cheerleader gossiping about the prom, complete with giggles and OMGs.

"We know he's not going to talk," I said. "The least I could do was show him some kindness."

"Did I miss something?" she asked with the heat still in her voice. "Jenny told me you wanted my help."

Mercury popped out of the water and shook like a dog. Drops flew everywhere. He said, *Bro, you finally asked Pia-Caesar-Sabel for help?*

I said, *Not intentionally. I need to improve my partner-communications. Jenny keeps yin-ing when I'm trying to yang. Or whatever.*

Mercury said, *If you're going after the big dogs, you're gonna need a Mastiff like Pia-Caesar-Sabel.*

I said, *Maybe things were different back in Ancient Rome, but in modern times, you don't compare a woman to a dog.*

Mercury said, *OK, Sabretooth tiger then—you get the picture. You're gonna need her help. Go on now, get up on your hind legs and beg.*

"Jenny thinks we need your help," I said. "To tell you the truth, you'd be better off not getting involved."

Ms. Sabel took the lounge chair on my left and opened a book. She wore a shimmering blue one piece that would've been modest except it was so tight you could see every muscle group it covered. If you looked.

Which I would never do.

I was reading Daniel Silva's *The New Girl* but wasn't sure what it was about since I'd lost my ability to focus after we left Cuba.

She opened her book, *Death and Conspiracy,* with exaggerated movements. Pissed. She looked over at me. "My shoulders still hurt from that pole, you know."

I looked up at the sky. "Do those clouds look like they're scudding to you?"

She looked up. "Scudding?"

"You'd think an author of Silva's caliber could use a better term than one from the sixteenth century."

"Read a decent writer then." She tossed her book at me. It bounced off my abs. "Do you need my help or not?"

I set the book aside. Her question made my stomach turn and my lungs collapse. I'd rather face down the Taliban than eat crow. Through clenched teeth, I said, "Yes."

"Then next time use my method. Stick him with a dart and wake him with smelling salts. By the third time, he thinks he's dreaming." She sat on the edge of her lounge and stared at me. "You want to be a one-man show, I get that. You want to do everything your way. I get that too. So why do this instead of dealing with Yeschenko?"

I couldn't blame it on my fiancé. It could get awkward if Ms. Sabel knew Jenny wanted me out of her sphere. And I couldn't tell her the truth. Going over the you-shot-me-once argument was uglier.

I sighed. "Yeschenko holds me responsible for the missing twenty-eight million."

"Really?" She crossed her arms. "I'll take care of it. Let's talk about right here, right now. You're not working well with others, Jacob."

"I need order and discipline. How I was trained."

"For what Jenny described to me, you don't just need my help, you need Peng and Danny. And that means you need to make room for the way other people work."

She got up, grabbed her towel, and strode away.

Before she left hearing range, I said, "I'm sorry. Next time, I'll check with you."

She stopped and turned and waited.

I said, "And I'd really appreciate it if you'd help me. I can't do this alone. As I mentioned earlier, it's a hopeless case, so there may not be another publicity stunt in it and it might get us all killed, but …" I thought for a moment while she waited. "I watched Mr. Baldy execute fifteen people. I don't give a damn about Peng and her magic rock. I'm going to terminate Mr. Baldy."

She stood still. Her face said *fuck you*, but she didn't voice anything for a long time. Finally, she said, "I never do it for publicity. Our marketing team brought me a layout of you with the French president that had 'Sabel' written all over it. I told them to make it about you. The company you worked for was one sentence near the bottom when they released it. I don't care about China or Mr. Baldy. I'm here because you care about this—and I care about you."

She walked away.

The birds sang and the bugs chirped and the monkeys squawked. The humidity felt like a warm washcloth. I looked over at Miguel. He'd finished his phone call. His chiseled face stared back at me. It was one of those times I wished I could take back all the stupid words and leave the good ones.

"I could've used a little backup just then," I said. "All these years I've known you, you never say more than five words at a time. Always the strong and silent type. But when I hear you on the phone with your family, you're talking a like a teenage girl, full-on chatterbox. What's with that?"

"Cultural bias," he said. "Every time Natives talk to white people, we lose a million acres."

I had no answer.

Danny stalked across the pool deck with Fiona-the-blonde one step behind him. He pulled up five yards away and crossed his arms. "We don't need your help."

I said, "Fine."

Mercury popped out of the water again. *Hey, homie, how come nobody likes you? Is it cuz you're a first-class asshole who thinks he's superior to everyone? Just cuz the President of France tossed you a ribbon doesn't mean you earned it all on your own. Maybe you're the Hero of Paris cuz the gods helped you out.*

I said, *I did some of that on my own. I can get along without you.*

Mercury said, *Get real, brutha. You had my help every step of the way.*

I said, *What about Chicago? Did you help me out there? Wait. You did. OK. Thanks for that.*

Mercury said, *And when I wasn't carrying you, Jenny was. She's your balance. And she says you need help. So, get balanced—ask for help.*

I said, *But what do I need Danny-the-Inexperienced for?*

Mercury said, *Numbers, if nothing else. If you'd gone to the temple with the Brotherhood, they would've all died, but you'd have the Stone.*

I said, *I'd rather lose the Stone than have the lives of innocent kids on my hands.*

Mercury said, *They'd rather have died than lose the Stone. See, these people believe in something. Maybe someday you'll believe in something enough to tell Jenny.*

"If you're fine with that," Danny said, "why is your girlfriend begging Peng to take you back?"

"Well, Fiona—" I turned to her "—did you need my help in Chicago, or were you OK with climbing into that cardboard box they were going to toss into the crematorium?"

"Oh. That. Thank you. But Danny freed me."

"He didn't tell you who freed him from a locked room at the top of the building next door?"

The two of them exchanged embarrassed glances. They shifted their weight from foot to foot.

"Why's it always you who gets the glory?" Miguel sat up. "What've you got against people helping you, bro?"

I said, "They screwed up an operation with their chaotic, undisciplined tactics."

"Don't disrespect my people like that," he said.

I looked over at him, surprised. Danny and Fiona did the same.

"Manuelito, Barboncito, Narbona, all the Navajo chiefs were guerilla fighters," Miguel said. "They never lost to the white man's army. Kit

Carson had to burn their crops and hogans and slaughter their livestock to starve them onto the reservation. Same for Crazy Horse and Geronimo and Red Cloud and Cochise—all the great Native chiefs. They presented no fixed positions, presented no target. The US Army rarely encountered them of their own accord. The few times they did, from Red Fork to Wounded Knee, the soldiers killed mostly women and children and old men. Natives used unconventional tactics. They attacked from unexpected positions, often at night or early morning. Never with an organized plan. Each warrior found opportunities and exploited them. If he found nothing, he retreated and looked for a different opportunity. They didn't teach that in Ranger School, but that doesn't mean it doesn't work. Let these people do their thing. Build on their strength. Maybe they'll save your ass next time."

Miguel picked up his book, grabbed his towel, and padded by me. As he did, he muttered, "That probably cost us Kayenta."

A few years ago, he took me to the town of Kayenta on the Navajo Nation in Arizona to visit his cousins and tour Monument Valley. Beautifully desolate, its magic was undeniable. I hoped they weren't going to lose it on my account.

Danny and Fiona watched him leave. When he'd disappeared down the path, they looked at each other. They didn't know what to say. Neither did I.

Mercury got out of the pool and dripped his way to the empty lounge chair where he flopped down. He said, *Now you got all the knowledge and help you need, homie. You can do this.*

I said, *What are you talking about this time?*

Mercury said, *You know what the Knights are after. You got Pia-Caesar-Sabel on your side. You got lots of cannon fodder, I mean, the Brotherhood to help you. Put it all together and you gonna be the Hero of the G20! Check it.*

I said, *They aren't looking to help. They're telling me to take a flying f—*

Mercury said, *You understand the problem, my brutha? They don't trust you. They think you want the Stone. I'll give you words to say that'll bring it all together for you. Trust me.*

I said, *You're not going to throw Neptune into it again, are you? That didn't work last time.*

Mercury said, *Will you let that shit go once in a while, homie? It's not healthy to be hanging onto your anger like that. Take a deep breath, Ima paraphrase Alexander the Great for you.*

"OK," I said after catching Danny's gaze. "I'm going after Mr. Baldy and the Knights of Mithras. To succeed, I need your help. And for your plan to work, you need mine. I make you this promise: I'll take Miguel's advice to heart. I'll work with you on your terms. I wouldn't blame you if you lost faith in my plans except that you saw me run every mile you ran. I took every risk you took. I wouldn't ask you to do the work and let others take the reward. You want the Stone and I want Mr. Baldy. We've shared the struggles, the successes, and the defeats so far. We will share in the rewards. The Stone belongs to you. Peng is a good and honest leader. She'll see that you're rewarded with what you value more than gold: respect. Two of Ms. Sabel's jets will be here in an hour. They'll take us to Germany. Before we go, I ask you to speak to every Brother, one on one. Give them a chance to stay here or go with us. No questions asked, no judgments made. The challenge ahead will not be easy, and this is a nice place to ride it out. But I promise you, I'll make those who go to Germany the envy of those who stay behind."

CHAPTER 40

JOE GRIFFITH PACED HIS SUITE at Claridge's in Mayfair, London. The video conference should've started ten minutes ago. Infuriating. Who did Amanow think he was? It was a poor strategist who made a play for Griffith's job and lost. He should've known the outcome with certainty before making such a bold move. Griffith resolved to shove the upstart Knight into his place. The Protector already showed the man Griffith's importance. Without him, the mission would have gone to Garmisch empty handed. If it had gone at all.

The demonstration of the Poison Stone had left Griffith unconvinced. He was a modern man. He believed in science. Though the incident did raise questions about the possibility of it having some unknown, unquantified properties that affected people in some way or another. The Protector was convinced. If Griffith wanted to be the next Protector, the current one had to believe that Griffith believed. He could go that far.

He checked his onscreen appearance one more time. He preferred standing for video calls. It made him feel more intimidating, more threatening. Now that the Protector had tied his fate directly to Amanow's, he would make it clear who gave the orders. There was one Guardian and thirty-two Knights for a reason.

Amanow's brazen play still chafed him. The fact that Amanow had agreed to the Protector's terms didn't fool Griffith for one minute. The man was ambitious enough to claim the Guardian role by killing him. Griffith had to stop the lunatic before the Protector eliminated them both. Which was exactly how the Protector would deal with any more infighting. Griffith knew this because that was how he solved problems in his organization. Over the years, the kleptocrats he laundered money for had taught him a valuable lesson: the best solution was cremation.

Griffith looked at his perfectly coiffed hair on screen. He looked sharp. He felt sharp. All he had to do was keep his goal in mind: Make Amanow understand killing him to get ahead would destroy them both. But what could he do to make the filthy Muslim appreciate him?

Finally, the system pinged with Amanow's call. Griffith clicked it on. As soon as the picture flickered to life, he asked, "Why are you late?"

Amanow sat in a drab room with beige walls behind him. He replied, "It is not so easy to find a good connection in Belize."

"Belize? Damn it, you were supposed to be in Garmisch by now."

"One of my Knights became separated from us. We have retrieved him. Even so, I will arrive there before you." Amanow smiled that smug grin of his. "Let us not waste time bickering. Our lives have been lashed together. I like it no more than you. Nonetheless, the Protector has made it clear: we succeed or die as one. So, tell me, my most esteemed Guardian, why did you ask for this call?"

"I felt it best if I explained our end game to you. We need to be on the same page. Now, I've sent an agenda—"

"You? Explain to me?" Amanow leaned back laughing. Then scowled and leaned into the camera. "Did you run twenty-seven and a half miles to arrive at Jacob Stearne's location yesterday? Did you establish a perimeter to ensure snaring him? Did you lose three of your Knights in a deadly—"

"Yes, yes—" Griffith waved his hands as if batting flies "—you have great tactics. You and your Knights performed admirably. But let me remind you where those coordinates came from."

"Information we would've had a day earlier by torturing Jacob Stearne and his girlfriend. An opportunity missed. A day wasted."

"This won't get us anywhere. You heard the Protector. We work together and succeed, or we die together."

"Indeed." Amanow sneered. "I have the Poison Stone. What thing of value do you bring?"

"A meeting with Pia Sabel and an informant in the Brotherhood."

"What good is Pia Sabel to us?"

"She has meetings scheduled with four of our five prime targets."

Griffith couldn't help but find Amanow annoying. "If you get everything in place, I can get her to include me in those meetings. And that means I can deliver the Poison Stone."

"Anyone can deliver the Poison Stone. We don't need you."

"The Germans earmarked €30 million for security." Griffith scoffed. "You plan to walk in as strangers and hand it to the German Chancellor and the Italian Prime Minister? Or do you think your remaining Knights can raid a place guarded by thousands of military and police officers?"

Griffith watched Amanow's smug demeanor weaken. Indeed, the man had planned to storm the conference. It wasn't a bad plan in theory; the mountaintop research center being used for the meetings was a bad choice for security but a stunning choice for photo ops. And politicians gravitated to photo ops no matter what their security people told them. But it wasn't the German's first time hosting world leaders. There would be no rocks to crawl out from under.

Griffith said, "I have business propositions of interest to the leaders we need to reach. Pia Sabel will help me drive these deals. That puts me in front of the leaders without a layer of security between us."

"You Americans." Amanow scoffed. "You think everything is about money. Power does not come from money. It radiates from one person to another. If Vladimir Putin gives you a medal, all of Russia will bow to you. No amount of money can buy that."

"Does Putin believe in you?"

"I too have connections," Amanow said in a less-than-convincing voice.

Griffith decided to let his silence speak for him. When Amanow retreated into his stoic look, Griffith said, "Your connections can get you face time with the leaders on our list?"

"I have other methods of deploying the Poison Stone."

"Captain Amanow, remember the Protector expects us to succeed. If we fail, we die. I'm offering you a plan that works. All we need to do is work out the details."

Amanow's jaw worked, contorting his expression as he ran options through his head. Griffith could guess what Amanow was thinking. Amanow considered him a dead man. It was only a question of whether to act before or after the mission.

As he watched the captain cycle through his options, he realized the man was not such a bad strategist. He must have worked out something with the Protector ahead of their last call. The damned Central Asian faction was planning to fill all the posts with their kind. The Protector and Amanow were about to rid themselves of Griffith, the last of the true bluebloods. If that happened, the Board—made up of good clean British and American men—would be powerless. Amanow and his Turkmen would run a global cabal untethered to the true ideology.

Only his meeting with Sabel had saved Griffith. The Protector changed their original plan and forced Amanow to get what he needed: Griffith to deliver the Stone. Then they would kill him.

It was so diabolically treacherous he had to admire it.

Nonetheless, it left him facing the most dangerous man he'd ever known. A cold-blooded killer. He knew only one way to stay alive with psychopaths. Sun Tzu said it best, *Build your opponent a golden bridge to retreat across.*

"Before we go any further," Griffith said, "I should apologize. I've treated you badly. I've been unkind. Your feat of strength in the jungle was unbelievable. I apologize for not recognizing it and showing my appreciation earlier. With so many things going on, it did not sink in until you reminded me of it. You really ran twenty-seven miles—and then ran back?"

The Knight leaned into the camera. "Yours may indeed be a more elegant method. Perhaps. Tell me about it."

CHAPTER 41

PIA SAT IN THE G-WAGON'S back seat watching the left side as they drove down the narrow street. Miguel sat in the passenger seat, watching the right. The driver, a Sabel Security employee from the Munich office, spouted tourist facts like a proud Bavarian. The cities of Garmisch and Partenkirchen had been combined for the 1936 Winter Olympics. Neuschwanstein Castle, only fifteen miles across the Alps as the crow flies but an hour's drive, had inspired Sleeping Beauty's Castle at Disneyland. Pia's hotel, the Schloss-Emlau Resort, hosted the 2015 G7 Summit but the Schneefernerhaus environmental station high on Zugspitze, the highest peak in Germany, had been deemed more on-message and offered better photo-op views for the G20 meeting.

Pia didn't tell him to be quiet, which she thought demonstrated remarkable patience. For a moment she found herself distracted by the early-morning scenery. Massive peaks surrounded the alpine town in every direction. Unmistakable among them was the gray slab of rock that formed Zugspitze and its sister peak, Alpspitze. Snow covered the forests and slopes from the base halfway up. The rest alternated between ice, snow, and rock depending on how vertical the surface. A wisp of cloud streamed from the ridge in an otherwise bright and clear sky.

"Why are we looking for the Chinese lady?" her driver asked. Except that the Ws sounded like Vs. "Vy are vee …"

"I owe her an apology," Pia said. She noticed him observing her in the mirror. "I was rude to her."

He returned his gaze to the road.

Pia considered Peng's masterful tactics. Pia had delayed her departure from the hotel specifically to sit with Peng on Sabel Two, departing

Belize half an hour behind Sabel One. When Peng noticed Pia's machinations, the old woman made sure to get on the first jet out of town. Why would she avoid Pia? Was she trying to build Pia's guilt? Was she trying to get rid of Pia? Her comment about wealthy people looking out for each other's interests was true for most ultra-rich, but not Pia. Or was it?

Miguel tapped his window, pointing at two men walking down a pedestrian lane. "Is that Dhanpal?"

"Definitely," she said. "The man he's with has one of those green tattoos. What is he doing?"

"Not undercover work," Miguel said. "He turned off his phone, we haven't been able to track him."

Pia turned to the driver. "What's down there?"

"*Einkaufszentrum*, ehm, open mall?" He shrugged. "Cafés, shops, ski gear."

"Cherry said Rafael took her for coffee at Der Laden, right?" Pia thought out loud. "That should be several blocks up the road."

"Der Laden?" the driver asked. "They don't open until nine. Two hours."

Miguel glanced back at Pia. They both sensed trouble.

Pia said, "Could you drop us off?"

In the heavy traffic of delivery vans, the driver took them around to the other end of the pedestrian mall and stopped. They hopped out and consulted a map for cafés.

While huddled, they spotted two more men with the green tattoos on their wrists. They walked purposely in the direction of the first two they'd seen. Wordlessly, Miguel took the far side of the broad cobblestone lane while Pia followed directly behind the Knights.

Miguel kept pace a few yards back, out of the Turkmen's peripheral vision. Pia scanned the area ahead of them. She didn't see Dhanpal and the other Knight coming toward them as she expected. Several courtyards and small alleys were set back from the central area. The men she followed angled toward an alley on the left. She caught Miguel's eye and nodded for him to overshoot her turn, then come back.

She followed the Knights into a short, bricked alley with an apothecary on the corner and a small café kiosk at the end. It was just opening for business. There were four customers: Peng, Rafael, Dhanpal, and the Knight she'd spotted earlier. Still twenty yards away and closing briskly, Pia couldn't hear their words but could sense an unpleasant confrontation.

Gu Peng raised her walking stick and shook it at Dhanpal's companion, her long gray braid swinging behind her. The Knight smiled, his Stalinesque walrus mustache spreading wide. Dhanpal flanked the old woman while the two Pia had followed picked up their pace. Pia sped up as well, catching up with them quickly.

Her many years on the soccer field taught Pia moves that came in handy when up against four men. She hooked her left foot around the ankle of a man on her left, sending him sprawling to the ground before the man on her right realized they were under attack. Twisting her core back to the right, she slammed her forearm into his neck. While she'd aimed for his head, the neck-blow choked his air supply. Close enough. Combined with the shock, both men were out of commission for the five seconds it took Miguel to weigh in behind her.

Pia used those seconds to slam the heel of her right hand into the lower jawbone of walrus-stache. He was already turning away from the expected punch, which sent her blow glancing off to the side, overextending her arm. She spun on her left heel hoping to use his avoidance maneuver to climb his back, but before she could complete the turn, Dhanpal clamped one of her biceps in his strong grip. An instant later, he had the other.

All her hopes that Dhanpal had infiltrated the Knights on her behalf evaporated when she felt the strength of his grip.

Behind them, what sounded like two coconut shells clapping together echoed in the narrow alley. Walrus-stache turned to see Miguel's six-foot-five-inch frame, holding his two comrades by the neck. Miguel banged their heads together a second time for dramatic effect, then dropped their limp forms to the ground.

Walrus-stache turned back to Pia, throwing a haymaker straight at her face. Held fast by Dhanpal, she pushed backward, forcing him to lean back. She pulled up her feet, planted both in the Knight's belly, and kicked off. He fell back two steps as his punch touched the tip of her nose. Pia dropped her feet to the ground and bent at the waist. Dhanpal ended up on top of her back. She flipped him all the way over, slamming him on the pavement where Miguel stomped a foot in his abdomen with such force the air whooshed out of him.

"Dhanpal!" Pia pulled his shirt.

His mouth opened and closed to speak, but her former employee couldn't talk after Miguel knocked the wind out of him. His eyes flamed with hate and anger.

At the mouth of the alley, the two head-bangers dragged themselves to their feet and fled around the corner.

Walrus-stache popped to his feet, a gleaming silver stiletto in his hand. He slashed at Miguel, holding the big guy at bay for the moment. He reached down, yanked Dhanpal by the collar, brought him to his feet, and the two sprinted for the exit.

"Are you all right?" Pia asked Peng.

"I very all right." The old woman smiled and reached up to cup Pia's cheek. "You act. First step, but good step."

Pia looked at Rafael. She thought he looked distraught. At first, she believed it was because professors rarely see such violence. Then she considered his time as a revolutionary. Perhaps the outburst had triggered long-buried memories. Under her observant eye, he gave her a nod devoid of any emotion.

Pia asked, "Are you OK?"

"Quite," he said. His voice wavered ever so slightly, as if he were lying.

Pia looked deep into his eyes. They were cold, emotionless. Most people's eyes are dilated, the lids wide open for many minutes after a violent confrontation. The human body opens its senses to take in all signs of danger. Rafael showed no concern about the violence, yet some concern about Pia's presence.

"You know in heart what need doing." Peng accepted a cup of tea from the kiosk's serving window. "Brotherhood of Claritas need women like Pia Sabel. Claritas mean brightness of mind. Claritas mean clarity. Like sunny day." She looked to the sky as Rafael took his coffee.

"Clarity hard for some people. Sometime what need be done very hard to do. Claritas mean knowing like sunny day how and when to act."

Pia sensed someone's presence nearby. At the end of the alley stood Cherry.

CHAPTER 42

WHAT STRUCK ME WAS THE scale of the place. The mountains were huge, angular blades of rock rising from the valley floor. Not soft and round like the Appalachians, not big distant blobs like Colorado, not dusty rock piles like Afghanistan. These were sharp, nasty, jagged peaks filed under "dangerous" in the dictionary. They looked like serrated knives thrust out of the underworld by Vulcan himself. I felt like I was falling to my death just looking at them.

Mercury floated down onto my suite's balcony. *Quit being such a drama-queen, bro. My boy Julius took Octodurus from the Veragri to secure the Great Saint Bernard Pass not too far from here. You can do this.*

I said, *Julius Caesar sent his soldiers home after the battle because it was too cold.*

Mercury said, *Yeah, but he won. Don't worry, if you win—and give thanks and praise to yours truly—I'll see to it that Pia-Caesar-Sabel takes you back to that resort in Belize so you can get a hot stone massage. Did ya notice how everyone else got one? Now quit yer whining and make your battle plan. You gotta find Mr. Baldy.*

I said, *I'm up against a well-trained, professional force and all I've got is Boy Wonder and the Misfits.*

Mercury said, *It's a poor craftsman who blames his tools, homie. Talk to the man. Have a meeting of the minds.*

I went back inside the suite where Danny, Fiona, Mark, and the guy whose name I still didn't know pored over a giant map of the region with Jenny. Next to the map was a portable whiteboard, currently blank. The map showed ski slopes everywhere. There were plenty of *seilbahns,* cable cars with big gondolas. Not to mention a cogwheel train that ran through a tunnel carved into solid rock. One cable car came from the Austrian side and a bigger one came from the German side, meeting at Munich's Haus, an observation deck, mountain lodge, and restaurant at the top. In the complex was a restaurant called Panorama 2962, the numbers referring to meters above sea level. Some of the G20 meetings would be held there. Across the ridge was the Schneefernerhaus Environmental Station where the presidents and prime ministers would meet. I looked up Schneefernerhaus on a translation site. It means, *snow distant house.*

"What do you expect the Knights to do?" I asked Danny.

His face twisted in thought. "They want to destroy democracy and return the world to despotism reminiscent of the Roman Empire. That means, they want the leaders of the remaining democracies to hold the Freedom Stone."

I looked at Jenny. She didn't get it either. I asked him, "I was thinking more tactically, but as long as you're at it, how does that work?"

"The legend says the holder flips personality-polarity," Danny said. "An autocrat becomes benevolent, as you saw with Carlotta. Conversely, an elected official becomes a despot."

"How do you know what happened to Carlotta?" I asked.

"Someone told me." Danny shrugged and pursed his lips. "Fiona, maybe?"

That either of them would have detailed knowledge of a scene they didn't witness struck me as odd, but I couldn't figure out why.

"There are eleven elected officials coming to the conference," Jenny said. "They think they can get all of them to touch the Stone?"

"Theirs is a long game," he said. "They will infect as many as possible. One, two, maybe five? Whatever works. They have other methods as well. They're the ones who create all the conspiracy theories that destabilize democracies. They're behind the disinformation campaigns that—"

"Those have been going on for years," I said.

"The Knights have been around for centuries. They persecuted people for witchcraft in Scotland in the fifteenth century. Among them, the Earl of Mar, brother of King James III, because he advocated for an end to feudalism and the introduction of a democratic system. They supported Franco and Mussolini. They support several well-known politicians today."

And I guessed they had supported Stilicho in his last-ditch attempt to stabilize the Roman Empire. I glanced at Mercury, who also referred to it as the Poison Stone. My lonely idol shrugged. He preferred plutocracies because it only takes one rich guy to believe in him and a whole cult of millions will follow along—he hopes. Which made me wonder why he was helping me with the Free China group. He had to have an ulterior motive.

Snap. I knew his motive. He wants me to be the rich guy who makes the Roman Pantheon popular. He smiled and touched his nose then pointed at me.

Jenny and I took a minute to process Danny's historical perspective. I'd always thought witch hunts were a handy way to steal money, land, and power from people you didn't like.

"OK," I said. "We want to stop them from doing that. So where is Mr. Baldy? How would he stage this? Since the meeting place is on the tallest piece of limestone in Germany, how would he drag in a hundred-pound magic stone? He would have to bring it in ahead of time. Security would never let him carry it in."

"Why not?" Danny asked.

"Anything that might be a bomb is assumed to be a bomb," Jenny said.

"Then he can't hide it in Munich Haus or Schneefernerhaus," Danny said, "because if security found it, they would cart it away."

"Geology display?" Fiona offered.

"Air drop, by drone maybe?" Jenny said

I wrote those down on the whiteboard and added, "Handoff."

Jenny said, "How would they hand it off? And to whom?"

"A security guard. We have to assume they've infiltrated one or more security forces. A guard could hand it off to whoever will present it to a leader. Still, where is the guard going to get it? He won't be allowed to bring it to work with him."

We stared at the map in silence, each of us visualizing the area, the approaches, and the buildings.

Then Danny said something very smart, which surprised me. "The lifts open in an hour. Security sweeps will close everything later today. We have three hours to figure this out. Let's scour the town first, then the facilities before they close at noon. I'll get the Brothers on this."

Jenny patted his shoulder. "I have a good feeling about this. We can figure it out."

"Where they stage the Stone is one thing," I said. "I want Mr. Baldy. We have to find his command post."

"Why?" Jenny's voice shook with worry. "You're not going to kill him."

"If the situation comes up—"

"You're not on a battlefield here. It would be wrong. And, the Germans won't give you a pass, Jacob. If we find him, we bring him in alive."

Jenny and I had two different views about killing people. I'd killed quite a few men while in uniform, and a few more in self-defense. Jenny had killed one man. A naval officer raped her, got off on a technicality, and came back for a second round. During the struggle, she stuck a pistol in his eye and pulled the trigger. She went to jail for manslaughter before getting a pardon. She only saw the downside of killing a guy. I only saw the upside. Hidalgo's next of kin would give me a medal. This was one area where the yangs outweighed the yins. Or whatever.

But she had a point: the Germans aren't keen on murder. They'd gone to great lengths to atone for their national complicity in the Holocaust. Despite having one of the highest gun-ownership rates, Germany ranks near the bottom of the world's nations in homicides per capita due to strict licensing requirements. They would drag any self-defense story I might offer through a lot of psych evals. And those usually brought up Mercury and his divine guidance. German officials might not take kindly to alternate religious theories. They'd done well after Luther and pretty much left it at that.

But Jenny's comment did cause me to recalibrate what I intended to do with Mr. Baldy. I decided I would kill him outright and not tell Jenny.

Problem solved.

"Promise me you'll bring him to justice," she said after reading my mind.

"If the situation allows, I'll bring him in."

Jenny looked at Danny for support.

"The Knights are protected around the world," Danny said. "If you have the chance, kill him."

CHAPTER 43

WHAT SHOULD'VE BEEN A PLEASANT stroll through Alpine villages to hunt down Mr. Baldy became an opportunity to improve my listening skills. My fiancé had new ideas forming in her head and she let them spill out of her mouth as soon as they came to her. There was something she didn't like about Danny's answer. She used phrases with words like *immoral* and *illegal* and *wrong*, plus a whole bunch of other words that mean nothing to me. Even after he explained that the Knights slipped through the justice system in every country because they had allies all over the world, she still didn't like killing a man without a trial. It didn't align with her understanding of the "light" of Claritas.

Her thoughts were lost on me. As far as I was concerned, Danny had uttered his first sensible sentence since I met him.

We walked by an alley where Ms. Sabel was deep in conversation with Peng, Rafael, and Cherry. Miguel caught my eye and gave me a nod that said: They have issues to work out. There was a little blood on the cobblestones, as if someone had run from there with a bloody nose. I kept walking.

Miguel texted me about their encounter with Dhanpal and three Knights. We'd lost our former brother-in-arms to the dark side. What I found most interesting was the man who threatened Ms. Sabel and Miguel with a switchblade. It meant the Knights weren't carrying firearms. Considering they'd executed people in Mexico, there had to be a good reason for them to observe local laws. The heightened security in advance of the G20 Summit would stop most people from carrying even if they were licensed. The Knights just didn't seem like the types to worry about it. That they did now told me they were close to their goal and didn't want anything to go wrong.

Which meant I was running out of time.

My eyes took in every shop and café. The houses and cars, the traffic patterns, the street alignments, the icy spots in the shade, the salted sidewalks, the muddy places where grass would grow in a few weeks. We walked the two-mile length of the town. Nothing shouted, *Knights of Mithras!*

Finally, one shop did catch my eye. Outside the front door was a life-sized sculpture of a woman reading a book to a child on a sofa. Something about it struck me as out of place. Garmisch was a ski town, not Santa Fe. The artwork stood out as unusual. But I wasn't looking for art, I was looking for Turkmen. We kept going.

I checked in with Danny. He and the Brothers came to the same conclusion. His people were combing the hundreds of hotels and resorts. They moved on down the valley to check more hotels big and small.

Jenny and I caught an Uber to the next town over, Untergrainau. From there, we drove toward Eibsee, a lake where the road ended. Along the way, I noticed many tracks running into the woods off the road. When I asked the driver where they went, he said they were forest service roads and campsites. We came to the Eibsee Seilbahn station, where the biggest gondolas in the region rose up the mountain. The cables swayed in a light wind and disappeared in the distance. The peak loomed high above us.

The lift was just warming up. While it wasn't open yet, Jenny used her German to talk our way into a ride with the work crews. The lift manager said he would allow it if the security team approved.

A security officer waved us over and asked Jenny a series of questions. I didn't need to speak German to know he was suspicious of our request. We willingly emptied our pockets, having wisely left all weapons at the hotel. The gondola full of workers left without us. We promised the man we would wait for the next one. While he wanded us with a metal detector, a large van dropped six important-looking security officers at the entrance. They wore different uniforms, each person from a different country.

One man looked familiar. Plump and middle aged with a gray

mustache, the man stared across the lobby at me. When I remembered him, I wanted to run. My nemesis in Paris, Major Pavard. He almost convinced the entire country I was a terrorist bent on mass murder. He managed to poison my reputation with European police departments across the continent before I managed to save a few thousand lives and redeem myself. Not the guy I wanted to run into at that moment. I was just about to tell the security man to forget it, we were leaving, when the Frenchman shouted my name.

"Jacob! *Ah, la vache!*" He waved and grinned. He tapped the man next to him and said something in German that spread the smile to the whole group. They waved me over.

"What does *la vache* mean?" I asked Jenny in a whisper.

"It's French for holy cow," she said. "He told the other guys you're the Hero of Paris."

The security guard stopped wanding us and gestured to the VIP crowd. He also had a big smile as if I were someone important.

As we crossed the lobby, Mercury showed up in his formal toga, full-length with red trim. *Do I treat you right or what, homie? See now, you be the toast of the town.*

I said, *That's Major Pavard, right? The guy who wanted me drawn and quartered?*

Mercury said, *That was before the Holy Public Relations team from the Dii Consentes descended from on high and talked the President of France into giving you his biggest medal.*

I said, *That was you? Not Sabel Security's public relations team?*

Mercury grinned from ear to ear and said, *They were divinely inspired, brutha. Drink it up. They love you. Now tell them all about me.*

Major Pavard stuck out a paw as if we were the oldest friends. In a thin accent, he said, "The President will be most pleased to hear you are with us."

He spoke English, which was a refreshing change from our last encounter when he barked accusations at me in French. His transformation was complete.

Another familiar face stepped from Pavard's shadow: Chief Dalsgaard from Denmark, now in charge of security for European Union officials. Dalsgaard was the one who turned back the tide of public opinion against me. I was genuinely glad to see him. The two of them shook my hand and introduced me to the group. They deferred to the German head of security, Luca Brandt.

Then the selfies started. Everyone wanted a picture with the one-time celebrity. One day they want to throw you in jail, the next day they want to show their friends that you're besties. They were headed to the top for a pre-lockdown tour and took us with them. As soon as the phones went back in their pockets, Jenny and I were old news. When we got on the gondola, they returned to their security conversation, pointing at things, and bragging about what their teams had done.

Considering I've jumped out of airplanes from forty thousand feet, killed terrorists with my bare hands, and defused bombs relying on the protection of a mythical god, I find it surprising that ski lifts give me the willies. Maybe it's crossing above the wicked spiky rocks waiting to impale me, maybe it's the gentle swaying that sometimes becomes rocking, or maybe it's the tiny metal connectors that keep the immense gondola slung below thin strands of wire that makes me sick. Or maybe I'm a control freak who would rather guide my chute and live or die by my own calculations than trust my life to a beer-swilling German engineer I've never met.

Jenny was quite the opposite. She looped her arms through the elbows of Luca Brandt and Chief Dalsgaard and together they started rocking the gondola from side to side. They laughed and hip-checked each other. The kind of risky behavior you'd expect from drunken teenagers. Pavard noticed me turning green and laughed. I gripped the rail next to the exit until the damn thing quit moving. I was the first one off.

It was cold. Bitter cold. The platform was an open area sheltered by glass, yet it was still freezing. Gusts of frozen air swirled up from the cliff below and surrounded us. I had on jeans and a leather jacket over a t-shirt that read, "I'm the terrorist's retirement plan" above a 75th Rangers logo. Pavard, Dalsgaard and their buddies glanced at me. I sucked in a deep breath, smiled, and imagined I was still in hot and humid Belize. The others zipped up their parkas and hustled inside. I stretched and admired the view, knowing they could see me through the glass. I'd rather freeze to death than let them think I had any other vulnerabilities.

Thankfully, Jenny wasn't into macho games. She shivered and tugged me indoors before my chattering teeth gave me away.

Pavard met us inside and declared, loud enough for his counterparts to hear, that the security arrangements were first class. He clapped my shoulder and said, "Luckily, we will not need the heroic services of Monsieur Stearne."

He laughed. His pals laughed. Except Dalsgaard. The Dane didn't speak English but instinctively knew Pavard was tempting fate.

I considered telling them about the Knights of Mithras. The upside would be having extra eyes and ears looking for them. The downside would be explaining it to them. An ancient order of fascists with a mythic hunk of obsidian planned to make their elected leaders go crazy. They'd laugh at me all the way to the insane asylum.

I could tell them about Mr. Baldy. Except that I hadn't found him and couldn't be sure the perpetrator of the Yucatán executions was here.

I laughed and smiled and told Pavard nothing could make me rest easier than knowing he was on the job.

Then I turned to the geology exhibit. There were no samples. Everything was written in three languages with arrows pointing to impressionist renderings of geologic events.

Jenny and I went outside to the observation deck for another round of freezing. The German side of the mountain formed a large bowl over a mile wide with a glacier filling the center. Half a mile away, a restaurant was perched at the top of the glacier, which the clever Germans named *Gletscherrestaurant*. Meaning, glacier restaurant. A gondola ran to it from where we stood.

Just above the glacier, the Schneefernerhaus had been bolted to the side of a cliff. There were no gondolas or lifts. Dalsgaard wandered outside for the view and Jenny asked him how the dignitaries planned to get there since walking would require crampons and possibly ropes. He told her they would take the cogwheel train to the restaurant, where snowcats would take them the rest of the way. He assured her security would keep them safe.

The Austrian side was vertical from the cantilevered deck I stood on straight down several thousand feet. The mountain terrain was so steep on their side, they kept the ski runs at the bottom. A razor-sharp ridge separated the two countries and shielded the Austrians from the morning sun. A smaller cable car came up from an Austrian town called Obermoos.

Again, Jenny dragged me inside before we both froze.

We took the gondola to the Gletscherrestaurant and checked out Schneefernerhaus as we passed near it. The Germans had already closed off the scenic science center with armed police. Snowcats were lined up, their engine compartments taped closed for safety.

Having been involved in the security arrangements for generals in a war zone, I couldn't see any detail Brandt's team had left to chance. At the same time, Mr. Baldy wasn't the kind to come without a foolproof plan. He had an angle the top security guys hadn't predicted.

"How is he getting a forty-pound rock through security and up the side of a cliff?" I asked rhetorically.

Jenny said, "You don't like my drone-drop idea?"

"Not if the weather holds. With air this clear, they could never land it unnoticed."

We checked out the restaurant and facilities. Cops roamed everywhere. They were tightening the security noose. We decided to take the cogwheel train back. We waded through a crowd of workers and police exiting the train on their way to work.

Among the people getting off was a guy who bore a striking resemblance to Joseph Stalin, walrus moustache and all. I turned to Jenny's ear as if telling her a secret as we passed him. He didn't see me. But I saw the emblem on his uniform. The word *Bundesnachrichtendienst* circled the German black eagle. The BND, Germany's version of the FBI. The Knights were here—and they were in deep.

Still, even as a federal agent, he wouldn't be allowed to bring a foreign object to the conference. Security men weren't allowed to bring anything that wasn't directly required for their job.

We got on the train. A few minutes later, the doors closed, and the train cogged its way down the mountain. I stared out of the window at the rock walls of the tunnel. It went by in a blur.

Then it came to me. Half of it, anyway.

I turned to Jenny, "I know where the Knights are holed up. Give or take a few miles."

CHAPTER 44

CAPTAIN BATYR AMANOW KICKED THE tool chest. In his native language, he shouted, "Our mission culminates tomorrow! Everything we have worked for is now at hand. Now is not the time to rest."

The stone walls echoed his words. His Knights didn't even bother to stand at attention. They trembled like frightened sheep. Their down parkas, boots, and snow pants made their bodies appear larger with smaller faces.

"Which one of you will fill Artur's shoes?" Amanow paced in front of their loose formation. He clapped his gloves together for warmth. "After he failed to retrieve Gu Peng, he reported for duty at the BND. Someone must take over his squad."

He looked at his men. They kept their eyes fixed on the hostage stations behind him. Giant wooden Xs with chains waited for their prisoners. The new man, Dhanpal, began to volunteer, then realized he would not be trusted in an important role. Which was true.

He marched back and forth, unable to sense what was wrong with them. Normally, three or four Knights would gladly take over a prestigious operation like Artur's. Yet they hung back, afraid to speak to him.

His phone rang. He clicked it over to voicemail.

Amanow had gone the extra mile to retrieve Zafar Muhadow. If he needed to conscript a volunteer, Zafar owed his life to Amanow's benevolence. Any other leader of the Knights would've left him to commit suicide for having been caught. Yes, Zafar would do the job.

His phone rang again. Artur. He took the call.

Artur said, "Jacob Stearne just left Gletscherrestaurant on the cogwheel." He clicked off.

Amanow kicked the tool chest again. And again. And again. "What must I do to make Stearne go away? How could he show his face after such a humiliating defeat? Do Americans not revere the Roman creed, *Aut cum scuto aut in scuto?*"

He looked expectantly at his Knights. They knew the Latin phrase, derived from their Roman founders, *either with shield or on it*. Meaning a soldier returned with his shield or his corpse was carried on it. Their eyes remained fixed beyond him.

His strange sensation of something amiss pinched his mind. He observed his men more closely. Only Mammet would look at him, and that was a furtive glance. Amanow tracked back to the young man and stared hard into Mammet's eyes.

"What is it?" he asked in a tightly controlled voice. "You wish to speak. Go ahead."

Amanow stepped back, spreading his hands wide, giving Mammet the floor.

The others turned to their fellow Knight with expectant faces.

"Sir," Mammet said, "the others asked me to speak on their behalf."

Amanow sensed trouble. "Yes, yes, I can see that. Go ahead. Speak."

"We are greatly troubled by your behavior, sir. We do not understand how to follow your orders."

"It is simple." Amanow spread his hands farther apart. "Do what I tell you."

"Yes, sir. And Didar did exactly what you told him. He picked up the Poison Stone."

There it was.

It was good to get things out in the open, Amanow decided. Perhaps he should've addressed it earlier. At least, he now knew why the Knights hesitated. With the right assurances and precautions, he could get them back on track for the remaining thirty hours of the operation. This mission needed to be successful. Not only did the future of mankind depend on it, but his future as well. His only question was how to settle their qualms.

"Command has many options," he said in a confidential tone. "Some options are opportunities. Others are disasters. The difficulty lies in deciding which path to take. We make these decisions and move on. The good decisions always outweigh the lesser decisions. The Protector ordered me to verify the Poison Stone was genuine. And with good reason. Jacob Stearne is a man of many deceptions. He could have replaced it with a fake. We needed to make certain. Didar was chosen for the honor."

The men shifted in place. They seemed unsatisfied. He turned to Mammet and raised his brows.

"Sir," he said, "Didar did as you ordered."

"Ah, yes." Amanow tapped a finger to his lips and marched back down the line. "You are concerned about his resignation. This is the most difficult decision to make as a leader. Do I follow the order to which I have sworn my allegiance and my life? Or do I allow a man to resign after he has sworn to remain a Knight of Mithras until death? There was no decision, really. It was a painful requirement of leadership. Not a required act I took lightly, I assure you. But it was necessary. Didar would have done the same had our roles been reversed. As I am certain all of you would execute your sworn duties without hesitation."

The electric charge in the air reduced a fraction. They were not happy, but they were no longer rebellious. Were they ready for the mission? He looked each of them in the eye before stepping to the next. They met his gaze.

"There is much to do. Mammet, you and Zafar take a squad each and find Jacob Stearne. This is a higher priority than Gu Peng. Stearne can do far more damage than an old lady. Don't mess about—kill him on sight."

CHAPTER 45

"HE DUG A TUNNEL," I said. Danny stared at me like a bird after his first encounter with glass. "He dug a tunnel in the cliff on the Austrian side. It's a sheer wall of rock for two thousand vertical feet. No one in security would expect an assault from that side. They'll watch it, but they aren't looking for a tunnel high on the mountain. I need you to get over to Obermoos and start looking for a mountaineering operation. A team of Knights climbed up with ropes and pitons and picks. They dug through a thousand feet of rock, so they probably started last summer. Ask around at the campsites, the local shops, grocers, places like that. Turkmen would stick out like a sore thumb."

Danny didn't like taking orders from me, especially over a video chat. Our weak alliance was about to break down altogether. I took a deep breath and considered different ways to reach him. I needed his help. Jenny and I had taken the train back to Garmisch, miles away. He was checking hotels near the Austrian border. He was closer and had more people to comb the cliffs.

"It would take months to dig a tunnel like that," Danny said. "You found the Stone two weeks ago."

"The Stone is a bonus to his plan. He's had a plan to bring the G20 countries to their knees for months. We have to stop it."

"They couldn't have an entrance into the building," Danny said. "Security would have it sealed."

"I'm working on finding the other end. It could be covered in snow if they had enough lead time."

"You're right." Mark stepped into the video frame behind him. "We can cover the stores, then find the most likely trails they would've used.

Whatever they excavated from the tunnel will be scattered below."

Danny gave his man a get-out-of-my-video-chat look, then turned back to me. "How will he get the Stone out of the tunnel and into the conference?"

"I don't know yet," I said. "That's the part I'm working on. If we find the tunnel, that will tell us his plan."

"Don't worry," Mark said, "we can find this, Jacob."

Danny added, "Let's make it a race."

I liked his new attitude toward me. Or was it my attitude toward him that had improved?

"You're on," I said and clicked off.

Jenny said, "You balance each other well. Let go of your need for order long enough to let his need for chaos to work for him."

A snarky reply about shoving his chaos where the sun don't shine came to mind, but I shelved it. I wanted this woman to stay with me the rest of my life.

"Do you have a phone number for Pavard?" Jenny asked.

"Until today, I thought he wanted me to die in jail, so … no."

I rented a car. With any luck, we could get back to the lift and catch Pavard on the way down. Maybe he would let us look around up at the top as extra eyes. The rental car company had only one car left, a hotrod Audi RS5. We took it and headed down *Bundesstraße* 23.

Mercury leaned in from the back seat. *There ain't no room back here for adults, homie. You gotta scooch over so I can sit between you.*

I said, *What? No. Why don't you fly along outside and yell through the window?*

Mercury said, *This is a mountain road, bro. Narrow lanes and big trucks comin' atcha like cannonballs. I could get hurt.*

I said, *I thought you were immortal.*

"Funny you should mention it," Jenny said. "I was just going to tell you I feel immortal when I'm near you. You always walk out of deadly situations. It's like you have a guardian angel looking out for you."

I said to Jenny, "Just lucky, that's all. But don't worry, I would never let anything bad happen to you."

She picked my hand off the gearshift and kissed it.

Lucky? Mercury said *What kinda bullshit izzat? She just opened the door for you with that guardian angel thing. All you gotta do now is tell her about your lord and savior: ME!*

I said, *That might be more dangerous than you think.*

Mercury said, *Oh yeah? More dangerous than the guy in the car behind you?*

I glanced in the mirror. An Audi just like mine passed the car behind me and snapped back into our lane. He was gaining on me with an extra twenty miles an hour. The sun glinted off his windshield. I couldn't tell if a Knight was driving or a local. In Germany, even the grandmothers drive like Sebastian Vettel.

The car careened toward me, recovering from his sudden swerving lane change.

I peeked around the semi in front of us by pulling into the oncoming lane. A car zipped by going the other way. He leaned on his horn. Behind me, the Audi closed in fast. A man leaned out of the passenger window. There aren't many scenarios where that's a good thing.

Shoving the gas pedal to the floor, I pulled into the other lane and forced a VW onto the shoulder. Mud flew up from his tires as his blaring horn raged past me. I overtook the semi with *ALDI* written large across a bright and colorful photo of fruits and vegetables. We were about to get squished like a blueberry. Another semi barreled straight for us.

"What the hell are you doing?" Jenny asked.

"Got a message from that guardian angel."

She noticed me checking the rearview mirror and craned around to check it out.

Keeping the pedal down, I snaked in front of the Aldi truck while the Knight behind us was forced back. The stretch in front of us was open for a quarter mile. Ahead of us, ten cars followed another semi. Mountain roads are always blocked by slow trucks.

"Do we have a rifle?" I asked. "A pistol? Anything?"

"You said they'd be a liability with all the security."

"How about a rock? Is there anything you could lob out the window at the car behind us?"

While she searched the empty glove compartment, I passed two of the ten cars. My nemesis caught up at the end of the line. I leapfrogged another car while he got around one. We both overtook another car, keeping two cars between us. Those drivers freaked out and pulled off the road, throwing up dust and dirt. When the Audi slid through, the reason became obvious: the passenger now leaned far out the window with an automatic rifle in his hand.

I downshifted and slid into the oncoming lane. A BMW met me and refused to put two wheels on the shoulder, which left an inch between us. We smacked sideview mirrors with a BANG that made me jump. An A-class Mercedes in my lane slammed on his brakes and pulled over. I flew by him. He caused panic in the lane, slowing my pursuers for the moment.

Jenny pointed to my left and started to say something, then changed her mind and grabbed the dashboard.

I remained focused on passing the remaining four cars and the semi. We shot by two when the lead car, oblivious to me closing in on him at high speed, pulled out to pass. I tapped his bumper, scaring both of us. He picked up the pace, passed the tractor trailer and pulled back in his lane. As I flew by, he tapped his forehead with his index finger, the German gesture for *you're an idiot*.

The holdup gave the Knights a chance to catch me. They were around the clot of traffic and gaining on me. Worse, I realized there were two cars chasing me. A blue Audi like mine and behind him, a white Honda Civic Type R. A Japanese pocket hotrod.

The road ahead was wide open. The engine screamed near redline. I upshifted quickly and maxed out on speed. Our two-lane autobahn swept through a valley, a railroad track on one side with a steep slope down to the river beyond it. On either side, massive mountains. Directly behind me, a man sat on the windowsill of an Audi with a raised rifle aimed at my head. Light puffs of smoke followed the bullets out of the barrel. His first shots went wide, smacking the pavement next to me.

"That was our turn back there," Jenny said. She'd been looking for a good time to tell me.

I couldn't answer. I needed to take out the gunman. I thought of ten ways to do it while more bullets pinged closer to me. He was learning how to compensate for the wind and buffeting. I settled on the quickest method of causing chaos.

I stood on the brakes. The driver had no choice but to do the same. Both our cars stuttered, chirping and burning rubber as the automatic braking system kept us from locking up. The tires stopped and turned fifteen times per second. The steering remained straight. The road did not. As we headed across the oncoming lane and toward a fifty-foot drop to the river, I downshifted and floored it.

When the Knight saw my maneuver, he followed me. He jerked his wheel to the right too quickly, nearly rolling the car before catching it. His slight left twist of the wheel to compensate for the overcorrection threw his passenger onto the pavement, rifle and all. His body rolled at high speed, leaving a smear of skin and bone behind him.

Which made the Knight behind the wheel exponentially angrier.

In the next sweeping left, he gained on me. I had the pedal down and tried downshifting, but the revs were too high. The transmission complained and I lost speed. The Knight tapped my rear bumper.

As I slowed ever so slightly for the next right curve, he dove into the small space between me and the guardrail. The side of his car screeched against the metal rail. I looked to my left. The train tracks. A few pine trees. A small river. Traffic coming the other way. I knew exactly what he planned. Before I could move my foot to the brake pedal, he did it.

He cranked his wheel to the left, shoving his car into mine.

My car careened out of control, crossing oncoming traffic in between two cars. We flew off the side. When we hit the train tracks, the car rolled over sideways. Time slowed down. I became aware of many things at once.

The blue Audi had accomplished his goal of forcing me off the road, but it had cost him the same fate. His car tumbled end-over-end in front of me. His engine compartment crushed into his passenger compartment on the first landing, ensuring his instant death.

The next thing I became aware of was a pine tree that had been snapped into a sharp spear by a lightning bolt. It loomed directly in our path. It stood out of the ground about five feet. We bounced into the air and turned upside down. I heard my fiancé's death-shriek as her fingernails dug deep into the dashboard.

The next thing I became aware of was my used god screaming *YAAAHHHOOOO!* like a twelve-year-old boy on a rollercoaster.

While we flew through the air for an eighth of a second, Mercury said, *Homie, remember that story I told you about Jesus and the stoner in Malibu?*

In a surreal dream, I answered, *Yes.*

Mercury said, *You ain't gonna be an ingrate if I save your ass, are you? None of this whoa-totally-rad shit, right?*

I said, *OK.*

Mercury said, *You're gonna tell Jenny about me, right?*

I said, *Sure.*

Mercury patted my shoulder and said, *Who loves ya, baby?*

If you can save me, I said, *I'll always love you.*

We landed upside down. The spear of pine ripped through the sheet metal roof and through the center console and through the floor—which was now the roof.

Everything stopped. Something creaked once. Then all was silent.

Jenny stopped screaming. Then she started again. Gasping and screaming. Gasping and screaming. Gasping and screaming.

"Jenny, are you hurt?" I called out around the tree stump between our shoulders.

I leaned around the log. My weight was suspended by the seatbelt on one shoulder. She leaned around to meet me.

She said, "I'll always love you, too."

We were silent for another second. Then I said, "You're all right?"

"Not a scratch. You?"

"Shaken, not stirred."

We both looked around at the impossible-to-survive scene.

"Whoa," she said and picked a splinter out of the pine. "Totally rad."

A knuckle rapped on my window. Someone familiar stood upside down. My head translated my position into something I could deal with. That's when I recognized the face.

Zafar Muhadow.

CHAPTER 46

ZAFAR RAPPED THE GLASS AGAIN. This time, the window disintegrated into light blue chunks of safety glass. He dropped to his hands and knees and tilted his head. "You live, Jacob Stearne?"

I was in the awkward position of being upside down, restrained, and unarmed. Not the best way to greet a foe. Yet he had drawn no weapon and made no aggressive moves. "Yes, Zafar. No thanks to you."

"And your lady?"

"Same," Jenny said lightly, as if she were sitting on a swinging bench in a garden.

"I help you," he said and reached for the seatbelt release.

"Uh, that's OK. I'm good here—"

"No. You misunderstand." He reexamined the situation. "I have difficult position. You spare my life. I spare your life. But I fail. Let me get you out. I explain. You see. I need help from you."

Without a good defensive position, I thought it best to let him extract us. Besides, if he'd wanted to finish us off, he could do it without getting me out of the car.

He released the seatbelt. My body weight crunched to the ground on my neck. I wriggled out of the window. Together, we managed to pull Jenny out. Then the three of us stood and stared at the knife of wood sticking out the car's undercarriage.

Zafar slapped my shoulder. "Allah favor you."

"Yeah. Or someone," I said, glancing at Mercury. "Thank you for getting us out."

He pointed down the hill where the blue Audi lay crunched to the size of a beachball. "Mammet not favor by Allah. He have order to kill you on sight. I have same order but not see you first. I try to stop him. I arrive too late."

Jenny looked the man over as if she planned to give him a hug. I'm a good deal more skeptical of battlefield conversions. Too many times I've seen Taliban or ISIS soldiers spin a good yarn and offer up seemingly good intel, only to blow up several good men the minute people relaxed.

Sirens rang down the valley. Travelers stood at the top of the slope, looking down. They called out in German. Jenny replied, directing them to the other car.

"Not much time. Explain quickly now. In Belize, you say my captain kill fifteen people. You say I have problem. You are correct. It get much worse." He pointed at himself. "For Knights, I mean. He kill one of us. Didar. No reason."

"He's a homicidal maniac," I said. The term was lost on Zafar's weak English. "Mr. Baldy likes killing people."

"*Hawa.* Yes." He nodded. "Too much killing. No thinking."

"You need a way out of this mess, Zafar?" I asked.

He looked left and right, then back at me. He nodded slowly. The admission pained him.

It pained me as much. Can you trust a traitor? He could give me the information I sorely needed to track down Mr. Baldy. He could also walk me into a trap that could test my immortality.

"We'll get you out. Don't worry." Jenny stroked Zafar's arm, then looked at me. She added in a definitive tone, "Won't we."

I gave her a look to make her back off.

She returned my expression with one that said we were going to help this stranger. "Jacob, he just saved our lives."

We had a long way to go working out our yins and yangs. Or whatever.

"It appears that way," I said. "And I want to believe him. But this could be a deception. We don't know if—"

"Don't worry," she said to Zafar. "We'll help you. What do you need?"

Zafar held up a hand. "No. Jacob right. Easy trust, easy betray."

Something I'd once heard a terrorist say just before he pulled the pin on a grenade. Were it not for a good friend standing between us, I might've been the one who died that day. Jenny tossed an apologetic glance my way. She stepped back.

"How can you prove your value to me?" I asked.

Two police officers started down the hill. Behind the cops came two more Knights.

Zafar saw the Knights as they picked their way down the steep and rugged hill. One officer stopped, turned to the Knights, and sent them back up the hill. Two EMTs appeared along with more police. The Knights had no choice but to turn back.

"Where is the tunnel?" I asked.

Zafar's jaw worked as he processed my question. It packed a lot of information. That I knew they had a tunnel. That I expected him to give it up as a condition of rescue. On top of that, I was asking him to betray his comrades. A tough ask.

"I show you," he said, "Infrared beacon from entrance. You see it from ground. I use IR strobe on 1PN121 frequency. Shine this afternoon. Maybe this evening. When I get opportunity."

"Thank you for saving us." I clapped his shoulder. "I'll get you out of there. After you show me the tunnel entrance."

He nodded.

The police arrived and started asking questions.

Zafar told them he had witnessed road rage by the blue Audi. He went on, doing his best to exonerate us with the cops. It was an honorable and effective effort.

But I still didn't know if I could trust him.

He'd just given me his promise to give up the tunnel's location by using an invisible infrared beacon, a signal only seen by someone dialed into the right frequency. That could work well. All I needed to do was calibrate my Sabel Visor for the frequency and I would see the tunnel from miles away.

The trouble was: the 1PN121 frequency was unique to Russian SVLK 12.7mm sniper rifles. The most powerful in the world.

CHAPTER 47

GRIFFITH STOOD BEFORE HIS COMPUTER and large screen on its hydraulic stand. He read the intelligence reports on Pia Sabel. His investigators had earned their keep. They'd dug up a damning transaction. He paced his suite at Claridge's in Mayfair, memorizing his talking points for Sabel. With anyone else, he wouldn't worry, but Sabel could be one horrific bitch when rubbed the wrong way. She had been known and feared for her temper in international soccer. And she was quickly earning a similar reputation in business.

A thought occurred to him. He crossed to the keyboard and typed out another bullet point and moved it to the top. She was a winner. Born that way, raised that way, ruthless about it throughout her soccer career.

His video conference app beeped. The Protector summoned him. Griffith glanced at the time. He had only minutes before Sabel's meeting. He checked his look on the monitor before clicking over.

The Protector lay in a bed. A nasal cannula delivered oxygen to his nose. He coughed and wheezed.

"You are shocked, Guardian." The Protector took a deep inhale of oxygen. "My secret will become public in a matter of days. Pancreatic cancer." He took another inhale and coughed and closed his eyes while pain passed.

Griffith realized why the Protector had not taken the lead with Pia Sabel. The cancer had moved too quickly. In his condition, no one would take his threats seriously. Now the old man was grasping for solutions before he died. Which, Griffith realized, could be a good or terrible thing for him.

"My plans must move quickly. The board is restless about Captain

Amanow." Another long pause followed by labored breathing. "He was to be my heir. The papers were drawn up. But the board is concerned." Pause. Breathing. Coughing. Breathing. "They find his unfortunate incident with Hidalgo … unsavory. They do not care for him."

No surprise to Griffith. He could only wonder why a man of the Protector's education hadn't seen it earlier. Mass murder might be standard operating procedure around the Caspian, but not on the world stage.

"All this leaves me," he wheezed, "in a particularly precarious position. You are too weak, unwilling to be brutal when brutality is required. Yet, he will not succeed me. And so, this is a delicate problem."

The old man left the sentence hanging for Griffith to unravel. If he had promised Amanow the position, it would be painful for the Protector to retract it, admitting to everyone he had chosen badly. He looked to Griffith for a way out.

And one came to Griffith in the moment.

"Succession is always a tricky problem," Griffith said. "It was a custom of the Roman cult of Mithras to determine rank by contest. You can easily draw papers to that effect and make the contest tomorrow's event. The loser will suffer the Roman fate for failure: to fall on his sword—or be beaten to death by his men."

The Protector coughed and smiled and coughed again. He closed his eyes for a long time. So long, Griffith began to wonder if he'd died. Then they opened again. "Your confidence … hmm. Well. It will be as you proposed. Good luck."

The screen went blank.

Griffith fell into the nearest chair. What had he just done? He'd played into the Protector's hands. The old man had a beef with the board and Griffith had just given him a way out. He could turn to the others and say, "It was a contest by Roman rules. Amanow won."

The crafty old bastard had just made him sign his own death warrant.

But he could be just as crafty as the Protector. Craftier. He couldn't let a grand society like the Knights fall to these impure Muslims. For the sake of the white world, he had to succeed. It was up to him to find a way through the machinations of the Eurasian imposters.

Pia Sabel was his ticket to taking over. If he could use his leverage to force her to open those doors, the board would see him as the logical choice to replace the dying old man. A smile crept across his face. It was a big "if," but not impossible. Yes, he believed he knew how to make it work. But how long would it take? Sabel would open one door at a time. How long would the Protector live? Months? Weeks? Griffith would have to move quickly. He would have to light a fire under Sabel.

But Sabel was no push-over. Winning her over would be like a woodsman felling a mighty oak. It would take a lot of work. She saw herself as an idol for young women, considered herself perfect in every way. A girl scout selling cookies. His research proved all that a lie. She had a dirty side like everyone else. Would she admit it? Or call him on his threat?

His life depended on making her see things his way in the next half hour.

He flipped the screen back to his notes. He had it down. He was confident of the win.

He looked at his watch. No more time. He grabbed his coat and umbrella, told the hotel's butler to order him a cab to White's Club, and left.

After careful scrutiny by the doorman, he was shown in and taken through the halls, upstairs to the Coffee Room. Sixty feet long and half that across, large windows brought in daylight on three sides. Intricately carved moldings trimmed the wood paneled walls. Portraits of members hung on every panel, the newest being two hundred years old. A few portraits dated to the club's founding in 1693.

Pia Sabel sat in a large leather chair, her back to the corner, a window allowing faint light to fall across her shoulder. Had she not been the only woman in the building, he wouldn't have recognized her. She wore a tasteful, conservative dress one might expect to see on the Queen. Her shoes and purse were made of the same material. A pearl necklace glowed around her neck with a matching barrette and pair of earrings. Her hair was uncharacteristically coiffed into gentle waves. She looked more mature, reasonable, and approachable than when her sinewy muscles flexed under stretchy athletic wear.

A man was seated facing her. When she spotted Griffith approaching, she waved.

The man looked over his shoulder. Well past the hump of middle-age, he had a familiar face. Perhaps someone famous. The man rose and greeted Griffith with a brief smile that was quickly replaced by a suspicious squint. He turned back to Pia and said, "Don't take this the wrong way, but allowing you in was a stretch at best. If we knew you were going to bring more Americans—"

"Joe Griffith, this is James, Duke of … Kent, was it?" She smiled in a way that made the Duke wince. "Thank you for the chat."

"Kingston, ma'am. Duke of Kingston." The Duke tightened his fists, worked his clenched jaw. He said, "Good evening then." He tossed a nasty glare to a large Native American in a chair ten feet away, then turned and walked away.

Pia directed Griffith to the man's empty seat.

Griffith took it. A server appeared at his elbow an instant later and leaned in wordlessly. Griffith looked at the man for a moment, expecting a menu or wine list.

"He'll have a gin and tonic," Pia said. The server disappeared as silently as he'd arrived. "It's the kind of place that makes anything you ask for, even if they have to fly someone to Zanzibar to get it. The only thing they don't tolerate is hesitation."

"My kind of place," Griffith smiled and leaned back.

"You can have it." She lifted her martini as a toast. "I don't expect to last long. They had to take me. At the time of my father's death they owed a stinking pile to Sabel Capital for an ill-advised renovation. They've been renegotiating terms ever since. Fuck 'em."

His gin and tonic settled on a coaster next to him. He raised his glass to her and remembered a quote of hers from her soccer career. "The power players will set the pace."

It earned him a smile. "Joe, in your call you included something about the 'perilous future of civilization.' From what I can see, you're the perilous future. You've bought struggling companies, soaked them with ridiculous fees, overburdened them with debt, taken out credit-default insurance, then forced them into bankruptcy, laying off hundreds of people."

He sipped his drink. It was perfect. He savored it while holding his anger in check. He said, "We've all done terrible things to keep the larger company afloat. Sabel Mortgages floundered out of existence in the Great Recession if I recall correctly. Closing it saved Sabel Industries—and sixty thousand jobs. Your father made a difficult choice, but the right one. Every time I walked away from a business that went sour, I told myself it was for a bigger cause. One I believed in. A business of grander scope that was worth the little sacrifices. Without that, we're lost."

"Your pile of little sacrifices grows every day. If you—"

"Sabel Capital transferred twenty-eight million dollars to a shell company controlled by Mikhail Yeschenko." He regretted snapping it out so loudly. But he relished the shock on her face. It was time to press harder, make her listen. "No regard for US sanctions against a murderous oligarch, Pia? Do the regulators know about that early morning transaction in Luxembourg?"

That shut her up. She might look cool and calm on the surface, but she hadn't moved so much as an eyelash since he blurted out his intel. He knew his men were good. And now she knew it too.

"You do cherish your threats," she said. She picked up her martini and stared at him over the rim, then took a sip. "I came to hear you out. So speak."

"Your soccer career was all about the powerful proving themselves over the weak. The winners moved on in the championship and the losers went home. What was it you once said? 'You can't just beat a team. You have to leave a lasting impression so they never want to see you again.'"

She sat still for a long time, then sipped. "Mia Hamm said that, but I get your point."

"You're a dominating woman, if you don't mind my saying so. You intimidate people and you don't take time to worry about those who can't keep up. I find that fascinating and admirable. You dominated the beautiful game, and now you dominate corporate America. You didn't take on Space X in the field of rockets. It's a crowded industry full of spectacular failures. Instead, you chose to dominate the field without competitors: satellites. Let someone else blow up a rocket. You put your product on top and make them pay for it if they don't deliver. When they fail, you actually make more money. It's brilliant."

"Thank you." Her gray-green eyes remained locked on his.

"You've done the same at Sabel Capital, Sabel Technologies, Security, and all the other companies."

She rolled her hand for him to move on. His research mentioned she didn't care for brown-nosing.

"I am inviting you to join an ancient order. Far older than White's Club. In fact, it traces its heritage to the founding of Ancient Rome." He paused, expecting her to make an inquiry. She gave him nothing. Those gray-green eyes never blinked. "The organization is headed by a man we call the Protector. His connections open international doors. At his suggestion, regulators end inquiries. From his office flow opportunities unbridled by the ever-changing sands that are our elected officials."

She leaned forward. "What's wrong with elected officials?"

"Imagine a business plan that allowed you to make investments without regard for whether the Tea Party or the Socialists were going to win the next election. Imagine how stable your company could be if the goal posts remained in one place."

She squinted. "But the people elect those officials. We simply have to adapt as the rules change."

"In the 1780s, before the US Constitution was written, the states were true democracies. The rabble voted into office whoever would promise to give them everything and take nothing. They taxed the wealthy and redistributed money to the poor. Businesses failed, jobs were lost, the economy was in ruins. That's what forced the Founding Fathers—all white, wealthy landowners—to frame the Constitution. They didn't form a democracy. They formed a plutocracy. And they did it for good reason."

Pia frowned. "That's not right. They—"

"Hear me out," he said. "John Adams warned against the 'tyranny of the majority.' Alexander Hamilton said, 'The people should have as little to do as may be about the Government.' And, having seen the economic carnage around him, George Washington himself said they had allowed for 'too good an opinion of human nature in forming our confederation.' The Founders put in the electoral college and two senators from every state regardless of population to prevent mob rule. The Senate was modeled after Ancient Rome. Only the rich could join. They knew the country could only grow when people like you could invest without having it all torn down every other year."

Her eyes fell to her drink. He was close. He could feel it. He reminded himself to be careful. Don't take too big a bite.

"While the Senate is hardly representative," she said. "I don't see anything wrong with democracy. America has had some bumps along the way, but we've survived and prospered."

"The future is not the past," he said. "With the population growing and the economy expanding, the complexity becomes exponentially more difficult to control. Volatile presidents and the ever-changing face of Congress fail to lead at critical moments. It takes a strong leader and a government under control to make things happen when crises occur. You can't sit around debating wars, pandemics, trade deals. Events move too quickly. In our class, our village of the wealthy, we need to look out for each other. We need to protect each other from the rabble who would tax us into poverty. With an unbridled democracy, that's exactly what will happen."

She swirled her drink and squinted. As best he could tell, she understood that part. She sipped and made no further argument. When she looked up, she had an expectant face, ready to hear more.

"You bear a tremendous responsibility," he said. He enjoyed another taste of his gin and tonic, letting her wait for it. "All those employees expect you to navigate thousands of regulations in hundreds of countries and make it all work. It's a deadly balancing act. At any moment, some politician wielding a 'wealth tax' or a new regulation could knock you over." He relished the drink again. "The Protector is building a network of like-minded power-players who set the pace in business as you once set it on the field."

He leaned back and waited for her to say something. To her credit, she thought it over before she spoke.

"I open plenty of doors on my own." She sipped and inhaled. "What power are you referring to?"

"You've opened doors with money. Real power isn't something you buy. It radiates from one person to another. When the President of the European Union gives you a medal, all of Europe bows to you, and Airbus buys jet engines from Sabel. When the President of China introduces you to his finance minister, Sabel Capital is the power player. These are the doors the Protector can open."

She pursed her lips and stared him down. "That's all very nice, but what specifically are you talking about?"

"That little deal with Yeschenko? The inspectors can be called off by breakfast tomorrow. Or they can raise red flags in Washington. That little problem of Sabel Technologies' spyware on the Italian Prime Minister's phone? Apology accepted by lunch. Or—a complaint filed with the Secretary of State. Pia, I can deliver the power you need to vanquish your enemies. I can make them fear your approach in the halls of power the way players once feared you running up the sidelines."

"This is what the Knights of Mithras are all about?" she asked.

Her knowledge surprised him for a moment. It shouldn't have. She had done her research, too. He said, "Ours is a simple cause, we quietly advocate—"

"You're the fucking Salvation Army. Get to the point."

"The Knights can do many things that you need doing. There are requirements for joining and certain fees for operations and introductions. All of which are well worth your while. You will do well to join our village of important people. But initiation is not monetary."

She nodded and tucked her purse close to her body. She tightened her ankles beneath the chair, leaned forward, and said, "What do you want?"

"Well." He sipped his drink and cherished her anxious expression. In the end, he'd felled her like a young sapling. "How can you prove your value to me?"

CHAPTER 48

IT WAS DUSK BY THE time we joined Danny and the Brotherhood of Claritas on a trail high above Obermoos, Austria. After we got free of the Polizei, a feeling of imminent victory crept through me. I could sense Mr. Baldy within my grasp. I had no reason to trust Zafar, but I felt good about him anyway. He felt real. And that could lead me to bring the dangerous bastard to justice before he killed a world leader.

The Stone was one thing, but when Zafar confirmed the tunnel's existence, I figured Mr. Baldy had a plan to kill a VIP—if not several. I didn't know how his concept worked, but one didn't dig a tunnel months in advance without a plan for going big.

I laid out the four ice-climbing kits I'd scrounged up in Garmisch. The Brothers had done an excellent job of canvassing a mile of cliff face for the tunnel debris. What they learned from hiking all afternoon was that the Knights had done a good job of hiding the tunnel. They didn't just dump dirt and rock out from the top. They carried it down and scattered it.

To their credit, the Brothers plotted out the extent of the Knights' tracks along the mountainside and narrowed the possibilities to a cliff on the north side of the ridge leading from the peak down to a thousand-foot rock wall. That made searching for Zafar's signal marginally easier.

So far no one had seen his signal. Which allowed me to relax a little. The possibility of Zafar setting me up for a sniper's bullet was no big deal if it was me holding the IR-reading binocs. But all afternoon the watch had been manned by several of the bright-faced kids in the Brotherhood. They'd put their faith in a couple old Kevlar helmets they owned. I hadn't worked up the courage to tell them it wouldn't even slow a round from the Russian SVLK-14. We were set up a mile from the tunnel's probable entrance—only half the rifle's range.

The Brothers scarfed down the takeout Jenny brought for them. She was thoughtful like that. I figured we could all go hungry until I killed Mr. Baldy at point-blank range. That would work up my appetite. But her mothering instinct won out and the Brothers were happy about it. I took my vegetarian sandwich. Jenny assured me it was good for my digestion on a mission like this. I walked off to take the lonely watch for Zafar.

I trained my binoculars on the wall above us from behind a large rock outcropping. A thousand vertical feet of rock covered in patches of ice faced me. The climb would be a serious technical climb. I had training. The Rangers didn't consider you ready for war until you could climb Everest, dive the Mariana Trench, and walk the Sahara without water. While Danny assured me that he, Fiona, and Mark were rated for AI7 climbs—the most dangerous rating for Alpine ice with overhangs—he never mentioned M13. M for mixed ice and rock. The climb would require transitions from two different disciplines, not to mention double the equipment. Ice and mountaineering axes are different beasts. Same for pitons and ice screws. It was going to be ugly.

Mercury slid in next to me, his back against the rock. *This is gonna be special, homie. Ima bet on you to die here at the rock. Bullet goes right through your forehead, through your brainpan, out the back, and three feet into the dirt behind you.*

Bored gods have a bad habit of wagering on the outcome of mortal lives. Not a lot to do after your believers wander off.

I said, *Thanks for the warning. So, you're telling me Zafar is setting me up?*

Mercury said, *Guess I shouldna mentioned that part, huh. Well, in that case, Ima bet on you dying on the cliff, bro.*

I said, *Why all the hostility? Is something bothering you? Are the other gods being mean to you again?*

Don't patronize me now. He worked kinks out of his neck and shoulders. *It's not cuz Saturn's laughing like a hyena. Remember when you were upside down, suspended between heaven and hell and I asked you if you'd tell Jenny about me?*

I said, *Uh. Yeah.*

Mercury said, *And do you remember what you said?*

I might've committed to telling her, yeah, I said. *I'm getting around to it. I'm gonna ... when I'm ready.*

"Well, now's a good time because it's cold," Fiona said. She was suddenly sitting where Mercury had been an instant earlier. "You can eat it whenever you want. It's just that the ants are coming for it."

I looked at my sandwich, half-eaten on a wrapper lying between us in the dark. Fiona took the binocs out of my hands while I picked up the food. I wasn't worried about the ants. I doubted they liked rubbery tofu either. I picked out a slice of avocado and wondered if the spinning wheel of yin and yang ever landed on steak.

"Ever wonder how the Knights knew which road you were on this morning?" Fiona offered.

"Blanket surveillance, spotters in a church steeple, bribed store owners, spyware on someone's phone."

"Or an insider," she said. "You walked right past Cherry and Rafael this morning."

People offering extraordinary statements without evidence puts me off. At the same time, any good cop will tell you the best clues drop out of nowhere. I kept an open but suspicious mind.

"Back in El Remate," I said, "you told Danny to be on the winning side. What did you mean by that?"

"I don't remember saying that," she spluttered. "Might have been encouraging him."

"You like tofu?" I traded the binocs for the sandwich.

She looked at the sandwich like it was a snake. "I had the bratwurst."

I fought back a tinge of jealousy. "Why Cherry? Is the Brotherhood only big enough for one beautiful woman? Or do you have—"

That's when it flashed. Zafar's IR beam. Dead in front of me.

I marked it on my visor's mapping software and measured vertical distance to the base. Eight hundred feet up a seam littered with frozen streams and dry rock ledges. Of course they put the entrance in the most inaccessible crevice on the mountain. When I trained the binocs on the opening, I could see Zafar himself. He looked at me through the scope of a wicked looking SVLK-14 Sumrak, the current record-holding rifle for distance. It was set up in a defensive position. The Knights intended to defend the tunnel with deadly force.

Zafar waved.

At the risk of giving myself away, I waved back. Zafar looked happy for a second, then moved back from the entrance into the dark.

It was time to make the final decision: Was it a trap?

He had a rifle that could've killed me before I knew he was there, yet he hadn't fired. That was as close as I could get to confirmation of his good intentions.

I ran back down the hill, Fiona on my heels, deeper into the trees where the others sat around a fire. The Brothers stood when I entered the circle. Their eager faces filled with anxiety as the upcoming fight became as real as road rash. As Mike Tyson famously said, "Everybody has a plan until they get punched in the mouth." The realization that they were going up a dangerous ice-covered cliff at night into the camp of a heavily armed enemy was that punch in the mouth.

CHAPTER 49

ONLY FOUR OF US WERE rated for ice climbing, Mark, Danny, Fiona, and me. Jenny and the others would wait until we could tell them more about where the tunnel came out.

We geared up with ice axes, mountaineering axes, crampons, ice screws, pitons, helmets, stiff boots, belts covered in carabiners, and enough dry-coated rope to rig a clipper ship. Our pistols and rifles went on last. The Sabel Visors turned the moonless night into day, which gave the team a measure of confidence.

We staked out four Brothers as shooters to cover our ascent from the base. Danny put the guy whose name I still didn't know in charge. Their HK417s had an effective firing range just short of the distance to the cave. They were at the mercy of the sniper rifle on high ground, yet they committed to their fate with grim determination. I visualized their weapons against the target in my head. They'd have to use their rifles like mortars to get a bullet to land inside the cave, but the attempt might scare off the enemy long enough to help us out. Maybe.

I mapped out our route for Danny, Fiona, and Mark. It was directly below the cave entrance and involved several icy sections. Danny didn't like the idea of climbing ice until I pointed out how much quieter it is than hammering a piton into rock.

We could make out a few carabiners left by the Knights from their previous climbs. They had a much better route technically. It swung wide to the left, using more rock and less ice. My path had a sixty-foot-wide overhang halfway up that could prevent detection and cover us should we need to retreat. But it would be a bitch to climb. Ice hanging from the bottom of a rock has a bad habit of falling off when you bury your axe in it.

We set out hiking over scree made of rocks the size of our feet. Like running up a two-hundred-foot sand dune only with a fifty-pound pack and ten-pound grains of sand beating on your boots. We were warmed up when we reached the base of the cliff. Fiona and Danny did well. Mark looked like our weakest link. They met my observing gaze and turned up their determination.

Our first encounter was a seventy-degree rock slope that we climbed quickly and efficiently. It led us to our first encounter with ice. A seep had formed a crevice which, under different circumstances, would have been a beautiful frozen waterfall of sixty feet. Layer upon layer of ice had formed in the alternating cold and warm of spring. I went first.

My left ice axe went in, followed by my right. I tested my weight, pulled up, and slammed the toe of my boot hard into the ice. I tested my weight before repeating the act with my right foot. Arching my back for leverage, I repeated the maneuver until I stopped and turned in an ice screw. It held our first carabiner and rope. Danny followed, offset a few feet. Then Fiona. Mark brought up the rear.

Despite having comms in our ears, we moved silently. There was nothing to say and every axe swing was critical to survival. We saved our concentration for the task at hand. The others were good climbers, moving only after planting a solid toe in the ice, keeping their heels flat, and not moving their feet the way they would on rock. We finished the ice section and gathered on a slope. I looked them over. No signs of overexertion. We were going at the right pace.

The next rock section was vertical. We pinged in a minimal number of pitons to keep the noise down. There was a seam that ran right up my path most of the way. I reached a six-inch ledge covered in ice and looked for a place to sink an ice screw.

That's when Fiona cried out, "Watch me." The technical term when a climber feels their grip loosening and a fall could be possible. Mark was her belayer. I heard him grunt as he checked his grip on the rope. I looked down. A split second later, she called out, "Falling."

And she did. She fell twenty feet, teabagging Mark as she did. She kept her legs bent like a pro and didn't push off the wall. She twisted as she fell, then slammed into the rock below Mark's position. She quickly said, "I'm good."

Her breathing contradicted her report. Her heart rate had to have gone sky-high because nervousness reverberated through the comm link. I considered sending her home, but that would cut my team in half since there was no way to safely return without belaying each other. I told them to take a minute.

Checking on her made me see the sharp rock and slick ice below us. And far below that, the ground. We were one mistake from dying. I felt my heart rate spike.

Mercury floated in the air next to me. *It's a mind game, homie. Panic is contagious. If you catch it, all y'all fall to your death.*

I said, *Does that mean you bet on me to survive the climb?*

Mercury said, *Most of it, yeah. I gotcha, brutha.*

I said, *You bet on me to make it most of the way?*

Mercury said, *Oh no you don't. I'm not going to let you trick me into telling you the future. I'll tell you this, though: if you get calm right now, you'll get off this mountain alive. If'n you don't, then I gotta take all four of you down the river. You know what I'm saying? So get it together and act like a leader.*

Mercury ferries the dead to the underworld in his spare time. But I got what he was telling me. The difference between living and dying is determined by attitude.

"Mark, did she hit her head?" I asked in the comm link.

"I don't think so."

"This isn't a 'think' situation, Mark." I used my commanding baritone. "Get your head where your partner needs it. She called for you to watch her. Did you?"

"Yes, sir. She fell feet-first. She did not hit her head. Her shoulder hit first, her knees second, then she had her feet out for a solid stop."

"I said I'm fine," Fiona snarled. "Climbing."

We resumed our ascent. Danny and I worked our way forward on the ledge to a sheet of ice fifteen inches thick. We worked our way up that to the underside of the overhang. We assembled beneath it in a place where, a million years ago, a chunk of rock the size of an office building fell away. Under better conditions, it would've been a great picnic spot. No ants.

I started the upside-down climb, stemming my way up a corner to a crack that offered finger grip for the transition. The others watched. If I fell to my death, they would take a different route. If I made it, they would follow using the same holds and moves. I moved across sideways to where the underside of the ledge was shortest.

Everything went by the book until I reached the lip and had to transition from upside-down, to vertical. The only way I could do it was to let my feet and weight swing out below, holding on with nothing more than my fingertips. I made the mistake of looking down. Six hundred feet of open air below me. If I fell, I'd bounce off a nearly vertical incline covered in jagged rock. It would take weeks to recover all the pieces of flesh left behind.

Mercury wouldn't let me die like that. I hoped.

I took my feet off the rock and let my body pendulum out over the deadly drop. I waited until my swinging slowed and my body hung still before making my next move. With a big, one-handed pullup, I managed to get an axe into the ice above and do another pullup. A third and fourth were required before my feet found anything to cling to. To my left, a smooth sheet of ice at a forty-five-degree angle offered a staging area for the last assault on Mr. Baldy's cave. I moved over a bit and secured myself before giving the others the go-ahead.

One by one, they made the perilous journey to join me. Danny refused a hand from me. There was something the size of a cigarette stuck to his helmet. It was barely visible, yet something about it set off alarms in my head. I tried to brush it off, but he turned to pull Fiona up. She took the assist. Mark brought up the rear.

Just as Mark reached the ledge but before he secured his position, Mercury whispered in my ear. *Take a big step to your left and take Danny with you. NOW!*

I heard a thump and a whoosh as I followed my abandoned deity's order. I grabbed Danny's wrist, took as big a step left as I dared, slammed my crampon into the ice, moved without testing my weight, and yanked him with me. He looked surprised, scared, and angry all at the same time. We stood toe-to-toe, three feet to the left of where we'd stood an instant earlier. His expression turned to pure rage.

A falling body hit Danny in the head and knocked him over the edge into the darkness below.

Instinctively, I knew the falling body was the corpse of Zafar Muhadow. It had been thrown from above. I don't know how I knew that other than its human form was unmistakable as it caught Danny at terminal velocity, around 120 mph, and took him over the edge. There was only one Knight likely to be used as a projectile to kill me, Zafar. What didn't register in that split-second as Danny's belay rope flew over the edge, was why or how Danny seemed to know what was happening before I did.

Danny's body slammed hard into the wall below us.

The weight tried to yank me over with him. I held fast to the ice axe in my left hand.

I knew he was dead. A man doesn't survive getting hit with 160 pounds of falling human and survive. I tugged at the rope. Even it had no life left.

That didn't stop Fiona from screaming into the comm link. "Danny! Danny! NO! Danny, say something!"

I let her keep trying for a few seconds, then started pulling him up. Mark reached around Fiona and helped. After ten lengths of rope went by, she grabbed hold and helped.

Danny was dead, all right. The angle of his neck told us as we pulled him into view. His glassy eyes made his condition certain. Mark tied the corpse to a separate ice screw.

"You did this!" Fiona pushed me. "You were supposed to be standing there."

She pushed me again. It took me a couple cycles to process her words as she swung an axe at my head. I caught her hand. She fought against me. Her crampons loosened in the ice. She yanked the axe free and reared back for a deadly, overhand blow. My weight shifted. I grabbed my ice axe, still buried in ice, to stop myself from falling over.

Her backhand momentum, combined with her grief, sent her backpedaling into thin air. She fell.

Mark and I watched as the first piton below the shelf popped out. The rope tensioned to the next safety point. We were watching what climbers call a zipper fall. Fiona's falling weight popped the second at the lip. Her third point popped out as well. None of them had been fully secured. She'd been in a hurry and Mark hadn't noticed her sloppy work. The net result was that Fiona's fall was about to pull him over with her. He planted his feet, hoping to catch her fall, which probably wouldn't work given her momentum and the fact he hadn't secured himself yet.

Suddenly, what Fiona and Danny were up to crystalized in my mind. The cigarette-sized device on his helmet. The fear and anger on his face. Her anger at me for yanking Danny into my position. Danny was Ephialtes, the traitor.

I slammed my razor-sharp crampon into Fiona's rope an inch from Mark's boot, severing it instantly. Her scream echoed all the way down to where she cratered at the bottom.

Mark looked at me like I was a crazed killer.

I held my ice axe to his throat and said, "Were you in on it with them?"

"What?" His eyes were wide as a watch face.

"They signaled the Knights. That falling body was meant for me." I leaned down and pulled the IR transmitter off Danny's helmet. The size of a cigarette, but a known device to most operators.

Mark stared at it for a long time before looking up at me. His shock and disgust appeared believable. But did I trust him enough for the rest of the climb?

He turned to the ledge and threw up.

That gave me the trust I needed. I said, "Mission scrubbed."

CHAPTER 50

Hours later, the Austrians released me with the warning not to leave the area. They were not happy and suspicious of the whole story. No cave entrance could be found at the position I gave them. A helicopter with a bright beam found nothing but rocks on a vertical slope. They let me watch the video feed live. But they agreed to let the Hero of Paris continue consulting with the conference's security teams. The investigation into the climbing disaster would continue immediately after the G20 meetings.

I had to admire Mr. Baldy's thoroughness. He managed to position a rock over his entrance without leaving a trace. Which pissed me off even more. Not only had he slaughtered fifteen academics, he'd also killed Zafar, the only decent Knight I'd met—and I was no closer to stopping him.

Jenny and I drove to the resort in silence, both of us lost in our own thoughts.

Jenny followed two paces behind me when I stormed through the lobby. She had been nice enough to say nothing through the entire ordeal with the authorities. While stomping down the hallway to Peng's suite, it dawned on me why she was so quiet. I stopped in my tracks. She stopped an arm's length behind me.

I faced her. She kept her head down.

I didn't know where to start. I decided to blurt out what was on my mind.

"You were right," I said. "There was something wrong with Danny wanting to kill Mr. Baldy. That kind of thinking fits my line of work, not the Brotherhood of Claritas. He was trying to avoid suspicion and tried too hard. I should've listened to you. You're right, you are my balance."

She fidgeted, her fingers writhing like snakes. "It's OK. It was just a feeling. I didn't have any logic behind it. No one suspected them. You did what you thought—"

"What I think isn't always right," I said. "I should've seen it. In Chicago, he wasn't looking for Cherry, he wanted Griffith. I thought he meant to take the man down, but it was to switch sides. Before we left El Remate, Fiona told him to be on the winning side. When they got caught in Chicago, the first time, they were making contact and offering themselves up. That's why Griffith had so many men on duty later that night. Then, during their 'attack' on the property, Mark got beat up but not Danny. And Danny was taken from the room where you were held for a quick consultation. Later, when we rescued the others, Fiona was being released from the coffin, not being shoved in it like I thought at the time. And Danny knew about Carlotta. Only Mr. Baldy would've known about her because he knew Hidalgo's team was short one benefactor. He told Danny. I should've seen it. After Chicago, nothing he did fit with Gu Peng's whole light and clarity thing."

"I didn't see it either," she said. "I'm also having second thoughts about helping Peng. I think you were right to begin with. This isn't our fight."

"Wait … you were so gung-ho about freeing China."

"Freedom must be won, not given." She met my gaze. "I think that's why all those civilizations died out. The change was forced on them. No one fought for it. The people weren't invested in the change."

Certainly a good point. One I hadn't considered.

"We can deal with that tomorrow," I said. "Just one more thing: you were right about the yin-yang thing. Sometimes an orderly guy needs a little chaos. Or a chaotic guy needs some order. However that works, we make a good team. Your dad's an idiot for undervaluing you. I don't want to make that mistake ever again. Next time I'm not hearing you, tug my ear."

Her gaze swept the carpet. She nodded.

I lifted her chin with my knuckle. She had tears in her eyes. I gave her a hug.

Rafael and Cherry slowed as they approached from the lobby. Jenny and I were hogging the hall space. We broke our embrace.

"We intend to pay our respects to Ms. Gu," Rafael said. "Would you be good enough to join us?"

We turned in unison, falling into pairs by gender. Rafael and I in the lead. It felt odd to pair off after realizing how partnership really works, but Rafael had a way of steering things. I sensed a purpose in his movement.

"We tend to see tragedy from our perspective and not others," he said. "Before you level accusations against Peng, have you considered how painful it must be for her?"

I hadn't considered her at all. I intended to storm in and ask questions about how the people she chose compromised my operation. I intended to blame her for blowing my chance to kill Mr. Baldy. Rafael's point was well taken. Those weren't nice topics for a wake. I stopped just outside her door. Rafael smiled, patted my shoulder, and went around me.

Jenny had been chatting with Cherry but understood what needed to happen next. She gave me a peck on the cheek and said, "I hope you and Pavard find the other end of that tunnel."

She followed Cherry inside. The remaining Brotherhood stood shoulder-to-shoulder in mute grief beyond the foyer.

It was a good division of labor. She did compassion. I took down killers.

Since I'd failed to get through the tunnel on the Austrian side, I still didn't know where it came out. I'd asked Pavard to help me find the German end.

I turned around and walked out to the entrance and caught a cab to the cogwheel train.

I arrived ten minutes before Major Pavard agreed to meet me, so I wandered the shops near the station. An art gallery featured a large sculpture next to its front door. I'd noticed it on my first sweep of the area, but it didn't register that it was a Gu Peng original. A mother and child read a book on a loveseat. Everything was carved from a single block of polished sandstone except two throw pillows, one black obsidian and one white marble. The black one looked like a replica of the

Freedom Stone except that it lacked the gold flakes embedded in the glass-like rock.

I picked it up and noticed gold flakes had been embedded in the pillow's back. As if Gu Peng had created a fake. Then I wondered if it was the real thing. I'd never seen it up close.

Mercury stood at my shoulder. *You know how you can tell it's fake, homes? You're still talking to me. See now, if it was going to change you, it would've done that already. If it were real, you'd be singing the praises of Jesus Christ or Quantum Mechanics or Buddha or some such nonsense right now.*

I said, *It weighs the same. It looks the same on one side. She planted this here?*

Mercury said, *You saw it this morning, dude. It's like she's expecting you to find it.*

I said, *Do the gods ever say anything straight out? Does everything have to be a riddle?*

Mercury said, *When I landed your car upside down on a tree stump— after you promised to tell Jenny about me—was that a riddle? When I told you to grab Danny and dance a step to the left, was that a riddle? I swear, damn ingrate mortals are going to be the death of me. I'm outta here.*

He disappeared in a blink.

OK, that was wrong of me. I should've asked nicely if I was supposed to take it.

"Are you Jacob?" a woman asked from the doorway of the gallery.

"Yes." I gently placed the black stone back where I'd found it.

"A messenger told me you would stop by to take that." She pointed at the rock.

"Messenger?" I asked. Sometimes the gods work in freaky and mysterious ways. "Ah. Yes. OK. Thanks."

I put the stone in my pack and headed for the last cogwheel going up the mountain.

Pavard waited for me on the platform. We got on and I explained a simplified version of my story. I left out any reference to a magical Poison Stone and the competing Knights and Brothers. I explained it was as much a hunch as when I charged into a Paris cathedral and took out two terrorists. He was patient. He listened well. He nodded.

He clearly wanted to go back to his room and go to sleep. Maybe he felt guilty after Paris when he had issued what amounted to a shoot-to-kill order for me only to have it all blow back in his face. Probably not, though. He wasn't the kind of guy who regretted anything. But he was being nice, and that I appreciated.

He got out his phone and called the head of the German BND operation, Luca Brandt. While Pavard begged favors on behalf of a guy who had nothing more than a tin-foil-hat conspiracy theory, I stared out the window. The cogwheel churned up the steep slope, its lights showing nothing but the dark gray limestone. Here and there were small caves formed in the layers of karst sandwiched between the harder layers of the mountain rock. The tunnel engineers used the niches for maintenance and tools. Flashes of yellow tape flew by. All had been taped off for the G20 meeting by inspectors.

We arrived at the *Gletscherbahnhof*—glacier train station—and were met by Luca Brandt in person. He was less-than-enthusiastic.

Brandt showed me an official BND personnel file for one Artur Titow, a naturalized Turkmen immigrant who'd gone to boarding school in the EU and university at Heidelberg. He'd been with the BND three years and had been recommended for promotion. Titow was the man I'd seen twice before. He looked as much like Stalin in his official records as he did in real life. He was assigned to the passengers. I asked if there were any other Turkmen in the BND.

Brandt clicked off his tablet and nearly called me a racist in German. He meant well. He was looking out for one of his men. Anyone in command knows with the utmost certainty that none of his men are double agents.

He gave us a tour of the building. He reminded me the crossing from the Gletscherbahnhof to the Schneefernerhaus—the environmental science station—would be by snowcat. He pointed to everything along the way, including the places where holes had been drilled in the glacier for ground-penetrating sonar. Standard procedure. There was nothing but rock beneath us for twenty feet. And that meant Mr. Baldy's tunnel didn't surface anywhere near the meetings. In Schneefernerhaus everything was clean and taped shut. I couldn't have done a better job myself.

I praised Luca Brandt and the BND. Highly. And I meant it. They hadn't left anything to chance.

Pavard and I made our way to the train platform in silence. He wasn't taking me home as much as I was retreating. Nothing showed up. The only thing churning through my mind was: How the hell is Mr. Baldy going to get the Stone through security? He had a tunnel, but where did it connect? We'd scoured the place. No tunnels in any of the buildings.

I needed another look at the venue. I needed to get back in there. I could ask Ms. Sabel to put me on her security team and I'd waltz right in. She'd do it in a heartbeat, but Jenny and I were trying to get free of our old lives. I could ask Brandt, but he was German. They don't break rules. Which left one option.

Pavard and I left on the last train back down the hill. When we pulled into the station at the bottom, we faced each other to say goodnight.

I held up a hand to pause the usual pleasantries and said, "Could you get me access tomorrow? Could I get in as one of your team? Please."

Pavard's face contorted in the dim light of the streetlight. His mouth began to form the French version of *no fucking way* when he stopped. He tapped his index finger to his lips, looked at the ground, then up at me. "Perhaps. If you could do me the favor in return."

I said, "Anything for you, Major Pavard."

I fully expected him to say, *Never call me again.*

He looked away, slightly embarrassed. "Two weeks it is my anniversary. My wife is very much the fan of Jacob Stearne. Would you be willing—"

"I'd be honored to be there, Pavard." I clapped his shoulder. "Absolutely."

A smile grew across his face. He beamed. "Excellent! I have your credentials at your hotel by morning. Thank you, Jacob."

We shook hands and parted ways.

When I turned to stride up the lane, Mercury stood in my path. *You serious? You're going to kiss some old French lady on the cheek but you can't be bothered to tell Jenny about me? Did I miss something here? Did Pavard save your ass on the side of a cliff four hours ago? Did Pavard save—*

I said, *Sorry. I've got a lot on my mind this weekend. As soon as this is over, I'll sit down with her and tell her all about us. I swear.*

Mercury walked away, kicking over flowerpots and sandwich boards. *Fucking mortals. Cannot believe I spend one second talking to you. What good are you? Shoulda let Zafar take you out.*

I went back to the hotel and crawled into bed. Jenny was already asleep. I dreamed about the train going through the mountain tunnel. I dreamed about Jenny. And the train. And the tunnel.

At 2:12 AM I sat bolt upright.

I knew where the tunnel came out. More or less. And that told me how they planned to get the Stone through security.

CHAPTER 51

RAFAEL TUM FOUND GU PENG sitting alone in a sunny corner of the lonely restaurant. A shaft of early morning light brushed her shoulder. She was dressed in a staid black dress, making him glad to have chosen a dark sport coat. He stepped up and silently gestured to the empty chair in front of her. She stared back blankly for a long, uncomfortable time.

"Misery unique to person," she said before nodding at the chair. "Forgive my manner."

Rafael slid in quietly and said nothing. He unfolded the napkin, put it in his lap, then folded his hands on it, sitting upright and still.

She turned her gaze to the massive picture windows framing the Bavarian Alps.

"You had many loss?" she asked without looking at him.

He nodded. "And betrayals."

She nodded for him to continue before taking her tea.

A waitress approached. Rafael ordered coffee and a fruit bowl. She left. He said, "The betrayals are always a shock to the system. Especially the ones above suspicion."

"Shock, yes." She set her teacup down and turned back to the window. Zugspitze loomed above them. To the north and west, a bank of black clouds moved slowly, relentlessly toward them. She muttered, "Above suspicion."

"The Brothers are not here this morning?" he asked.

"I send home. Pia very generous, very gracious. No need for them here now. Jacob Stearne say, 'Mission scrub.' Pia say she know a way. I say not for Brotherhood. Not for Gu Peng. Too much danger. All around, too many people above suspicion."

Rafael nodded. He knew the weight on her shoulders. For leaders, the loss of one soldier sometimes weighed heavier than a thousand. "Once, I lost a trusted aide. I lashed out at anyone and everyone around me. My darkest moment in life. My soul burned."

"It should."

He looked up to find her glaring at him. He leaned back just as the waitress returned with his coffee. The young lady sensed tension between them, set it down, and scurried away.

"You find Pia Sabel difficult to trust?" he asked.

"All rich people come from same village, have same interest."

"You suspect her of working with the Knights of Mithras?"

"Not her. She different." Peng sipped and thought. "Not too much different. After all, she meet Joe Griffith last night."

Rafael tilted his head and opened his palm, inviting her to speak more.

Peng picked up her tea, held it a moment, sipped, then looked out the window with a pensive gaze.

He considered probing deeper into her statement but decided to let her grief work its way out. It was nothing personal. Pain had a way of making the nicest people cold and prickly. He sipped his coffee and joined her in admiring the view.

His phone vibrated in his jacket pocket. With a surreptitious glance at the screen, he saw Griffith calling. He sent it to voice mail.

"I wonder why Pia would meet Mr. Griffith?" he asked quietly.

"Find out what kind deal you make with him." Peng's gaze swung back to cut through him.

He flinched. His phone rang again. He sent it to voice mail without looking. He couldn't glance away from Peng at this point. He asked, "Why does she think—"

"Above suspicion. Your soul burn, Rafael Tum. Cherry not know where we go for coffee. Pia not know where we go for coffee. But Knight of Mithras know. Pia follow Knight. Good thing too." With a hot and angry glare that drove through his heart, she yanked the napkin off her lap and slapped it on the table, rattling the silver. She rose with her walking stick and pounded away.

He let out a slow breath.

The waitress brought his bowl of fruit, gave him an empathetic smile, and turned away. He stared at the dish.

His phone rang again. He dragged it to his ear. "Yes?"

"Rafael, is that you?" Joe Griffith sounded out of breath.

"Yes." His voice felt distant and estranged.

"Our deal is not finished. I need you to—"

"I'm done." Rafael closed his eyes and saw Gu Peng's hateful gaze piercing through him again. "No more."

"Oh no you don't. The ICC has not ruled and will not rule until I give them the go-ahead."

"I don't care about the ICC." Rafael felt his chest close as if a horse lay on it. "I will not do anything more for you."

"You say you don't care," Griffith said. "Your old Eton roommate is dying. He has days to live. And he's the only reason you walk free today."

It took him a minute to evaluate Griffith's tone of voice. Was it another manipulation or was it a statement of fact? He decided it had to be both, given the source. "Indeed? That is quite sad. I'm sure the Knights will sorely miss the Protector's leadership."

"He's named me as the next Protector."

Rafael tried not to gasp. "Congratulations, Joe. That is why you left the Keepers in the first place, is it not? I am delighted you have reached your goal."

"You're not delighted," Griffith snarled. "Don't give me that upper-crust bullshit. The ICC business is up to me now. As you well know, my threats are not idle. You'll do as I say, or the Germans will round you up before lunch."

CHAPTER 52

I CLICKED OFF THE PHONE and looked at Jenny across the hotel room. "Pavard could get only one set of credentials. Sorry."

"You didn't ask him for two, did you?"

I couldn't lie to her, but I couldn't have her going along either. At some point, if all went well, Mr. Baldy and I were going to face off over iron sights. There's no way I could let her near the line of fire. I said, "It never occurred to me."

Her face contorted in a way that I could read like a book. She contemplated calling Pia Sabel for a favor. We needed her help. At the same time, we didn't want too much help. She understood why I decided to ask Pavard instead of Ms. Sabel. The fact that I'd only asked for one made her angry.

Jenny stuck out her jaw and glared. "I don't need you to protect me, you know."

"No. But I need to protect you. It's my yang thing." I slung my jacket over my shoulder and opened the door. "Or whatever."

Mercury walked down the hall with me. *Dude, you don't mind bringing Pia-Caesar-Sabel to a gunfight.*

I said, *I'm not going to marry Ms. Sabel.*

The credentials waited for me at the front desk, just as Major Pavard promised. A lanyard with photo ID sealed in a plastic holder and some papers. He'd included a note on procedures: No weapons, no unauthorized baggage, and phone verification of employment would happen at the checkpoint. All of which were problems for me. I'd rather swim in a pool of vipers than chase down Mr. Baldy without weapons. Pavard had listed my employer as Sabel Security, which had been accurate up until I quit. And I was carrying a forty-pound rock.

Miguel strolled out of the breakfast buffet and crossed the lobby to me. He punched my shoulder and grinned the way old friends do. He looked at the lanyard. "Contractor for Major Pavard? Didn't he want you dead?"

"No one can resist my charms forever."

His eye stopped on the listed employer. One eyebrow went up. Slowly, his gaze turned to me.

"Say," I said, "would you do me a favor?"

"No."

"They need phone verification of current employment."

"No."

"C'mon, just get me on the payroll for one day."

"No."

"You're going to make me call her?"

"Yep." He turned and walked away.

There was only one person at Sabel Security who could get me a job for a day. I looked at my phone for the time. I didn't have any. If I flew, I would have thirty seconds to spare before the train—and Pavard—left the station. It took me all of that to screw up the courage to call her. I took a deep breath and dialed. While it rang, I heard Miguel's distinctive laugh coming from the elevator banks around the corner.

Ms. Sabel answered my call by saying, "He just told me. I'll make it happen. I've got to run."

She clicked off.

Mercury leaned against the front desk. *She's not such a bad person, homie.*

I said, *It's an abusive relationship.*

Mercury said, *She never abused you.*

I said, *She shot me. That's abusive.*

But did you die? Mercury held up his hands.

Take it from me—arguing with gods never gets you anywhere.

I grabbed my backpack and caught a cab. Dark clouds covered half the sky, moving into the valley like an invading army.

Running from the cab to the train, I squeezed through the door as it started to shut. I found Pavard in the forward cab. His men filled the rows behind him. The only seat open was next to him.

I dropped in with the pack on my lap. "Thank you, Major. This means a lot to me."

He eyed the backpack suspiciously. His gaze rose to me skeptically. With an eye roll of resignation, he took the pack off my lap and put it on his. "Tell me it is not a bomb."

"It's a rock. It looks exactly like another rock that—"

"I don't want to know." He sighed. "Things for you … they always work out. Crazy things that make no sense. Maybe the gods make fun. But in the end, everyone think Jacob Stearne is the big hero. Let me know when you need it."

We rode the rest of the way in silence.

When we pulled into the station, Pavard gave his men a pep-talk. I wandered nearby, watching the working class streaming off the train and up the steps to their jobs. Half were security personnel; the other half were service staff. Of the security people, most were *Bundespolizei*— BPOL, the federal police. They coordinated with a small number of BND officers. The remainder were small contingents from the individual countries like France.

I heard my name shouted out across the platform in a Southern accent. I tried to ignore it because it sounded familiar. But Brynn Pickett was insistent. "Jacob Stearne, get yourself over here. Let me have a look at you." Only it sounded like, "lemme hava look itchoo."

I turned in her direction. Brynn waved her hand high in the air. She stood with her cameraman and two extras. A young woman brushed her face with makeup. Brynn, a reporter for French TV, did me a solid when I needed it back in Paris. I couldn't refuse her. I ambled over to her corner of the platform while she spewed French to her crew. They parted for me, looking me up and down with typical Parisian disdain. Hero of Paris only works with certain classes.

I tracked around behind her to keep a clear view of everyone on the platform. My position forced her to turn. Which made her makeup girl crab around with her. And that earned me a second dirty look.

"What in the world are you doing up in these parts, Jacob?" Brynn asked.

"Sightseeing."

She pulled my lanyard and read it. "For Pavard? Are you two sweeties all a'sudden?"

I tugged my lanyard back.

She frowned. "Hold up. Are you meeting your buddy, the Pres-i-dent of France?"

"We're not buddies."

"Oh, Jacob. Y'all gotta let me in on that one. You owe me." She waited for me to promise her an interview with the French president. Then her expression changed. She realized she had it wrong. "Y'all found a threat to the G20, haven't ya? Pavard wouldn't call you in to chase pole cats. What is it? Terrorists? Arms dealers? More of them Red Jackets still lurking around?"

She twirled around in a full circle, looking over the platform at the people heading up the stairs. The makeup girl tried to follow.

"The Knights of Mithras," I said.

Brynn twisted back to me with her don't-bullshit-me scowl so fast she knocked the makeup girl over. While the girl scrambled to her feet, she gave me a third nasty glare.

"I'm not kidding." I kept Brynn staring up at me while I used her for cover. In this position, I could see the entire platform. "They're a bunch of whackjobs who believe in a magic meteorite. They're probably harmless, but I thought I'd check it out just in case."

She studied me while my eyes roved the crowd milling about behind her.

"They handle plenty of whackjobs without a guy of your caliber." She brushed the makeup girl aside. "That means you know something about these … knights? What did you call 'em?"

Right then, I saw someone clawing his way up from the blackness of the track bed to the platform. It was four feet from the track to the platform. The figure placed his palms on the concrete and pushed up. His knees landed on the deck. A thick messenger bag lay next to him. He pushed to his feet. Artur Titow, in his BND uniform complete with lanyard.

Brynn rattled off words intending to spark a reaction. She snapped her fingers for her cameraman to start rolling.

I kept an eye on Titow. He picked up his heavy messenger bag, slung it across his chest, and walked calmly toward the exit. I looked back at the train track. He'd come out of the tunnel. My hunch was right. Titow was the one responsible for taping the caves closed. Which gave him access. And that meant I could find Mr. Baldy.

But where was Titow going? Should I follow the Poison Stone he carried or go kill Mr. Baldy?

"Excuse me, Brynn." I grabbed her shoulders and moved her aside. "Stay here and I guarantee you first interview. But I've got to hit the men's room first."

I pushed off, grabbed my bag off Pavard's shoulder, and followed Artur Titow up the stairs into the main building. People scattered in different directions. Titow paced directly to the men's room. I scanned the area for anyone looking vaguely Turkmen-like and saw mostly Germans. He had no backup.

I gave Titow a few seconds' head start, then strode in and went straight to the first stall. I pulled my monocular periscope with the laser-mirror and stood on the toilet to rise slightly above the partitions. It was a busy morning. A guy in the stall next to me sat on the toilet reading his phone. The one after that was empty.

I found Titow in the second from the end. He had the trash receptacle taken apart. Using what looked like gloves for handling molten ore, he placed the Poison Stone at the bottom of the trash bin, put the gloves on top, then replaced the plastic bag. He pushed the assembly back together and covered the hinge with official yellow inspection tape.

The door to my stall slammed open. Two BPOL officers shouted at me in German. I didn't know the language, but the last sentence was easy enough to figure out. *"Du verdammter Perverser!"*

CHAPTER 53

JENNY STOOD ON THE BALCONY, staring at the knives of morning sun striking through dark clouds to Zugspitze's snow-covered peak. Her insides churned like berries in a blender. Pavard had backed up Jacob's story about having only one set of credentials. But then guys always stick together. She tried Brandt, but the German was all-German and refused to break the rules. She could only get Dalsgaard's voice mail. She paced while thinking about going up the hill anyway. Nah. They wouldn't let her on the train without credentials.

She shivered in the cold morning air and went back inside, where the food on the room service cart held no appeal.

Someone knocked on her door. When she answered it, she found Cherry standing in the hall looking downcast and depressed.

"You need to talk?" Jenny asked before deciding not to wait for an answer. "Come in."

Cherry trailed her to the couch and sat on the opposite end. Jenny jumped up to retrieve the tea service from the breakfast cart and poured cups for them both. Cherry took hers with a nod of thanks.

Jenny gave her guest time to think up a way of presenting whatever news brought her to the door.

After her third sip, Cherry set the cup down and tossed her hair back. She said, "I did a terrible thing and I don't know how to fix it."

Jenny stayed quiet.

"My uncle is not who I thought he was." Cherry reached for a tissue and started crying. "I spoke to my mother last night. She told me the truth about why she disowned him. It was the war crimes. The charges were true."

Cherry broke down in sobs. Jenny gave her time, then reached for her hand and squeezed it.

"I know how it feels to have your world torn up." Jenny felt like crying herself. Her parents' recriminations and angry denunciations of each other coupled with demands to take sides came back to haunt her. But Cherry had taken sides and apparently chose poorly.

Cherry brought her sad eyes up. "A village had been helping his rebels. The government soldiers came and threatened to kill the villagers unless they revealed Uncle Rafael's base. He and most of his men survived the government attack. They went back to the village and slaughtered every man, woman, and child—on his orders."

Jenny felt bile rising. She shook her head, unable to reconcile the calm professor with a ruthless rebel leader. She squeezed Cherry's hand again. "You didn't have anything to do with that."

"The government gave him amnesty when they negotiated peace. Only a few Central American countries honor that pardon. The International Criminal Court doesn't recognize it. He can't, or shouldn't, travel outside Guatemala or Mexico. If they know he's here, they'll arrest him."

"Then why did he come on this trip?"

"He said he wanted to help Gu Peng. I believed him." She started crying again but pulled herself together quickly. "Back in Chicago, Joe Griffith made me a deal. Griffith and my uncle once worked together at the Keepers. He told me if I helped him find the Poison Stone, he would get Uncle Rafael's charges dropped. I thought I could trust him. But he lied. Griffith made it look like it was all going through, that the ICC would honor the Guatemalan pardon, but he called Uncle Rafael this morning. Griffith threatened him unless he stops Peng."

"Stop her how?"

"I don't know. He told me about Griffith's demands and left."

Jenny rose and paced. "What was that about the Keepers? What are they after?"

"What is everybody after? The Stones. Power. Control. They see themselves as the Keepers of the Stones. They have three safely hidden somewhere and they want the rest. They've all been revolutionaries like

Spartacus, Robespierre, Trotsky; the list is long."

"Not terribly successful."

Cherry shook her head. "They're the ones who didn't have the Stone. Babylonian King Nabopolassar used it to overthrow the Assyrian Empire. Arminius used it in the successful Germanic revolt against Rome. The list goes on."

"I'll take your word for it." Jenny hugged herself as she thought about what Rafael might do and how to stop it. Or had Jacob been right all along? This wasn't their fight. "Do you think Peng can free China with it?"

Cherry wrung her hands. "I don't know. Uncle Rafael believes in it. Griffith believes in it. Peng believes in it. But it's just a fucking rock. I can't believe Uncle Rafael would do anything bad to Peng. I hope he … All this killing and death …"

She broke down in tears again.

After a few minutes, Cherry blew her nose and rose. "I can't believe I trusted him; can't believe I'm related to him. I screwed up in Chicago. All of you risked your lives for me and it was all bullshit. I was wrong. Everything I do just makes things worse. I'm going home."

Jenny gave Cherry a hug. The girl was broken. Her carefully curated world turned upside-down inside a week. Jenny walked her to the door and waved goodbye.

It was time for action. She couldn't sit in a hotel room and let things unfold. She needed to be on the mountain, tracking down whoever Rafael and these Keepers really were. She dialed Jacob. On the fourth ring, a strange voice said, *"Guten Morgen, Bundespolizei."*

"Where is Jacob?" she asked. Jenny checked her phone to make sure she dialed right and confirmed it was Jacob's number. "I need to speak to Jacob."

"American? Ja. He is not coming to the phone right now. I am officer Sven Kroos. Who is calling him?"

"His fiancé, Jenny Jenkins."

"I will tell him of your call." The man clicked off.

Jenny stared at her phone. What the hell happened to Jacob? That man could get in more trouble than an unsupervised five-year-old in a candy store.

There was only one option left. The one option last on her list to try. But only one person could still get her in. She dialed.

Pia answered on the first ring. "Jenny, what's up?"

Jenny spilled everything Cherry had told her in a single gush.

Pia was silent for a moment. Then she spoke to someone before muting the phone. A few seconds later she was back. "Meet me at my suite. We'll have Dhanpal's credentials changed over to you. We'll figure it out on the way. But I'm leaving in two minutes, so run. Oh, and welcome aboard. As of right now, you're an employee of Sabel Security."

CHAPTER 54

JOE GRIFFITH WAITED FOR PIA on the platform at Gletscherbahnhof. She was dressed better than a queen today. Same conservative, yet tasteful dress, this time with more decorative embroidery. Flashier. On the platform around him industrialists, reporters, and cabinet ministers did their *so-good-to-see-you* greetings. He felt sweat on his palms. He wiped his forehead just in case it was showing. Calm would serve him better, he told himself. But time was running out and Pia had chosen this moment to pick a fight with the BND over a new employee. Did she expect everyone to bend over backwards just because the great Pia Sabel decided to hire one of her rich-kid playmates at the last minute?

He glanced at his watch again. Amanow told him the security sweeps of the restrooms happened at random intervals at least once every half hour. And Pia's big Indian never took his iron gaze off Griffith. That added to his concerns.

"I'm going to the men's room," Griffith told Miguel. "I'll meet her back here. It doesn't look like she's going anywhere soon."

As soon as the Indian nodded, he trudged off. He hiked up the strap of his day pack as he slid through the crowd. In the restroom, his memory failed him. End stall? He pushed open a door. No trash bin. He pushed on the next one, but it was occupied. He tried the third. No trash bin. Sweat formed on his forehead. If only he had thought up a different way to become the next Protector. This kind of stress was not his preferred method of doing business. He could negotiate and argue, but carrying what looked like a bomb to a world leader? He could be shot on sight.

He ordered himself to get a grip. If Amanow could handle this kind of pressure, he could too. Besides, he had Pia Sabel over a barrel. No one suspected her of anything. And they always listened to her.

Then he found the bin, second from the end. He stepped in and closed the door. He dropped the toilet cover and set his pack on it. With the hidden razor in his fountain pen, he sliced the seal. The key fit as promised. He swung the bin outward and removed the trash bag. He put on the special gloves and pulled out the Poison Stone.

He admired it for a moment. It was lighter than he expected. And there were more flakes of gold than he thought. But it was beautiful. He placed it in his day pack, tossed the gloves on top, zipped it closed, and hoisted it to his shoulder. Putting the trash bag back in place, he shut the bin, locked it, and sealed it with the piece of tape provided by Artur. Done. He sighed a breath of relief.

Exiting the men's room, he passed three officers on their way in. Just in time. The gods favored him.

Pia Sabel hadn't waited for him. He found her marching up the stairs from the platform. Her Indian shrugged at him. No apologies would be coming from her. The Jenkins girl wasn't with them. He could thank the gods for some things in life: The great Pia Sabel couldn't pull every string. He caught a glimpse of Jenkins looking nervous at the bottom of the steps.

Griffith fell in line with Pia. They made their way through the building to where a herd of luxury snowcats idled. A queue of dignitaries waited for a second round of credential checks before climbing in for the ride to Schneefernerhaus.

"What's in the bag, Griffith?" Pia asked.

"A chunk of meteorite of incredible beauty. World leaders love people who present them with rare and unusual gifts."

He watched the security people. No one was being searched. Good news. He inhaled the cold mountain air and felt his confidence building. In a few minutes he would make his first conversion. And Pia Sabel was trembling in his palm. Was it luck or hard work that uncovered her little end-run around international sanctions for Mikhail Yeschenko? Whatever it was, the boys in research deserved a bonus. He smiled to himself.

"What does the Poison Stone do?" Pia asked.

"What you call 'poison' others call freedom," he said. "What you're facilitating here today is the release of leaders from the restraints of mob rule. You'll be proud of this moment, Pia. This is the day you stepped up while others wavered."

"So glad I could help." Her gray-green eyes settled on him. Her jaw flexed. He was looking into the eyes of a caged tiger. He flinched.

A security officer checked their lanyards and waved them through. They crunched onto the snow.

"What do you expect it to do to the Prime Minister?" she asked.

"Amaze him," he answered.

Her tone bothered him. He wondered if she needed another reminder of her $28 million problem. Better to hold the stick in reserve. He said, "You've heard the carefully-crafted lies coming from the government. You've heard media outlets sensationalizing stories to confuse us. Decades of law and order have been shredded in the name of political correctness. No one cares about a safe society anymore. Crime is up sixty percent around the world. In every country, immigrants are invading. Syrians in Europe, for god's sake. Mexicans in America. Uighurs in China. Why should we sacrifice our children to give a terrorist a warm place to sleep?"

Pia raised a brow and didn't move a muscle. Those damned eyes bore right through him.

They reached the front of the line as their snowcat arrived. It was awkward, but they climbed aboard. The big Indian stood at the open door, not speaking, and not getting in.

Finally, the Indian said, "Something's wrong."

"Check it out," Pia said. She pulled the door closed without another word. The Indian jogged back toward the building.

The snowcat lurched forward. They rode in silence. Her stare became annoying. He had explained things politely once, his patience wore thin. It was time to remind her of his stick.

"What did you pay Yeschenko to do?" he asked.

"I stole it from him a couple years ago and gave it to charity. The man has no sense of humor. He recently threatened a friend of mine about it, so I covered it."

Her smug answer pissed him off. It was all he could do to stop from lashing out at her. "Flaunting sanctions just to help a friend. Was it worth it?"

Pia tightened her lips and turned to the window.

Now he had her where he wanted her. A tiger on a leash.

The snowcat clattered to a stop. They hopped down and went inside. Policemen checked them again. A young man in a suit met them. He gushed about Sabel's recent consideration of Winnipeg for her new satellite manufacturing site. He led them down a long hallway with glass windows. They stopped and admired the view of the Alps, the glacier, and the valley far below. Black clouds obscured half the region and moved toward them like a plague. They continued to a meeting room. The young man opened the doors.

This was it. This was his moment.

Pia stepped ahead of him and through the entrance. In a booming voice, she said, "Justin, so good to see you."

CHAPTER 55

PAVARD FOUND THE MONOCULAR PERISCOPE amazing. Three times I explained how the laser formed an invisible mirror, but he didn't care. He kept looking at people around the corner and up the steps like a Peeping Tom.

"No, really," I said, "it's all yours, Major. I'd be in a German jail if you hadn't rescued me from that little misunderstanding in the toilet."

As handy as having a top official in my pocket was, I didn't want him following me on my last quest: The hunt for Mr. Baldy. Officers of the law had a bad habit of objecting to my plans for summary execution. I patted his shoulder again and said, "I'll be right back."

Marching through the station, I saw Miguel coming the other way. We exchanged nods, telepathically communicating what would happen next. He swung by Pavard and greeted the Major in French. They chatted. I went on with my mission.

I waited until Brynn Pickett's cameraman flicked on his light and started live-casting an interview with someone from Argentina. With her distracted, I slipped into the crowd getting off the latest train and made my way toward the end of the platform.

Across a handful of people, I saw Jenny standing alone against a wall. Our eyes met. What in the name of Jupiter was she doing here? I left her at the hotel for a reason. Besides, she would insist Mr. Baldy go to jail, same as Pavard. I put my finger to my lips and pointed, indicating I was following someone. She nodded and stayed put.

After pushing through a herd of photographers festooned with cameras, I made it to the end of the platform and jumped down. The track bed was rough stone, the crushed remnants of the tunnel walls. A hundred yards down the line, there was a small, shallow cave. Inspection tape stretched across the opening. I easily ducked under. Inside were three shovels and a sledgehammer. I wondered if they were the tools Mr. Baldy and his crew used. The back and sides of the spur tunnel were solid rock. No connection to the Knights' tunnel. Twenty yards farther down the tracks was another shallow cave with no tools and solid walls. Another hundred yards down the hill, there was a siding where they could stash extra train cars. From the look of the rusty switch, it hadn't been used in my lifetime.

At the end of the rail spur was a set of railroad ties standing upright with a large reflector attached. An assembly from the early postwar era. Beyond it, a chain link fence sealed off the remaining depth. The inspection tape hung loosely across the fencing and made a sad attempt to stick to the rock on the right side. Many footprints marched to and from that side. Both boot prints and dress shoes, an unlikely mix. Artur Titow would be wearing dress shoes.

The fencing peeled back easily from the right and rolled up toward the left. The inspection tape stayed with it. The right side was secured with a series of magnets made to look like bolts. If a security officer didn't tug on it, they would expect it to be shut down tight. Clever.

A cold breeze whirled around me. My jacket and t-shirt combination wasn't working any better than the last time I'd tried it. You'd think my favorite deity would remind me to check the weather.

If this tunnel connected to Mr. Baldy's, the narrow space formed a venturi. With cold air freezing my ears, I knew this had to be the place. I needed backup. I called Miguel. He answered but the signal was less than weak beneath that much rock. After not getting much across, I texted him to find me at the spur. A few seconds later, the message failed to send. Perfect.

I hung my lanyard on the reflector. Any Ranger looking for me would see that and know what it meant.

I peeled back the fence and ducked into the opening. Another bit of cleverness by the Knights: the first thirty feet formed a letter S. Anyone shining a light into the space wouldn't see the turns or the main tunnel beyond. Combined with the fence and the inspection tape, they could fool the best security sweep. These guys were not amateurs.

I moved through the tight passage into a larger space and stopped to reconnoiter. Indirect light came from a distant opening. Judging by eye, it was a fifteen-hundred-foot tunnel. The Austrian end was open, letting in weak daylight. The tunnel took advantage of caves in the karst sections. The walls and floor were rough and rocky, built for purpose, not for show.

There was a wider area near my position. Something moved in the dark. I couldn't make it out. I didn't sense any Knights nearby, it was too quiet, and my senses weren't tingling. I crept out from the S portion into the straight part of the tunnel. I kept my back to the wall and felt my way along. The rocky floor slowed my progress. As I reached the wide spot, I noticed a camera mounted on a tripod to my left.

Across from me were three large objects, one of which thrashed against bindings.

A male voice said something muffled and desperate in what I guessed was Japanese. I didn't answer. Neither did anyone else. The Japanese speaker stopped moving, hoping to hear a response in the brutal silence. I joined him. I heard nothing. No movement, no spoken words. Only the breathing of four people. Me, a Japanese guy, and two others whose breathing was ragged.

I strained to hear anything else. If the Knights were aware of my presence, they could be lining up a shot through the Sumrak's infrared scope right now. I could be dead in an instant. Unlike the movies, the bad guys don't pop out and explain their whole evil plan, then leave you hanging over a shark tank from which you can escape. They just shoot you. Dead. Why explain anything to a guy you're going to kill? What's the point?

I waited a few more seconds, listening and wishing I'd brought a Sabel Visor. The monocular was hard enough to get through security; I couldn't imagine explaining what I needed with night vision during a daylight meeting on a bright-white glacier. Still, I listened. When up against pros, it's important not to underestimate them. Using my ears for radar, I zeroed in on the breathers in front of me, then tuned out those frequencies and listened for any other movement in the tunnel.

Nothing.

I clicked on my phone light for a split second to process the scene. It was risky, but I couldn't think of any other way to figure out what I was up against. Three men in business suits were splayed out on giant Xs. Chains bound their wrists and ankles. They were tightly gagged. One man was passed out. The next had been savagely beaten; a backpack lay at his feet. The Japanese man had a bloody nose but was alert. They looked like important guys. Their suits were not politician or uber-rich-guy material, but a step or two above pencil-pusher and three steps above journalist. Hostages of some importance. But who?

The Japanese guy started talking into his gag again. He was trying English but he had too much cloth in his mouth.

Mercury said, *What is the G20 all about, homie?*

I jumped out of my skin. Then took a deep breath. I said, *Don't sneak up on me like that.*

Mercury said, *I didn't. I've been waving at you for a minute. I'm always with you but sometimes you don't see me. Anyway. Answer the question—what's it all about?*

I said, *Rich countries exploiting poor countries?*

Mercury said, *Yeah, duh, but who and how does that work?*

I said, *Rich people like Pia Sabel talk to prime ministers about who has to get bribed to build a factory where lots of poor people will work cheap without a union?*

Mercury sighed. *I coulda used you back when Trotsky was on the rise, but you missed the era by decades.*

I said, *Yeah, well, it didn't go so well for him.*

Mercury said, *We'll get you enrolled in Capitalism 101 later. Right now, who do these guys look like to you? I'll give you a hint: They're not politicians so they didn't have tons of security.*

I said, *Which made them ripe targets for hostage taking. Which means, they're bag men?*

Mercury slapped his palm to his face. *Dude, when you get to the Caesar-level, they're not called bag men, they're called...*

I said, *Bankers! Oh, these guys are central bankers for Japan and—I* tried to remember which countries were part of a global cabal that meant nothing to me—*a couple other places.*

Mercury said, *Which means Mr. Baldy is going to do what?*

I said, *I don't know. Hostages are taken for ransom. What would that have to do with the Poison Stone?*

By asking, I answered my own question. Mr. Baldy would hold these guys until the leaders touched the Stone. An odd request but impossible for the leader to turn down when the life of his bag man, I mean, central banker, hangs in the balance.

I crossed the space toward the chained men. As soon as I stepped forward, a bright light next to the video camera came on. Motion sensor. Not a great thing to miss when you're sneaking around. But it was too late. The area was lit up like a TV studio.

I pulled the gag from the Japanese guy's mouth

The Japanese guy nodded at the floor and said, "Bomb."

I glanced at the backpack on the floor. A few dim LEDs flashed inside it. It wasn't just a bomb. It was a remote-controlled bomb. Beneath the controller, it looked like a twenty-pound sack of ANFO, the most common industrial explosive in use today. That much would kill anyone and everyone within a thousand feet. That meant everyone in this end of the tunnel would die. Due to the far end being open, allowing some of the blast to escape, they wouldn't collapse the mountain on top of the bodies.

Mr. Baldy wanted to threaten the lives of these three so their corpses could be found later. That indicated a level of evil intent I'd rarely seen in my wanderings. Knowing the authorities would scour the world for the killer, he had enough confidence to know they would never find him.

Then I remembered something Danny had said: *The Knights are protected around the world.* Mr. Baldy had no reason to fear an international manhunt. His organization had global resources. Which he proved by getting his hands on a rocket launcher in Flores, Guatemala. And that meant he could kill with impunity. So how was all this going to work?

My head swiveled fast to the camera on the far wall. Looking past the bright light, I could make out speakers and a transmitter. A two-way communication system.

I sensed someone behind me. Few people in the world could get the jump on me. I turned in time to see Dhanpal—my former co-worker and friend—swing a bat at my head. It hit me. Hard. Black stars twinkled in my vision.

I collapsed.

CHAPTER 56

I STRUGGLED TO REMEMBER WHERE I was. Somewhere dark and freezing cold. Europe. Pyrenes? No, Alps. My head throbbed. So did my wrists. Which was a strange sensation. On closer examination, I realized they were chained next to some guy's ankles. Nice shoes though. My arms were spread wide. My legs sprawled on a cold stone floor. A cave in Bavaria. Bayern, in the local language. Germany. I took a deep breath.

My brain kept fritzing out. I caught snatches of the situation.

I was in big trouble. I just couldn't remember why.

Nausea came in waves. I felt like puking. But I didn't. I needed to concentrate. Because … Why?

It was dark. A dim light in the distance to my right. In front of me, a video camera and speakers. Then I remembered one word: hostages. Were they my hostages? Nah. That wasn't my style. Usually.

I tugged my chains. "Hey! What the fuck, man? Anyone there?"

There were two other guys chained next to the guy over my head. One of them grunted. The guy above me tried to say something but he was gagged. Blood dripped from his face onto my shoulder.

Danger.

What was it? Who was it? I couldn't remember the name of the town we were in, much less what posed a danger to me. I rolled through the few things I could remember. A mountain. A train. A glacier. A Frenchman. Pia Sabel. Damn it. Did she do this? None of that jogged my memory of a cave.

A bright light came on, directly in my face. The speakers in front of me crackled. A British-accented voice I recognized—but couldn't place—started talking. "Jacob Stearne. You owe me your miserable life!

Yet instead of showing even a modicum of gratitude, you come here to sabotage my brilliant endeavor."

"Guess so." I desperately wanted to put the pieces together. I knew that voice. A bald guy named … I had nothing.

The Japanese guy tried shouting through his gag again. Sounded like "mom."

"Why couldn't you leave it alone?" the voice on the speakers asked. "We are men, just like you. We bleed when cut. We die when poisoned. But when we are wronged—we will have revenge."

"Shakespeare," I said. "Misquoted, but you've got the gist. You know, Marcus Aurelius said, 'The best revenge is to be unlike him who performed the injury.'"

At least I remembered Mercury's teachings. Not that it helped with the chains or anything. Where was that delinquent god of mine anyway?

The Japanese guy kept repeating his word through his gag with a lot more urgency.

"Such a grasp of the classics," Mr. Baldy said. "Aurelius is philosophically advanced for a little man of your breeding."

That was good. I remembered calling him Mr. Baldy. A step in the right direction. Didn't care as much for him disrespecting my ancestry, though.

"Bomb." That's what the Japanese guy kept saying.

It brought my brain back from the edge. I glanced over at the backpack a few feet away from me. It wasn't my backpack. I remembered thinking it held a bag of commercial ANFO. Mr. Baldy planned to blow up the Japanese guy. Since I was chained to the Japanese guy's feet, I had a problem.

"It's the saddest thing of all," Mr. Baldy said. "I trusted your friend, Dhanpal to kill any intruders. He couldn't bring himself to kill you, though. I assure you; he has been appropriately chastised. But it leaves me with the irreconcilable situation at hand. I can't kill you until I am ready to dispatch the rest of my hostages. As much as it grieves my soul, the bigger picture requires that you live a little while longer. It will all be over soon enough, I suppose. I shall have to live with that."

The speakers stopped rattling. The light went out.

The Japanese guy repeated his complaint.

I kicked at the bag. It lay three inches beyond my outstretched toe. I looked up at the Japanese guy. "Believe me, brother, I'd love to do something about it."

I heard running behind me. Hard breathing. The motion sensor tripped the light. A woman's silhouette appeared to my left. Jenny.

"Jacob!" she screamed.

"Run," I said. My brain wasn't working fast enough to explain the danger. "Get out."

She burst into tears and ran to me. She tugged on my chains and quickly realized they weren't coming off.

The Japanese guy said, "Mom" again but Jenny didn't get it any quicker than I did.

"Get out of here," I said.

"Yes, I'll get you out of this," she said. "I need bolt cutters."

She looked around the jagged floor for tools and found nothing. The Japanese guy repeated his single syllable word over and over. She ran a circle around all three X frames before coming back. After nearly stumbling over the pack, she peered inside.

Immediately, she looked up at the Japanese guy and understood.

"Run!" I said. "Get help. Go! Now!"

"Bloody bastard!" Mr. Baldy's voice on the speakers returned. "You've brought help. Now I must kill the lot of you and regroup. Ten months of hard work destroyed!"

"Who is that?" Jenny screamed.

"Mr. Baldy," I said. "Get out of here now. Go get help."

Jenny looked at the bag. Then she looked at me and tugged my ear. The action I told her to use when she wanted me to listen to her. She said, "Let me be the hero for once."

She ran to the pack.

"NO!" I shouted.

She picked it up and slung it over her shoulder. She was fit and strong, but it was heavy. She staggered a step as the weight swung to her shoulder and threw off her balance.

"NO!"

She looked back at me with a sad smile. "You were the one who said it: She who can, must."

She ran down the low tunnel toward the dim blue light. That much ANFO would kill anyone near it. The only way she could survive would be to throw it off the edge of the cliff five hundred yards away. She stumbled and cursed and regained her pace.

"NO!" I yanked my arms against my chains. I twisted and writhed and pulled and strained. The bindings were tight; I couldn't find any slack.

Two hundred yards away, she tripped and fell on the uneven rock floor. She struggled to her feet and kept going.

"Jacob, where did your little tramp go?" Mr. Baldy shouted through the speakers.

"NO!" Tears streamed down my cheeks.

Miguel appeared at my side. His head swiveled to the camera, the light, the Japanese guy, the dim shadow of Jenny growing smaller in the distance. He tried to process the scene but missed one critical piece of information.

"Damn it all!" Mr. Baldy shouted. "Did you bring everybody down here?"

"She has the bomb," I shouted at Miguel. "You have to take it from her. Throw it over the edge."

His eyes snapped to mine.

Suddenly, I realized what I was asking of my best friend: to die in Jenny's place. In that same instant, he understood the same thing and took off running.

Jenny neared the tunnel's far end—yet was still a hundred yards short.

Major Pavard reached me next. He tugged at my chains.

A blizzard of French and German security officers flooded into the cave. Pavard shouted at his men in French. Luca Brandt shouted at his in German.

Pavard looked down the cave at Miguel and beyond him, Jenny. Pavard took off running.

The bright light reached me first. Then the shockwave. Then the sound.

CHAPTER 57

"NO! NO! NO! NO! NO!" I couldn't hear my own voice. Or anyone else. I couldn't hear the German officer shouting in my ear. I could only feel the strain in my neck and vocal cords as I raised my voice to its greatest volume. Futile.

Pain electrified my entire body.

Pavard was running down the tunnel toward the damage. Miguel was ahead of him, picking himself up off the ground after the blast knocked him back ten feet.

I didn't hear as much as feel the snap of bolt cutters. The tension in my chains slackened on my right hand. Another snap and the same result for my left. I wrenched myself free of them and scrambled to my feet.

Brandt tried to push me back. As if he were far away, I could make out his words as my hearing slowly returned. He was saying, "It is not safe. The rock may not be stable."

I shoved him aside and ran.

Miguel and Pavard stood a hundred yards short of where the daylight spilled in the opening. Their faces were downcast.

I shoved between them.

She lay mangled on the stone. Her broken body blown from the remaining backpack fragments. I dropped to my knees and cradled her in my arms. Limp. I felt for a pulse. Nothing. I touched my cheek to hers. Cold.

I kissed her.

She was never going to kiss me back.

She was exceptionally beautiful. Even more so in the peace of death. Maybe she had finally found solace from her life of pain and hardship.

What were the last words I said to her?

"Jenny, Jenny, Jenny," I said, "what did you do? Risking your life to save others is my job."

It was a selfish thing to say. Everyone who joins the military, from the generals on top to the mop-and-bucket guy at the bottom, signs up for the ultimate sacrifice when called upon. Service is in the blood of volunteers. And she had volunteered for the Navy.

It was my fault. My life had endangered hers far too many times. The car chase that ended with us impaled on a tree came to mind. My luck had covered her for a while, but now it had run out.

I choked. Tears fell from my cheeks to hers.

Memories of our moments together flooded into my head. We read books on my sofa. Did I tell her how much I loved Sunday afternoons when she leaned against me and read her trashy romance novels? No one loved my cooking more than Jenny. Did I tell her how much her compliments meant? She listened politely while I played my jazz collection. I never listened to her hip-hop; maybe I should have. We went to her therapy sessions together. We worked our way out of her rape-trauma. Those were scary times for both of us. I learned a lot about what she's made of and what she had endured.

That's why it can't end like this. This can't be real. Someone has to make time go backwards and start over. There are things I need to tell her.

I became dimly aware that I had been sitting with her for several minutes. Neither Miguel nor Pavard had moved.

Mercury knelt an arm's length away.

I said, *You have to fix this. You're a god. If you're real—FIX THIS!*

Mercury said, *You already pushed fate, my brother.*

I said, *No more riddles. You can bring her back. You have to bring her back.*

Mercury said, *Don't put this on me. Don't you dare give yourself a way out. This is about you.*

I said, *How can you play stupid guilt trips when I'm in this much pain?*

Ain't no guilt trip, bro, Mercury said. *Her fate was to die in Basel-*

Stadt, Switzerland. But we gave her a pass. Her fate was to die from sarin gas on the Black Sea, but we were merciful and gave her another pass. What did you do with the extra time we gave you, Jacob? Did you argue with her? Did you fight? Did you tell her how you feel about her? Did you trust her with the strange things in your head? Did you cherish every extra minute we gave you with her?

I hated that he brought all that up. Lessons I thought I'd learned after losing good friends in battle. That every minute of your life and every person in it is precious beyond measure. That any opportunity to express love and gratitude cannot be ignored. That every minute of every day is a minute that should be filled with appreciation and thanksgiving. I knew all that and still I took it for granted that we would grow old together.

Emergency people arrived with a mountain rescue stretcher. Pavard stayed them with an outstretched arm.

In my head, Jenny said, *You can be the order to my chaos...* I longed for another moment of her chaos. We had our partnership worked out. How could it end before it began? I closed my eyes and saw her repeatedly smashing the door into the face of our attacker in El Remate. Who has that kind of spirit? To take on an armed man with nothing more than a door? She was the one who got us out of that hotel in the water taxi. No one could think as fast on her feet, knowing what was at her disposal and how to use it. Did I tell her how smart that was? She put her Navy training to use on Lake Michigan, expertly piloting the getaway boat. How did I react? Did I say *thank you for being there*?

I remembered her little speech about symbols and saving China when she didn't believe in the Stone. She believed in helping people. An honorable baseline of principles. I couldn't remember if I said anything about it. What about the time she told me to feed Zafar? It turned out to be the key to turning him. As ill-fated as his life was, without him, we would never have found Mr. Baldy's lair. She made that happen. She got Dalsgaard and Brandt to rock the gondola like rambunctious teenagers. So vigorous and full of life.

Lost.

I let the technicians take her from me and put her on the stretcher. I stood there with Miguel, Pavard. Brandt joined us, and together we watched them carry her away. No one said anything. No one moved.

One more memory of her surfaced: she worried I'd go to jail if I killed Mr. Baldy.

I was going to kill Mr. Baldy. I didn't care if they put me in jail.

Miguel gave me a look of solidarity, followed by a quick glance at our two companions. He knew my thinking. He knew what I would do next. His glance was a warning to me: Premeditating murder in front of two high-ranking police officers is a bad idea.

They were men sworn to the rule of law. They were professionals who lived to serve justice. In court. Before a jury. And a judge. They would never condone vigilantism.

I didn't care.

I snarled, "I'm going to kill that motherfucker."

Brandt looked at me with sympathetic eyes and sniffed and looked into the distance. He remembered the pretty woman who rocked the gondola. He pursed his lips and shook his head. "Nein. The BND will handle this."

Pavard put an arm around my shoulder. In a whisper only I could hear, he said, "Soon, my friend. Patience."

CHAPTER 58

GRIFFITH TOOK A DEEP BREATH and followed Pia Sabel. She was ten feet ahead of him in a room filled with bankers, executives, and politicians. Everything was red and white. A nearby table featured a pyramid of maple syrup bottles. Another table was stacked with autographed hockey sticks. Beer bottles from Molson, Moosehead, and Labatt's topped another. And the maple leaf covered every surface.

Pia and the Prime Minister were frozen mid-handshake with sparking smiles while photographers flashed a thousand pictures. They held the pose for a ridiculous length of time before breaking it off. The photographers took the hint. They turned their lenses to Griffith. A couple flashes went off before they realized he was no one, and away they went. Even the young man who'd ushered them from the entrance turned his back.

He squeezed his eyes shut and screwed up his nerve. His life was on the line. Should he lose to Amanow, a sniper would end his life in an instant. There would be nowhere to hide. The only question he would contemplate was when. This was it. Pia got him in the door, as promised. He had a prepared statement. He was ready.

But Sabel was hogging the conversation. She was supposed to introduce him. Instead, she turned her back on him.

He recalled the words of his school's motto: *Audentis Fortuna iuvat*, Fortune favors the bold.

Griffith moved to form a triangle between Sabel and the Prime Minister. They were deep in a discussion about building the next generation of Canada's communications satellites. Her concerns centered around building a science and engineering college near the factory. The

Prime Minister assured her it could be done. She argued there were better resources closer to Montreal. He countered that the rural areas had a larger under-employed yet highly educated population. And few unions. Sabel took a moment to consider this.

Then she turned to Griffith as if he'd surprised her.

"Oh, yes," Pia said. "Have you met Joe Griffith, Mr. Prime Minister? You might have heard of him. He uses his wealth to lure young women to his home in Chicago where he keeps them as sex slaves in bedrooms that lock from the outside."

Griffith choked. How did she know about that? What the hell was she doing?

She went on, an icy stare cutting him like a knife. "He has a meteorite for you."

What the hell was she talking about? Why did the Prime Minister have a smirk on his face?

"How unfortunate to meet you." The Prime Minister leaned back without offering a hand. "I will not accept a gift, no matter how well-intentioned."

Griffith glared back at Pia. If he had a pistol, she'd be dead right now. As it was, his life was on the line. Amanow would gladly kill him. It was now or never. He had to push on. Fortune favors the bold.

"She's making fun for some reason," he heard himself say. Good recovery. "It is an offering for the people of Canada. Allow me to show you. It is a stone of great beauty."

Griffith set his bag down and quickly donned the gloves and pulled out the Poison Stone and thrust it into the Prime Minister's hands. The Prime Minister stared at the gold flakes in the fathomless black stone. Pia didn't. She stared at Griffith.

Pia said, "Not her best work, to be sure. It looks rushed. The finish doesn't have that smoothness she's so famous for. Turn it over and see if it has her signature."

The Prime Minister turned the stone over as if it were a funny joke and he were about to read the punchline. The bottom was smooth as silk. A button carved in the center had *Gu Peng* chiseled in immaculate letters across the face. Her trademark signature found on all her works.

Griffith reeled back. Obsidian art by Gu Peng? Where did that come from? Amanow was supposed to leave the real thing, not a fake. Had Amanow tried to burn him in public? What purpose would that serve? It couldn't have been Amanow, Pia knew in advance. So did the Prime Minister.

They both smiled at him. They were in on it. Pia must have called the Prime Minister and set this up just to make him look like a fool.

Griffith looked up at Pia. "You fucking bitch!"

"Hey!" The Prime Minister shoved the stone in Griffith's stomach. "There's no call for such language."

The young man who ushered them in appeared at Griffith's elbow with two Canadian officers. The young man said, "I'll see the stone is returned to the art gallery where it belongs. These gentlemen will see you out."

The officers grabbed his arms roughly. As he tried to shake them off, Pia said, "The $28 million is part of a Treasury Department trace operation designed to flush out Yeschenko's shell companies. The exception to the sanctions bears President William's signature. Your intelligence—if you can call it that—let you down. As for the Stone, I couldn't be sure Jacob could make the switch until after you presented it. We owe Major Pavard our thanks for helping out at the last minute."

The officers shoved him toward the door. He could hear Pia and the Prime Minister laughing at him. They went back to their discussion of satellite manufacturing.

The officers quick-marched him down the hall and outside to an empty snowcat and tossed him in and slammed the door and patted the hood. The snowcat chugged forward.

He had never been so humiliated in his life. His first worry: How did Sable know about the young women he kept? Who told her? But he would worry about that later. He knew the call he had to make right now. He had to report to the Protector. The call was expected. No, it was required. He dialed the number and closed his eyes.

"Griffith, is that you, old boy?" A familiar voice answered the phone. The voice indicated he was in far better health than the Protector.

"I'm trying to reach the Protector," Griffith said.

"This is James." The voice paused, waiting to be recognized. "We met. At White's? James, Duke of Kingston. You were meeting with that dreadful Sabel woman. Terrible thing I couldn't reveal our connection at the time. But then, it wouldn't be a secret society if we didn't keep secrets, eh?"

"Oh, yes. I'm sorry, you caught me off guard."

"Quite alright. Listen, your friend the Protector … he's not made it, I'm afraid. He arranged some sort of contest between you and that Eurotrash captain of his. We had to do something." James snickered. "So, we've gone and pulled the plug, you see."

Griffith felt his neck twitch. "I'm sorry, I don't see. What happened?"

"Oh, I've gone and left out a rather crucial detail. Sorry. I'm the Chairman of the Board. We were—that's the board of the Knights, not the royal 'we' this time—unhappy with the Protector's choices of late. This whole business of setting up Captain Amanow as the next Protector just didn't match our expectations. Imagine, a Muslim running the Knights of Mithras. Heaven forbid."

Griffith sifted through the man's words about the Protector and came to the phrase, *pulled the plug*. Literally?

"Yes," he said quickly. "I found that prospect hard to swallow myself."

"Ah, good then. We shall install you as the 312th Protector of the Knights of Mithras on an interim basis. A full search for the permanent Protector will commence forthwith. There were some concerns about you, to be frank. Some of our members are concerned you are unwilling to be brutal when brutality is required. Nonetheless, we are unanimous that our foray into the ways of Caspian Sea is at an end. You will be good enough to take the helm in these trying times?"

A thousand thanks to Mithras, god of order, rolled through his mind. Timing is key in life. Failing was no longer an issue. James had not brought it up. Amanow was suddenly a problem of the past. They needed him. Now was the time to negotiate.

Griffith said, "Before I commit, I have a few questions."

"By all means, go ahead."

"I was thinking the Knights should be drawn from—how can I put this delicately—a more northern race?"

"Do you have a chapter in mind?"

"I'd like to interview before making a determination, but I know some Scots, Welsh, and Norwegians who I feel better suited to the role."

"Indeed. There is a good deal of Asian blood mixed in with those Turkmen, after all. Then it's settled. You are the right interim."

"About that. As interim, would I be considered for the permanent position?"

"Young man, since the Reagan-Thatcher era began, we have made great strides toward ending the wasteful pursuit of equality and charged straight ahead to rewarding each according to his birth and station. We did this without relying on sixteenth century myths. If you can get us past this ridiculous pursuit of the Poison Stone, you'll be our front-runner."

"I'm very glad to hear that."

"There's one other thing," James said. "Is it possible to do something about that Sabel woman?"

"Where she is concerned," Griffith grinned, "I am prepared to be brutal because brutality is required."

CHAPTER 59

PIA FOUND GU PENG SITTING on a bench outside the Chinese hospitality pavilion. A beautiful box decorated in Chinese motifs sat next to her. She stared out the picture window at the glacier spread before them. Black clouds covered most of the sky, moving slowly, inevitably southward. Soon they would be overhead, and a blizzard would descend on the region.

Pia picked up the box. "I see Miguel found you and gave you the Freedom Stone."

Peng nodded and rose, hoisting herself up by her walking stick. The older woman's face bore a hard and determined look. Pia hadn't felt this proud since the last World Cup. At last, she could play a small part in changing the world. Even if the Freedom Stone was a myth and the whole thing a waste of time, Pia felt pride in helping the famous artist.

They were close now. Close enough to accelerate her pulse and excite her senses.

A guard opened the door for them. They entered a room decorated in red and gold. A giant embroidered panel depicted the Great Wall. Nearby, another panel illustrated the Imperial Palace in glowing colors. At the far end, in front of the General Secretary, were five early narrative paintings. Treasures of the ancient culture representing thousands of years of civilization. Pia felt the awe and wonder intended to humble those brave enough to approach the powerful nation.

Three meticulously organized reception lines snaked through the room. A greeter checked Pia's name against the list and pointed to a line. Following it up to the head, she saw the First Vice Premier.

Pia turned back to the greeter. "I'm sorry, I had an appointment to see the General Secretary, President—"

"No mistake." The young woman checked her tablet and bowed. "On the advice of our specialist, we reassigned your meeting to the First Vice Premier. He can assist the expansion of Sabel Capital in Shanghai."

Pia felt like a dog who'd had her snout gently smacked. If they were trying to snub her, they made their point. The Party Secretary, in charge of the People's Bank of China, would be the logical choice if the General Secretary cancelled. She scanned the room, looking for the advisor who demoted her schedule. Standing next to the General Secretary was a high-ranking official staring at her.

On closer examination, the official was not staring at Pia, but at Gu Peng. Pia noticed the old woman give him a shake of her head. The official's face fell in sadness. He nodded his understanding. Pia realized it was the Brotherhood's ally in Zhongnanhai. The usurper waiting for his moment.

"We go now." Peng touched her elbow and nodded in the direction of security men who were eyeing them. "This not good place cause trouble. China security not tolerate protest."

"I can fix this," Pia said. "I need to find the advisor and pull rank."

"You big deal in America. You big deal in Europe."

Pia slowly brought her gaze down to the older woman at her side. Her implication was clear. North America and Europe combined didn't have the population of China, much less the greater Asian sphere they influenced and controlled. While Sabel Industries would rank somewhere between American Express and Lockheed Martin on the Fortune 500 if it were publicly held, the People's Liberation Army could buy it in minutes should she entertain an offer. Pia Sabel was no big deal in this room.

Then she saw the advisor who'd trashed her plans. Her competitive nature drove her to consider punching his lights out. She felt her fists tighten. He held her gaze from the center of the room, where he stood in a smart business suit with his arms crossed. Peng saw him too and hissed lightly under her breath. He approached them and nodded toward the exit. Just as Cherry told Jenny he would, Professor Rafael Tum had stopped Gu Peng from meeting the Chinese president.

Without protest or comment, Peng turned on her walking stick and led them out of the pavilion.

When the doors closed behind them, Pia turned to Rafael and opened her mouth to berate him. Before her first syllable formed, she felt Peng's hand on her arm and held back.

"We so close," Peng said. "There be another day. Another chance."

Rafael nodded.

"That's it?" Pia asked. "You're giving up?"

"No question me." Peng glared up at her. "I lose husband, daughter. I never see granddaughter except for video call. Now, she drowned. One day China take your family. Then you say go or no go." She wagged her finger at Pia. "Today, is my say-so. I say this not time. Better to bend like reed when tank come. Sometime lay low to survive. There be other time."

Pia reeled back a step. "I can't get a meeting with the General Secretary whenever you feel like it. This took months to set up. This isn't just about you—I had serious business to discuss in there." She turned to Rafael. "Not with the First Vice Premier, either."

Rafael Tum said, "This is hardly about you. They need your resources. The Party Secretary will be in touch."

"Where did you come from?" Pia faced him. "How did you pull that off?"

"I am with the Keepers." He folded his hands and looked down. "We keep balance in the world. Today, you defeated the Knights of Mithras. To balance that, we blocked the Brotherhood of Claritas."

"Keepers keep nothing," Peng snarled. "Keepers spawn evil. Joe Griffith a Keeper once, now evil Knight." Peng shook a fist in his face. "Keeper of balance? Every day, more and more despot take over. Less and less freedom for people. Every day, worker go work. Rich go to glacier have meeting, drink Mai Tai, ski. No work, just make money while other people work. Do not say balance."

Rafael shrugged.

Pia couldn't believe all this was real. Three ancient secret societies held each other in check? One of the groups acting like a referee? She wondered if this whole escapade were a dream from which she would wake.

She held up the box she'd been carrying and asked Rafael, "Is the Freedom Stone for real?"

"What happened to your man, Dhanpal?" he asked. "For thousands of years, people believed the universe existed because a creator said, 'Let there be light.' Now people believe it all started with a Big Bang—of light. What will we believe a thousand years from now?"

"I suppose you want the Stone?"

"Not yet." Rafael held up his hands. "You're responsible for it now. Keep it safe."

Pia turned to Peng and held the box out.

"You keep it," the old woman said. "The struggle continue every day. When time come, I call. Freedom Stone need Pia Sabel help."

Peng walked away, her walking stick tapping the slow rhythm of a dirge.

Reluctantly, Pia turned back to Rafael. "Why stop her? Why not see what happens? Maybe she could set China free."

"Freedom must be won, not given." Rafael sighed. "To force change on people, good or bad, wreaks havoc on a civilization. People must invest in change for that change to succeed."

"What did they offer you?" Pia asked. "Was it just dropping the ICC charges?"

"I don't care about them." His eyes misted. "Karma is hardest on those who fail to see their own evil. My sins are not something for which I can atone, regardless of the ICC. It is my burden. Nothing Joe Griffith does will change that. I will return to my classroom and the students therein. Every day I create a small portion of hope for the future, perhaps a small portion of my sin will be lifted."

"You don't care about the murders of your associates?"

"Guilt does not become you, Ms. Sabel." He waited for her to regret her statement. "The Knights have sealed their fate. Theirs are deeds with which they will have to live. However, unlike me, they fail to recognize the evil within them. And that makes their fate so much the worse."

He turned and left.

Pia wondered what had happened to the black-and-white world she once knew. Everything used to be simple and clear. She should have stayed in soccer. The boundaries were marked. The rules were the same for everyone. The referees made sure everything was fair.

She still had eighteen more meetings to attend.

Her phone rang. Miguel. She answered.

He said, "It's Jenny—"

CHAPTER 60

LUCA BRANDT LISTENED WHILE ONE of his detectives took my statement. Two paces away, Miguel and Pavard stood side-by-side with their arms crossed, listening and waiting. I understood the need for following procedure. I understood the Germans were doing their duty. But I was itching to get on the trail of Mr. Baldy. I was going to look him in the eye when I pulled the trigger. And Brandt was slowing me down. Which made me edgy.

"I said that already." I clenched my jaw and took another breath. "I've seen ANFO. I used ANFO in the military. I've seen others use it. I know what it looks like. It was ANFO. Maybe you guys call it something else."

The detective nodded and made another note.

"We call it ANFO," Pavard said. The detective shot him a nasty look for interrupting his interrogation. Pavard raised his brows and shrugged in a half-hearted apology.

"And the bankers?" The detective nodded at the former hostages being treated by the EMT personnel. "What did they want with these persons?"

"No idea. I don't follow international finance. Ransom? Extortion? Better soaps in the guest room? Your guess is as good as mine."

More Germans approached in tight-knit formation. One of them whispered to Brandt.

"This is enough for now." Brandt tapped his detective. "We have someone of interest to Mr. Stearne. He may wish to observe our interrogation."

The new Germans pushed Artur Titow out of their midst. Brandt started interrogating in German. Titow kept his mouth clamped shut and his gaze fixed on me. Pure hatred flowed out of him straight to me. The stream was so hot and angry that Brandt looked between us a couple times. Undeterred, he kept pestering Titow with questions. The hardened Knight had no intention of answering.

After a few minutes of trying, Brandt turned it over to his detective. This gave Brandt more time to observe the staring contest between Titow and me. His detective had no better luck than the boss. Titow refused to respond to anything. The detective poked him and pushed his shoulder but still got no response.

Brandt pulled his detective out of the fray. He looked at me while he spoke. "We will release him. He refuses to answer, and we have no evidence to hold him. He will remain under observation and will not be free to leave the area. That is all we can do. Unless there is something more you have not told us, Mr. Stearne."

Mercury stood behind Titow with a dark and serious look. *Why you putting up with this crap, homie?*

I said, *He knows I'm holding out on him, and he's right. If I told him about the Knights of Mithras or the Poison Stone, he'd lock me up in the looney bin.*

Mercury said, *Are you looney? You talk to me every day, and that makes you as sane as they come. So why put up with this crap?*

I squinted at my discarded deity. *What do you mean?*

Mercury said, *Dude, he ran out of questions to ask you a long time ago. He can't hold you here legally, and he knows you're going to hunt down Mr. Baldy the minute he releases you, so he trotted out Artur Titow just to make you stick around. So, like I said, why are you putting up with this?*

My mythological god had a good point. I didn't have time to hear Brandt's elaborate presentation on how much he was doing to find Jenny's killer. I didn't care what, if anything, he did about it. He could never do enough because the Germans got rid of the death penalty in 1949. Killing Mr. Baldy wouldn't bring her back, but it would make me feel better. And at that moment, I'd never felt worse.

Releasing Titow could work for me. I could follow him back to Mr.

Baldy. But, come to think of it, he was a professional. He wouldn't go back if he thought I might follow him. Therefore, Titow served no purpose to me. And, from what I could tell, he served no purpose to Brandt or Germany either.

I figured most Muslims in Europe, practicing or not, spoke Arabic to keep up socially. It was a distant cousin to the Turkish dialect of Turkmenistan, but it was worth a shot. In the language I had learned during my many years fighting Middle Eastern wars, I said, "You are a disgrace. You failed to complete your mission and you failed to fall on your sword like an honorable Knight of Mithras."

His expression leaned to curious. He refused to speak, but he communicated his inability to fall on his sword by rattling the handcuffs that bound him.

Brandt looked at me with shock. "What is this? What are you saying to him?"

Continuing in Arabic, I said, "Did they take your cyanide capsule from you?"

Titow scowled. Then he realized I was right. It was the only honorable way out for a man belonging to a Roman society. He turned up his resolve. His jaw started working. In a few seconds, I heard him swallow.

Immediately, the officers around him knew something was wrong. In seconds he convulsed and foamed at the mouth.

Brandt turned to me. "What has happened? What did you do?"

"Never touched him," I said.

I turned and marched to the exit. Miguel and Pavard fell in behind me.

CHAPTER 61

CAPTAIN BATYR AMANOW GLANCED AT the low-slung clouds darkening the sky, then checked his ringing phone. Griffith calling. Amanow had heard nothing from the Protector all day. Would Griffith gloat or offer himself up for slaughter? Only one way to find out. He answered.

"It's been good competing with you," Griffith said. "It made me stronger. For that I thank you."

A concession? The tone of voice contradicted that idea. "Get to your point, American."

"No chit-chat, Captain?" Griffith snorted. "Then here it is. Someone pulled the plug on your Protector. Literally. He's gone. Dead. Useless to you. The Board amended his last orders and installed me as Protector. I'm calling to let you know—you are hereby decommissioned, effective immediately. If you've committed any crimes, and I'm sure you have, it would be best to turn yourself into the local authorities. Your legal expenses will not be paid. Good day."

Amanow stared at the phone. Griffith had disconnected.

He pulled up his email. One from the Protector had arrived minutes earlier. It confirmed Griffith's statement. He replied. Seconds later, the email bounced back, undeliverable. He tried texting the Protector. An automatic reply read, "This phone is no longer in service."

As he stared at his screen, a new message appeared. "Remote security wipe in progress. This phone will be decommissioned in sixty seconds."

Amanow tried to catch his breath. How had everything gone so wrong, so fast?

He looked at his men as they staged their equipment for their planned exfiltration. Everything before him was all he had left. Twenty-six men, several tons of gear, and plenty of firepower. He would have to rethink his exit strategy. Again.

His plan had been to force three world leaders to handle the Poison Stone in exchange for the safe return of their central bankers. The exchange was an easy decision for the leaders to make. Griffith was the patsy who would deliver the Stone and no doubt be detained as a conspirator. A conspirator the BND officer, Artur Titow, would later dispatch for him. It was a perfect plan. One that would have won him the job of Protector.

Then Jacob Stearne came into the picture, bringing his little bitch, and half the BND. The Knights had been forced to abort. Now his men were in the middle of a rushed exfil plan. They had to get out of the country before the authorities closed in on them. And on top of it all, that racist American controlled the Knights of Mithras. Without the Protector, the Board had turned on him. They had only tolerated the Protector and his cadre of Turkmen because he solved so many Eastern European problems for them. The Board had always looked down on Amanow and the Turkmen. They'd been used. And now that they were no longer useful, they were discarded like trash.

To hell with them. He would kill them in their sleep.

An aide ran to him. "Sir, our scout reports roadblocks on all roads leaving town. The train station is guarded as well."

"Local or Austrian Federal?"

"Both, sir. Local police set them up; EKO Cobra reinforcements are arriving in squads." His man referred to Austria's national SWAT team.

An ad hoc operation. Effective nonetheless. With twenty-six Knights, Amanow could easily rush one barricade. But given the narrow confines of the Alpine valley, it would only serve to alert a larger force against them. He considered his advantages: superior fighters, mountain terrain, two interconnected caves behind him, and a tremendous cache of weapons. An all-out battle against EKO Cobra would be a losing proposition in the end. But his Knights would die defending him.

He checked the rounds in his silver Scorpion. It was fully loaded.

He gathered his Knights. When they settled before him, he said, "Gentlemen, you are the bravest, most resolute men I have ever led.

When we were home, preparing for this trial, I observed each of you. You were then the most humble, honorable, and peaceful men the world has ever known. When our hardships and battles began, you did not shrink and did not falter. You rose up like ferocious animals. You drove your anger, flexed your muscles, and raged against our enemies. No fear overcame you, no conscience held you back. For that, I am most proud.

"And now, with great sadness, I must report, the enemies of law and order gather in the valley below us. Before nightfall, they will attempt to overpower us. But we will fight to the last man. Whoever survives this night will avenge our deaths."

Amanow examined their eyes.

"Now is the time to fight, my friends," he continued. "Think of your fathers and your grandfathers, who fought like wild beasts to protect you. Set your mind to the task, breathe deep and hearty as they once did. Don't let your mothers hear anyone speak of your cowardice, but only of your unrestrained bravery. Make yourself an example to the man who stands next to you. Let everyone admire you, the greatest Knight of Mithras. No, not Knights. When I look at you, I see kings."

His Knights all rose to their feet and held their heads high. Amanow swelled with pride. Even Dhanpal, the man they saved from Pia Sabel, joined in. They shouted their oath and hugged each other.

Amanow consulted with them about where to build their redoubts and barricades. Together they plotted where the authorities would approach and how best to ambush them. They set about making the cave at the base of the mountain their last stand. Sandbags were filled, body armor distributed, ammunition stacked, and the last of the ANFO placed with trip wires.

Amanow looked over the preparations. It was only a matter of time before the authorities figured out where they were. And they were ready.

Then one last precaution occurred to him. He looked at the cliff above them and decided no one could approach that way. They would be a sitting duck. Little more than target practice. But Stearne would never come up the main trail.

He turned to his aide. "From which direction would you least expect an attack?"

The aide pursed his lips and considered the terrain. He pointed at a little-used hiking trail winding toward them from the forest.

"Stearne will come through there." He looked to the side, where the cliff met a steep slope of scree. "Take two men and set up along that edge. Ambush him."

CHAPTER 62

EVERYONE KNEW WHERE I WAS going. Brandt was the only one who tried to stop me. He gave up when I climbed back onto the station's platform. Miguel gave Pavard a boost up, and I offered a hand. Between the two of us, we got the Frenchman to his feet.

The cogwheel was in the station. A few passengers were already onboard. I marched toward the first car.

Pia Sabel descended the stairs. We both stopped when we saw each other. In spite of her dress pumps, she broke into a run, handing off the Stone to Miguel as she passed him.

She tackled me with a hug, tears streaming down her face. My arms instinctively wrapped around her. But stiffly. She sensed my anger. She stepped back, wiped her nose and eyes with a tissue. She said, "I'm so sorry."

"She was safe at the hotel." My voice was as cold as the glacier outside.

"She was my friend too."

"A dangerous occupation." I regretted my angry snap as soon as I said it. Her father was killed right in front of her, in part because I failed to keep him out of a firefight.

We both breathed to settle ourselves, to keep our anger from flaring.

She said, "I want to go with you."

"No."

"I can help."

"No." I started walking to the train. Then I realized I was doing exactly what led me into this nightmare in the first place. What would Jenny want me to do?

"Sorry." I stopped and faced Ms. Sabel. "I need your help."

With a sad glance at me, she tugged at her dress. "I'll change and catch up with you."

I boarded the train and walked to the forward car so I could be the first one off when we hit Garmisch. Miguel and Pavard followed me. The train started off while we were still moving down the aisle. We grabbed railings to steady ourselves, not because we lost our balance from the motion but because the steepness threw us off. After the train traveled a hundred yards, we got the hang of it and continued.

A familiar man occupied the seat closest to the door. I took the seat next to him. Miguel and Pavard took seats across the way. Rafael Tum looked like a different human being in a suit. He looked like a guy who went to English boarding school and became a professor. He stared straight ahead.

After listening to the keening of the steel wheels through half the length of the tunnel, Rafael turned to me. "I joined the Keepers to atone for my sins. We keep the Stones in a safe place."

"I offered it to you several times. Why didn't you take it?"

"You're not finished, yet." He looked away. "Your responsibility was to make sure it didn't fall into the wrong hands."

Those were the words he used when I first met him. He had warned me. Would Jenny still be alive if I'd left the damn thing in Seven-Death's temple? Screw it. No good would come of second-guessing my actions.

"Well," I said with a nasty glare, "it fell into the wrong hands. And now the love of my life is dead. Your advice turned out to be useless then and still is now."

"Don't let it fall." He accented the last word.

"Quit talking in riddles. I hate that."

"Use it."

"How? I don't believe in magic rocks."

"Then use it on those who do."

The train came out of the tunnel and crossed the valley toward the town. It was dark out and snow was falling. Big fluffy flakes, the kind that piled fast and high and wet.

He rose and stood by the door. The train came to a stop. Rafael Tum strode out across the platform and down a narrow lane. Miguel stood next to me while I watched the professor vanish into the falling snow.

Miguel hoisted the Stone to his shoulder. "What the man said made sense."

"What do you mean, using it on believers?"

"Exactly."

"They have rifles," I said.

"I didn't say it was going to be easy."

Major Pavard stood next to me with a phone to his ear. He held up a finger, telling me to wait. While I did, I saw Mark of the Brotherhood approaching with the guy whose name I still didn't know. Eleven men and women followed them. They worked their way through a herd of black Mercedes G-wagons. He came straight towards me. Everyone in his group watched my eyes.

"I thought Gu Peng sent you home," I said.

"She did," Mark said. "We heard about Jenny. We came back to help."

Miguel pressed his big shoulder against mine. A signal not to overreact. Not to send them away.

"Help?" I asked.

"Look," Mark said, "I know you don't like our methods, but you saved my life on the mountain. And everyone loved Jenny. We're not letting this go. We're here to take out as many Knights as we can before we … as many as we can."

Mercury whispered in my ear. *Homie, know anyone whose ancestry includes famous guerrilla fighters? Maybe that someone could lead these guys like Crazy Horse.*

I said, *You mean like Manuelito?*

Miguel turned to me. "Sure, I've studied Manuelito's tactics. Not as much got written about him as Crazy Horse and Sitting Bull. We can do this. If you go in the back way, we can take on the main force."

We had been through too many battles together. He could read my mind.

Pavard put his phone away. "I must return to my duties. But I have spoken to the Austrian authorities. Their drones have identified an area near the base of the cliff warranting further investigation. At my request, they have pulled all their resources back from the town. They wait for the snow to stop. About two hours." He smiled and patted my shoulder.

Then his smile turned to tears. "When I met her, I thought you two would have many wonderful years together. As many as my wife and I. There must be balance in life. You get these men, Jacob Stearne. They do not deserve to breathe the air she breathed."

He wiped his eyes and gave me a bear hug. Then he turned and went back to the train.

"I'll be there, Pavard," I called after him. "Your place, two weeks."

He waved without looking back and got onboard.

Miguel tapped my shoulder and pointed at the row of G-wagons. He said, "I called the Munich office. Asked for volunteers and all available hardware."

CHAPTER 63

WE PASSED AN ABANDONED ROADBLOCK outside Obermoos. The village looked like a ghost town. On the edge of town, we found a chopper landing. Ms. Sabel stepped out, fully dressed for battle.

The coordinates Pavard gave me were a mile up the steep slopes from the last building. We had seven volunteers from Sabel Security's Munich office plus twelve Brothers and an arsenal that would make my old Ranger platoon salivate. Body armor, suppressed MP7s, Sabel Visors, handheld Sabel Darts, green lasers to find tripwires, and other goodies.

We put up a recon drone and found the Knights quickly. We could see they'd built a U-shaped redoubt against a wall of rock hundreds of feet high. Directly behind it was a cave of undetermined depth. Before we could see much else, the drone crashed inside their fortress, weighed down by the heavy snow. So much for the element of surprise.

As the snow fell and the wind picked up, Miguel pulled the group together for a plan of attack.

He said, "It's a common misconception that Natives attacked like a swarm of bees. They had well drawn concepts and strategies. Each tribe had their own objectives and methods. At Little Big Horn, all the chiefs carried different colored flags to rally their warriors to direct different points of attack. They coordinated with war whoops and whistles made of eagle bone. Lucky for us, we have comm links.

"The warriors were driven by an overwhelming desire to be the bravest. At the battles of Powder River, Arrow Creek, and Little Big Horn, Crazy Horse rode up and down in front of the US Army, letting them shoot at him. He did it because he knew their Springfield rifles would overheat and jam. When that happened, his warriors attacked."

The Brothers snickered nervously.

"To the whites," he said, "our attacks looked like chaos. Natives would ride straight at them, then run away. There were no firing lines, no squads, no apparent coordination. Yet each was trying to do something brave that would benefit the other warriors. The whites never realized they were being distracted. Natives confused the whites, then went for the flank. When the soldiers regrouped to face the flank, the warriors would reverse roles and attack head-on again. Just like a pack of predators. One wolf will attack at the nose of an animal while the real attack comes from the flank. And that's what we're going to do today. You're now honorary members of the Wolf Tribe."

He had them choose the chiefs they wanted to serve and created squads of four and five. They would form the traditional Native half-moon formation around the Knights. Wild and crazy attacks followed by retreats, followed by attacks on the flanks. First one side, then the other. The Knights would think a horde had descended on them.

And that left Ms. Sabel and me free for our mission: to find Mr. Baldy and kill him. If I could get to him quickly enough, I hoped the Knights would surrender. More likely, they would keep fighting for their cause. They had proven themselves dedicated to their cause.

Miguel left his operatives while they donned their battle rattle and came to wish us luck.

Ms. Sabel said, "Good speech, great plan."

He smiled. "Yeah, I probably cost us the Hopi reservation." He checked my body armor and brushed snow off my helmet. "Stay frosty, brother."

Ms. Sabel gave him a hug.

I nodded at the group. "What role are you playing? Are you going to be Crazy Horse?"

"Crazy Horse rode a fast horse and got lucky. Sitting Bull saw what the younger chief did, and went out, sat down, and smoked a full pipe while bullets buzzed his head. That's the kind of chief I want to be." He pounded his fist to his chest, formed a peace symbol, then strode away.

We slipped into the trees and climbed the hill toward the base of the cliff parallel to the Knight's position. I scanned our path with the green laser visible only in my Sabel Visor searching for trip wires. When we got to the tree line, we turned left and stayed in the trees.

The snow came down faster. Clumps the size of soccer balls fell from branches. Tripwires would get buried in the snow, eventually making my green laser useless. We slowed and looked for footprints. Early in a snowstorm, they would be visible. As fast as it was coming down, that trick wouldn't work long.

After a hundred yards, I saw them seconds before they saw me. Two Knights opened fire as I crouched behind a pine. Ms. Sabel laid down suppressive fire over my head. I backed up, reusing my tracks. When I'd backed up twenty yards, I jumped out of the tracks and over a fallen log. She did the same thing at a different angle. We waited.

A full minute went by before curiosity got the better of the Knights. They followed my footprints with a professional separation between them. I couldn't see Ms. Sabel, and it was too quiet to use the comm link without giving away our position. We had to count on each other to maximize our element of surprise. Because of their separation among the trees, I could see only one of the Knights. I popped up and missed the first guy. While he wheeled to face me, Ms. Sabel dropped him.

The second Knight vanished.

Which was a problem. I circled his last position in a wide arc. He wasn't there. Thinking like a Turkmen wasn't my forte, but it occurred to me he might try the same trick. If he'd made his in a counter-arc, I was safe, but if he were on the same path only deeper, he could be behind me. I couldn't find him. I figured that must be what he was doing.

I dropped and rolled as his three-round burst blew the bark off the tree nearest me. I heard Ms. Sabel firing. From where I'd last seen her, she couldn't possibly have him in her sights. She was distracting him. I spun, rolled, and got off a three-round burst of my own. The last one hit him in the back.

Mercury popped up out of the snow. *If they're expecting you on this route, homie, maybe—just maybe—you oughta consider a different route. Seeing as how you can't see tripwires and all, definitely take a different route.*

I said, *Where else is there to go?*

Mercury looked at the cliff across two hundred yards of snow-covered scree.

No way, I said. *If he sees me, I'd be a sitting duck. Besides, I don't have any hardware.*

Mercury said, *Crazy Horse wouldn't need no hardware. Besides, you got Pia-Caesar-Sabel with you and she's as brave as any Native chief.*

The worst problem about having a personal relationship with god is when he tells you to do something and you know he's right, but you don't want to.

I took a deep breath and started trudging toward the cliff. Ms. Sabel stayed to the trail, a few yards back to cover my exposed position. If someone looked up, she would shoot him. If he didn't, she was a sitting duck.

I climbed the steep slope sideways, keeping my rifle ready in case someone saw me.

But they didn't. They were certain I was coming through the woods. And the skirmish had proven them right.

When I reached it, I walked at or near the base until their stronghold was below me. From there, I had the perfect view of Miguel's battle. It had just begun.

True to his word, Miguel walked out into the open waving a white flag and carrying the Poison Stone cradled in a blanket. He held it high and took a step left as someone shot at him. He stepped right as another round came in. Then he set the blanket and Stone down gently, as a round skimmed his armor. He raised his rifle and fired back. That silenced the Knights. They dove for cover.

But his challenge was clear: the winner keeps the Stone.

Miguel let out a frightening war whoop. One I'd heard on our many death-defying missions. Three Brothers ran out of the woods behind him racing for the ramparts, shouting and screaming and firing. Every Knight in the compound watched the attack. No one saw me.

Brothers attacked the left flank. The entire group of Knights turned to face the new danger. More Brothers ran in from the right. They were able to toss flash-bangs inside the perimeter. The Knights shot back. The Brothers ran back to the trees. Thirty seconds after it started, the area was silent.

A terrific plan. The Knight's defense started to unravel. Two leaders took control, ordering their men to focus only on their assigned areas. Discipline in the face of chaos. It was the orderly thing to do.

On the trail behind me, a bomb went off. The explosion grabbed everyone's attention. Ms. Sabel reported herself safe and surmised a tripwire had been weighted by the snow. I couldn't make a sound being directly above three Knights.

On the comm, Miguel said, "Pia, Jacob, speak to me."

"The reports of our deaths are greatly exaggerated," Ms. Sabel said.

"Jerks. I'm busy here." He went back to work.

The Brothers attacked again. This time coming from different directions with different patterns. While the Knights were bewildered, Miguel and Mark ran to the Freedom Stone. Each man grabbed one side of the blanket and carried it between them. While the Knights focused on the attacks from both flanks, Miguel and Mark used the blanket like a slingshot, launching it into the thickest group of Knights. It hit one man in the head, knocking him down. Two others picked up the Stone. Suddenly, they looked confused.

I heard Mr. Baldy's voice shout, "Don't touch it with bare hands, you fools!"

A man with gloves on picked it up, but one of the first men to touch it, snatched it away from him. Confusion engulfed them.

From where I was, I could see a group of Brothers crawling on their bellies through the snow to the right flank. When they reached the bulwark, they rose and fired.

Instead of pressing the attack, they ran away as fast as they could go. Several Knights gave chase. A fatal mistake. The retreating Brothers led the Knights into an ambush. Inside the fortress, the leaders tried to reassign Knights to the abandoned posts. But the Stone's chaos continued, thinning their defense even further.

In all the years we served together, Miguel always took orders and executed battle plans according to the military officers. They should've asked him for advice. The man Mercury called Monster Slayer was Sitting Bull reincarnated.

Satisfied he had it under control, I scaled the icy rocks with toe and fingerholds. I needed only enough height to be unnoticed should a Knight turn around. People don't look up unless they see movement. I climbed to thirty feet, not a deadly elevation but a potential leg-breaker. I found a ledge a bit higher and made my way until it thinned out. From there, I had nowhere to go but down.

Below me, Ms. Sabel approached the perimeter wall and waited for another attack by the Brothers to distract the Knights nearest her.

Directly below me was the center of the Knight's fortress. With Miguel keeping them occupied, I lowered myself an inch at a time.

Then the wind buffeted me at the same time my fingers slipped from an icy ledge. I fell fifteen feet, landing on my back on stacked gear. My rifle flew off my shoulder and landed ten yards away. For a few terrifying seconds I couldn't breathe.

A Knight ran to me, his rifle aimed.

I played dead.

A bullet whizzed by the man's ear. He returned to his assigned position.

I rolled off the stack to my hands and knees and took a deep breath.

Directly in front of me stood a man in ninja-black with a smooth and shiny scalp. Mr. Baldy stretched a sick grin across his face and raised his silver Scorpion.

CHAPTER 64

WE GLARED AT EACH OTHER over the iron sights of his pistol as he brought the barrel up. When the alignment was right, his finger squeezed the trigger. And I rolled right. I spun three times, trying to get my knees under me. Dirt puffed next to me on each turn.

My escape attempt ended when I rolled to the legs of a large, angry Knight. He picked me up by my arms and dragged me to standing. He held me in front of him in a bear hug. Mr. Baldy had lost his angle, having been too deep in the cave to follow my roll. But his grin returned when he stepped out.

He lined up his shot more carefully this time. As the barrel aligned to my eye, a strange look came over him. Instead of pulling the trigger, he ducked. Blood and brains from the man holding me sprayed out in several directions, his grip slackened, and he fell to the ground. I turned to see Brother Mark standing fifty yards away.

Mark gave me a quick salute. I nodded thanks, pulled my pistol, and chased after Mr. Baldy. At the edge of the cave, I peered around the wall hoping to get a look inside. Instead, rock fragments exploded in my eye. I spun away and let tears wash out the debris. I felt Ms. Sabel's soothing hand on my shoulder. She returned fire while I was blinded.

Karst caves are formed when the softer sandstone erodes away from harder limestone. In this case, remnants of the softer stone formed a flat gravel floor. A more solid layer of rock formed an angular ceiling, giving the cave a triangular look. I hadn't examined the back, but a large boulder filled the space forty feet ahead. Whether that was the end of it or not was hard to tell. But it gave a serious advantage to Mr. Baldy.

Even though the snow was coming down fast, there was still more daylight outside than in the cave. Any peek I could take would be backlit. I'd make a perfect target.

Mercury leaned over my shoulder to look inside. *What would Sitting Bull do, homie?*

I said, *I'm not at that level of bravery yet. What would Crazy Horse do?*

Mercury said, *He would ride in, frontal assault, preserving his ammunition and aim because that's the scariest way to do it. Of course, back in those days, soldiers were poorly trained, and officers insisted on firing their revolvers single-handed, so he had that going for him.*

I said, *Thanks. Not helpful.*

Mercury said, *No need to get saucy, bro.*

I reached my pistol around the entrance and fired blindly inside. With no hope of hitting him, my intention was to keep Mr. Baldy from coming out. I ran back to where I thought my rifle landed when I fell. It wasn't there. One of the Knights saw me as a rear-guard threat and started shooting. I dove and rolled. Ms. Sabel covered me, firing back at the man. I would stick with my pistol.

I scrambled to my feet and ran back for the cave. When I got to the entrance, I repeated my firing blind method before rolling in on the gravel.

Mr. Baldy was waiting for me. I felt one round hit my armored shoulder as I stopped my roll in a prone position. There was no sign of him. I flipped my visor to high-sensitivity thermal and found heat rising from behind the boulder at the back. It appeared to be a fallen section of the roof with a crawl space to the left. There must be a chamber behind it.

Pinging a couple bullets through the small space made the heat signature retreat. Enough space for him to move around, but trapped? I could only hope. If there was an exit on the back end, he hadn't taken it. That didn't mean I had him cornered. I'd have to crawl in or talk him out. Crawling in would be braver than Sitting Bull and Crazy Horse combined.

Ms. Sabel landed on the ground next to me. Outside, the fighting reached a fever pitch. More rounds than ever were being fired. To me, that meant Miguel was storming the barricades. He would never risk lives without absolute confidence in winning.

"It's over, Mr. Baldy," I called out. "Crawl out with your hands up and I'll let you touch the Freedom Stone."

"You are the worst, Jacob Stearne." His breathing was irregular. "You are a tool of the overeducated elite. They lie to you and still you do their bidding."

His ragged breathing tipped me off to a problem. I looked around at the gravel, curious if he'd been wounded. I didn't see any blood. I said, "I'm here on my own."

"When will you realize that democracy is a lie? Only a strong individual can rein in the forces that attack police and let terrorists roam the streets."

"You killed Jenny Jenkins. You're the terrorist."

I heard scrambling in the gravel. The son of a bitch was getting away. I had to crawl through the tight space. No option.

Ms. Sabel pushed to her feet and ran out. I didn't know her plan, but I was confident she had a good one.

Crabbing to the crawl space, I realized little of my battle rattle would fit through. I stripped off all my gear except for the body armor and an extra magazine. I pushed my 9 mil into the space and fired three rounds.

Bad idea. The ricochets pinged around furiously. I barely got my hand back without a hole in it.

"You believe the lies you see in the media?" Mr. Baldy's voice had risen an octave and echoed more.

The echo meant he was in a second chamber.

"I'll believe double-confirmed reporting curated by professional editors with their reputations on the line over some clown with a Twitter account making baseless accusations."

"Your country has been invaded—"

While he waxed poetic about his personal paranoia, I crawled in.

It was a cramped, dark space. The visor did little to reveal the confines. It felt like a rock coffin.

Feeling around, I determined the gravel floor ended under my knees. The exit Mr. Baldy took was up a slick piece of stone and to the left. I knew spelunkers were contortionists because Mother Nature didn't make caves like Disney rides. I would have to repeat all my dangerous maneuvers again on the other side of the narrow passage.

At any moment, he could push his pistol through the opening and fire blindly. Since he hadn't done that, I guessed he had moved deeper into the cave.

I reached the top of the slick part and felt an opening smaller than the first. Mr. Baldy waited on the other side with the clear advantage of knowing my entry point. I pushed my 9 mil in and fired off a couple rounds. This time, no ricochets. But Mr. Baldy let out a scream.

Fake or real? A seasoned veteran often makes a wounded noise to fool an amateur into charging in.

I pulled out my new monocular, a gift from Miguel to replace the one I gave Pavard. I aimed it at the opening and got a look at the other side. A large domed space with a flat floor waited four feet below the opening. On the left, indirect daylight lit a corner. On the right, Mr. Baldy cowered with his shiny pistol. I put away the clever device and positioned myself to somersault into the cave.

Two more rounds brushed him back. I could hear him scrambling.

I rolled in, landing on sharp gravel as Mr. Baldy fired in my direction. The shots were wild and went wide.

He was running for the source of the daylight. Getting away. He rounded the corner into what looked like a doorway that had been hacked into the rock just for this purpose.

Instead of disappearing outside, just as he stepped through the exit, his head snapped back quickly.

He fell backward and landed on his ass.

An extended fist appeared silhouetted against the light. The owner of the mysterious arm moved forward cautiously. Ms. Sabel.

She stepped through the opening and gave me a nod.

I ran to Mr. Baldy and pressed my weapon to his forehead. He relinquished his Scorpion without a word.

Ms. Sabel stood next to me. After a silent moment, she said, "Remember Viktor Popov?"

I recalled watching her shoot the murderous Russian monster nine times with a sickening but satisfying coldness. I said, "Yes, I do."

She took my pistol and kept it trained on Mr. Baldy.

I checked out his Scorpion. It was the competition model. An odd choice for operations. Not exactly practical but one slick-looking weapon. In the end, he was just a showman. I checked his pockets and came up with a second magazine, still full.

Ms. Sabel took a step back.

Mr. Baldy rose to his feet.

"There are many more chapters of Knights," Mr. Baldy held his hands up. "They will—"

I fired the first round into his left shinbone. I said, "That's for Hidalgo."

He groaned and clenched his jaw to stifle his pain.

"I didn't know the names of the others," I said. "But you executed them."

I fired another round into his right shinbone. And then another in his left. The pain was too much. He fell on his back and screamed.

When he got his pain under control, he asked, "Are you the kind of man who shoots an unarmed man when he's down?"

"Normal, no," I said. "But this is a special occasion."

I slowly fired a pattern into the flesh of his legs for a total of fifteen severe, but not deadly, wounds.

The pain overwhelmed him. He stopped screaming. He rose on his elbows and stared at his shredded legs. He looked up at me with hate in his eyes.

I checked the magazine. Four left. I slapped it back in. "This is for Zafar, one of your own."

I shot him in the abdomen. He screamed again.

"This is for Danny." Another hole in his belly blossomed blood. One more punctured his lung. "That was for Fiona."

I squatted down next to him, getting as level as I could with the worm. I pulled his face to mine and held his gaze.

He couldn't take it. He turned his eyes to Ms. Sabel, tears streaming down his cheeks. He said, "Please! Help me!"

"No." Her voice made even me shiver.

Mr. Baldy dropped back. I yanked him upright by his coat. I put the barrel between his eyes and watched him look at it cross-eyed. I pulled it back to make it easier for him to focus. I wanted him to see the bullet leaving the muzzle. I said, "And this is for Jenny."

CHAPTER 65

MS. SABEL AND I WALKED out into a blizzard and made our way over rough ground to the Knight's fortress. It was a scene of carnage.

The Brotherhood lost three; the Knights lost twelve. The remaining Knights had surrendered and were pressing their bare hands to the Freedom Stone. Miguel stood in line with one hand on Dhanpal's shoulder. I wondered if it would turn him back into the friend we'd lost or someone else altogether.

The Austrians arrived and began taking over operations.

Ms. Sabel and I sat on a case of equipment to watch.

I used to think life followed a formula. You serve your country, follow the rules, they give you a medal, you get a wife and one-point-nine kids, you keep following the rules, you keep getting the good things in life, and you grow old in a suburban bungalow. Neat and tidy and orderly and safe. It's a lie. Nothing about life is safe. I'd finally found the woman I could spend a lifetime with—and that fragile dream was destroyed in an instant. Few things are as shattering as losing your future.

I glanced at Ms. Sabel's stoic profile. She knew more about loss than I. At the age of four, she'd watched her mother strangled. She'd been adopted and raised by Alan Sabel, only to watch him get shot in the head while she was strapped to a chair. All the connections to her past had been violently ripped away. Despite having sixty thousand adoring employees, she was alone in this world. Despite having a loving family, I felt the same.

Ms. Sabel was all I had left. And I was all she had left.

She reached over, took my hand, and held it. We didn't look at each other. We didn't need to. We understood each other. Not like star-crossed lovers, more like fragments of the same falling star. We sat in silence. Our hearts pounded with grief and anger while the snow fell.

We watched Miguel talking to the Austrians some distance away. They were barely visible through the piling snow. We lost track of Dhanpal.

After a while, she took a deep breath and said, "Why do you want to leave?"

"You keep stringing me out," I said. "You shot me. You publicly fired me. You've let me take the risky missions all the time. Why?"

She breathed. Then she said, "To save the others."

"What does that mean?"

"You've walked through explosions and war zones and firefights and come out unscathed. Every time. You're immortal, Jacob."

Mercury tried to push his way between us. I shouldered him out. He said, *Say what, homie? You're immortal? Oh, she's got that wrong. You bleed like the rest of them—if I let them touch you.*

I said, *No.*

Mercury said, *So introduce me.*

I said, *No.*

Mercury said, *You owe me one.*

I said, *No.*

Mercury said, *You promised you were going to tell Jenny.*

I looked him over and said, *No.*

Ms. Sabel squeezed my hand. "It's like, I know I shouldn't. I know it's unfair. But when I took Cody on one mission, his leg was shot to pieces. He almost died. If I'd taken you into that warehouse with me, you would've killed them all and walked away without a scratch. Even though I know it's not real—and your mythical god is a cute story that helps you get through the day—I can't help thinking, 'Jacob can get it done without getting killed so he should do it.'"

Mercury slapped my shoulder. *Whoa! Dude. '...a cute story that helps you get through the day?' You're letting her trash talk me like that? Speak up, cuz there could be a lightning bolt in this blizzard. One word from me and Jupiter tosses one on ya.*

I said, *I've talked to her. She built a temple for you back at Sabel*

Gardens.

Mercury said, *Yeah, she did. And put a statue of a wimpy-looking white dude what looks like a ballerina in the middle. You gotta TELL her about me.*

"You mean…" I squeezed her hand back. "He who can, must."

"Exactly." She looked at me.

"That's what Jenny said when she grabbed the bomb."

A tear formed in her eye. "She wasn't immortal."

"She taught me something that will last with me forever." I took a deep breath, trying not to break down. "I can't do it alone. I work best with a team. She was going to be my team." I choked. "I don't want to start my own company anymore. Not without Jenny."

Ms. Sabel hugged me.

CHAPTER 66

MS. SABEL PREFERRED TO WALK the cobblestone streets of the Montmarte neighborhood in Paris. We got out of the limo and headed up the hill. Major Pavard's address was two blocks off the tourist-packed approach to Sacré-Cœur, the famous basilica on a hill overlooking the city. We passed a postcard stairway, a mouth-watering boulangerie, and two sidewalk cafés on the cobblestone Rue des Trois Frères before the street turned more residential.

Up two flights of stairs we were welcomed by the Major's wife Delphine. Plump, white-haired, and babbling her native language as if I spoke it, she ushered us into a tiny apartment filled with friends. She made a big deal introducing me. The small gathering applauded. I did my best to smile and wave. I hoped to pull it off as bashful and not depressed.

Life without Jenny had little meaning.

Ms. Sabel had stayed near me—or kept me near her, I'm not sure which—ever since the funeral. It felt like she had me on a suicide watch. I wasn't that distraught. There was a hole in my life where Jenny used to be. It hadn't healed. The pleasures of life meant nothing. Food was tasteless, odorless, useless stuff. Music sounded like chirping insects. Friends felt like distant relatives. Every day was overcast.

For a while, I distracted myself by tracking Joe Griffith's movements. Just to send a message, Miguel and I set charges on all his bedroom door handles under the noses of his personal guards. We blew them at 3 AM when he had "guests" locked inside. We called the police for him.

Even that brought little more than a short-lived smile to my face.

Delphine Pavard poured wine and brought out cheese and crackers.

We chatted. I hoped my contributions were amicable. From the look on Delphine's face, I was failing miserably. She kept trying to tell me jokes but her English was worse than my French.

A knock on the door allowed me a moment to myself. I told myself to perk up, if for no other reason than to make the Pavards happy. A man at the door handed Delphine a huge bow attached to a ribbon trailing down the stairs behind him. It was a surprise gift from Ms. Sabel. The Pavards started rolling it up. Their friends followed them down the steps.

Mercury grabbed my shoulder and pulled me to the balcony. He said, *I got a message for you.*

I said, *I don't want to hear it.*

Mercury said, *It's from Jenny.*

I said, *C'mon. Don't be yanking my chain like that. I'm not in the mood.*

Mercury smacked the side of my head, *Dude, I'm the messenger of the gods. I took her across the river. You listening to me now?*

I said, *Yeah. OK. Fine. Go ahead. What's the message?*

Mercury said, *Life is about balance. She wants you to know you need to balance the grief with joy. Otherwise, her legacy on Earth is nothing more than a depressed guy. She wants to be remembered as the woman who rocked the gondola with Dalsgaard and Brandt, not the woman who turned Jacob Stearne into an emotional black hole.*

I looked at the city view. In the distance, the Eiffel Tower turned its lights on. At some point in my life, I recall someone telling me hell wasn't a place you went when you died, it was a place you made for yourself in life. You had to actively choose to live there. This man also told me choosing to see life as heaven was much more rewarding. To celebrate everything from the joys to the pains is how you turn hell into heaven. That man might've been Mercury. But I doubt it.

I turned around and saw the last of Pavard's friends holding the door for me. I jogged to catch up.

Ms. Sabel clutched my arm as we followed the group down the sidewalk. She nodded toward a man sitting alone at a sidewalk café. Professor Rafael Tum sipped a coffee with his iron gaze locked on us. With a slight wave of his cup, he acknowledged us when we passed by.

"I offered the Stone to him. He said he didn't want it yet," Ms. Sabel said in a hushed tone. "Do you think he wants it back now?"

"Where is it?"

"Somewhere in the Sabel Security ops center." She referred to a massive armory in the countryside. "Uhm. They lost it."

"If he asks," I said, "let him go find it."

The merry parade followed the Pavards to a nearby hotel and inside. The ribbon led up to a small ballroom. Judging from the size of the hotel, it couldn't be a big ballroom, but it was larger than the apartment. Four serious gendarmes patrolled the small lobby. Two guards in dress uniform manned the ballroom doors. They opened them as we approached.

A band, balloons, and a cheering crowd welcomed them in. The President of France shook their hands first. Then Luca Brandt of the BND stepped forward. Behind him lined up Dalsgaard and the other police chiefs of Europe. Dignitaries from around the region joined the line.

Ms. Sabel pulled my elbow. We stepped to the side and watched the beaming Pavards soak up the attention.

"You did this?" I asked.

"Called a few people—it kinda escalated." ·

We stood there watching human kindness in action. It is amazing how wonderfully people respond to the love of friends. All too often we wallow in anger when it's obvious we need each other. We need kindness. We thrive on upbeat, unbridled optimism. When we work together, we build things up. Like bridges, hospitals, schools, rockets to the moon. And we work best when we compensate for each other's strengths and weaknesses. Jenny was right about balance.

When they'd greeted everyone, the Pavards took to the dance floor. Everyone watched and applauded them. When the song ended, the anniversary couple came straight to us. The Major asked Ms. Sabel to dance. I asked Delphine.

As we stepped out to join them on the dance floor, I asked Ms. Sabel, "Do you know anything about yin and yang?"

THANK YOU!

Thank you for choosing my book. I hope you enjoyed reading it as much as I enjoyed writing it. As an independent writer, I am dependent on word-of-mouth referrals and book reviews. If you liked this book, please tell everyone, and leave reviews all over the place. I will be eternally grateful.

When you do write a review, send me a link to it and I'll put you in the next drawing for an autographed book. I run at least three or four drawings a year.

If you can't get enough of Pia, Tania, Miguel and Jacob*, checkout the series at SeeleyJames.com/books. While you're there, join my newsletter to get discounts, drawings, fun, news, outtakes, and more about the Sabel Agents club on Facebook! Every week (or so, sometimes I'm lazy), I'll let you know about the book in progress, personal triumphs & tragedies, what I'm reading and other fun stuff. I even had one person write to me to say, "I don't like your books, but I love your newsletters." To which I replied, "Thanks, Mom." Yeah … whatcha gonna do?

I'd love to hear from you. Please write, message me on Facebook, let me know what you think.

*I like you already.

NOW THAT YOU'VE READ THIS BOOK, WHICH ONE SHOULD YOU READ NEXT?
HTTPS://SEELEYJAMES.COM/BOOKS

ACKNOWLEDGMENTS

My heartfelt thanks to the beta readers and supporters who made this book the best book possible.

- Extraordinary Editor and Idea man: Lance Charnes, author of the highly acclaimed *Doha 12, SOUTH, THE COLLLECTION, STEALING GHOSTS and CHASING CLAY.* If you like beautifully written art heists, visit http://wombatgroup.com
- Medical Advisor and Character Diviner: Dr. Louis Kirby, famed neurologist and author of *Shadow of Eden.* http://louiskirby.com Without his help, the ending would've been a snoozer.
- Amazing Editor: Mary Maddox, horror and dark fantasy novelist, and author of the Daemon World Series and the fantastic thriller, DARK ROOM. http://marymaddox.com

A special thanks to my wife whose support, despite being a tad reluctant, has gone above and beyond the call of duty. Last but not least, my children, Nicole, Amelia, and Christopher, ranging from age twenty to forty-seven, who have kept my imagination fresh and full of ideas.

ABOUT THE AUTHOR

His near-death experiences range from talking a jealous husband into putting the gun down to spinning out on an icy freeway in heavy traffic without touching anything. His resume ranges from washing dishes to global technology management. His personal life stretches from homeless at 17, adopting a 3-year-old at 19, getting married at 37, fathering his last child at 43, hiking the Grand Canyon Rim-to-Rim several times a year, and taking the occasional nap.

His writing career ranges from humble beginnings with short stories in The Battered Suitcase, to being awarded a Medallion from the Book Readers Appreciation Group. Seeley is best known for his Sabel Security series of thrillers featuring athlete and heiress Pia Sabel and her bodyguard, unhinged veteran Jacob Stearne. One of them kicks ass and the other talks to the wrong god.

His love of creativity began at an early age, growing up at Frank Lloyd Wright's School of Architecture in Arizona and Wisconsin. He carried his imagination first into a successful career in sales and marketing, and then to his real love: fiction.

For more books featuring Pia Sabel and Jacob Stearne, visit: SeeleyJames.com.

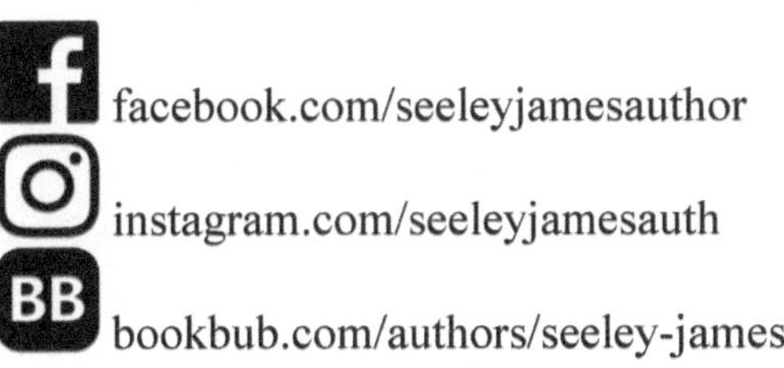